The Warrior Priestess

This first edition published in 2022 by
Blue Moon Rising Publishing
www.ektaabali.com

ISBN ebook: 978-0-6452939-0-6
Paperback: 978-0-6452939-1-3
Hardcover: 978-0-6489830-9-5
Paperback (Pastel Edition): 978-0-6454650-5-1
Hardcover (Pastel Edition): 978-0-6454650-6-8

Illustrated Cover design by Carly Diep
Hardcover Case by Jessica Lowdell
Maps by Najlakay
Chapter Header by Jessica Lowdell
Book Formatting by E.P. Bali with Vellum

CONCUBINE. WIFE. PRIESTESS.

Captured by a demon king, Drake, with his memories
returned and Saraya, must now come to terms with a
surprising truth:
That Drake is not only Saraya's true mate, but is also the son
of a monstrous deity who bound his powers at the age of
thirteen. But now the demon king wants Drake's true powers
to be unbound for his own nefarious purposes.
Forced to marry each other, Drake and Saraya must now gain
the trust of the Court of the Demon King in order to escape.
But there are even bigger forces at play here.
Will Saraya give into her desire to be Drake's fated mate? Or
will she do the unthinkable?

Join Saraya and Drake the seductive adventure in Book 2 of
the Warrior Midwife Trilogy

Due to the mature nature of this novel, its content is suited to
readers aged 18+

The author acknowledges the Traditional Custodians of the land where this book was written. We acknowledge their connections to land, sea and community. We pay our respects to their Elders past and present and extend that respect to all Aboriginal and Torres Strait Islander Peoples today.

A NOTE ON THE CONTENT

I care about the mental health of my readers.
This book contains some themes you might want to know
about before you read.
They are listed at www.ektaabali.com/themes

E.P. BALI

The Warrior Priestess

HUMAN REALM

REALM OF THE DARK FAE

OBSIDIAN COURT

BLACK COURT

ECLIPSE COURT

FARLOUGH CITY

SERUS

PEACH TREE CITY

KAALON

SAMPATI CITY

KUSHA

TRAENARA

SHOBNA CITY

WAELAN

BALNOR CITY

QUARTZ

LUMINOUS QUARTZ DESERT

LOBRATHIA

THE TEMARI FOREST

TEMPLE RUINS

THE SILENT MOUNTAINS

THE ONYX MAGIC ACADEMY

THE LOTUS SEA

ELLYTHIA

LOTA

THE JUNGLE ACADEMY

QUARTZ

KAALON

LOBRATHIA

The Temari Forest

Temple ruins

SILENT MOUNTAINS

FAE WARRIOR ACADEMY

BLACK COURT

THE BLACK GROVE

OBSIDIAN COURT

ECLIPSE COURT

MIDNIGHT COURT

TWILIGHT COURT

INTER-REALM PORTAL

SKY COURT

BLOSSOM COURT

VALLEY OF THE JACARANDAS

COURT OF FLAMES

COURT OF LIGHT

COURT OF TIDES

N

REALM OF THE DARK FAE

REALM OF THE SOLAR FAE

To the first woman whose baby I caught as a new midwife. You looked into my eyes, held my hand and said, "Thank you so much, Ektaa. You are kind and patient and I can't thank you enough." I rushed out the door before you could see me cry because it was you who showed me the might and patience of a woman. I will never forget you.

.

1
JERALI JONES

I held my sword like a lover.

A sword had been my first love.

And as far as I was concerned, it would be my last. This battle that had begun in the Sticks and spread like a rampaging ox through Quartz City filled my veins with fire. War was where I was home. And against demons this vicious and bloodthirsty, I was a happy match.

I had been skulking through the shadows— scouting the Sticks past curfew to gather information on the fae scum who had invaded my home when I heard two fae guards gossiping. They were talking about how Saraya's wedding to Prince Daxian had been expedited to tonight. The information had frozen me because her marriage would change everything about our current dilemma. But the fae guards didn't even get to finish their sentence before they abruptly began sniffing and retching. There was a choked-out *"demons"* before I saw the first of the massive horde that would descend upon the city. They were demons alright, with mouths full of fangs and skin colours ranging from blue to red. They were headed straight for the palace.

There had been no time. I knew it would be a massacre, and that reality chopped at my heart like a meat cleaver.

But perhaps there was one way a single, skilled swordsperson could help. I had friends in the castle, and they needed a warning. Saraya might be the one getting married, but there was also Tembry, who was with child, and Blythe, who had once painted a portrait of me as a bloodthirsty warrior for my birthday.

I cherished that painting.

So, I ran for the secret tunnel that Saraya had helped Captain Starkis and I escape through a few days ago. If I was quick, I could get into the palace at the same time as the demons and get to the girls.

All I could hope was that Starkis and the other human rebels would catch on and work to free the soldiers kept in the barns—before the demons came down on them as foxes tore apart a chicken coop. Without weapons, those soldiers would be dead in the space of a few heartbeats.

I ran for the tunnel on farmer Thompson's land and thanked my lucky stars that I had the presence of mind to kick a rubbery tree branch into the door before Saraya magically closed it. I had never seen her do magic so openly before, and it had stumped me for a fraction of a second before I made the split decision, knowing that we might need access to it later.

It was just unfortunate that I had imagined a contingent of soldiers would be with me when I re-entered the palace. So much for that plan.

Through the dark, the sounds of distant screams spurring

me on, I felt my way through the bushes and vines, scraping my skin on brambles and thorns.

I found my branch, stuck my fingers into the side of the door and hauled it open an inch at a time. After a minute of sweating, I was able to hold my breath and squeeze into the tunnel, closing the door shut behind me.

I ran like fire was on my heels.

By the time I entered the palace, the demons were making the foundations shake and there came a distant roar. I clenched my teeth and made my way into the labyrinth of servant's tunnels. Saraya's maids would not have been permitted to attend the wedding, so there was one place I would check first—her personal rooms.

I knew the entire palace like the back of my hand because, as armsmaster, I was one of those responsible for training our military. I needed to teach my cadets how best to protect the palace. The first thing I had done when Saraya's mother had enlisted me was to memorise the palace maps. The only thing that hadn't been on there was Saraya's secret tunnel. Other than that, I knew every inch of the place.

I had known that one day, an invasion like this was possible. Lobrathia's quartz quarry was too valuable for anyone to overlook. And apparently, the demons had thought this very same thing, just as the fae.

I slammed through Saraya's servant's door, only to find Tembry, Blythe, and Altara's maid, Lucy, cowering in Saraya's closet.

A ball of rainbow-coloured fur launched itself at me with a snarl.

"Opal, no!" Tembry screamed, running out of the closet, a bundle of blankets held close to her chest.

3

The rainbow ball of fluff abruptly closed its snarling mouth and scrambled up my chest and onto my shoulder.

"Jerali's a friend!" Tembry said. "Thank God you're here, armsmaster. We don't know what's going—"

"A horde of demons is invading the land," I said simply, going to the side window and peering out. "We need to get out of here immediately."

When I turned around, the girls were gaping at me. Tembry, red-headed and slightly swollen from pregnancy, dark haired, stubborn Blythe and cherub-faced Lucy.

"Why?" asked Blythe. She was always the most fiery of the three. And the best fighter. "Demons? I mean—are you sure? They've never come above ground before." She stared at the others.

"I'm sure," I said darkly. "There's too many of them. If we stay, we are dead. I saw their numbers. They're here to take over."

Tembry clutched the bundle tighter, and it took me a beat to realise what it was. "Oh, Tem!" I rushed forward to peer at her child. "The baby's here!"

"A few days ago," she whispered. "I've called her Delilah —but now I almost wish she was still inside me. I can't let them take her. What if—"

"No one is taking her," I said firmly. "Blythe. Lucy. Help Tembry strap the baby to her back. You might all need to fight if you want to get out of here."

"What?" Tembry blanched. She was terrified. I knew that feeling, and I had discarded it years ago, condemning it as useless. Lucy and Blythe began leafing through the clothes in Saraya's wardrobe.

"What about Saraya?" Tembry asked as Blythe carefully took the tiny rosy cheeked babe from her. She was healthy, that was good. The creature on my shoulder made a distressed noise.

I shook my head. "She'll have to look after herself. There's a bunch of fae warriors with her. She should be…"

But I had no guarantee she *was* going to be fine. Because, in fact, if I let that dark thought at the back of my mind peek through, I knew that these demons would come for her first.

The creature still sitting on my shoulder, Opal, leapt onto the bed where the girls were arranging the baby's blankets. She was the size of a kitten, with pointed, cat-like ears, a sweet, round face, and a long tail she kept coiled. Her rainbow eyes filled with tears. I stared at the obviously intelligent creature—she could have only come from the fae realm.

"Oh, Opal," said Tembry, rushing to grab the creature. "You're only still a baby too. Oh!" Tembry's eyes lit up. "Opal can make illusions, Saraya told me! We can get out of here, unseen, with her help. Can you do that, Ope?"

The creature patted its eyes with a paw and nodded, sniffing.

"Well, that's helpful," I said, eyeing Opal thoughtfully, "but let's hurry."

Tembry had just strapped the baby to her back when there came a thud behind us. The main door crashed open, and a hulking crimson faced demon in the shape of a man, complete with black plate armour, stood there, bearing a naked sword. He sniffed the air with giant nostrils.

"Opal!" Tembry cried. The three girls huddled together, a sheet of glitter fell around them, and instantly, they were invisible.

But the demon warrior had already seen them and made to lunge. Except I got there first, levelling my sword at him. He stopped short and appraised me with yellow, slitted eyes.

"Are you a woman or a man?" His voice was like a heavy boot over gravel.

"Does it matter?" I asked. Honestly, to women, I was a woman. To men, I was a man because that's what they were comfortable with. No one gave a tinker's cuss what *I* thought. Only Saraya's mother had accepted me as I was when she found me on that ship a long time ago.

"It makes a difference in what I do after I kill you." He showed me all of his summer yellow teeth.

A rabid smile curved like a scimitar along my mouth. "Oh, but it makes no difference to me." I lunged.

He met me at the first strike and the second, but on the third—alas, he had never been trained by me—I feinted and proceeded to slice him precisely in the carotid artery. Blood burst from his neck and he gave one half-hearted swing before collapsing to the floor.

Shaking my head at the folly of plate armour, I picked up the demon's sword.

"Madam Opal, can you shield me too?" I asked politely.

After a little bird-like warble, I too was enveloped in the shimmering light. Now I was a part of the illusion, I could also see the girls.

I gave Blythe the demon's sword. Since she was undoubtedly the best of the three in swordplay, it was best that she have it. She took it with a wrinkled nose.

"It kills the same as any sword you've trained with," I said lightly.

She nodded.

I gave her an approving smile. "Let's go."

Leading them down into the servant's stair, I wondered which screams were coming from where. But I knew none of them would be Saraya's. I'd trained her and Altara to rival even me. I wasn't even surprised when I heard a rumour that she'd bested some of the powerful fae during her time with them. I hadn't doubted her for one second. Not only did she have magic in her that would help her best the fae, but she had a determination and strength of will I'd never seen in a person before. Part of that reason was her stepmother— a vile, cruel woman I'd known from the start would be trouble.

But I couldn't afford to think about that now. The best thing I could do to help Saraya was to make sure our loved ones got away from this mess.

The palace foundations shuddered again, and just as we reached the wooden panel in the wall that led to the secret tunnel, I heard the presence of others in our corridor.

Silently, I opened the panel and ushered the wide-eyed girls into the darkness. Goddess bless them because they went in without question. Silently, I took Opal from Tembry's shoulder and placed her on my own. I put a finger to my lips and shut the girls inside.

Booted footsteps thundered down the wooden floorboards of the passage, and I pressed myself against the wall. They didn't sound like the heavy boots I had seen on the feet of the demon I'd just dispatched.

Opal trembled on my shoulder and I placed a comforting hand on her tiny body. She quietened as we waited.

But it was not the enemy's feet shuffling uncertainly down the passage. It was Derrick, the king's manservant, closely followed by the royal contingents from neighbouring king-doms: King Osring, teenage King Junni, and his older regent. They had all come for Saraya's wedding to the fae prince. A neat present for the demons.

"Stop!" I called.

Opal's magic fell away around me. Clever little thing.

7

Derrick and the others froze, their faces contorting in panic. But it was Queen Helena, the Rubenesque leader of the Waelan Kingdom, who spoke first. "Who goes there?"

"Just me, Jerali Jones," I said, coming into view. "I have a way out. Follow me, Your Highnesses."

I opened the tunnel entrance and didn't wait for them to follow.

Tembry and the girls took one look at who was behind me and immediately started down the darkness of the tunnel.

"It's about a thousand paces long!" I called as Derrick shooed the royals in. "Let's not tarry here."

They murmured in agreement or complaint; I couldn't tell. Couldn't care, for that matter. We reached the exit point after a number of stumbling and falling incidents but all in one piece.

Farmer Thompson's lands to the east of the palace where the tunnel came out was dark and absent of demons. We could still hear the screams and sounds of fighting in the distance.

"Make for Kaalon," came a deep voice. King Osring, Lobrathia's eastern neighbour, shuffled his wiry frame to the front of the group, clutching a walking stick tightly.

"We have no supplies, no horses, no nothing," Queen Helena huffed, wiping dirt off her regal, lavender gown. "We must think this through. Where is a safe area we may hide?"

"M-My parent's house," stammered Tembry boldly. I looked at her in surprise and then remembered her parents had a large farming property. "They're in the northeastern fields. We have horses and supplies there."

"But where are the demons coming from?" Helena asked. "We don't want to walk straight into a trap."

"No indeed," said Osring darkly. "I do believe they are

coming from the quarry. There have always been old stories of demon sightings around there. That has to be it."

I had to agree that was the most likely story. The quarry was deep and vast, a perfect way for subterranean creatures to muscle their way up here.

We stood in the dark, only the sound of the trees rustling and human voices screaming— and then the sound of a demon roaring as if it had been skewered in the gut. My heart beat rapidly with excitement.

"The demons will be focusing on the city proper," I said. "If you hurry to the farm now, you'll have a chance."

"Lead the way, young lady," boomed Helena to Tembry. The other royals had no choice but to agree.

"You go on," I said to them as I handed Derrick my sword. "I'm going back to the city."

"You can't!" cried Tembry. Her newborn squeaked from her back.

"I'm going to make sure you are not followed," I said calmly. "And I need to see if Saraya is okay. I am sure they are here for her."

"And Eldon," Osring said. "Your king will be who they want."

I gave him a short bow as Tembry kissed Opal on the forehead. "Opal, protect Jerali. And you be careful," she murmured.

"I'm coming too," said Blythe firmly. "I can fight, Jerali. You know I can."

Tembry began crying, but Lucy pulled her into her arms and began whispering about her parents in her ear. I nodded to Blythe. The girl was strong and determined, excellent with a sword to boot. She had a craving for adventure, something we'd long spoken about while training. She wanted to paint the world, she said. And that gave her an eye for detail. I could very well use her.

I gave her a grin and beckoned to her as I strode off. She kissed Tembry and Lucy on their cheeks and ran after me.

But we were too late.

We arrived at the palace, crouched in the shadows of the trees lining the palace wall. Saraya, the fae commander Drakus Silverhand, the sergeant Lysander, and King Eldon were being carried, magically paralysed, in a morbid sort of procession. In the lead was Queen Glacine, now bearing a strange black tattoo on her neck.

I quivered with rage. She had been tricking us all along, that turncoat!

"Opal, listen to me," I said. "We're okay now, but Saraya is not. I need you to follow and help her. Do you understand me?"

From my shoulder, the tiny creature gave out a sad, crooning noise, sort of like a cross between a bird and cat. Her small tail flicked irritably.

I plucked her from my shoulder and commanded her as I would any of my soldiers. "Stay hidden, eavesdrop where you can, and help her get out of wherever they are taking her." I looked up at the palace. "Blythe and I are going to stay here and make sure these bastards don't ruin Lobrathia. Do you understand me?"

Opal looked me in the eye, nodded, and leapt from my hand into the lawn, becoming invisible under her own illusion.

I beckoned to Blythe to follow me. Keeping to the shadows, I snuck up upon a dawdling demon. I grabbed him and snapped his head to the side, breaking his neck. I took his demon blade and wiped the human blood off it using the creature's pants. We needed to find what happened to our men. I listened intently.

"There's fighting at the back," Blythe whispered, wiping her own sword.

That's where our people needed help. "Let's go."

We skirted around the side of the palace and found ourselves in a melee of demons and fae warriors.

Blythe let out a battle cry I was proud of, stabbing at a smaller demon. I covered her back, knowing that as skilled as I had made her, a melee was a different skill set entirely. As I ducked and swung at a demon warrior, severing his femoral artery, I came up to find one of the fae sergeants, the massive dark-haired brute, fighting alongside me.

"Where is Drake?" he called to me in that deep boom of his.

Never mind that this was one of the fae who'd imprisoned me— I supposed we were fighting on the same side for the darned moment.

"Taken." I stabbed another demon and stopped one from coming in behind Blythe. "Along with the blonde one, Saraya, and the king."

The fae oaf swore and tore through another three demons in quick succession. I was impressed. I had never seen fae fight before, but this was something to behold.

Blythe cried out as, from nowhere, a swarm of demons jumped into the melee, surrounding us and the fae. As I cut, stabbed, beheaded, and ducked, I tried to carve a path to the outside of the mess. I pulled Blythe away from a demon's downswing just in time. She was sweating, covered in demon ichor. I was proud of her, but this was not a fight we could win. There were too many. I caught the fae brute's eye.

"We need to get out of here!"

Blythe grunted, going one on one with another demon. I let her for the moment, but I could see her strain.

The stomping of boots made us all turn. It was a contingent of demon warriors, all bearing a scorpion crest.

The fae brute roared in anger and began chopping and slicing his way through them, alongside his remaining warriors.

But we were overcome. No less than six demon warriors pinned the fae brute to the ground and got out a set of glowing black shackles. A dark snake wound its way through my heart.

"Blythe, run!" I cried.

This had been a mistake. I should have let Blythe run with the others. I had come to terms with death years ago, but Blythe had more to live yet. Except the raven-haired girl was not listening to me, instead she grunted as she skewered another lesser demon.

"Blythe!" I cried. We were now separated by fifteen paces. I needed to get her out. I needed to drive the attention away from her.

Blythe suddenly let out a cry as a demon blade pierced her arm. She fell to her knees. My heart twisted.

I had worked my way to the outskirts of the melee. Behind me, the dark night awaited. I looked back at the horde where Blythe was now surrounded by those scorpion-bearing monsters.

Never in my life had I run from a fight. I wasn't going to start now.

I let out a cry and lunged towards them.

2

SARAYA

"Wake up, human."

Cold water struck my face, and I came to with a start.

Gasping in the darkness, blinking the droplets of water away, I tried to make out my jeering tormentor. But my vision was too blurry. I'm guessing a residual effect from the potion my stepmother—*no*, she was not family to me now—Glacine had shoved down my throat.

My hand flew to my neck only to find a cold, hard band of thick metal around it. Chain links were attached, leading away from it, and someone yanked on the end.

I jerked forward, my face hitting wet stone. Guttural laughs assaulted my ears from above.

They had collared and chained me by the neck like an animal.

Clawed fingers dug into my skin where my mother's purple Ellythian wedding silks had been torn and shredded. The smell of blood, decay, and sulphur filled my nose. I gagged as I was roughly pulled to my feet. My own hands

13

were useless, shackled in glowing cuffs that cut me off from my magic. A dark, oily curl of despair wound its way around me.

My father. Drake. Lysander. Tembry, baby Delilah, Opal. I had no idea where anyone was—if they were okay. If they were even alive.

"How long was I out?" I managed to choke out.

But they did not deign to answer me. Instead, they dragged me forward as if I weighed nothing, the sound of the metal links rattling like defeat in my ears.

These were the warrior demons, I knew, as I squeezed my eyes shut and opened them to find some semblance of focus. The scorpion-bearing fighters that had come to overrun us. To take my father, the king of Lobrathia, and me away. But they had also taken Drakus Silverhand and Lysander, the commander and sergeant of the elite forces of the Black Fae Court.

All this time, I had thought the fae were sending the demons to steal human magic at birth. We had never suspected the demons themselves were doing it of their own voilition.

Demons, much like the fae, were a fairy-tale to most humans. They were supposed to live their subterranean lives, separate and content, away from us.

Luminous quartz light shone beyond me and I made out the forms of multiple man-sized demons. *Luminous Quartz.* The demons had come into the human realm from the quarry where we mined the precious, light-giving, magic-collecting crystals. We'd never once suspected this could happen. How could we have been so stupid? How could *I* have been so incredibly stupid?

My vision slowly returned as they guided me down a low-ceilinged earthen tunnel, the walls lined with luminous quartz crystals that shone brilliantly like they were brand new. They must have been mining them from under the earth only recently. Luminous quartz needed to be charged with solar light to give off light. That, or magic.

Demons had been prowling the earth for hundreds of years in their astral form. A transparent, ghost-like version of themselves, collecting the magical seed from human infants at birth. Stealing magic from humans so that we'd never come into our own powers. But when they had stormed my palace the night of my wedding to Prince Daxian of the Black Court, they had been in their very real, physical form. That had to mean that they had only recently opened a portal into our realm.

I would have to find out the truth. Because wherever they were now taking me wasn't likely to be for my own benefit. Why they wanted us, why they wanted my father, and why Glacine had tricked us and planned this marriage to him and then progressively poisoned him so that his brain became permanently addled, was beyond me. There were things at play here that I clearly knew nothing about.

I wondered how much of this my mother knew. She had been training me in preparation for joining the order of warrior midwives from infancy, and I'd had no idea. How much more had she known? But it was useless thinking about that now because she was long dead, and here I was, in the demon realm, under the earth, probably going to meet my death. I wanted to vomit, scream, and flail about. But I was tired, I had fought a hard battle and at every turn, my efforts to save my kingdom were thwarted.

They tugged me up a series of stone steps, and I had my wits about me enough to observe these demon warriors.

These were stronger, elite versions of the pesky, easy-to-kill beings that I'd been hunting these past few months. They were all over six feet, riddled with heavy muscle, and clearly trained to hunt and kill. They wore a light type of fighting armour, black and brown, with that black scorpion on their chests. But I knew nothing about the demon kingdoms. I had no idea whose house bore the scorpion sigil.

We were joined by a contingent of demon guards when I was led outside, and I only knew it was outside because of the foul wind that rustled my wild hair, long since come loose from my bridal hairdo. The sky above us was a completely all-black void, but of course, this realm had no sky at all. That made sense seeing as the demons lived under the earth and could not suffer sunlight for long, if at all. The land beneath my sandalled feet was a yellow sand-like substance that I was sure had no fertility to it. I wondered what the demons ate and shivered.

One of the demons came forward, a captain by the way the others parted to let him through and took over the thick black chain leading from my collar. He gestured to another demon, and this one carried a second chain, roughly fastening it to the shackles on my magic snuffing handcuffs.

"If you fall, girl," the captain snarled, his red eyes taking in my barely covered form, "we're draggin' you." His breath smelled like rotting fish and I suppressed the urge to gag, instead meeting him solidly eye to eye.

They began walking at a fast pace, pulling me along by my chains. It was only sheer adrenaline that kept my tired body hobbling fast enough to keep up. There was a gash in my thigh, as well as other sharp pains of the bruises and aches in my body. But pain was something I knew. So, I distracted myself by making observations of where I was.

We seemed to be on some sort of military compound where one-story buildings were set in neat lines. But then we rounded a corner and I almost stumbled in my step.

In the distance, looming before us like some mysterious jewel in the dark, was a magnificent palace of gold and silver, lined with black. Luminous quartz lights of all colours shone from the windows, the turrets, the spires, and towers. It was larger than my own palace in Quartz and larger indeed than any palace that I had seen in the human realm.

They dragged me through black curling gates and up a circular drive, where a fountain depicting a lewd scene between a man and multiple women made me raise my eyebrows. But that fountain was nothing compared to what waited for me inside this demonic palace.

The entrance was no less than twenty feet high, flanked with black metal doors and guarded by seven-foot-tall monsters—black, rotund, powerful creatures with snarling mouths full of yellow, serrated teeth. It was made all the worse by red luminous quartz light glaring from behind them.

I cringed as we passed these guards, and they leered down at me before my breath was taken away by the black and marbled entrance hall. But drenched in the garish, red quartz light, the effect was rather sinister and anxiety-provoking. Something, I suspected, that was done on purpose. It reminded me of Glacine, how in her rooms, she preferred to use the red quartz light. That realisation made my stomach churn. She really *was* from here after all.

The demon warriors veered towards the right, and immediately, I recognised the tall doors of a throne room. I knew that I was going to meet some sort of king. Though I knew nothing about the nobility in the realms below the earth, I suspected that the vile creature I had known as Stepmother for five years would be in there. Anger unfurled within me, fresh and bright.

I knew I looked awful. My mother's bridal silks were torn around my lower half, showing more leg than was proper. The blouse that bared my upper midriff now had one sleeve hanging off my shoulder, showing the curve of my breast on that side. My clothes and arms were stained with my own blood and that of the demons I had killed during the melee at my own palace.

I was in no state to meet a king, but I would do it with all the pride of a princess of the human realm. I straightened my spine and pushed my shoulders back, the glowing cuffs on my hands clinking. The demon beside me growled in warning but I paid him no heed as we headed straight through the second set of double doors.

The throne room was like none I'd ever seen before.

All matte black walls, and a long black carpet that was wide enough for a group of people to walk through, led up to a huge golden throne, haloed by an ornate gold panel. It wasn't just this that had me surprised. A further six thrones lined the long walk—silver inlaid chairs, each on their own dais. In each sat a demon male, some type of nobility from the looks of their rich dress and sparkling jewels. Behind them, taking up the rest of the hall, no less than a hundred lesser demons milled about, murmuring in low voices as I came into view.

But as we walked down the long carpet, I saw who were standing by the smaller thrones, and my blood ran cold. In each seat sat a demon lord, but standing next to them were a number of women in sheer dresses. While the number of women ranged from two to six, the way they were chained did not. Each woman bore a black metal cuff around her throat, black metal links adjoining it to a matching silver, gem-encrusted cuff encircling the lord's wrist.

My fingers twitched in a habit that, if I didn't have on these Goddess damned magic cuffs, would have me summoning my astral sword in a flash. But as it stood, I had no magical ability right now. All I could do was clench my fists so tightly that the blood stopped flowing to them. Because as I walked down the carpet, minor demons crowding around the thrones to jeer at me, the lords' gazes sat heavily on my body, weighing me down. The gazes of the women seemed latent, dazed, their faces pale and drawn.

Yet again, I could do nothing.

I was powerless.

And no amount of rage or anger would help me. But I would be damned if I let them do to me what they wanted. I would fight it every step of the way. Fight it like they'd never seen a human woman fight before.

Because no matter what they did to me. I was now an initiate of the Order of Temari. Touched by the wild and ferocious Goddess Umali, whose sign I bore, hidden on my forehead.

So as I looked up at what awaited me on the main throne, I repeated the oath I'd made in the ruins of the ancient temple of the seven goddesses in the Temari forest.

I am the sword in the night. The protector of human potential. The shield against all that is evil. I accept this pledge.

My eyes found my stepmother first. She was standing next to the throne, in a new slinking dress of black, a strange green tinge to her skin, and that awful dark tattoo on the side of her neck. She had hidden her true self from us for five whole years. At that time, she had flogged me every other month, and as a girl of thirteen when it started, I'd had no idea what to do except protect my younger sister. So I had done nothing and borne her abuse.

Little had I known that she was a demon through and through.

And looking at her now, my shame and hopelessness were magnified, creeping through my core like a suffocating poison.

Breathe, I bade myself. *Just breathe.* I would get through this because I had no choice. Just as I had gotten through the years of her torment.

Despite Glacine's dark presence, the being who sat on the throne dwarfed her completely.

He sat on his gold throne, exuding a malevolent presence —a thing of nightmares. He was a large demonic male with a face made by the devil himself. Corpse white skin, frightening alabaster irises, and low cheekbones. He was completely bald and black tattoos marked his entire skull, neck, and arms. His lips were black in a jarring way, and a crown of black sat atop his hairless head. He was huge, full of hulking muscle that didn't look quite real.

Unnatural, a voice in my head screamed. *Run.*

But of course, I could do nothing.

Kneeling on the floor on the other side of the throne were three human women, dressed in sheer metallic shifts, their eyes trained on the floor. On their necks was the same scorpion tattoo Glacine had on hers. From what I could see of their downcast faces they were beautiful, with skin a bronze shade slightly darker than mine.

The backs of my eyes burned ferociously at the realisation that every single human woman in this room appeared to be a slave. An angry scream crept its way up my throat, but I swallowed it forcefully back down. My hands trembled slightly and I irritably flexed them.

As we came up to this strange demon king, one of my demon gaolers pushed me onto the floor, where I landed awkwardly on my fists, the tight, glowing handcuffs preventing me from using them properly. I bit back a cry of pain as my clotting thigh wound tore anew. I managed to push myself onto my knees and then back onto my feet. The crowd around the hall fell silent.

"Princess," drawled the deep voice of the demon king. "So you are the new Warrior Midwife. The one who's been killing my collectors."

I looked into his eyes, those eerily white irises ringed in black, and suppressed a cringe.

"That's me," I said calmly.

His head cocked to the left, just a fraction, and I knew he was surprised at my defiance. He did what any man would do when faced with a half-dressed woman. He dragged his eyes down my form, taking in every inch of brown skin— courtesy of my dark Ellythian mother and white Lobrathian father. But I did revel in the fact that my skin was also caked in dried demon blood. The blood of *his* warriors. I saw his eyes take *that* in too.

The king leaned back on his throne, and just as he opened his mouth to speak, I blurted out, "Is someone going to tell me who you are? Because I have no idea." I looked him up and down like he was dirt on my shoe.

His nostrils flared in anger, and I watched his every movement carefully for signs of what type of being he was. He flicked his wrist.

My legs were kicked from under me. I lurched to the black carpet once again, this time landing on my face to avoid splitting my thigh wound further. Dazed, rough hands hauled me up, and I just managed to get my knees under me before they plonked me back down.

Blinking the pain of my face away, I was just able to concentrate as Glacine's icicle-ridden voice said, "His Royal Highness, King Havrok Scorpax, is speaking to you. And you *will* address him with respect."

I glanced up into her cyanotic coloured eyes, and she regarded me coolly back. I said, "And who is His Highness, King Havrok Scorpax to you, *Stepmother*?"

Her upper lip curled, but it was the king who answered simply, "Glacine is my wife."

SARAYA

I felt like my soul had left my body.

His wife.

I stared at Glacine in horror, and she smirked back at me.

"All that time," I said hoarsely, "you were married to my father, you were *already* married?"

"We in the demon lands are more *progressive* when it comes to marriage," she replied smoothly.

Clearly, if your husband was allowed multiple, scantily clad female slaves. I wanted to strangle her. "Why?" I asked through clenched teeth.

She glanced at the demon king, *her blasted husband.*

The king flicked his wrist again, and two demons sprang to attention. "Bring forth my cousin. Let us discuss this with him."

I frowned, scanning the crowd on either side of me. Who was his cousin?

"What have you done to my father?" I croaked. "Have you killed him?"

The king's white eyes simply stared at me in that cold, menacing way before a blow to my left cheek sent me careening back down to the floor. I hated myself for the cry that escaped my throat, but there was no mistaking the strength in the arm of my demon guard.

Pain bloomed through the bones of my face, and I squeezed my eyes shut, not moving any muscle as I lay on the floor, trying to control myself. But tears still gathered in my eyes. If I'd had my magic, I would've numbed my face—I could manipulate my body intricately like that—just so I could continue this situation without looking weak. It hurt me to the core that I couldn't.

Defenceless, I lay on the floor like a child, unable to summon the energy to push myself back up. Shame grated through me, a dull slice through my spirit. But I was tired, so tired after fighting for my life, my muscles felt like liquid, my bones like rubber.

It wasn't until the squeak of wheels and a metallic creak approached me that my eyes flew open. Kneeling in a tall, cast-iron cage that glowed with a faint green light, was a tall, muscled fae male with short mahogany hair and a tanned, chiselled jaw. I would know that face and form anywhere.

Drakus Silverhand, the fae Commander of the elite forces of Black Court, glowered where he knelt, hands bound in black shackles that sizzled with a foul and potent magic. Whatever they had used on him was clearly taking a toll because his breathing was obvious and ragged, and sweat gleamed across his handsome face, plastering the longer parts of his hair to his forehead. His hazel eyes darted around the room, and as they wheeled his cage to a stop next to me, his eyes found mine, lying like a fool on the floor. He blanched at the sight of me, and I would never forget what he said before they'd taken us from my palace.

"I am Wyxian's firstborn son. My mother lied to the king."

And then the words that shattered everything I had known to be true.

"Your father's contract bound you to me. Not Daxian. They took my memories away. But I still felt you then, in the fae realm. I feel you now."

During the war with the fae thirty years ago, my father, and the fae King Wyxian of Black Court, had signed a contract in their own blood. That I, my father's firstborn princess, would be married to Wyxian's firstborn son across the mountains. My father had done it to stop the war, and then he'd lied to everyone about it. He had told me he was going to try to get around the contract, but he never found a way. As soon as I came of age at nineteen, the dark fae of Black Court came for me, and Daxian and I confirmed our engagement in blood. But just as I had walked down the aisle to marry the sorry brute, these demons had invaded the palace.

And then Drake had revealed this—that *he* was Wyxian's bastard and firstborn. Meaning that I was...*his.*

But who was Drake's mother, and why had she lied? There had to be more to it. I was still confused and worse, now befuddled by the blow to my head.

"Cousin," jeered King Havrok Scorpax, leaning forward to get a better look at Drake in his cage.

Drake frowned up at the king, a tic in his jaw pulsing.

"I'm assuming with Wyxian's death," Havrok said. " Your memories are returned? Our mothers are sisters of a sort, did you know?"

25

I dragged myself off the floor in a painfully slow manner, my bones aching, feeling every bruise and cut from the battle before. The long gash on my thigh stung something awful as I twisted to get to my knees. I needed to listen to this.

Drake's voice came out as a ragged rasp. "My mother is—"

"The deity of the tree known as the Black Widow, yes," the king said lazily. "My mother is the deity of the river that runs around her, the Black Scorpax river. That makes us *cousins*."

I had to stop myself from gaping. Drake was the child of a minor goddess *and* a fae king? That explained why he seemed stronger than a regular fae. Why he just seemed something *more* in general.

"You see those tattoos on his arms, little Princess?" The king nodded towards Drake's rolled up sleeves. I glanced at the runic black tattoos that covered Drake's hands and arms. They started with symbols down his fingers, runic wheels on the backs of his hands, then snaking up his arms like the branches of a tree. I had looked at them often, in passing, wondering at their meaning. "Well," said the demon king. "Drake was born of a monster goddess—that makes him a *monster*. His powers were so vast and the need for his mate so...fierce that at age thirteen, his mother had him bound. Those tattoos shackle him, control him—prevent him from being the monster he was born to be."

I looked at Drake in wonder as he glowered at the king. "How do you know all of this?" he asked.

"I have a friend of yours here. Captured on his way to you —the mage, Dacre Liversblood."

Drake's jaw ticking was the only sign of any emotion.

"He was the one your parents used to bind you, so he tells

me. We caught him coming across the mountain border. Strange things he's told me, the mage of Obsidian Court."

This was beyond anything I had imagined. Drake was completely someone different than I thought he was. But then again, anything I had actually known about him was a rumour or an educated guess.

"See, I've been curious about your...abilities," continued Havrok, white eyes gleaming with greed and envy. "Wyxian's been using you all this time—to murder and mutilate on his behalf. Tell me, how is it you are rumoured to be more powerful than any fae even *with* your magical bindings?"

Drake bristled but did not reply. I licked my lips. Where was this going? What did Drake have to do with my father? With me and Lobrathia?

"Imagine my surprise," said Havrok, rising from his throne. "When I heard tell of a...prophecy."

"Don't," said Drake through clenched teeth.

Havrok stilled, and Glacine shifted behind him.

The demon warrior that had wheeled in the cage stuck a metal rod through the bars, and magic whirred through the air along with something that sizzled.

Electricity.

My mother had first taught me the word. Like lightning but smaller. It was the same spark that I saw flying through nerves in the body and the brain.

Drake's spine straightened so quickly when it struck him that I thought he might've pulled something, but he didn't utter a sound. His eyes slid over to mine and the pain in them tore through me so unexpectedly that I had to clench my fists tight in empathy. This fae had been my enemy, but I had been fooled. There was someone even worse to contend with. All I could do was meet Drake's gaze, and when the current stopped, his body sagged only a little.

"See?" the king whispered, walking down the steps from his throne. "Even bound, his strength is unparalleled. That current should have killed him."

I felt my own face twist in disgust at the demon king as he prowled down his throne stairs towards us with his face lit up in a gross sort of wonder.

"I would like to see what would happen if your runes are taken off."

My blood ran cold at Drake's reaction. His head whipped up, his lips thinning. "You can't," he rasped. "You—" He then looked at me, and those hazel eyes struck me like a hammer. It was like he was trying to tell me something, but I couldn't understand.

Havrok laughed, a blood-curdling sound. "You would be compelled to claim your bond mate, I know." He then looked at me with a smirk.

"I don't understand," I said.

"They never told you why Wyxian chose you?" Havrok's brows lifted, but his eyes sparkled maliciously. "Oh, how brilliant, indeed. How depraved. Oh, the cunning of the dark fae."

I frowned, looking from Drake to Havrok then Glacine.

"When a fae is made King," Havrok continued, towering over me, "they are allowed counsel with the all-knowing Mother Jacaranda tree in Blossom Court. Upon his coronation, Wyxian was told that his firstborn son would destroy the realm as he knew it. And that the only way to ensure that didn't happen was to bind him to another of royal blood. But that union would destroy her."

My blood chilled in my capillaries. The day my father

had told me that he had sold me like cattle to the fae king, I had thought it was the worst possible thing that could happen to me. But I was wrong. This was so much worse than I could have imagined. Wyxian had wanted a princess to *sacrifice*.

"And Wyxian thought his firstborn son was Daxian," I muttered.

"Magic does not care for human law," sneered Havrok. "A son is a son, legitimate or not. Blood is *blood*. So, he made the human king swear a blood oath that they could use you. In doing so, both of you were bound."

Use you. My skin crawled. If all this was true, what exactly did this Havrok want? I would've asked, except my face still pounded painfully with every beat of my heart. I knew another blow would cause permanent damage without my magic to heal it. But I was desperate to know if my father was alive. My eyes found Glacine, still standing next to the throne. Her face remained imperious as she looked back at me. I wondered what her vile, aggressive mind was thinking. Every mark on my back suddenly stung anew, and I looked away from her to the king.

"I have plans for you two," Havrok smiled with all his teeth, and I saw that his canines were elongated into sharp points. "Soul bound, eh?" he sneered at Drake, whose lip curled. "Husband and wife-to-be? The blood contract is still in place after all."

I grimaced. I had signed a blood contract with Daxian on the day of our engagement. But this knowledge rendered Daxian's blood on that old piece of paper obsolete. But *my* blood was still on there. One-half of the union had pledged themselves.

"By now," Havrok said with a smile, "my warriors will

have taken over Lobrathia, and the humans already know Glacine as their queen. Therefore, I am now your new king."

So, this had been their plan. To use Glacine as a familiar face to take control of Lobrathia. With her by his side, the citizens would have no choice but to accept Havrok as King. A snarl crept out of me, but I forced it back down. To my horror, it came out as a strangled noise instead. Glacine tossed a smirk my way.

"I would like Drakus Silverhand to join me as one of my liege lords. Your power is…" Havrok spread his palms out, "…too valuable to have elsewhere."

The implication was clear. *Be mine or be no one's.*

Drake remained abnormally silent and still in his cage. All around us, the demons in the hall were listening keenly, excited murmurs bubbling at the thought of a new monster, no doubt.

"Bring out the mage. I want it done now," Havrok barked.

Drake's head whipped up as another set of chains clanked, and a black-robed figure came through a side door. With his hood down, I could see he was fae, appearing to be in his late twenties. He was onyx-haired and might have been handsome if his entire face wasn't covered in black runes, symbols, and numbers. He glowered as the cuff around his neck rubbed the skin red raw. He bore a black eye, and he too, had glowing black shackles binding his wrists.

"Dacre Liversblood." Havrok grinned with those sharp teeth. "I just want it half un-done, you understand? We need to see how mad he gets. I need to see the monster peek through."

Dacre glanced at Drake apologetically and then back at the demon king. "You might live to regret this, Your Highness."

Havrok tilted his head back and laughed madly, and then glared at the mage. "Do as you're told."

Maybe he *was* mad.

As they shoved the mage of Obsidian Court forward, he peered at me curiously, and a small frown graced his tattoo-ridden face. The points of his fae ears, also tattooed, twitched.

The demon guards removed the shackles from Dacre's hands and held tightly to the chain bound to his collar.

From behind Drake's cage, the guards shoved that metal device through, pushing Drake to the other side of his cage.

"Princess," Drake rasped. "I'm sorry, I won't be able to control—"

"Quiet!" Havrok shouted.

My heart clenched as the demons shoved Drake forward with the electricity once again. He jerked forward, his lips pressing together in pain. An angry heat flared in me. I had always been drawn to Drake in some way I couldn't explain. In a way that hadn't made sense. Now I had this explanation before me—the fact that we were soul bound, the fact that as a child, he had tried to cross the mountains to find me, if what Havrok said was true. I felt a prickling vine cramp around my insides and pull me forward. I was hot and cold all at once.

Drake had no choice but to press himself up against the bars of the cage on Dacre's side as a demon held out a roll of fabric. Within it was a set of sharp wooden tools. The mage reached for a pencil-like one, its tip filed into a severe point.

He began at Drake's right hand, and I cringed as Dacre's lips moved in some silent fae spell before he pressed the tool into Drake's skin. A crimson droplet welled before blood dribbled to the floor. Drake turned his head to look at me, and his eyes bore such a great and terrible sadness that it coiled around my own heart.

"I'm sorry, Saraya," he rasped.

Surprise flew through me, ragged and cold. I had the sudden realisation that his voice bore the weight of an entire life of seeking me. *Me*. I couldn't fathom that he had known of me long before I'd ever known about him. How could I have never known?

The demons didn't stop me when I stood and went to Drake's cage, but they yanked me back when I reached to touch the bars.

"Look, she feels it already," Havrok said gleefully.

Only *I* knew the pull towards him wasn't a new sensation. I was just giving into it for the first time.

Drake rumbled low in his throat, like the sound of distant thunder. And the entire time, he didn't take his eyes off me.

Blood dripped.

Drake's jaw ticked.

And still, he didn't take his eyes off me.

The mage wiped the blood off Drake's arms with a rag while he remained impossibly still, eyes searching my face as if seeing it for the first time. It made goosebumps erupt all over me, to see a male looking at me that way—desire, I think, mixed with an intense curiosity that seemed so out of place given our situation. I wondered what he saw in me.

But all I could do was look at him back in sympathy as the mage cut into him. I knew pain. From looking after women in labour for eight years, and enduring Glacine's whippings, I knew pain inside and out. And Drake handled it like a veteran.

I wondered if that ability was a part of the monster that was inside of him. But as I looked into his eyes as the fae mage worked, I couldn't help but see the eyes of a young man who had been through a lot. Not a sort of killing machine

Havrok seemed to expect. Emery and Briar back at the Academy had called Drake and his sergeants 'psychos' and had been terribly afraid of them. But I had only ever seen Drake be protective of others.

Then again, I hadn't been there when he took over my own palace by force. What exactly was this person capable of?

I could see the magic of his bindings coming undone. It began slowly. A darkness overcame Drake's eyes, and black spread from his pupil all the way out to the edges. Something in the air shifted, and the particles felt charged. It felt like the very air was waiting.

Then Dacre wiped the last of the blood away and stepped back, placing the wooden tool back into its pouch. Drake looked down at his arm, and we both saw that his tattoos had been hollowed out. Their lines were still there, but they were no longer a solid colour. It was done. He growled low in his throat. I swallowed down the lump that had grown in mine and took a tentative step away from the cage.

"That's halfway," the mage said, warily looking at Drake, who was staring at his forearm with those new, midnight eyes.

The mage's voice dragged me back to reality. Behind me, the demon lords shifted, and all around us, the minor demons craned their necks and whispered in hissing voices.

Glacine was still. Havrok leaned forward on his throne. "What say you, Drakus Silverhand?"

Drake slowly looked up at the demon king, and when he spoke, his voice was a gravelling rasp that sounded barely like the fae I had known back in Lobrathia. "I want my mate."

Heat coursed through me like a king tide. I took another step away from the cage.

33

Havrok laughed. "And so, you shall have her. But soon, my monster. Soon." He gestured to the mage.

"Now do the rune to bind him to me. He needs to listen to every command I make."

My blood ran cold as I stared in horror, first at Drake, then the mage. Drake didn't do anything except grip the bars of his cage with white-knuckled fists as Dacre Liversblood strode over to the king and began tattooing a fae rune onto an empty space on his forearm. Drake's breathing quickened, and all I could do was watch him as he stared at the king with such rabid hate that I thought he might actually crumble those metal bars with his bare hands.

But he didn't. And a silent sigh of relief escaped me. *I want my mate.* Would he even be cognisant in this form? Would he know himself, or was he now like an animal, reacting to his own instincts?

King Havrok was waving his arm at us with a smirk, the new tattoo shiny with residual blood. The fae mage turned, solemn-faced, his nostrils flaring with controlled anger or despair, I wasn't sure. But the way he was looking at Drake suggested to me that he cared for him.

Havrok gestured to his warriors again.

"Return them to their cells, empty the hall. I need to speak with my demon lords."

Just as Drake turned to look at me, the warriors reached that instrument through the bars again and shocked him with the current. Drake thrashed silently and fell to the floor of his cage.

A small flower of pride blossomed in me. Whatever he was, Drake took the pain like a warrior. I couldn't help but respect that.

As they wheeled him away, my own gaolers yanked me

backwards by my collar chain, and I fell to my knees, just barely able to scramble back up before they could start dragging me along the floor.

I was walked back down the black carpet, surrounded by demon warriors once again. The lesser demons murmured and jeered around me, but I only had eyes for one thing. The human female slaves standing on the podiums next to the demon lords. Dejected faces, in chains that clanked so heavy.

And I could do nothing about it.

4

DRAKE

aged.

I wanted out of this gods-damned cage. I bared my teeth and paced the small confine in the darkness of the prison cell they'd wheeled me into, trying to burn off the sudden murderous energy that had taken over me.

Blood. Kill. Destroy.

I took a huge breath, trying to still my raging thoughts.

The monster now prowled freely inside my skin. While the runes had bound the darkness inside a cage of magic, I was finely-controlled violence. But now that control was slipping. I was scrambling at a cliff's edge, struggling to maintain my grip on humanity. The two sides of me were fighting and I was starting to think my humanity was on the losing side. The darkness was too familiar, too alluring, too powerful. And stuck in a prison, power was something I badly wanted.

Getting my memories back turned out to be as jarring as a spiked mace rattling around in my brain. They'd been taken away from me as a thirteen-year-old.

The fucking demon king Havrok Scorpax was my cousin in name only. We shared no real blood, and he was as depraved as they came down here. His sick fascination with my power was going to get Saraya killed. In all of my travels, I'd never heard of this demon's name. I had been down in this realm before, but never to this palace, which I knew had been ruled by another demon king not long ago. But that's how demons were, their search for power led to volatile, ever changing thrones. Someone was always plotting in a demon court. There was always someone younger, and stronger. And that person was Havrok right now, the son of a goddess, just like me.

I remember the day my power came into focus as a teenager. It was like something had sprouted in me overnight —a wild, ferocious, insatiable tree and its branches were willing me to do things. To kill, to maim, to destroy. And most of all...

Get to the one person who was going to make it all better. The person who was going to sit in the dark tentacular branches, caress them, sing them a song, and make them calm again.

It had given me a primal, unforgiving urge to seek her out and claim her as mine. I had wanted to leave my forest home and run beyond the mountains to find her because I always knew where she was. When she'd gone on summer holidays to Peach Tree City, when she returned, when she travelled around her kingdom. I felt her movements, tracked her, and pined for her.

It wasn't until I did actually run away from the treehouse in which I lived, deep in the Black Grove, that my goddess mother petitioned my father to come after me. They found me in the Temari forest and dragged me all the way to Obsidian Court. I had screamed until my throat stopped working. I'd gotten so close to my mate, and they'd taken it all away. That sense of despair was something I would never forget.

Until they made me forget.

At thirteen, I was getting too powerful for my mother to control, and when Dacre, in his high tower, had tattooed the runes around my fingers, I felt the bond between Saraya and me dampen a little. When he'd completed the runes along my arms, I almost couldn't feel her—she lay at the back of my mind, distant but still there. By the time Dacre had tied the binding off at my chest, I couldn't feel her at all. That night after my mother—in an unusual display of mothercrafting—tucked me into bed, I fell asleep looking for Saraya in the corners of my mind. By morning, I had no recollection of knowing her presence at all.

Now, the anger I felt at having those precious memories taken away from me stung so badly that I wanted to rip someone's head off. Only one thing kept me from jumping up and down in my cage like a rabid beast: the intense desire to find Saraya at all costs— at any cost. In order to get back to her, I needed to have my wits. I needed to think. I needed to hold the beast back.

The memory of what I had been like that day I had tried to run to her haunted me. It was a feral and all-consuming desire. I had been thirteen then, but now I was a male grown.

A monster fully grown.

My runes kept a monster at bay. A monster that wanted its mate and would let no force in heaven or hell get in the way of that.

Naturally, something like me, capable of mass destruction,

is terrified of nothing. But this? This was my one true fear—hurting Saraya. And now that they'd taken half of my binding off, I could barely contain myself.

I had loved Saraya my entire life. And the monster inside of me didn't know the gravity of that emotion. I couldn't be certain what would happen if Havrok had Dacre taken my runes off all the way.

The demons had taken great pains to secure me since they knew what I was capable of. Not only did they have me in tourmaline shackles, which weakened me magically and physically, but my wheeled cage was also made of tourmaline. They had then wheeled me inside what looked like a dungeon, with only a tiny flame on the wall sconce outside to keep me company.

It was lucky I was made for the dark.

My eyes caught a darting movement hobbling into my cage. I frowned for a moment before the jolt of realisation caught me, and I yanked the kitten-like creature up. It was Saraya's lumzen. The fae illusion-making creature that she always had with her—first, at the Mountain Academy, and then it had watched over her and Tembry's newborn baby at Quartz Palace.

Half of my brain was telling me to squeeze the creature dead in my hands. The other half was telling me that she belonged to Saraya and that I couldn't do that. She was important to Saraya, and that meant she was important to me.

The lumzen was still a juvenile, easily fitting into the palm of my hand, her tiny heartbeat rapid against her ribs. But she was weak and injured. She cooed softly at me, and I saw that both her back legs were broken. Anger shifted within me like a dense shadow. That urge to kill and destroy waking up again. Someone had stepped on this lumzen perhaps, but she'd been smart enough to drag herself away and find me.

"Why didn't you find Saraya?" I asked in what I thought was a curious voice, but it really came out as a monstrous gravelly sound. I set her down, trying really hard to be gentle as the opalescent sheen of her coat glittered dimly in the low light. Her wide, rainbow coloured eyes looked imploringly up at me and I nodded. "I know, little guy. I know." The pain she must be in would be incredible.

My magic was not the healing sort. Not like Saraya's— that joined, sewed, created. No, my magic was all serrated edges like a roughly hewn blade. It was made to take, to destroy, to hurt.

So if only because I needed something to do with my hands, to distract me from wanting to eat the thing, I set to work.

I took off my shirt, tore off a strip, and rolled it up tightly to make a miniature splint. I tore off another few clean pieces to make bandages. Fuck the shirt, honestly. It had blood all over most of it anyway.

"This is going to hurt." For some reason, I was concerned about her pain.

She warbled, and it struck me in a way that it shouldn't have. Perhaps as a monster, I now related more to animals than humans or fae. That's certainly the way it had been for me as a child.

But I took her little hind leg and felt it up and down and set her bone so the pieces were straight. She was lucky they were fairly clean breaks, so I then splinted it and tied the bandages around it. I repeated the process on the other side. She made no noise but began trembling like a newborn pup.

I sighed and laid down on the bottom of my cage so I could set her on my chest.

"Sleep, little one," I whispered. "Because that's all we can do right now."

The sight of Saraya, her mother's clothes torn, lying on the floor after what had clearly been a horrible blow to the face, had brought a rage in me so fierce that I thought, just for a moment, that my power would tear me open.

I traced a finger down one of the tourmaline rods of my cage, feeling the dull ache of tiredness enter me. I wondered what it would take to bend them apart, escape, find Saraya and get out of here. But I would still need to know what became of my sergeants, Lysander and Slade. I knew Lysander was down here, but Slade, I had no idea about. He knew the demon lands well due to his prolonged stint here as a child. But for him to return here could very well destroy him.

I exhaled, long and slow, trying to get rid of the irritation that consumed me. But it didn't work, so I settled for stroking the little lumzen instead.

"I think I will call you Fluffy," I said in my new gravelly voice. "I have no idea what my mate called you."

She let out a little faint squeak before her breathing evened out and she fell asleep.

My mate. It felt right. It felt like the only true and good thing in this world.

When I got out of here, I was going to rip Havrok apart from spinal cord to head. Saraya could have Glacine as she desired, but the demon king would be *mine*.

I WAS AWOKEN SOME HOURS LATER BY THE SOUND OF BOOTS ON the stone floor. I hid Fluffy under what was left of my shirt. One of the demonic captains came into view, his yellow eyes reflecting the light of his shiny new quartz lamp.

"His Majesty has called for you."

5
SARAYA

I had spent some number of hours alone in my cramped, damp cell, lost in a daze of my own pain, when two girls came into view, creeping along the dark prison passage. They were in their mid-teens. One was olive-skinned with mahogany hair, the other dark of complexion, with long flowing black hair down to her lower back. They both wore black slave collars and the transparent gauze dresses that was all women seemed to wear around here.

The olive-skinned girl, petite, with the large doe shaped eyes peering at me, spoke first. "You're the princess?" she asked. "My name is Flora. This is Tarangi."

I smiled kindly at them both, though I think it ended up being more of a grimace. But the other, Tarangi, had caught my eye. "Are you Ellythian, Tarangi?"

She nodded sincerely, toying with her long, black pony tail. "Are you half-blood?"

"My father was Lobrathian, yes."

But it was Flora who giggled. "I've never had a Lobrathian before."

My brows shot up, but Tarangi rolled her brown eyes. "I apologise for my friend. They feed some of us a potion that makes them desire a man."

I shivered in horror as I saw it for what it was. Control. My mother had thought that Lobrathia was bad for the unequal amount of legal control that men had over women. But this…this was a whole new domain. These women were property. They were cattle.

I touched my own metal collar.

Now I was cattle too.

I gripped onto that thought and held it like a talisman. "That's awful."

"It's really not," breezed Flora, stepping from foot to foot as if she were swaying to her own slow, music. "It's quite pleasant. Makes everything…better."

I looked at the girl with concern and noticed her pupils were slightly dilated. I hoped whatever they were giving these girls was not addictive. I would have to find out more about it. Meanwhile, Tarangi was staring at me with great interest.

"How did you get here from Ellythia?" I asked her.

She shrugged her narrow, bony shoulders and I wondered how much these girls were given to eat. "The demon lands extend all the way around the earth. They can gain access to humans anywhere there is a portal."

"But I imagine portals are few and far between, or they would roam freely, no?"

"The portal in your quarry opened only a few days ago," Tarangi explained. "It takes a great amount of power to make one. That's why it took so long gathering the magic for the Reaper to make it."

I guessed the Reaper was what they called Havrok and

wondered if she knew he'd been stealing the magic from newborn infants. But if she didn't, I wasn't about to tell this poor girl.

"How do you know all of this?" I asked.

Flora giggled. "They never expect the pretty ones to listen," she whispered as if revealing a great secret. "We hear *everything*."

"You've never tried to escape? To get back home?" I pressed them. "Is there no way out?"

Tarangi sighed in a way that told me she had thought about this a great deal. "The Ellythian portal is in the middle of the Lotus Sea," she explained. "It opens with a maelstrom once every decade. That's how they got me."

"There must be a fae portal as well," I thought out loud. "There just has to be another way to get out."

"But why would you want to leave?" asked Flora, pink lips agape. "I've been here ever since I can remember, and they treat us so nicely as long as we're good. I remember as a child, I never had enough food or a warm place to sleep. Here..." she giggled again, "...I am warm *every night*."

Suppressing a grimace, I wracked my brain for knowledge of herb lore, wondering what Flora was possibly being given.

"I heard," Tarangi licked her lips, looked over her shoulder, and leaned forward, lowering her voice, "that you are also a trained midwife? Is that true?"

I nodded, wary of what this might lead to. "I am, do...do the human women get pregnant here?"

"All the time," said Flora, googly-eyed. "Through the breeding program to make more warriors. But there are separate slaves for that. The first-concubine chooses them based on physical strength."

"First concubine?"

"The king's consort, Glacine Eyesmith," Flora said, a note of resignation in her voice for the first time.

My stomach twisted. Of course Glacine was responsible for this! It was typical of her to want to be in a position of power. But I had never heard this surname before. I added that to the list of things I was learning about my old step-mother. We had been told her family hailed from Kusha king-dom, which was so far north in the human realm that no one in Lobrathia could have possibly caught her out if when had given a fake family name.

"The problem is," urged Tarangi, "human women were never made to mate with demon males. The process usually kills them."

Fingers of ice crept down my spine. "Usually kills them," I repeated dumbly.

The girls nodded—Tarangi sadly, Flora absent-mindedly.

"Do you think you could help somehow?" Tarangi asked. "I have a friend who's expecting. I just wonder...I mean, I don't think she'll survive it. Her tummy is really big."

My stomach churned violently. How many of these women were dying to make more soldiers for this insane king? "I can help," I said softly. "But there's no way they'll let me have my magic back."

Tarangi chewed on her lip, eyeing my glowing shackles like they were a riddle she could solve with her eyes alone.

"There might be—" she began, but Flora cut her off.

"The reason we came in the first place, Princess," she said, completely unaware that Tarangi was glaring at her, "is to give you new clothes for your next meeting with the king."

She held up two gold slippers sitting atop a gold gossamer material that was completely see-through.

"I'm not wearing those," I said flatly.

46

"Oh, but they're lovely, Princess!" Flora cooed. "So lovely against the brown of your skin."

"I'll practically be naked."

Flora pouted and made goggle eyes at my torn wedding silks. "Please?"

I sighed. "Absolutely not, *Flora.*"

"Oh, bully. You'd rather wear the dirty ones?"

"Yes. I'm fine." I crossed my arms as Tarangi hid a smile.

"We'd better go," the Ellythian girl said. "We'll get in trouble for taking too long."

I WAS ESCORTED TO THE THRONE ROOM AN HOUR LATER, THE demon warriors keeping the same formation around me, chains clanking from my neck and from my shackles. Yesterday, Havrok had wanted to speak to his demon lords after I left, but I couldn't fathom about what. I wondered how Drake was faring, and I still didn't know what had become of Lysander and Slade. The sergeants could very well be dead for all we knew. And Drake could very well be a rabid animal for all *I* knew as well. From the way he'd looked as I'd left the throne room...all I could think of was the raw power he exuded and that voice. That deep, molten voice speaking of his need for his mate.

Me.

Goosebumps erupted all over my skin. Drake was a handsome fae, and it was no surprise that I might feel butterflies in my stomach looking at him. But his sudden and obvious desire for me had me feeling uncomfortably dizzy. I'd been on the receiving end of desire before, but...not like this. And not when I desired him back. I would have to shove that all away. We needed to focus on getting out of here.

When I entered the throne room this time, the crowd of demons was making such a racket that I wished I could cover my ears. The ones closest to me were jumping up and down excitedly as if they were celebrating something. The demon lords sat on their podiums along the aisle, their slaves perched or standing next to them. But this time, there were chalices in their hands, from which they happily drank.

Drake was standing at the end, right in front of Havrok's throne. To my surprise, he was not in a cage or shackles but stood alone as a free fae. In front of him were what looked like a neat row of seven boulders.

It wasn't until I was practically standing next to him that I saw, with horror, that they were not boulders at all.

They were seven severed heads. Each one covered in dark hair and definitely not human.

I felt all the blood in my body pool at my feet. Air wouldn't enter my throat. I took a slow, shaky breath to try and calm myself, but all I could see was Drake, brown hair a little tousled, a hint of scruff now on his cheeks. He was standing with his large silver-tipped, clawed hands clasped in front of him, all-black eyes staring straight at Havrok, his expression terribly blank.

I wanted him to look at me. I wanted to see what was in his eyes. Was he a completely different person now, or was there some semblance of his old self in there? He was the only familiar face I had in this awful place and I needed to know that some of the fae warrior I had known in Lobrathia was still in there. I needed to know that I was not alone.

But my attention was quickly diverted to Havrok, loudly clapping his hands.

"Look at what your mate has done!" The demon king said cheerfully, and he still managed to look obscene, with those white irises staring at the severed heads fondly. "I have lost many a demon warrior to this creature of myth. And in less than twelve hours, Lord Drakus has executed all seven heads and delivered them to his king."

They cheered behind me, the minor demons, and I tried not to look rattled by it.

"As your king," Havrok said, "for your reward Lord Drakus, I command you to wed your blood mate."

My jaw went slack, and I gaped at the king. "No!" escaped my mouth quicker than I thought was possible.

But all too quickly, Havrok flicked his wrist, and a demon from behind me shifted. But Drake got there first and, before anyone could do anything, caught the warrior's foot and snapped his tibia, the shin bone, in half. The demon screamed. Demon Warriors surged towards Drake.

"Stop!" Havrok commanded.

Drake stilled as if someone had magically frozen him. I looked back at the king, and he tapped the rune on his forearm. "That's enough, Lord Drakus, but you *will* punish your consort for speaking out of turn."

Drake advanced on me, and I recoiled from him and his all-black eyes. But the hand he put around my throat was gentle, his silver finger blades barely touching my skin. The closeness of him shocked me just enough that I froze like a deer as he leaned down from his great height.

"Behave," he growled into my ear.

My breathing hitched as I felt the heat coming from him, felt his breath against my ear. Something in me reared, and to my embarrassment, something tingled in my core. I desired him, I realised breathlessly. I wanted him to move closer—

49

But then he was standing a foot away from me, a cold wind in the place where he had just stood.

I let out a shaky breath, pushing away the desire unfurling within me. I couldn't be giving in to what was surely the magic between us. It wasn't real.

The king nodded in approval, and I simmered. I couldn't believe I was being forced to be married again. That was two weddings in one week to different fae warriors.

"You will consummate the marriage within the week. If there are children to be made, I will have them."

Drake growled low in his throat. My head whipped to look at him, but his rugged face gave nothing away. I frowned. What exactly was he thinking? I would make damn sure I wasn't getting pregnant by *anyone,* anytime soon.

"I'll take that as a yes, Lord Drakus." The king levelled him a look and flexed the broad muscles of his own forearm where the fresh ink sat boldly. A grating symbol of our captivity. "I will have the slaves prepare the hall for the wedding. And I expect—" he levelled a look at me, now, "that your mate will be appropriately dressed."

Appropriate. He meant wearing nothing. I wanted to scream at the unfairness of this, at the injustice. The way Glacine just stood there, goading and useless, letting these men take all the power from the women. She had no right to be smirking the way she was. No right, when the scars on my back twinged every time I looked at her. She was so powerful in Lobrathia, someone I couldn't fathom, couldn't outsmart or defeat. Was it going to be the same here?

After all this time, she still had a hold on me.

Fresh anger tore through my spirit. I had sworn a vow to my father before I had walked down the aisle to marry Prince

Daxian. I had sworn that I would kill Glacine for poisoning him. And I had *every* intention of fulfilling that vow.

"My mate's father should be at the wedding." Drake's voice was the scrape of sandpaper against woodgrain.

I glanced at him in surprise.

Havrok waved his hand in dismissal. "The old human king is too far gone. I may breed him with one of the stronger demon females," he said casually, casting a look at Glacine. "He was supposed to be a warrior in his prime, was he not?"

Glacine inclined her head with a marble-perfect smile at her king.

"A shame you poisoned this girl's mother. She would have made an excellent breeder as well."

Every particle in my being froze in time and space.

No.

The filaments that held me together all this time began to tear. I was going to rip into a million pieces and never be recovered. I was—

Drake was in front of me, his heavy presence filling my vision.

"Not now," he murmured. "Saraya, *the lotus is patient.*"

I blinked at him in surprise. A monster stared back at me, those black eyes boring into mine. I could feel the feral in him, sitting like water under his skin. I felt the concealed violence in the way he blinked, the way he moved. But now, there was a softness in his voice, a timbre I could not deny meant me well.

A voice that now spoke my mother's words. I closed my eyes and focused on an inward breath. I folded myself back together. Edge by edge, corner by corner, I gathered and pressed into myself until the roaring in my ears stopped, and the fire that threatened to tear me apart slunk back down my spine.

A single finger brushed my cheek, and my eyes flew open, but Drake was standing a foot away from me again.

I didn't look at Glacine. Because I knew she would smirk at me. I knew that if I saw her terrible face, I would lose the fine tether of control that I had right now. It was lucky Drake had been here because I probably would have ended up dead from lunging to attack her. So instead, I looked at the seven heads lying on the floor.

Because it was a reminder to me that all monsters eventually get slain.

6
SARAYA

When the guards led me from the throne room, they did not take me back to the dungeons on the military compound outside the palace. Instead, two girls waited for me in the entrance hall.

Naturally, I recognised Tarangi and Flora right away.

Flora bobbed up and down, reaching for my hands excitedly.

"A wedding!" she squealed.

"Sh!" one of the guards said sharply, a white X on his chest marking him as potentially a captain, or the equivalent in demon terms.

Flora pushed out her bottom lip and looked up, doe-like, at him. He grunted back at her and unclamped the chains from my collar and handcuffs.

Tarangi immediately pulled me away from the demons before something caught her eye behind me and she immediately let me go, bowing her head and dropping her shoulders into a curtsey. Flora did the same.

I turned around, my heart sinking as I saw Glacine, strutting towards us, her long black gown swishing behind her. Her gaze was fixed malevolently on me. I clenched my jaw, wondering what she was going to do with me now.

"Let us get one thing straight," she said loudly. "You are no longer a princess, you are no longer royalty or nobility. You have no palace, no land, nothing. *You* are nothing."

I ground my teeth together in an effort to maintain my calm. But I was seething. She looked like she'd been waiting years to say this, and there was no way I would let her have any satisfaction with a reaction from me.

When I spoke, I enunciated with a staccato filled with venom. "I am a princess born and bred. Nobility is in the blood, no matter what titles one may or may not have." I looked her up and down. I knew nothing of her parentage, but I doubted she was any type of royal.

Her lip curled before she gestured to the white X marked captain of the demon guard, still standing and watching. He strode up to me, lips curled into a smile and I reflexively held my hand out to summon my sword.

But of course, no sword came, I had only made my shackles clank.

He struck me with a backhand across the face that stung a million times worse than any blow I've had before. As I staggered to the side, my cheeks reddened with embarrassment.

I had no magic and no means of defence. I squeezed my eyes shut against both the physical and mental anguish.

Straightening, I looked at Glacine, pushing my shoulders back. A satisfied smile sat on her mouth and I wished to the Goddess I could swat it off her face.

She said, "A reminder. Of who holds the power here. You will follow my rules, you will be quiet, you will do as you are told or risk the consequences." She turned to Tarangi and

Flora. "Girls, you have your instructions. Saraya is no better than any of you. Treat her as such."

The girls stuttered and curtseyed again.

With that, Glacine turned on her heel and swept away.

Tarangi waited for her to be out of sight before she grabbed me by the elbow and guided me out of the entrance hall and down a narrow corridor. "Come on, Princess, you are staying with us now."

A small type of relief flooded through me, despite the stinging in my face. Flora glanced at me and bit her lip, tears glimmering in her eyes.

"I'm alright, Flora," I said softly.

The olive skinned girl sniffed. "The first concubine has all sorts of rules she makes us follow. And she's always sure to punish if we don't. You mustn't speak out of turn again!"

I grimaced as I followed them down a set of stairs and underground. Speaking out of turn was a habit of mine and something I had no intention of getting rid of.

Suddenly keenly aware that I had no chains on, and no guards were around, I looked around wildly, trying to find some way I could exit this place and get away.

"Don't even think about it," muttered Tarangi, observing me. "They'll catch you before you get ten paces. They're fast and will sniff you out like a bloodhound. Especially with all that *blood* still on you."

I looked down at my tattered silks. She was right. I needed new clothes, and I had no idea where I was, how far from the quarry portal, and in what direction to go. I would have to wait.

The lotus is patient.

Drake must have been paying more attention to me than I had realised. I remembered when I'd spoken my mother's house motto after Daxian had told me I was to marry him the next day. And now, just as I'd been told I was marrying Drake, he'd repeated those words back to me. Oh, how life was a vicious cycle. It seemed destiny was determined to have me marry a fae.

But it was different this time. Drake had called me his mate, and that bore more weight than any marriage, I was sure. But what did it even mean? The thought that someone thought of me as *theirs* made the hairs on the backs of my arms stand on end. I had no idea what to feel about it. Was it supposed to be an honour? It didn't feel that way, especially as I'd no say in it. It had been done *for* me. There was no choice. At every turn, my choices had been taken away.

I sighed. "So, where are we going, exactly?"

"The miscellaneous slaves," Tarangi said glibly. "We serve the upper ranks of the demon army and the lower nobility that live in the palace. We wait on them like maids."

"On their *every need*," Flora said happily, skipping along the black tiles of the hall. "We work in shifts—I serve the Earl of the Rot, Jessingu."

"What do you mean, Earl of the Rot? Is that his name?"

"They're all given some awful title," said Tarangi. "The Duke of Waste, The Viscount of Murder. That type of thing. The six lords that sit on the podiums in the throne room get better names. There's the Lord of the Feast, the Lord of Gold, the Lord of the Pyre and so on."

I wondered if Drake was going to get a new name. The king seemed determined to make him a part of his court. If only to do his dirty work. I remembered accusing him of the very same thing the day Wyxian was going to arrive, and I was being kept hostage in my own palace. I had said he was no better than a lapdog. I felt bad for saying such a thing now, although it had felt right and accurate at the time. Just like me, Drake had been pushed and pulled by the whims of kings and queens. Neither of us had chosen to be bonded to one another. We just were.

For some reason, that made me feel better.

The girls led me to a sort of dormitory, which was hardly better than the sour cell I had been staying in. There were twelve bunk beds for just as many girls. But the room was cold, the beds hard, and there was water dripping from one section of the ceiling.

They immediately pulled me into another section of the servant's wing where there was a large communal bathing room, filled with steam and perfume. Flora pushed a set of towels and strong soap into my arms and shooed me into the water.

Once I'd bathed, Tarangi led me to their room and provided me with a threadbare nightgown. Which was, thankfully, a full covering of cotton. Half of the girls filed in, apparently finished working for the day. The other half were working the 'night' shift. Although there was no apparent clear night and day in this realm, they used a clock to tell them the time.

As the girls got ready for sleep, I lay on a pallet next to Tarangi's bed. She had insisted that we swap, but I wouldn't have it. It felt like Tarangi had so much taken away from her when she had been stolen away to live here—I couldn't take the girl's bed away from her as well.

The next day, Tarangi and Flora had their shift in the palace, so they had to leave me alone in the dormitory with the other girls who had returned to sleep after their night shift. For the rest of that day, I remained on my pallet, eating whatever the girls brought me and otherwise being silent. I stretched in the pattern Jerali Jones had taught me from child-hood and did push-ups and sit-ups. By the time the demon night fell, Flora and Tarangi returned, tittering with excitement about the wedding.

They, and four other girls from their dorm, escorted me into another room, where there was a full-length mirror and a table full of beauty utensils. I grimaced at the sight of it all and had no choice but to let them do to me what they wanted. Only Tarangi seemed to understand my sullen mood.

Flora was practically bursting at the seams. She ran in, holding what looked like an elaborate piece of jewellery

"That's pretty," I said hesitantly. "Is that for me?"

"Oh yes. The king said you are a gift to his new lord, and a gift must be wrapped to perfection."

I was a gift. From one man to another, I was being 'given.' I muttered under my breath as Flora and Tarangi strung the sparkling jewels out between them. It hung in the shape of a woman's body with glaring spaces between the strings.

I looked around. No one held any sort of dress or material that could be construed into a dress.

"No." I said in disbelief, looking around wildly. Both girls sighed, each with the opposite cadence. I looked to Tarangi. "Is this it?"

She nodded stiffly.

The entire thing was only made up of elaborate strings of precious black jewels. I could see how they intended it to sit. "But there's—there's no—it'll show everything?"

"How about we put it on," said Flora gently, as if explaining something to a child. "Just see what it looks like, hm?"

I swallowed and said nothing as another one of the girls floated forward and gently pulled off my nightgown.

Midwifery had taught me to appreciate a woman's body for the sheer power it contained. Not only the creation power of growing a baby but also the colossal physical feat that was birth. So I had always appreciated my own body, whatever it looked like. The only thing I put to the back of my mind— tried not to think about—were the old wounds on my back. And now, the whole thing would be on display for the entire demonic court to see. How I viewed myself was one thing. But how others viewed scars like these?

I waited for the sneers.

Behind me, the whispers began immediately, and I stiffened— then frowned. Because the hushed voices behind me were saying something I had not expected.

"Warrior," one whispered.

"Fighter," breathed another.

"Battle wounds," said Flora, her eyes shining as she rounded me. "Princess, you didn't tell us you are a warrior as well!"

"Didn't you hear the guards talking?" asked Tarangi. "The king was angry about someone killing off the collection demons in Lobrathia. They discovered it was the princess with her astral sword all along!"

I managed to press my lips into a tight smile as Tarangi beamed up at me, simultaneously tightening the knot I had folded myself into back in the throne room—because they were wrong. They were not scars from a battle I had fought on a field of honour. They were a reminder that I had lost to the darkness that was my stepmother. Once again, here in the demon realm, she got her way, and I was losing to her.

I stood there lamely as the girls cooed over me. The 'bridal jewels' were so intricate that it took all six girls to work together at clasping, clipping, and moulding it into place.

The jewels pressed into my skin uncomfortably as they fastened each section and my cheeks got hotter and hotter as they wound the jewels from my ankle and up my thigh. When they reached my crotch, I was sure I was bright red. No one seemed to notice, intent on clipping the jewels in place around my lower stomach, right above my curls of pubic hair. They were careful to avoid touching my various healing wounds, mostly the big one on my thigh, which was still red and inflamed, but I had thankfully avoided an infection for the time being.

"There we are!" Flora said, clasping her hands under her chin.

We all turned to look at me in the full-length mirror, and I made a face at the six girls. It looked like I was locked into a cage of jewels. They began around my neck, flowing down to cup my breasts and just cover my nipples—otherwise leaving the entirety of my breasts on display. They then trailed down my abdomen as if they were the bones of a corset before encircling around my waist seductively.

"I'm not—I'm not showing my pubic area and rear end for the wedding?"

"It's customary," said a lovely blonde girl demurely. She cast her eyes down as she said it, but it made no difference because the words coming out of her mouth were the opposite of demure. "Your lord husband needs to see what he is marrying. This is the demon way."

"So everyone else needs to see my bare backside too? No, thanks."

"Oh, alright," Flora groaned as if I'd denied her something wonderful and then beckoned to one of the girls. She brought forward two strips of black cloth, and they clipped them onto my waist chain, front and back.

I had thought my Ellythian bridalwear had been daring with the exposed midriff, but it was nothing compared to this. I looked like some minor Ellythian sex Goddess, a variation of the Goddess of Lust. I blew the air from my cheeks. I had seen the whores at Madam Yolande's back in my home city dress more respectably than this. Though I suspected Madam Yolande would've instated it as an official uniform immediately given half the chance.

"This is *not* good."

Flora took this in high offence. "This is traditional royal demonic bridal attire!" she exclaimed. "It is made to show off a woman's body, that she might bring pride to her husband and inspire envy in others. And with your curves, you were *made* for a piece like this!"

I said nothing as I let Tarangi pat a pink tint over my cheeks and lips. This entire thing was ridiculous. Demons were honestly the worst sort of creatures if this was their custom. I kept brushing my fingers across the jewels, half wondering at the make of the skimpy beads and half trying to cover myself.

A flowing figure entered the room, and the first thing I saw was the glowing blue of magical handcuffs. I jerked my eyes towards the woman's face and found magical green eyes just like mine. There was a heaviness there, a weight that told me she bore an undeniable sadness, and yet her full lips were curved into a smile.

I recognised her immediately as one of the three women kneeling beside the king's throne, her black scorpion neck tattoo garish in the face of the beauty I could now see. I had no doubt she had been chosen for her appearance. Her ample breasts were like mine and sat heavy under the transparent gossamer, her chestnut skin shining through the gold material.

"The king's chosen," the other girls murmured and curtseyed for her.

She nodded in a flippant way that suggested she was long used to this.

"Sarone is going to do your hair. She'll know what to do with it," whispered Flora. Indeed, the king's chosen had the same type of hair as mine, wild and unruly if not tamed by a firm hand.

"Kinswoman," Sarone said, her voice deep and melodic.

I blinked up at her, knowing her confident way of walking, smooth and restrained, was of one who had been born noble. "You're Ellythian too?"

She nodded in that heavy way. As if a great weight were holding her down. "Though it has been a long time since I have been to our island home."

"I've never been," I admitted, "but my sister—"

I stopped short, my throat clamping shut with emotion and sudden terror. I had been about to reveal my sister's location at the Ellythian Jungle school. She'd stolen herself away with our elderly nursemaid the same day I had left with the fae to start my new life. We had thought it best she be away from my stepmother after my own leaving. To our luck, it had been the best decision we'd made. In Ellythia, she was safe. No fae and no demons were likely to find her in the dense jungles over there. But I had not seen her in months now, and my heart ached at the thought.

Sarone touched my shoulder with long fingers that I noticed bore old scars. "I know, my love. I know."

I pressed my lips together and nodded my thanks, trying

not to stare at her in the mirror as I undid the hair tie hidden within my messy waves and tried to comb it down.

"Are you nobility?" I asked in a low voice. The other girls hushed around us, paying close attention.

She titled her chin up. "I am, Princess. I had heard a lot about you before I was taken."

"They took you?" I could see Tarangi had gone stiff, hanging on to every word. Flora looked like she was itching to say something and glanced about the room in a twitchy way. I knew then that this conversation wasn't strictly allowed. The demon king must keep a tight rein on what conversations his concubines were entertaining. But it seemed that Sarone was a true Ellythian noble through and through because, like my mother, she wasn't afraid of anything.

"Five years ago, they took me and a few other girls, including Tarangi," she said, running a wide-toothed comb gently through my hair. "We were out on a voyage with my father. The maelstrom hit, and we were captured and brought through the portal. I know not what happened to my father and the rest of the crew."

"I'm sorry."

Sarone was silent a moment, and then she said, "My mother knew yours."

Something pulled at the forces that kept me together. My throat clamped up, and I choked out thick, "Really?"

She nodded and smiled as if the memory was a good one and my heart lifted in my chest. "I hadn't been born at that stage but my mother spoke about the parade as Princess Yasani left to marry the new Lobrathian king. There was such fanfare, my mother said, and everyone was so excited. We are second cousins, I believe, you and I."

I gaped at her. That made her a Lady at the very least. "I

knew we had relatives in Ellythia, but we were not ever permitted to visit."

She nodded understandably. "The Ellythians limit their contact with the outside world. That was always our way." Then her voice took on a terrible quiet. "And for good reason."

I couldn't stop the single tear that spilled from my eye. "I never suspected it was foul play that killed my mother. Not once. Not ever."

The other girls in the room suddenly found a reason to keep busy, fussing with some material in the corner, avoiding eye contact with Sarone at all costs. My eyes flicked from them to the older Ellythian woman in the mirror. She could only have been in her late twenties, but her eyes held the rage of someone who had been through great atrocity. I wondered what horrors she was subjected to on a daily basis as the demon king's chosen. It took my breath away. I felt that look in my core.

She leaned down to my ear on the pretence of pinning a curl.

"The lotus is patient, Saraya," she breathed. "And every enemy has their weakness."

That did it. I lifted my chin and met her eye, my breathing ragged with the thunder of emotions roiling inside of me. "My father's people have another saying," I whispered. "Lightning does not yield."

It was then that a tiny flicker of light over my forehead came through. Sarone froze. The flicker came again, and for a moment, quite clearly, we both saw, on the skin of my forehead, the symbol of the Order of Temari.—a crescent moon over a lotus. The goddess Umali had marked it into my forehead by her own hand when she had inducted me in the ruins of the temple of the seven goddesses.

"I am the first initiate of the Order of Temari in one hundred years," I said in a voice that did not waver. I wanted everyone in the room to hear. "The goddess Umali herself marked me as a warrior midwife and I executed demons for weeks before I was taken."

A ragged breath emerged from Sarone's throat as tears gathered in her eyes. "Oh, dear Goddess. We might have a chance…"

She clutched my shoulder with incredibly strong hands, and I knew she had probably been trained from birth to fight, just like me. She breathed, "We will rise again, sister."

My gaze never left her eyes as I nodded to her, just as a demon captain pounded on the door, making us all jump.

"It's time!" he barked.

Sarone and I both looked around at the six girls in the room.— teenage girls who bore an uncertain future. I looked back at Sarone's eyes and the fire I saw there told me only one thing. She wanted to get out of here and could stomach the risk. All she needed was a plan. A way out.

Perhaps I could give her that.

I would need to watch, to observe and learn. And if I needed to get married to a monster to do that, by the Goddess, I would.

7
SARAYA

The demon warriors ended up opening the door and leering at us, so Sarone quickly pinned the last of my hair up at my crown and then set the massive veil in place.

What my 'bridal gown' lacked in material, the veil made up for. The thing was an enormous length of sparkling black lace, easily ten paces long.

I turned in the mirror to see that the dark scars on my back would still be entirely visible beneath the veil. But at that moment, a cold voice came from the door.

"It's entirely symbolic."

As Sarone and I whipped our heads towards the door, the six younger girls all fell to their knees, touching their foreheads to the stone floor.

Glacine stood there, stunning but stony faced, in a black, shimmering gown, looking at me down her nose. I suppressed the urge to grimace as she stalked forward, circling around me as if to assess the girls' work. I bit the inside of my cheek as I felt her gaze on my back, knowing she was admiring her own handiwork. I bore her marks on my skin, and I always would. I had never been able to heal them as I could heal my other wounds. Try as I might, my magic had never been able to breach that awful chasm that would lead me to them. The most I had ever been able to do was numb the area.

"I can see what you really are, Saraya," she said quietly, "and so will everyone else in that hall."

I frowned incredulously. "All everyone can see is my naked skin. And really, I'm not the one with anything to hide."

"You and your parents were pathetic excuses for rulers," she said snidely, coming to stand before me. "And I simply made sure the dirt was taken out. You were all too stupid to see what we planned."

I forced my expression into nonchalance, clenching my fists tightly to let out my furore. I refused to show her any sort of weakness. I might be her prisoner, but I would *not* give her the satisfaction of seeing me cower. The lotus is patient. And I was patient enough to wait for the right moment so I could plunge my sword into her neck, right through that scorpion tattoo.

I also did not fail to notice that Sarone, while she had gone terribly still in Glacine's presence, had not dropped to her knees as the others had. Instead, she moved forward to set another pin in my hair. I could not help but see that as an act of defiance. And sure enough, when I observed Glacine's face, her ice-chip eyes were narrowed on my Ellythian cousin, her mouth twisted in hate.

"Enough." Glacine snapped. "She is done. Send her to the hall."

Sarone leisurely adjusted something, perhaps needlessly, in my hair. Then she turned on her heel and stalked out of the dressing room, ignoring the warriors that lined the hallway outside as if it were a daily thing for her.

Glacine waited a moment and then gave me a taunting smile. "I do look forward to Drakus getting you pregnant with his seed. Hopefully the process kills you."

She swept out without another word, leaving me stunned and sick to the core. Glacine had hated Altara and I from the moment she'd met us, though she'd hidden it well. But now, she had free reign to say and do as she pleased to me, no matter who was in the room.

I felt Tarangi by my side first, as the girls all got off the floor. "From the moment we arrived here, Glacine's hated the Ellythians. Her place was always beside and beneath the king and though her word might be law, Sarone is still the king's favoured. She is just as untouchable. None of the guards or lords one would even *think* of touching her. Rumour is, that the king's first wife was an Ellythian."

Perhaps that explained why she hated me so. And it had the cogs in my head turning—the realisation that there were full-blooded Ellythians down in the demon kingdom and the fact that Sarone looked like she would be extremely happy to have a sword back in her hand. It went unsaid, but I had seen the old scars on her hands and forearms. They were like mine. Arms used to managing weapons. Arms that knew how to fight. The threads of a plan began to form in my mind.

Two girls accepted a large bundle from the demons—black material attached to shiny black poles.

"Ooh, now it really feels like a wedding!" Flora squealed, grabbing my arm. "It's black tourmaline to ward off any negative energy."

I raised my brows at Tarangi, grimaced, glancing at the many demons waiting outside. In Ellythia, such things were common— the warding off of dark entities with talismans and rituals, but in the demon realm? It was laughable. Dark beings were *all* we were surrounded by.

Flora and Tarangi took the lead with the poles, being the eldest. The others each took a pole and assumed positions all around me, three to a side, spreading the black cloth, marquee-like, over me.

I had never felt more like a bride. Even when I had been preparing to meet Prince Daxian at the alter back in the human realm. For the millionth time, I wondered how Tembry and Blythe were doing, sending a prayer to the Goddess that they, along with Altara and Opal and all the others were safe at the very least.

With each stride I took down the gilded corridor, the jewels bit into my skin. It was definitely not an outfit made for comfort, and I was sure there would be marks all over me after. More to add to my lovely collection.

The demon warriors made way for us seven young women, their slitted pupils raking my bare skin all the way from my face down to my toes. Muscles flexed, nostrils flared, and some hissed slightly at me or the other girls—but they seemed used to the attention and kept their eyes downcast.

However, *I* was still a princess of Lobrathia as far as I was concerned. So, I met them stare for stare, with my chin thrust out and my spine impossibly straight. But at the back of my mind, a strange sort of satisfaction sat smugly. It was a strange thought of power, having the lust of so many warriors being directed at me.

Perhaps it was some womanly instinct taking over, but I found that unbidden to me, my walk turned into a sort of wanton strut. My hips swaying with each step, cutting jewels be damned. It amused me to be seductive, being so used to

69

being a straight-laced midwife in my city. But my mother had always taught me that there was no shame in sexual expression. The Lobrathian goddesses might have been limited to their roles as maiden, mother, and crone—women defined and bound by time, but my mother's people had a much more broad definition of women.

My mother had glared at the temple of the triple goddess, saying it was an affront to women to deny the other facets we had in us. She had said that the teachings of the seven goddesses told us that women were also warriors, seductresses, and artists.

In Lobrathia, I had been taught a woman should sit and be quiet, but my mother's teachings had always sat in the background of my brain. It had then been cemented by my meeting with the goddess Umali, who was feminine rage personified. I knew then that I was made to be so much more.

So I let myself sway through the palace of the demon king. Because there are different types of power women had, and why not use every one of them to my advantage? I might have not been used to showing the entirety of my skin to this many...beings, but I could handle it. I had handled much worse. The goddess Umali assumed a naked female form and the image became my guide, and I gripped onto it with everything I had.

The demon warriors gathered behind us as we passed them, forming a sort of procession through the palace.

"Try not to giggle," Flora said, and I wondered who she was talking to. "This is serious."

"Do all weddings happen in the throne room?" I asked.

Tarangi glanced warily back at me. "Only for the demon high lords. The king forms the unions for them. He likes to oversee the whole process."

A chill ran down my spine. There were no "ladies" so far as I'd seen sitting on the podiums with the demon lords. They had *all* looked like concubines. I'd have to pay closer attention this time around.

I wondered if Drake was being submitted to the same fanfare and almost snorted—if he was, I doubted anyone was leering at him like they were at me.

As we entered the eerie red light of the entrance hall, my skin crawled. Two weddings in just as many days—it must have been some sort of record.

But this one couldn't have been more different from the last.

Where my wedding with Daxian had been demure, with only my father's liege lords and the royals of the neighbouring lands present, no more than twenty humans, *this* wedding was a raucous party of over three hundred. As we approached the open doors to the throne room, by the shouting and cheering, I could tell that the hall was even more packed than the previous time.

Flora tittered, gripping her tourmaline pole tightly as we came to stand by the door. She glanced at me with a beaming smile as if this was the most exciting thing that had ever happened to her. For all I knew, it probably was. If she'd been here all her life, she hadn't seen all that much of the human world and all it had to offer her.

But I was distracted by the sudden and violent roar of the demons packing the hall. Common demons were all dressed in what was probably their version of finery— strange scraps of clothing and feathers that barely covered multi-coloured, fanged bodies. They pressed on each other as if this were a holiday parade, surging around the podiums of the six demon lords to try and get a better look at me.

They had wisely placed a line of demon guards standing close together all the way down the aisle. They elbowed or rammed their shoulder into anyone who tried to get too close to either the podiums or the black carpeted aisle.

"We have to walk slowly," whispered Tarangi back at me. "The king wants everyone to get a good look at you."

I suppressed a scowl at the audacity of it. But I supposed it wasn't every day that, in their realm, a human princess married a fae monster.

I wished my mother was here. I wished my father hadn't been fooled by Glacine. I wished that I hadn't sent Altara away. But it was no good to wonder what could have been because here I was, with only my wits about me. And it would take everything I had to get out of this.

Flora and Tarangi began the walk down the aisle.

A shining blond head of long hair caught my eye and I found Lysander's blue eyes staring back at me.

My breath caught in my throat as I realised he was standing on the first podium amongst a group of blonde women and men. Next to him was a throne, upon which sat an obese demon lord covered in a silver fur, his mouth full of fangs. He was dressed in silver cloth and a ridiculous amount of silver jewellery. Lysander, on the other hand, was not wearing anything except a loincloth and was covered in a slick oil with a slave collar around his throat.

When I caught his eye, he gave me an easy smile as if to say, *I'm alright. Worry about yourself.*

It made the backs of my eyes burn to see him like that. He had told me his story. That Drake had saved him from being sold as a courtesan. Now, he was no doubt a sex slave for a wolfish demon high lord.

My stomach churned.

Lysander had been my fae enemy back when Drake had taken over my palace. But he had always been kind to me, in that forever flirtatious way of his. Seeing him with a collar made an angry heat flare up in me. But from his expression and posture I could tell that he was accustomed to this game and willing to play the part.

As I passed his group and lost sight of him, I decided if this was going to be excruciating, I might as well make the most of it and play the game like Lysander. He knew more about this type of thing than I did, after all. So I reset my hips into that saunter I had come to appreciate and hoped that the fire in my eyes looked like a salacious smoulder. The crowd seemed to enjoy it because their roars reverberated in my ears all the louder.

But it was an odd thing because as I allowed myself to fall into my seductive side and acclimatised to the cheers around me, I felt drawn to look at the end of the aisle, where the king sat on his throne.

Standing below him, like a tiger with eyes only for his prey, was Drake.

He'd been given a black plated armour that he wore like it weighed nothing. It made him look even more terrifying than he normally did. His mahogany hair was neatly combed back, tattooed hands clasped formally in front of him. His posture was stiff, wide shoulders set as if they were ready to move and grab the black blade at his belt at any second. The first time I'd lain eyes on him, I'd known that he was a dangerous person to avoid. And now, in his half monstrous form, that feeling more pronounced, the threat of violence was obvious and open.

My body reacted immediately to his gaze and heat spread through my core. Even though his eyes were all black, I could tell that he wasn't looking at my body like the demon warriors were. He was just staring, an unblinking gaze fixed on my face.

The warrior part of me marvelled at the power in his form, the raw capability to inflict damage. But that female part of me, that was barely dressed and walking seductively towards this fae creature, shuddered with a primal sort of tingle. I chastised myself. I was still at war here, and this feeling must be the magic that bound us. I couldn't let myself forget that, whatever my body thought about him.

Eventually, we walked past the final set of podiums, and my breath caught. Someone had definitely been sitting on the last podium to my left the last time I came through here, but now it sat empty. I knew that whatever had happened to that particular demon lord could not be good.

The girls halted just before we reached Drake and turned their faces up to the king.

Havrok sat regally with his arms on either armrest for a moment before he stood with a smirk and descended the stairs. The demons in the crowd immediately quietened. I was impressed. He had them well trained—or well afraid. I found Sarone's beautiful form kneeling beside the throne with the other two girls, all with their eyes downcast in that familiar position.

Drake turned to watch the king.

"What do I do?" I hissed to the girls.

"Stay where you are!" whispered the girl directly on my left.

Once the king reached the ground floor, Drake gave a smooth bow that irritated me to no end.

"Bring forth your bride, Lord Drakus Silverhand!" Havrok boomed, the muscles on his pale neck bulging. I could see the blood vessels lining his neck even from where I stood under the black gossamer. I wanted to see them bleed, I wanted to tear them open and—

Then Drake was striding towards me, his form filling my vision. He stopped just infront of Tarangi and Flora, and in a move that I found strangely endearing, he bent a little so he could see me under the cover. The girls recoiled from him, terrified out of their wits.

Drake didn't seem to notice them and offered me his hand. I stared at it for a moment, large and calloused, and I noticed he'd taken off his signature silver claws just for the occasion. I took so long that Drake curled his fingers, the corner of his mouth twitching upwards.

"Scared, Princess?" His voice was that frightening, monstrous rasp, but the tone was teasing. Tarangi cast me a worried look.

I narrowed my eyes at Drake, the challenge snapping me out of whatever reverie I'd been in. Sashaying forward—to which he lost the smirk immediately—I placed my hand in his, allowing him to feel my callouses over his own. He needed to remember that I was no trembling Princess. Not only had I been delivering the babies of Lobrathia since I was sixteen, but I had also been killing demons with an astral sword no one else seemed to be able to summon. He needed to remember exactly who I was, and if he forgot, I would be there to remind him each and every time. Whatever this sham of a wedding was, he would be a monster first, my husband second.

I didn't take my eyes off his as I stepped out of the protection of the marquee and together we stepped up to Havrok. I tried to ignore the growing heat between the skin of his hand

75

and mine, but Drake let me go as we faced the demon king side-by-side.

Havrok looked at us each in turn, looking me up and down in the process. Then he procured a key and roughly took my handcuffs, unlocking them. As they fell away and a servant rushed forward with a tray to take them, I felt my magic released as if a blacksmith's billows were blowing the life back into me. I sighed, resisting the urge to close my eyes and revel in the return of an old friend.

I didn't get to enjoy it for long because the demon king's voice boomed so everyone in the throne room could hear.

"Take one another's hands, and under the eye of the king, recite the bond mate's binding oath."

Like he was the only king. But I bit my tongue because I was panicking—I didn't know the bond mate's oath. I'd never made it to the altar for my wedding with Daxian. So I turned to face Drake and he held out both of his broad, battle-scarred hands.

I placed my hands in his, a traitorous tingling sweeping up my fingers, arms, and straight into my chest. Shadows crept at the sides of my vision, and Drake curled his fingers around my hands as if to steady me. Struggling to control my breathing as the torrent of power surged through my body, I simply stared at Drake as he dropped my hands to accept the dagger from the slave now next to him.

I realised with a pang that on her black tray was a familiar yellowed parchment with magically written words in opalescent ink. They must have stolen it from my palace.

Drake pricked his left thumb with the knife and pressed the thumb to the paper a little aggressively over Daxian's old blood print.

Then he took back my hands and spoke in the softest voice

76

I'd heard ever come out of him. As if he and I were the only people in the room.

"I willingly bind myself to you, Saraya Yasani, daughter of Voltanius House. I am now bound to you in soul, in heart, in mind. My life is yours. I give it to you."

The tenderness in his voice struck me. He meant it, I realised with a horror that was like a blow to my stomach. He truly meant every syllable of this oath. But he didn't even really *know* me! To what extent was the magic affecting his emotions?

I suddenly realised they were waiting for me. I took the knife from the black tray and scored my finger, letting the blood well and pressing it again onto my own, old print. I put my hands in Drake's again and cleared my throat. "I willingly bind myself to you, Drakus Silverhand, son of..."

But he wasn't Wyxian's legitimate son. I didn't know what else to call him.

"The Black Grove," he said.

Ah, he meant the land his mother's tree lived on. "Of the Black Grove."

"According to this contract," Havrok interrupted. "Drakus is the firstborn son of King Wyxian Darkcleaver. Those were the terms, after all."

"Right...Your Highness." I swallowed the lump in my throat as the image of Wyxian's dead body being dragged across the tiles of my palace home flashed across my mind. I looked up into Drake's all-black eyes and felt, rather than saw, his breathing turn heavy as he clung on to each word of mine as if his life depended on it. My voice emerged breathy, taking on a life of its own. I felt separated from my body as if some magic that was not mine was taking over.

"I willingly bind myself to you, Drakus Silverhand, firstborn son of King Wyxian Darkcleaver. I am now bound in soul, in heart, in mind…"

I couldn't say the last bit. I just couldn't.

But it turned out that I didn't need to because a magical wind blew wisps of my hair, and I jerked. Drake turned to look at the contract.

I followed his gaze. Before my eyes, the entire parchment turned to stone.

8

DRAKE

As the fae blood contract made between our fathers thirty years ago turned to stone, the magic that bound me to Saraya tightened as if she had embraced me herself.

I had waited for this moment ever since I could remember. And now it was done, my body was telling me to bed Saraya, right here on the floor of the throne room. I pushed that urge back with the same violence I dealt to any of my opponents. *Not now, you fool, the room is full of our enemies.*

When Saraya had walked down that aisle, every filament of my body wanted to pounce towards her. To devour her curves, to cover her bronzed skin, to—and then I realised that every single person and creature in the room was staring at her. Staring at my mate. *Then* I had wanted to tear out the eyes of every male in this room and cut up their retinas into little pieces.

"Calm yourself, Lord Drakus," the king had muttered as he'd walked down from his throne.

I'd felt the pull of the rune on Havrok's arm. Like a leash

being yanked, my mind tugged itself into submission. I stood under his spell, like a dog waiting on his master.

Gods, I wanted to tear his face off his skull. Instead, I kept my own face like stone as I gave the demon king a stiff nod and walked to Saraya, pretending to gaze upon her serenely.

But now, with the wedding done, we were bound by word and my body screamed for us to complete the bond physically.

I had claimed her as mine in front of these creatures. The monster part of me growled in approval. This way, no one could hurt her ever again. No one could whip her or slash a sword at her while I was by her side. The fae part of me knew she could defend herself, that she was a capable fighter who had beaten my half-brother Daxian on his ass that time she was pretending to be a fae male at the Mountain Academy.

But as far as the monster was concerned, it was going home into the arms of a woman who was now its entire life.

"I now pronounce you, Lord and wife!" Havrok called.

The demons around us cheered, rasping throats, guttural squarks, and gnashing teeth creating a cacophony of sound that had me wanting to exterminate the lot of them. But one thing concerned me more, and it was the fact one of the demon lord's podiums stood empty—as if it were waiting for me.

Havrok raised his white hands in the air, but all I saw was the rune that controlled me. I wondered how quickly I could rip his arm off right here.

A slave carrying a black tray shuffled forward, trembling, as she offered it to the king.

"New metal, for a new bond," Havrok said, lifting two black circlets linked by metal chains. "Stand still, Lord Drakus."

80

That fucking rune held me in place as Havrok clamped the metal cuff to my wrist. It took me all of one second to realise what he was doing before he moved to Saraya and clamped the attached metal band around her neck. His fingers brushed her skin as he came away.

I couldn't control the animalistic growl that came from my throat.

Havrok bared his teeth at me, and my muscles tensed, ready to lunge at him. But he lifted a finger.

"Turn around and face my court, Lord Drakus."

My eyes met Saraya's bright emerald ones, which were currently burning with fury and shame as the glowing metal of the chain linking her throat to my wrist clanked far too loudly.

Havrok roared to his court, "My new Lord of the Kill!"

Through our mate bond, I felt Saraya's shock. I had known this was coming, but I'd had no way of warning her.

The crowd roared and I suppressed a sigh. I needed a way to get Saraya out of here and to a safe place so we could figure out what we were going to do. We had no business being members of Havrok's court. But while he had that controlling rune on his arm, I couldn't simply escape.

I held my hand out to Saraya and she frowned up at me, her beautiful face suspicious. After a moment, she placed her hand in mine, and with heat flushing through me at her touch, I led her to the podium that was now ours.

In a normal situation, I would have asked her to step up first, but this was not a normal situation, and we had to play the part of Demon Lord and Lady. So I stepped up and turned, trying not to watch the curves of her perfect form, the bare skin of her body, as she came up after me.

Letting go of my mate's hand, I begrudgingly took my

seat on the silver throne. If I hadn't taken up the whole seat, I would have pulled her to sit next to me, but these thrones were deliberately not made for that. Saraya stood next to my throne, her face stony. She was too proud to be murderous about it but it irritated me to no end that she was standing while I was sitting.

Unbidden by me, my monstrous self took over and grabbed her by the waist, pulling her to sit on my knee.

"Fuck you," she muttered. It wasn't the first time I'd heard her swear like a soldier and I delighted in it every time. Even more when her cheeks were flushed with pink and her arms were crossed under her breasts. I licked my lips as I let the desire overwhelm me. She was soft in the most wonderful way, but firm where her muscles showed obvious training. I was convinced that her curves were made for my hands and I had to curl my fingers around her waist to stop myself from caressing her skin.

My mate wasn't the type to be physically forced to do anything, but I think our magic was mingling together at our touch. The new sensations were catching her off guard because she let me arrange her black veil around her. I could feel her heat, her desire for me on her scent, and this close, it was overwhelming.

I couldn't help but grin at her as I broached her mind. But even without her magic, her walls were still strong. So instead, I physically said, "Just go with it."

She scowled back. "Just because we're married doesn't mean you can do what you want with me."

But the lecherous crowd seemed to love this lovers quarrel because they cheered and stomped like the savages they were.

"I know that," I growled, "but they don't."

She looked up and away from me—at the demons surging around us, trying to get a better look—and seemed to understand that we had to play this game. I felt her calm a little, and she settled on my knee.

However much the sweet scent of her skin or her heat on my thigh was distracting me, I turned to look at Havrok, who had assumed his position back on the throne. Beside him, Glacine's face bore no emotion. I was pretty sure she was still figuring out how to feel about this new situation her pseudo-step-daughter was now in.

Saraya wiggled uncomfortably, and I struggled to maintain my fae-focus. I kept stock still, trying to clear the red haze now clouding my vision.

"Stop it," I whispered.

Something in my voice made her freeze. It was probably the monstrous rasp. I mentally shook myself and tried to pay attention to what Havrok was saying.

"...have been trading human slaves without permission, without paying their taxes. I will be exacting with the king's justice accordingly. What say you, Lord of the Kill? Do you accept this task?"

The controlling rune on the king's forearm tugged on my magical leash. The words were a mere formality. Mere entertainment.

I inclined my head. "I accept, my king."

Havrok nodded imperiously before standing and walking down the throne steps. Glacine glided after him, leading the way for the rest of his marked concubines.

I felt Saraya hold her breath, her entire body tensing as Glacine passed us. But her old stepmother did not pay us any attention. I took my cue from the Lord of Gold opposite me as he and his slaves got off their podium. Saraya eased herself off my lap, the chain clinking annoyingly. I offered her my hand, but she turned her nose up at it and trudged down to the carpet, tugging me along as if I were the one with the slave collar around my throat. I suppressed a smirk as she continued ahead of me but became immediately aware of someone staring at her.

The Lord of Gold's leering eyes were hungrily fixed on Saraya's rear end.

"Lord of the Kill," he drawled as he noticed me watching him. He was a tall demon, almost as tall as my six foot four, but was fleshy and plump all over with a bulbous nose and yellowed, leering eyes. The hand around the chalice he was still holding was pudgy and full of gold rings. His slaves trailed behind us, ranging from deeply tanned to rich brown skin. Every single one of them was Ellythian.

"Lord Braxus," I growled back. Naturally, I had memorised all their names as soon as they'd been introduced to me yesterday.

He assessed me with those yellowed eyes, his thick golden necklaces sparkling in the lights as we walked slowly behind Havrok's party. I wondered if they would be strong enough to choke him with.

"I pay a handsome fee for what I want, Lord Silverhand," Braxus slurred. He was tipsy from the strong wine these creatures drank. I doubted that he would have been speaking to me if he was sober.

"All that caramel skin..." He bit his lip and nodded at Saraya.

I could've torn his beating heart out, right there. Instead, I clenched my jaw and looked at my mate, seeing her dark scars glaring through the bridal veil. But all I saw was her strength. I should have been there for her when it happened.

Although she hadn't told me outright, the moment Glacine had appeared in Saraya's palace with the purpose of taking us, I'd known straight away that my mate's scars had been her doing.

The sound that came from my chest was so vicious and serrating that Braxus raised his hands in supplication. "Of course, My Lord," he said magnanimously. He inclined his head and hung back, but not before pulling one of his dark-skinned concubines roughly over to him.

All I could do was watch Saraya walking with that strut in front of me. The demons on either side of us began whistling at her as we passed.

I'd had enough of this. I reached into my pocket and fit my silver tips back onto my fingers.

Quicker than any of them thought was possible, I lunged between the demon warriors meant to protect us, grabbed the closest demon male who had whistled, a bright yellow one with scales and red eyes, and slashed his throat. Everyone around him surged backwards, screaming, as the demon sunk to the floor, gurgling in his own blood.

Saraya had been tugged forward on her chain by my sudden movement, so I put my arm around her shoulders just as she regained her balance and continued walking down the aisle as if nothing had happened.

I'm sure they all got my message.

"That was unnecessary," Saraya murmured irritably.

"Really? I thought it was."

She pressed her pink lips together, eyes darting warily around us. I hoped that whatever she was thinking, she knew that now she was with me, she would be safe. Dragging my eyes off her lips, I looked around us.

As we passed the last podium, a particular shade of

golden hair caught my eye. Like a daffodil mixed with sunlight, Lysander liked to say. I had seen him on the way in, but we'd not had time to converse.

My sergeant watched us pass from the podium of the Lord of Feast and gave me the barest nod. He was alive, thank the Gods, but only my heightened sight noticed the way he winced when he walked. He was probably in bed with that monster every night. I had cunningly taken him out of this life half a decade ago and I had every intention of getting him back out if he didn't do it himself first.

He was a strong fae—one of the strongest I'd ever met. That's why I'd chosen him as my sergeant, along with Slade. His mental scars had calcified by now and I knew he could withstand anything. But that didn't mean that it didn't kill me to think of what he had to endure now.

As for Slade, I had not seen him down here. I hadn't seen him since I'd sent him with a group of fae warriors at Quartz Palace. I hoped he was in Lobrathia somewhere, fighting off the demons with our other warriors.

As we reached the glowing red entrance hall, Havrok swung one of the Ellythian concubines over his shoulder and, roaring with laughter, disappeared into a corridor at a full pelt. The demon was a physical menace. He would be difficult to defeat in combat.

Lord Braxus left with his group into another corridor.

"If anyone tries to touch you, Saraya," I said darkly, "I will destroy them."

"Well," she said lightly. "Start with him, will you?" She nodded at the corridor the king had left by, where Glacine pathetically strode after him, her nose in the air. My mate's old stepmother was an interesting puzzle. It had been hidden from me before, but with my super-heightened senses returned, her scent proved to me she had some fae blood. I would have to keep an eye on her.

I was about to reply to my mate when two demon guards broke off from the rest and hurried towards us, bowing low, their slitted eyes wary of me. No doubt they'd just seen my display down the aisle.

I came to stand by my mate's side.

"We will show you to your marital rooms, My Lord," said the marked with a captain's X.

The other demon lords left the hall in varying directions, some heading outside. But I knew Havrok would want me close by. No doubt our rooms were deep in the palace close to his.

I turned out to be right because we were led quite a way into the palace. This meant that we got to see a good deal of it. Some hallways and rooms were brightly lit with quartz lights, and through these I could plainly see the obscene paintings and statues with which the demon king chose to decorate the place. Other areas were dark and shadowy, giving me an overall feeling of malicious acts and dark deeds being done. There were even fake interior gardens, with the grass and flowers being made of a cloth like material that shone in an unnatural way.

It wasn't until I heard a muffled scream that I knew I was correct about the dark deeds. We were walking through a communal living space when we saw them. A demon guard had a human female slave against the wall. One hand around her throat and the other hitching her skirt up. I froze mid-step, as did Saraya. Without another thought, both of us lunged toward them and I yanked the guard back by his collar. He let out a roar as his charge sprinted out of the room and made to follow, but I slugged him in the jaw. He was thrown backwards onto the floor and I could feel Saraya's rage next to me, palpable like a hot wind.

One of our demon guards strode up angrily. "That is our way. You cannot—"

I turned and strode up to him and shoved my face in front of his, snarling."Tell me, Captain, do you like your heart where it is?"

He let out an angry grunt but to his credit, he stepped back submissively. "This is our way, Lord Drakus. You cannot stop the guards from taking a human."

Saraya was raging behind me, though her body was still and alert. But I didn't want her to have to deal with this. "I don't give a *fuck* about your way. Speak against me again and I will tear your heart out. The only person who can command me is your king. Understand?"

The demon captain's eyes passed between my mate and me, enraging me more. He seemed to sense this and quickly gave me a bow. "Yes, my lord."

"Then I believe we are done here."

The captain blinked then turned, the second guard nervously looking at the unconscious assailant still on the floor, out cold. I took Saraya's hand and she followed me without complaint as we continued our way to our rooms.

Fuck these demons, honestly.

Eventually, we came to a set of tall double doors made of tourmaline. I scowled when I saw that crystal, knowing suppression magic when I saw it. The new cuff linking me to Saraya glowed with a magic that would stop a human from casting magic, but not a half-fae monster like me. Instead, Havrok was going to suppress my magic inside the palace using tourmaline on the furniture. So be it. I always liked a challenge.

The two demons opened the doors, bowed low, and left.

Saraya strutted into the room, and I let her tug me along, trying not to step on her veil. It was a beautiful series of three rooms, airy and bright with yellow quartz chandeliers and lamps spaced around. The furniture was red and black. Saraya peered into the first room, branching off the main one. It turned out to be a bathing pool.

She pressed her lips together, brushed past me, and continued to the next room. Her long veil twisted around, and I ended up picking up the mesh material and bunching it in my hands. Saraya turned to look back at me, pulled some pins out of her hair, and the veil detached from her head. I tossed it onto a black leather couch before following her.

She stopped in her tracks, staring at the final room, which held three things. A massive bed and two wardrobes on either side. A marriage bed, if I ever saw one.

Heat swept through my core in a tidal wave of lust. We would be sleeping there tonight. Both of us. Together. And Havrok had declared that we would have to consummate the mating bond as soon as possible.

When my mate said nothing, I cleared my throat. "That's a strange dress they made you wear."

She didn't move. "Is it enough skin for you?" she asked bitterly.

I swore internally. "Saraya, you could be wearing a monk's robe, and I would still be as infatuated with you as I ever was."

She whirled around, her mouth twisted in anger.

Was I a bastard if that reaction excited me? "You should know how beautiful you are."

"Oh, so all of a sudden, you're telling me these things? That you—" She pressed her rose-petal-like lips together in a way that had me wondering what they would feel like against mine.

I shook my head, trying to keep up with the conversation. I couldn't very well be sinking into the animal sort of lust. "That what?" I asked, trying to keep my tone light. "My memories have returned to me, Saraya, and you...don't know what it was like for me. To crave knowing you from so far away. At such a young age."

She considered me as if she were really imagining what I would have looked like as a young boy, staring at the ceiling of my treehouse while I got fleeting wisps of her scent, glimpses of her skin, notes of her emotions. But now her defences were so good, I could only feel these things when she lost control. Like when Glacine had revealed she'd been the one to kill Saraya's mother. I would allow her to feel my own emotions, though, as my mate, I wanted to give her that right.

She shook the chain leading to her neck with her hand. "I'm not wearing this. I'm not your slave."

I didn't like the chain, but I didn't hate it either. "There's no way in hell I'm letting you out of my sight."

"Are you sure this *isn't* hell?" she grumbled.

"Good point."

Something in my pants pocket squirmed, and I remembered Fluffy was in there. I reached into the pocket and scooped her out. "Sorry, Fluffy."

Saraya gasped loudly. "Oh my Goddess, Opal!" she cried. My heart did something strange in my chest as Fluffy warbled loudly in my palm. With horror, I realised the creature was crying, track marks darkening the fur under her eyes. I watched Saraya take in the creature's injuries with both her back legs splinted with my old shirt.

"What did you do to her?" my mate screamed at me. "I'll kill you!"

Fluffy screeched loudly, and Saraya stopped short of trying to lunge at me. "I'm sorry, Opal!" she whispered. "I didn't mean to scare you."

She gently took the creature from my palm, and I relished the gentle feel of her hands against mine. But all too quickly, the touch was gone, and Saraya began crying, pressing the creature up to her face.

"Oh, my Goddess, your legs are broken. I'm so sorry, I'm so sorry!"

Something in me shifted as Saraya's emotions hit me like a blow between the legs, and I suddenly wanted to tear this place apart. Rip the walls down, break the bed and these wardrobes and kill every fucking creature living in here.

And Goddess fucking mark me. I swore by my mate, that's exactly what I would do to our captors.

9
SARAYA

Working as a midwife in the Sticks, where the poorest citizens of Quartz City lived, I had come to learn what real difficulty was. Where the battle of life and death was faced on a daily basis by hardened people who saw children die, women beaten, and young girls bravely selling their bodies to provide for their families.

It was seeing all of this, by the elbow of my midwife mentor, Agatha, that had taught me to value what I had. Perhaps that was part of how I stood tall after my stepmother arrived and began beating me month after month.

But seeing my little baby lumzen in this state, both of her hind legs broken, skinny, and weary, had me seeing red. She'd been with me from the start, from the moment I'd left the fae convoy to join their Warrior Academy. She'd seen it all alongside me. My one faithful companion, even guarding Tembry's newborn baby, Delilah, when I couldn't.

The knot I'd folded myself into was trembling, shaking, knotting further. How could everything have gone so wrong? I was now married to Drake, apparently half a monster, and we were stuck in this mad place of nightmares. I had just seen a human woman being assaulted as if it were a normal day. If it weren't for us coming into the room, the implications were obvious.

I set Opal down on the bed and knelt on the floor, so I was eye to eye with her. She licked my face, her own tears still falling. Drake had taken out that demon guard with the ease of someone taking a morning stroll. And now he'd helped Opal like a healer. What exactly was going on in that mind of his? He wasn't completely gone rabid all the way then.

"You must be hungry, Ope," I whispered.

She gave me a croon and nodded behind me. I turned and looked up at Drake, who was looking at Opal like he wanted to eat her.

"Drake!" I cried, affronted.

"What?" He jumped, coming out of some sort of reverie.

"You looked like you wanted to eat Opal!"

His mouth dropped open. "What? No! No, she's trying to say that I was feeding her while she was unwell."

I looked back at Opal, who nodded sombrely. I noted the dark fabric that had been neatly tied around her legs to hold them in place like miniature splints.

A lump grew in my throat. Opal was family to me, like a child or little sister that I would willingly die for. I wiped my eyes roughly and got to my feet. Standing in front of Drake, his eyes widening in surprise, I sniffed. "Thank you for looking after her."

He twitched a little bit as if my words were the last thing he'd been expecting. He looked back at Opal. "I...my magic does not heal, so that's all I could do."

I sighed as a tiny weight lifted off my shoulders. Finally,

knowing that one of my own was safe was a good thing in the midst of this mess. I tapped my collar.

"If I didn't have this stupid thing, I'd be able to try. I've healed animals before, and Opal is a female, so it should definitely work."

Drake looked down at the cuff that bound him to me. "The chain is a common demon tool used here, so I've seen. I think it's made to go longer and shorter. I've seen the other lords do it at least. Hold on." He frowned at the links and they multiplied, allowing it to lengthen.

"Oh, thank the Goddess," I murmured. I had been wondering how I'd use the bathroom with this thing on.

"And I can give your magic back for a short period." Drake squinted at it again, and the magical blue glow dulled. "I don't know if that was an intentional function of the demon magic, but it won't last long."

My heart soared as my magic rushed back into my body, the feeling euphoric, like the whirling joy you get dancing with a friend. It sparkled and sang within me, infusing my brain with power. As it settled within my skin, I felt out for Opal's body. "I'll give it a go, Ope."

As I knelt back down beside the bed, by the new magic of the mating bond, I felt Drake's emotions sailing towards me like a boat on calm water. I felt his happiness, his satisfaction at seeing me happy. I glanced back at him and he smiled at me. I quickly swung my head back around, my heart pounding in a giddy rhythm. I definitely had not expected to be affected by his smile *that* much.

So I focused on Opal instead, but she wasn't helping because her eyes were wide, set on Drake as if he held some answer she wanted. I bid my heart to stop its stupid arrhythmia. Drake was just the fae commander I'd fought back at my palace. The enemy fae that sought to take over my land before someone else had tried and succeeded in his place. My stupid body wanted to make something more out of it, but I couldn't let it. I couldn't let one smile, one piece of kindness, sweep me away. In a way, he was still my enemy.

I sighed and closed my eyes, looking into Opal's tiny body, seeking her skeleton, the bones of her leg. I started with the left leg, and to my surprise, Drake had set the splint so that the fractured pieces sat flush against each other. I made a tiny sound of surprise.

Behind me, I *felt* the darned fae commander grinning. I didn't even have to look at him, but I could feel through the mating bond that his lips were set into a curve. I shut him out with my mental defensive wall and frowning, focused on accelerating the healing process that was already taking place in Opal's femur bones. I multiplied the bone cells and bone marrow, fusing and joining, encouraging and invigorating with oxygen and nutrients.

Once I was done, I moved to the other side, feeling Drake sitting in the chair in the corner of the room. I ignored the clanking chains as I bonded Opal's bones together. There was still inflammation, and she would be in pain, so I would have to make sure she was well fed. I had just a little bit left to do before I felt my power snuff out. I opened my eyes to find the chain humming its suppression magic once more.

I made a face at Drake, who was pretending not to observe me.

"That's all I could do," he said as if irritated by the fact. "The tourmaline in the walls suppresses my magic as well."

"There's nothing else we can do then." I shrugged and stood. Opal crooned sleepily in thanks. "I'll have to find her some food."

"I'll ask the maids."

I looked around the room, feeling a draft on my skin. I needed to get out of these ridiculous jewels. I headed to one of the wardrobes and pulled it open to find a rack of female clothing.

Drake's heat followed close behind me. "You don't have to do that," I snapped.

He jerked back as if I'd slapped him. "Do what?"

I motioned to the space between us, or lack thereof.

"Oh," he said softly, before taking two reluctant steps back. "I'm sorry, it's just this mate bond is hard…to deny."

"What does that mean, exactly?" I said, my voice carrying the frown on my face. "Deny?"

He moved two more steps away from me and put his hands behind his back as if to convince me he meant no harm.

"It means, Saraya, that my body needs to mate with you. To take you as mine fully. To consummate the mate bond." He swallowed as if it hurt him. "I…have to constantly fight the need."

I flushed at his words, a bright tingle shooting through me. I put my smooth midwife-face on and tried to think about this rationally. As if it were an illness of the body I needed to fix. "Is this a part of your binding being taken off? Would you be like this if you were still bound?"

"I'd still feel it, but it would be easier to control."

I chewed on my lip in thought. "There was always…something between us."

He smiled again and my stomach flopped on itself. I pressed a hand to my abdomen as if I could push it into submission. When my hand met my skin, I was reminded that my standing here half-naked probably wasn't helping him to not think about my body. So I turned and began rummaging through the closet while he spoke.

"I agree there was something between us. I didn't have my memories, but I felt it too."

"Hmm." I disguised my breathlessness by pulling out a dress. It was silk. Everything in this wardrobe was either silk or transparent, and all were revealing. I'd have to do something to change that. I turned and my eye caught the wardrobe on the other side of the bed. I led Drake over to his side of the room and opened the cupboard. These were larger men's clothes with enough fabric to cover every bit of skin. It felt very unfair, but at least I had a solution. I began digging around but could feel him watching me. I was trying to think of another question, but Drake beat me to it.

"Before Tembry gave birth, you promised you would tell me about your magic. Your Goddess mark and why you went to the Mountain Academy—"

I spun around, a black cotton shirt in my hand. "You made me swear under duress. That was hardly gentlemanly."

He cocked his head in such an animal-like way that I looked back at Opal lying on the bed to see if there was a similarity. But of course, Drake was closer to a predatorial tiger than a sleeping creature that resembled a kitten.

"What gave you the impression that I was a gentleman?" His grin was so predatory that I stabbed a firm finger into his chest.

"I make the decisions here, *Commander*," I sneered. "Not you. Don't forget it."

He crossed his arms. "I'll think about it."

The response was so unexpected I barked a laugh. "Well, right now, I'm demanding privacy so I can change my clothes. Get out."

His face fell, but he nodded and turned, the metal links multiplying by the second. He stalked out of the room and closed the door, slipping the metal links under the door, which was, luckily, high enough to admit them.

So I began the arduous process of unclipping and unbuttoning the various strings of jewels, starting with my legs. They were easy enough to unwind, but once I'd undone the belly chain, I swore out loud, staring at the pieces of it in my hands.

"Flora, you sneaky little monster!" I groaned out loud.

Drake was at the door and I knew it without even turning around to see his shadow. "What's wrong?"

I sighed. The thing wasn't made to be taken off by one person. And I just knew these bridal jewels were intended for my *husband* to take off. Probably for some ridiculous pre-consummation thing. I swore under my breath and Opal covered her ears.

I turned to the door and stood there for a moment, staring at Drake's shadow. He had actually already seen me naked. Back in Lobrathia, with my Ellythian bridal ritual, he had come to guard me as I took a naked dip in the lake behind the palace. I knew he'd seen me then, and I hadn't actually been bothered for some reason. Some part of me had known even then that we'd had *something* significant between us.

But that had been at dusk and from behind trees. *This* would be up close, yellow quartz lights glaring, his fingers brushing my skin...

I shivered as desire pooled in my core.

"Saraya." Drake's voice was deeper, grating, filled with need.

I swallowed and took a deep breath, trying to control myself. "I need help," I said softly.

"With what?" His voice upturned at the end, as if wondering what I could possibly need.

"One moment." I turned and rushed to his wardrobe, pulling it open and yanking out a pair of pants. They would be long and ridiculous on me, but I didn't care. I needed some type of coverage.

I slid them on, then opened the door, holding his shirt against my chest to give me some semblance of modesty. Some semblance of control for both our sakes.

I had been right to do so because the veins around Drake's eyes had turned dark and inflamed, his grip on the side of the door jam white-knuckled. "You know I can feel it when you—"

"Stop." I held up my hand. "No hanky panky."

He straightened suddenly. "What did you just say?"

A burst of laughter suddenly erupted from my mouth and I tried to smother it with a hand. "Sorry, it's just something we say...something we said to husbands after their wives gave birth, to enable healing."

He nodded slowly. "Tembry said you were a midwife. That's how you knew what to do that day she gave birth."

I beckoned him into the room and decided that if we were going to try and get out of our situation, he had better know more about me. "I was taught from a young age when my mother felt the time was right for my powers. She taught me how to protect myself and how to use it before Agatha took me under her wing and taught me midwifery art and science at thirteen." I turned to face him and could tell he was listening and weighing each word. "And then my mother died, and my stepmother came, and everything changed—I need you to find all the clasps on this thing and undo them. The girls did it for me beforehand."

He stepped forward, and though I couldn't see it, I felt his hesitancy. I turned around and looked at him over my shoulder, saying as lightly as I could manage. "I trust you, Commander. And I'll keep talking, so you don't think about anything else."

He nodded stiffly, all-black eyes glistening. "I can do it."

He placed the tips of his fingers lightly on my waist and guided me backwards. Sitting down on the bed next to Opal, he began running his fingers along the beads, searching for the clasps. I noticed that he was careful not to touch my skin, but I still found the heat rising in me at the closeness. At least I wasn't in his lap like I'd been in the throne room—

"You were talking about when your stepmother arrived?" Drake's voice led me back to where we were.

"Right." I clutched his shirt closer to my front as I felt one clasp come undone. "She was cruel, though no one knew it except me—" One of his knuckles grazed one of my scars and I suppressed a hiss.

"I'm sorry," he murmured.

"It doesn't hurt," I said quickly. "It's just embarrassing. She told me she'd do it to my sister, too, if I told anyone. My mother raised me to be a fighter, and yet I could do nothing to save myself. It's a shame I'll carry for the rest of my life."

I felt the anger in him rise like a dark cloud. He took my hips in his broad hands and spun me around.

With him sitting, his eyes were level with mine. Opal had crawled into his lap and curled into a solid sleep.

"You got those scars," his voice was a growl so soft it was almost a whisper, "to protect someone you love. And that is the most honourable thing a person can do. It's the *only* thing in this life worth doing."

I tore my eyes off Opal and looked into his. I was startled

to see that the monstrous all-black of his eyes had cleared, leaving his regular, hazel irises to show through. But the pupils were dilated and fixed on my face. The emotion rolling off him hit me like a wave.

"Are you speaking from experience?" I asked softly, clutching his shirt to my chest so hard my hands were going numb.

The pad of his thumb moved, just barely, across my bare hip. "Yes," he whispered. The longing, *his* longing for me, swept through me from crown to my toes, and the force of it took my breath away. He pulled me closer, his face inches from mine. He licked his lips.

"I've thought about you since I was little. Saw glimpses of you…felt tiny bites of emotion. And then, one day, you must have learned to build your shields properly, and I couldn't see anything detailed that often. It was just the feeling of you being there. Far away. I always knew exactly where you were and it was torture not to go and find you. It felt like a part of me was somewhere else, lost without me—"

"I wasn't lost." I stepped away from him. "I was busy with studying and midwifery and training with weapons—"

"Did you ever feel something was missing?"

I watched as the black seeped back across his eyes once again, starting from the pupil and spreading outwards—and remembered who it was that I was talking to. He didn't love me, didn't know me at all. It was just the monstrous magic in him that craved me. I turned back around and indicated the remaining jewels. "I don't know," I said honestly. "I didn't have much time to think about it. But…"

As Drake's fingers found another clasp at the small of my back and freed it, I thought about what I had been like as a child. I wanted to move out into the city. Had only been too eager to go out at night. To head southwards and just *look*.

"My shield has always been incredibly strong," I said. "My mother pushed me and pushed me. More than my sister, even, to build it until it was impenetrable. Not even Daxian could get through…"

Drake made a noise of agreement as his fingers swept along the jewels. "She knew what she was doing. My mother tried to do the same thing, but I think my sense of wanting you, of hunting for you, was stronger than her insistence to block you out. I liked feeling you. Like a constant friend, by my side."

The corners of my own mouth twitched upwards as I imagined what that would have been like for him, getting flashes and glimpses of me but never a full image. I should have been creeped out, but I wasn't.

Another two clasps fell away in quick succession and I felt the whole set of jewels sliding off my body. I let it fall to the floor, then quickly stuck my head through my new shirt and pulled it over myself.

He sighed. "I can take the couch."

I turned around, glancing at Opal, still fast asleep. Weariness clung to me as well. If Opal trusted Drake enough to sleep on his lap, then I decided that I could too. Not sleep on his lap, of course, but beside him. At least for one night. Animals had good instincts about these things. So I said, "No, it's a big bed, and you're too tall. Just—" I levelled him a look, "stick to your side."

Drake nodded so earnestly I could have laughed. "I will."

10

DRAKE

I have slept with many a fae female in my life but never had I this jittery sort of heat cutting through me at the idea that Saraya and I would be sharing a bed. That she had given me permission because I might be uncomfortable on the couch outside. The thought that she cared for my welfare gripped me like something strange. It was at once warm and foreign.

She went into the bathing room, and I made sure the chain extended long enough that it wouldn't go taut from under the door. These chains and I would have a love-hate relationship because though it meant that she would never be far from me, I knew she hated being bound— and it was now my purpose to hate everything she did.

I carefully brought Fluffy to the common room and put her down on the couch just as there was a knock at the front door. I smelled a human female slave immediately, along with food that was distantly familiar.

Opening the door, I found two slaves carrying large trays of food. In the fae realm, we had feasts after weddings, but I knew it worked differently in the demon realm. I'd observed that the demon lords didn't like to eat together. Probably some deep-seated demonic instinct to protect their food from others at all costs.

The maid set the food down and left as fast as she could. Fluffy had put an illusion over herself, so she wasn't seen; lumzen were clever creatures and I had no idea how Saraya had come by this one. I only ever saw them in the Solar Fae Realm.

Fluffy and I sniffed at the strange food and I couldn't find any reason to think it was poisoned or unfit for human consumption. But I would have to taste everything first and see if it was safe for Saraya to eat. I chose a mushroom-like fungus and, finding it to be reasonable in taste, gave a bit to Fluffy.

She chewed the small piece with an exaggerated sigh, somewhat like Lysander when forced to eat Mountain Academy turnips. Slade ate anything, and I think I understood why. These demon foods could only be grown without sunlight and so they were all variations of root crops, onions, mushrooms. Some of them were bitter, so I shoved those aside to make sure Saraya or Fluffy didn't accidentally eat one. I fed Fluffy until she shook her head at me, laid her head down on her paws, and closed her eyes.

"Were you feeding her?" came Saraya's surprised voice from behind me.

I stood and showed her the second plate. "This is for you."

She gingerly took it, a coy smile playing on those lips I wanted to taste so badly. "I never imagined I'd see *you* feeding a tiny animal."

We sat down and I watched her inspect each vegetable before taking a bite out of it. I began eating the meat, not entirely caring where it had come from. "I'll admit she did look tasty when she first came sliding into my cage. But I'd thought I'd better fatten her up first."

She almost dropped her plate. "If you eat her, I'll kill you."

I honestly didn't even know if I was being serious or not. I *had* thought about eating her for a moment, but I'd stopped myself. "Fluffy's too important to you, so I'd never do that."

My mate put her plate on her lap and crossed her arms. "Her name is Opal."

Although I made a face, I knew it just looked like I was baring my teeth, so I straightened my features out. "I call her Fluffy and I think she likes it." When really, the name 'Fluffy' was a reminder for me that she *was* a tiny creature that I wasn't supposed to harm. Opal was a stone regularly found in the fae realm and I needed the name to be more endearing.

We both looked at the baby lumzen, curled up in a deep sleep. A wave of adoration swept through me and I knew the emotion wasn't mine. I looked back at my mate and a tear trickled from her eye. Startled, I put my plate down and made to move towards her, but the look of warning she gave me stopped me in my tracks.

"I don't really know you, Drake," she said softly.

With her in front of me, wearing my clothes, the smell of us both filled my nostrils, and a dizzying wave of lust pushed me back into the couch. The monster in me growled in annoyance at her wanting distance. But the fae in me knew she was right. The only thing that was stopping me from pulling her into my arms was the fact that I knew she didn't want that. I would always know what she wanted. I could smell it on her, taste it in the air, see her micro-expressions with an acute sight.

"Are you scared of me, Saraya?" I asked.

"I'm not scared of anything," she shot back. After a moment, she sighed. "Except for the people I love getting hurt, that is."

That cut deep into me because I knew I didn't count amongst that number. She meant her sister, her father, Fluffy. Not me. Some emotion I wasn't accustomed to made my throat go tight. Alarmed, I shot to my feet, confused as to why my chest hurt like someone was gripping my heart.

"Are you—" she began, but I cut her off.

"Fluffy is okay. You said your sister is safe..." I ticked them off my mental checklist. "That leaves your father."

"Drake—"

"I'll make the enquiries tomorrow. The demons go to sleep now. And they'll want me to exterminate that problem demon lord as quickly as possible." What my mate wants, she gets. Even if that doesn't include me.

Saraya lifted the chain questioningly. "Does this mean I come with you?"

Looking down at the chain linking us, I nodded. "I guess it does."

I saw the thoughts turning in her mind. She would get to see me work. I wasn't sure if that was a good thing or a bad thing. But I did know that right now, Saraya needed space. She had almost been married to Daxian and now was married to me. It would have been a shock for me, too, if marrying her wasn't all I'd thought about my entire life.

"Fluffy and I are going to bed," I said, scooping the creature up. She warbled in protest, but her eyes remained closed.

Saraya nodded, and it meant something to me that she trusted me with the creature she considered her family. Small steps were small wins. That was Slade's favourite saying.

I trudged to the bedroom and found a small blanket in my

wardrobe. I opened the drawer of one of the bedside tables and made a nest in there, shaping the blanket until it looked like something I would sleep in if I were a small creature. I placed her in and she buried underneath the folds until I couldn't see her at all.

I took off my shirt, made with buttons so they'd go around the chain, and, for Saraya's sake, put on a pair of soft sleeping pants.

Pulling back the blankets, I climbed in and lay there, not feeling tired at all. But I had to be in this bed. Perhaps it was because I knew I'd have to be up in the demon's equivalent of the morning to see what Havrok planned for us, or perhaps it was because I knew that my mate, as a human, would have to sleep soon and this was where my place was.

I listened to the sounds of her picking at the food and eating. A satisfied, cheery feeling lit me up—as if the monster was happy that she was being fed and cared for. But then she got to her feet, the chains chiming, and headed straight for our room.

My body tensed and I closed my eyes, pretending to be asleep as she padded around the room and crawled into bed beside me. But the bed was huge, and she was so far away from me that we might not have been in the same bed at all.

She sighed deeply as she lay down and then sat bolt upright, anxiety coursing through her. I sat up on reflex, looking around for the threat.

"Where's Opal?" she asked, whipping around to look about the room.

"Oh." I laid back down and gestured at the drawer next to me. "She's in there."

Saraya lunged over to my side of the bed, peering over me into the nest of blankets. I inhaled her scent, resisting the urge to lean upward and pull her face down towards mine. To kiss her, to caress her skin and feel her moaning with desire…my entire body hardened and my hand flew between my legs in an attempt to hide my arousal. But she didn't seem to notice and shifted backwards. I immediately rolled on my side, away from her.

The last thing I needed her to think was that I was some lovesick fool who couldn't control myself. I barely could, but that was beside the point. But she must have sensed it through the bond because she said, "Stay on your side, Lord Drakus, and I will stay on mine."

A smile crept across my lips. I loved it every time my name came from her lips. And she was all mine. "You're Lady Silverhand now."

"Don't remind me," she grumbled.

Well, that wiped the fucking grin off my face, didn't it?

I spent that night listening to my mate's breathing. And maybe on some mately instinct that had her subconsciously aware that I would keep her safe, she slept soundly.

11

SARAYA

I woke to find myself all the way on the other side of the bed, curled against the side of Drake's body. To his credit, he'd refrained from touching me, so it was with great annoyance that I had been the one to succumb overnight.

I quickly pushed myself backwards, stifling a yawn. Since there was no light in this realm, I had no idea how to gauge the time. The best strategy was to detract from my awkwardness with conversation. "Is it time to wake up?"

When Drake didn't answer, I finally looked at him. He was studying me in a way that was eerily similar to Agatha, my old midwife mentor. Even with his all-black eyes, I could tell that it was the carefully assessing manner of a person who had been studying others for a very long time. I wondered where Drake had learned that particular skill. I thought it was something only experienced midwives and healers had.

So I studied him back and suddenly realised he wasn't wearing a shirt. I must have kicked the covers back in the middle of the night because now I could see his wavering black tattoos all across his chest muscles, thin lines where the

109

mage had undone the spell, bleeding into the solid and dark black section that was remaining of the binding. I realised it was a black tree, the branches long, curling and malicious. It was not the type of tree I hoped I'd ever see in real life. But under his tattoos, my eyes were drawn to the hard planes and valleys of an incredibly muscled torso.

Drake's morning voice was a deeper rasp than I thought possible. "You snore, did you know?"

I was jolted out of my reverie. Embarrassed that he knew I'd been staring, I grabbed my pillow and threw it at him. "I do not!" It bounced and fell off the bed. Opal gave a frightened shriek from her drawer. "Sorry, Ope!" I cried. But annoyingly, Drake beat me to it, scooping the entire bundle of blankets out and unravelling Opal on the bed. Rubbing her eyes with a paw, she glared at me. Drake patted her gently on the head though it looked like he did it with great restraint.

"You'll have to stay here, Fluffy," he said as if speaking to one of his warriors. "Keep hidden in your drawer. I'll leave you food."

The chains clanked as he slid off the bed and put her back into her drawer as I stared at him in dismay. Opal could *not* choose sides like this and she clearly liked him. Though, perhaps he deserved it, since he'd looked after her when I couldn't.

I tugged at my baggy clothes, wondering what I should wear if we were going to be walking around this awful place. Whatever we were going to be doing today, I didn't want to be caught off guard. Midwife's motto: Always be prepared.

I went back into Drake's wardrobe, rummaging around to see if there was anything worth trying to alter with what little I had. Pants were a must, as would be a shirt.

"I can make it shorter," said Drake coming up to look at a shirt. "With my own magic."

I felt like an idiot. "You can do that?"

He nodded. "Just like how you can alter bones and flesh with your magic, fae magic can alter other materials. Depending on the fae, that is. Because my magic is destructive, I can take off parts that are too big."

That was certainly handy, but I wouldn't trade my magic for anything in the world. I picked out a set of pants. "Can you do these?"

He turned around, pulling on a new shirt himself. "Put the new ones on."

I hesitated, glancing around the room as if some invisible person would help me. Yet again, being naked in front of Drake was not something I particularly wanted when he was this close. And these darned demons had not given me *any* underwear in my stock of clothes. But I was being stupid, of course. We were both adults...and, I thought darkly, *husband and wife*.

Sighing, I had Drake turn around and changed clothes as quickly as I could.

He altered the fabric and was incredibly efficient at it. The pants shrunk around me until they were a good match for the fighting pants I used to wear back at home when training with Jerali Jones. Then he did the same with the shirt.

"In another life, you could have been a tailor," I joked, slapping him on the arm and trying to ignore how hard his bicep was. I was quite happy with this outfit. I'd be able to fight perfectly well if I needed to. But when I looked back up at him, he was staring at me. "What happened?"

"Turn around while I change my pants, wife."

I flushed and did as he asked. Fair was fair, I supposed.

"I did actually make my own clothes," he mused as he changed, "when I was a boy. As a deity, my mother often left me alone for long periods of time. So I had to learn a lot of things myself."

Hiding my surprise, I thought about this in silence. Yesterday, I had told Drake that I didn't really know him. Whatever I'd thought his childhood was like, it was not this.

"And," he continued, turning back around, "you never finished your story from yesterday. We got to the part about—"

I turned to face him and absently pulled at the metal around my throat, something that was becoming a habit for me. He frowned and I could tell by the angle of his head that his thoughts were distant.

"What's wrong?" I asked nervously.

"Slade," he growled, clenching then unclenching his hands. "He used to do that—" he made the same tugging motion around his own neck like I just had, "—and I never knew why. Now I do."

"Slade was a slave down here?" I said aghast. When I had asked Lysander what Slade's story was, he'd said that we'd need a stiff drink to get through it. My heart clenched as I imagined a child version of Slade down in this awful place.

Drake nodded, inhaling deeply as if it strained him to speak of it. "I know he and Lysander are both capable warriors but being here again…I don't know what that would do to him."

"We need to get out of here, Drake," I said. "What are we even doing? Playing husband and wife for a king?"

"I'm playing *assassin* for a king," he said darkly. "We just need to figure out what this place is like and make a plan, because Havrok sure as hell has one for us."

And Glacine. I was sure she had some say in what happened to me as well. But I knew one thing I didn't tell Drake. If I was getting out of here, so were the other female slaves. Because there was no way I was leaving Tarangi, Sarone, and even Flora here. They would wither and die in this place. I had not yet seen any women over thirty here. No doubt that was by design.

We went to the living room, where someone had placed breakfast at some stage. It unnerved me that I hadn't heard them come in and out. Last night had been my first sleep in a proper bed in a few days, so perhaps I had slept deeply. But I was sure Drake had heard because he showed no concern at all. He offered me a plate first.

"You were telling me about your midwifery yesterday."

I recalled halting my story with Glacine's arrival, but he courteously didn't bring that part up again. I looked at him curiously. This man who was supposed to be a monster—who I knew was a monster, with his black eyes and overall murderous demeanour, was *courteous*, even gentlemanly in many ways. I didn't know what to make of this juxtaposition. So I settled for telling him the rest of my story. Even about how I had met the three ghosts at the temple and how they'd told me that I'd need to learn to be a better fighter at the fae Academy before I was ready to fight real demons. And then how, after my capture by Drake himself, Arishnie had taken me to meet the goddess Umali and had anointed me into the Order of Warrior Midwives.

Arishnie. My ghost mentor had been meeting me at every full moon to teach me, to check in with me. I didn't know if she'd be able to find me here in the demon realm. When was the next full moon anyway?

"Temari is an old fae word, did you know?" Drake said after swallowing a mushroom.

That jerked me out of my reverie. "What?"

He nodded. "I wrote to the mage, Dacre, when I saw the mark on your forehead, and, I know he looks young, but he's actually so old he recognised it straight away. There was a blade named Temari. I don't actually know what it means. I meant to ask my mother."

There was a loud knock at the door and I jumped.

12
DRAKE

I loped to the door and Saraya trailed behind me. A soft bubbling of nerves sailed through the bond and I knew she was nervous. Other than act as Lord of the Kill, what exactly were we expected to do here, as husband and wife?

A human girl I had not seen before, bobbed a curtsey. She must have been a palace runner because instead of the ridiculous see-all dresses the other human girls wore, this one wore a shirt, pliable trousers and closed shoes that were worn with use. She kept her eyes on these shoes when she spoke.

"I'm here to escort you to the arena, My Lord."

Anger flared in me because I knew exactly what arena she was referring to. They were famous, the gladiator tournaments of the demon realm. Slade had been trained from boyhood to fight in them. Now, I would get my turn to see them for myself. "Very well," I said, glancing at Saraya.

Her face was a little suspicious but there was a hint of stubbornness that I had become familiar with.

Saraya had been right. Though as a child, I had thought that I'd known her and loved her from afar. I didn't really know her. But the woman I was getting to know was remarkable. I could not have hoped for a better mate.

The runner, Jessie, she told us, led us all the way to the back of the palace and out a wide back door.

The arena was huge.

A short walk down a path, the circular stone building loomed over us. Saraya tensed and I think she might have realised the implications of such an arena when a series of human male slaves came into view. They were walking in a long line, bound to one another with chains leading to each set of hand cuffs and ankle shackles. Led by a set of demon guards, the group were covered in dirt, frightened out of their wits and headed straight into the arena.

Saraya grabbed my arm immediately. I glanced at her and saw a great terror and rage etched onto the fine planes of her beautiful face, her green eyes wide. "Lobrathians," she whispered. "Those are—"

The hand around my forearm went awfully tight and I looked at her in alarm. Her sharp gaze was fixed upon someone in the queue of humans. I followed her line of sight and saw a familiar form.

I would not be forgetting that human any time soon. The Quartz palace armsmaster had taken down four of my warriors during my invasion of Saraya's palace. Fighting with an insane amount of skill, we had all been taken off guard. Lean of frame, with a shaven head, sharp features and an impeccable steel gaze, I could see that Jerali Jones hailed as neither man nor woman. In this place, it wouldn't matter, because I knew that the armsmaster was a force to be reckoned with. It was no wonder they had put Jerali in the number of men they had wanted to test in the arena. I bet the armsmaster had fought tooth and nail before being captured.

The demons would be making a lot of money off Jerali Jones.

But my mate was a pool of red hot anger, so I turned to her and placed a hand on hers, still fixed on my arm.

Ahead, our runner realised we had stopped and came back to us, wringing her hands nervously.

"We need to get to the king's seat," she said hurriedly, looking from me to Saraya. "Please, My lord—"

"Let's go," Saraya interrupted. She removed her hand from my arm, shook herself a little and nodded. "I'm sorry, Jessie. I just saw someone I knew. I didn't know Lobrathians were being brought down here."

"I heard the guards talking. Most won't stay," Jessie said in a low voice, glancing nervously at the demon guards. "They will only keep the strongest for fighting and building, and then send the rest back to the quartz quarry for mining. But please, we must go."

I glanced at my mate, assessing her emotions, but her face had smoothed out, the only tell that she was upset was a clenched fist by her thigh and the rapid beating of her heart. I wanted to kiss her, to tell her that I was working on a plan, but I knew she wouldn't want that from me right now. So I turned and we followed Jessie right up to the arena's entrance and up a wide set of stairs.

Down a dim stone corridor with a few orange quartz lights along the wall, we came to a door guarded by a set of armoured demons. Both immediately shifted their eyes to Saraya.

The growl that escaped my throat was purely reflexive, but it made both demons look at me instead.

"The king's balcony," Jessie said in a hushed voice, eyeing me nervously.

I gave her a polite nod. Before the guards even opened the door, I could hear male demon voices, including Havrok's.

I couldn't help it. I turned and offered Saraya my hand. Her jaw was set defiantly, but she put her calloused hand into mine anyway.

Warm emotion gushed through me. She trusted me on some level and I couldn't have been more satisfied about that. Perhaps she would trust me even more once we'd spent more time together.

I drew her forward to walk into the room in front of me, though I was so close to her I could've stepped on her heels if I wasn't careful. If we were to be surrounded by demons, I wanted to have her in my line of sight at all times.

The room was wide and circular, its fourth wall absent, opening into a view of the stadium proper. Seats were spaced around for good viewing and two were currently occupied.

Thankfully, for my mate's sake, Glacine was nowhere in sight. Instead, an Ellythian woman in her mid-twenties was perched on Havrok's lap, a large courtier's smile on her face. Her green eyes were identical to Saraya's. Shock coursed through me and I glanced at my own mate. Surely they were not kin?

I glanced at the other chair's occupant. In it was the Lord of Gold, Braxus, and a deep brown skinned girl with a plump frame. The moment we were in his line of sight, Braxus' eyes fixed upon Saraya like an eagle and he eyed her hungrily.

I turned my back on Braxus and swept a bow at Havrok, who lazily waved a hand at us. "Finally, I get to show my new Lord of the Kill my gladiators. Sit." His last word held a note of firm command that had me seething. But of course, I could do nothing as the controlling rune forced me into the remaining seat, leaving Saraya standing next to me. But I couldn't stand Braxus staring at her so I pulled her posses-sively into my arms.

Having noticed Braxus as well, Saraya didn't protest as she settled herself on my knee and to my great satisfaction, put an arm around my shoulder. With her delicious scent enveloping me, I instantly calmed. I noted everything about her. Especially the way her lips were tightly drawn and that she pointedly would not look at Havrok or her kinswoman in his lap.

Taking a deep breath to settle the lust pouring through me, I looked down into the stadium.

"There they are, Lord Drakus," Havrok said, sliding his fingers up and down his charge's leg. "He will be the best one, mark me."

I looked to where he was pointing and with a sudden and electric jolt of rage saw why Havoc wanted me to pay attention.

The huge, muscled fae male, with short black hair and a matching slave collar, dully surveyed his surrounds.

Slade.

I wanted to leap out of my chair and strangle Havrok. But from the side of my eye, I could see the demon king was watching me carefully. Of course the bastard knew Slade was one of my sergeants.

So I forced a half interested nod. "Indeed. Slade is the best fighter, after me."

Havrok nodded and turned his attention back on the sandy arena floor. I needed him to think I was a monster, that my true self was psychotic, emotionless, a rabid animal with no care. Only then would he let me into his inner circle and I could get Slade and Lysander out of here. Slade, from the way he was looking now, grey-faced, his nostrils flared, had turned to stone. He had grown up here, and thought he'd escaped the horrors of it for good.

Saraya's fingers were tracing circles on my neck. I glanced at her in surprise as heat hardened me, but her eyes were trained on Slade. As I watched her, the graceful plane of her neck calling me in like a siren's song, she turned and looked at me. As always, her gaze tore me open. Not just because of the brilliant emerald colour, but because of the compassion in them, the fire, the raw emotion.

She must have sensed my anger and was trying to calm me down. Perhaps, she cared about me after all.

I could have kissed her, she was so close, the urge to explore her mouth with my tongue was so strong I licked my lips.

But her lips twitched as if she knew what I was thinking and she ceased the movement of her fingers and looked back at the arena.

I forced my eyes off her and back to Slade, feeling better that I had my mate by my side to face this with.

The gladiators were now being forced against the walls. I spotted Jerali Jones immediately, eyes darting around, assessing everything and anything all at once. The other humans shuffled worriedly, armed with dull practice swords.

"And now," Havrok said excitedly, "we will see who survives."

Saraya's breath hitched and I placed a hand on hers where it rested on her thigh, squeezing it. Jerali would be fine and so would Slade. They were the best fighters I'd ever seen, barring my own mate.

From the other side of the arena, a horn blared. The grating sound of a metal door being lifted was promptly followed by guttural shrieks as twenty lesser demons stormed out with wooden swords.

I knew what would happen before the two groups met.

Saraya trembled where she sat, but I knew it wasn't fear. She was angry, her face flushed, her fists clenched.

But for the moment, we could do nothing.

After it was done, the dead were cleared from the arena, leaving anyone with mild wounds to be attended by human female slaves. Jerali was unmarked, a rough scowl on that angular face, that, as I watched, faded completely, replaced by smooth relief.

Because by the bench where Slade was being attended to, for a shallow scratch on his arm, a familiar face was pushing another human slave aside.

Saraya's second maid, Blythe, the raven haired, stubborn girl who was currently muttering something to Slade. Smart girl, that she was trying to communicate with the others.

Saraya shifted, her hand suddenly grabbing mine, and I knew that she'd spotted Blythe as well.

But it was relief that flew through her like a cool wind-floating towards me through the mate bond. So we knew that these two of her loved ones were fine.

Suddenly our plan to get out of here became a lot more complicated.

From the corner of my awareness, I noted Havrok's head swinging around. He was eyeing Saraya with interest and I knew it was plain for all to see that she was upset. So she should be. It was the genuine response that Havrok had expected.

But he hadn't known what *my* reaction would be. He had done this as another malevolent test. To see the type of creature I'd become. If I really was as monstrous as I was supposed to be.

So I made a sound of interest low in my throat and glanced at the demon king. "I look forward to the tournament once they are trained."

Havrok's smile was slow and approving. "Oh, I have so much planned, Lord Drakus, so much planned."

13
SARAYA

We returned to our rooms silent and seething. Well, at least I was. Drake had taken in everything from the arena with barely any emotion at all. The only time he had, was when he'd seen his sergeant, Slade, and his shoulders had stiffened. I thought he might've lashed out at Havrok then, and I'd tried to distract him. Luckily, it had worked.

I couldn't believe Jerali and Blythe had been forced into the demon realm as well. I had hoped they'd escaped somehow and run off to Kaalon. Jerali was clever and it was something my armsmaster should have pulled off. The fact Jerali hadn't...

I clutched my stomach, feeling sick to my core as I sat down on our couch next to Opal who crooned sadly when she saw our faces. The fact I was sitting down in our room and not out there fighting for our freedom irked me to no end. I looked up at Drake who was taking a swig of water, his face a stony mask.

"What do we do?" I asked dully. It hurt my pride to even ask, but I was out of my depth here.

"Nothing. For the moment." He patted Opal on the head and she pressed herself against his hand.

The movement was strangely endearing and in terrible juxtaposition to what he was saying.

"Nothing." I repeated numbly.

Drake looked at me and took a deep breath and I was able to see a fleeting moment of the wariness that clung to him.

"Tomorrow we go to Zengistas," he said calmly. "That's the city where this demon lord lives. The one they want dead. It's also actually where I first met Lysander."

I gaped at him as it all fell together. "The demons keep fae down here as well? Why do the fae not rescue their children?"

Drake shook his head in dismay. "It's only ever the orphans. The ones without anyone to speak for them. I did my best, the few times I found myself down here."

He'd rescued both Slade and Lysander and he would have only been a teenager at the time. I looked upon Drake with new eyes, trying to imagine him as a sixteen-year-old, running around the demon lands.

"We wait, Saraya," he said. "We wait and watch."

THE NEXT MORNING, WE WERE EATING BREAKFAST WHEN SOMEONE knocked on the door.

Drake growled, "demon," before striding to the door and yanking it open.

The crimson-skinned demon stood tall and imposing in black armour, the white X marking his station across his breast. His eyes were an unnerving yellow, just the same colour as the many incisors in his mouth. I recognised him immediately as the captain whom Glacine had instructed to strike me. The first chance I got, I was coming after him.

"My Lord." He bowed, addressing Drake and ignoring me completely. "I am Captain Argoth. I will take you to Zengistas. I've got your armour—"

"I won't need it," Drake said shortly.

I looked at him in surprise but hung back, seeing if I could glean anything about what awaited us. I wondered what Jerali and Blythe were doing down in their prison cells. There had to be some way I could go and talk to them, see if they were okay, or give them food perhaps.

"Yes, My Lord." Argoth bowed again, his sword sweeping backwards. He turned aside, ready to escort us out.

Drake turned to me, and I nodded, passing a warning glance at the spot I was sure Opal was sitting in, covered in her illusion. It would not do for anyone knowing she was here. She might be able to help us get out of this—she'd helped me in many precarious situations, after all.

We headed out the door and after Captain Argoth, who escorted us through the maze that was the demon palace. I didn't fail to notice that Drake had shortened our chain so much that I had no choice but to walk exceptionally close to him. I tried to pass him a glare, but he only had eyes for our surroundings.

Although I had my own magic muffled, I just knew there was magic all around us, as if it were steeped into the very paint, the very bones of this palace. The strange sculptures and the dark paintings all exuded the same malicious energy.

Outside the palace, a group of demon warriors in full armour awaited us along with a carriage tied to long necked reptilian creatures twice the size of any horse I'd ever seen. Their heavy tails swished solemnly as they waited.

"From the king." Argoth handed Drake a parchment written with a scrawling hand as well as a small sketch.

Drake scanned the paper and then handed it to me. Thankfully, written in a common tongue, I made out an official notice for a death warrant of one: Lord Bringu Gangrene. The picture was of a many-jowled male demon with sagging skin and a multitude of boils. The reason was cited as *Tax Evasion*. I handed it back to Drake, who pocketed it.

"I work alone, Argoth," Drake rumbled.

"I know, My Lord," the captain replied, his eyes darting nervously to Drake's hands where he'd attached his sharp silver tips. I suppressed a smile, relishing the fact they knew Drake's skill. They should have given me a sword and I would've shown them what *I* was capable of too. Argoth gave a short bow. "We will escort you to the city gate and will await your return there."

"Very well. And we don't need a carriage. I will ride a haxim with my princess."

I raised my brows at Drake's words because he was indicating one of the giant humpbacked reptiles before us.

"They are difficult to ride, My Lord," gruffed Argoth. "I do not think the female—"

Drake stepped threateningly up to the demon captain so that they were nose to nose. The air around him suddenly became charged with the promise of violence. "I will decide what is difficult, Captain." His voice was so low I could barely hear him. All around us, the warriors went still. "And she is 'Your Highness' when you address her, understood?"

The captain's red cheeks became mottled, and if he didn't hate us before, he certainly did now. "Yes, My Lord," he managed to say through clenched teeth.

I could never let myself forget what Drake really was.

These demon warriors, who by all rights shouldn't have been scared of anything, would not speak back to him. It made me shiver to think of the power Drake had.

Without another word, Drake tugged me along to a particularly massive reptile, who snorted through large nostrils as we came up to him. 'Him' because of the particularly large and obvious testicles hanging under his long tail. The haxim's red slitted eyes followed us as we approached. A forked tongue snuck out, tasting the air—tasting Drake's scent as he came up to pat the creature's rough, scaly skin.

"You bore me well on the last job," Drake growled. "You will have both me and my mate this time."

The creature hissed and swung around, falling onto his haunches. He was already saddled and bridled with a modified tack. Drake turned to me and offered me a hand. I steeled myself, trying to show no weakness, and swung myself up as I would any horse.

All around us, the demon warriors muttered. But I stared straight ahead as Drake swung up, not in front of me, as I'd expected, but behind me.

"I'm not a child riding double saddle," I protested.

"No," he whispered in my ear, and a shiver ran through me. I could feel the bastard smiling. "But you are my mate. And besides—" he did something with the reins, and the haxim lurched to its feet, the only thing keeping me from sliding forward as it got up was Drake's arms around me, "—don't you want to see the view?"

The creature trotted forward in a loping fashion and I was suddenly extremely happy Drake had his muscled arms around me. Then it began running at full pelt, and I kept my mouth pressed firmly shut. Goddess, help me, I would *not* scream in front of the warriors now scrambling to catch up to us.

"Have you done this before?" I asked in an attempt to distract myself.

"The other day was my first time," he said into my ear as the wind passed us. "These bastards thought they'd have a laugh at my expense, but they don't know the odd creatures that exist in the dark fae realm. I grew up quite wild, and I used to play this game where I'd try and ride any monster I came upon and see how long I could stay on while they tried to buck me off. That was before I was bound, of course. But even after, I was always good with animals. You never met my steed, Razor."

He sounded sad as if I'd deprived him of some great opportunity. I found myself saying, "Maybe one day." All the while, trying to ignore the fact that his incredibly solid body was pressed flush against mine, warming more than just my back. My insides tingled as his arms flexed around me. *Safe* one part of me was saying, *dangerous*, said the other part.

The demon land we passed was barren and bleak. I had no idea why anyone would want to live here under the always black sky—a place where the land was never fertile.

Then it hit me. That was why they wanted to leave. This was why they wanted to take over the human kingdom.

"Why are we doing this, Drake?" I said. "I want to go home."

"I know," he murmured in my ear. "But as long as Havrok wears that controlling rune, I'm bound to him as much as I am to you. And while he wears it, he trusts me to do as he says. We must make him trust me more, trust *us* more. He needs to think that we're completely under his thumb. Only then will he let his guard down and *then* we can attempt to get away."

"So we're resorting to doing his dirty work?" I said, aghast. "While he's doing Goddess knows what to my father? While the demons plague my people? We just play Lord and Lady and pretend to be in his court?"

Drake's arms around me tightened, and through our bond, I sensed that he too, was irritated, but underneath that was a determination. "We have to Saraya. Unless you can see any other way around it. He has me by the balls, so we need to be as cunning as him."

I had nothing to say about that because he was right. If we were going to get out of here with our friends' lives intact, we needed to play the game.

14
SARAYA

We rode for an hour under that suffocating, unnatural starless, black sky. The air was cool on my face as I observed the barren demon lands, dotted with villages as one would find in the human realm.

Eventually, the tall black brick walls of a bustling city came into view. As we approached, I made out a line of reptiles similar to our haxim, that were tied to a long wooden bar along the wall. Some were variations of the same breed, smaller or bigger to hold more than three or four people. One even had a litter tied to its back.

Drake led our group to a spare space in the lineup and our haxim, apparently familiar with this process, groaned back down to his knees. I gratefully climbed off after Drake, and he led me to the demon warriors, jumping off their own haxims.

"We will meet you back here, My Lord." Argoth bowed. He offered Drake what looked like a black silk cravat.

Drake inclined his head and accepted the silk, pocketing it. Together, he and I walked to the city gates. I was suddenly very aware of my slave collar and the chain that very obviously glinted in the great fiery sconces on either side of the city entrance.

Demons, with mostly humanoid features but varying in colours and sizes, trickled into the city gates. We joined the queue to head inside and I realised that I needn't be conscious of my chains because there were chains and leashes everywhere. One demon lord strode through with three demon females on a joined leash. They wore scraps of clothing covering their breasts and thighs, but nothing else. My stomach twisted with unease.

With great dismay, I understood the power balance of this. The richer you were, the more slaves you owned. It was barbaric and almost exactly what I expected of such a malicious place.

We entered the city and I observed it with curiosity. It was mostly made of towering black stone or brick buildings, clearly old, because many were crumbling at the edges. The smell of decay mixed with alcohol and sweat crowded my nose, almost making me gag. I breathed through my mouth— I could hardly complain because if I was overwhelmed by the smell, no doubt Drake, with his heightened senses, had it all the more worse.

But Drake's face was stony as he took out the silk from his pocket and held it to his nose, sniffing delicately. He growled irritably, low in his throat, put it back into his pocket, and took my hand, guiding me through the paved road.

Seeing him hunt was like something out of a...nightmare? Except I wasn't scared. It was entirely animal, purely predatorial. Not unlike a bloodhound, but more like an apex predator. His head was low, and though it was hard to tell with the black in his eyes, I knew he was looking at everything all at once.

As we moved through the dark city streets, I made a note of the differences between the demon city and my human one in Lobrathia. Even in the main district, whores flaunted their wares, and merchants sold dark and gruesome objects from carts and stalls. Strange creatures roamed on chains or were tethered to metal stakes wedged into the stone. In the dark, shadows made terrifying shapes and glowing animal-like eyes fell upon me, greedy or sneering.

I stuck close to Drake as he sought our mark. But what would happen when we got there? This demon lord Havrok wanted, bore a certain power over this region and must certainly be wealthy if he was withholding taxes. That might also mean that he had guards and defences.

I gritted my teeth in annoyance as we rounded a corner. I had no weapon, no magic— no defence for myself. I knew hand to hand combat as well as any fae warrior did—I had trained with them after all, but there was no denying that even with the extra strength awarded to me by being a warrior midwife, I didn't know if I was a physical match for these excessively muscled demons.

Drake halted at a crossroads, looking left and right.

"Hello, pretty," purred a demon female, emerging from the alley on our right, her bust popping out of a tight black corset. Drake ignored her, and we continued on the left, quickly, but not before a fiery heat tore through me. *That* was confusing. Was I jealous of another woman wanting Drake? He was my husband now—perhaps I *did* have a right to be jealous. Or was it just the magic of the mate bond influencing me?

Then Drake caught onto some scent because we flew through the streets for ten minutes before coming to a stop at a regal townhouse trimmed with gold and silver. Without hesitation, Drake strode up to the front door and rapped his knuckles against it.

It opened within seconds.

A beefy demon with a long black beard took one look at Drake, turned, and ran.

"Lord of the Kill!" he screamed as he bolted down the hall.

Chairs scraped, voices hissed, and feet pounded all around the house. Drake and I waited on the doorstep as he picked at the silver blades on his fingers.

I looked up at Drake questioningly, wondering how they knew of him already. But his face was stony and trained ahead of us.

Only once it quietened did Drake then lead me into the house. Our boots creaked on varnished floorboards and I wondered where they got the wood from—probably pillaged from other realms. We turned left and emerged into a parlour room wreathed in red and gold.

The elderly, fat lord sat still on a gilded chair, the spitting image of the sketch on the death warrant, only his skin was a pale mildew green. He wore a robe of glittering gold. "Havrok has finally come for me, eh?" He asked in a thick voice, fingering a silver goblet in his lap.

When Drake spoke, his voice was so gratingly animalistic that I stared at him, startled. "I have a warrant for your death, Lord Gangrene."

"Your reputation is known even here, Drakus Silverhand." Gangrene sipped from his goblet. "Unfortunate that Havrok has you under his thumb, we might have been great allies. I hear what you're capable of. However much Havrok is giving you. I will double it."

It was a struggle to hide the surprise from my face. We

had been here for a few days, and already Drake known by these people. And here was a tempting offer.

"I am not here to talk," Drake rasped.

"Are you quite sure?" Gangrene asked, brows raised.

Drake was silent. But just as I was about to open my mouth, his huge shadowy presence at the door of my mind, silently bade me away. Frowning, I held my tongue.

"No? Well—" Gangrene shifted his chair and reached into his pocket. "I'm old and have lived a good life. And in that life I have done many a terrible thing. Even so, I will not let Havrok have me the way he wants. I will do this my way. Take my head after, will you?"

Drake ceased his advance and we both watched as Lord Gangrene took out a tiny black glass vial and said softly, "Lily of the Valley."

My heart leapt in my chest. He uncorked it, gestured 'cheers' with the vial, and swallowed it down.

Lily of the Valley was rare in Lobrathia, but I knew my herbs. Taken in concentrated form would cause a cardiac arrhythmia within minutes. Sure enough, Gangrene closed his eyes and gasped a few times before his head dropped onto his chest.

"Look away, Saraya," Drake rasped.

I could only stare.

"*Princess.*"

I came to my senses and turned around, wiping an eye. Death was death, no matter whose it was. This man had no doubt committed all sorts of crimes other than tax evasion, but even then, we were here to murder, and I was a part of it. I hated Havrok for making Drake do this. Hated even more that Drake was so good at it that this demon lord didn't bother putting up a fight.

There was a slashing sound and a short gurgle before Drake fumbled with something and strode towards me. My stomach churned, bile rose up my throat.

Reluctantly, I turned to look at Drake, but he was looking around the room. A shadow had fallen over his form. Relief flooded through me. I had worried that he might enjoy this—enjoy killing people. But I could see that was far from true. Even though he was half a monster. I couldn't look at the bundle of gold cloth he had in his right hand.

I swallowed. "We could have—"

"This whole thing was a test, Saraya," Drake said, not looking at me. "The kill was easy. He didn't even need me to do it. Havrok would have known if we'd taken the offer. His spies are everywhere."

"But we could just leave, even *now*, we could just—"

"He has guards surrounding the city at all exits," Drake said. "Did you think that I wouldn't have thought of that? I've been listening, Saraya, and my senses are so much more heightened than they were before. I can listen to the guards gossiping in whispers, even if they thought it impossible for me to hear them. I'm constantly watching. I'm constantly thinking of a way to get out of this. And even without the controlling rune, today is not the day."

The folded knot inside of me tightened with this knowledge. Very conscious of the headless body sitting just behind us, I nodded glumly and followed him back out of the townhouse.

People stared at us as we made our way back. They parted when they saw Drake's heavy golden bundle, especially when blood began seeping through the bottom of it.

I shivered as we passed the group of brothel workers. The

woman who had spoken on our way past initially opened her mouth and closed it before a smile spread over her lips.

"Come in any time, Lord of the Kill. We'll look after you here."

Neither Drake nor I said anything, that shadow of Gangrene's death hovering over us.

When we found our way back to our escort, Drake silently handed the golden bundle to Captain Argoth before leading me to our haxim.

"I don't miss it," Drake said softly, looking up at the sordid excuse for a sky. "The cloud that always followed me around."

I gave him a long look before looking up at the strange, black sky as well. "So it *was* a magical thing. I suspected that it wasn't a mere coincidence. How did it come about?"

"It's a long story," said Drake warily, offering me a tentative hand.

His uncertainty came through the mate bond like oil, and I knew he was worried about how I felt about this business with Gangrene. But I found myself wanting to know more about him. "I'm assuming the ride back will be just as long as the ride here."

A slight turn of his head let me know that he was looking at me, finally. I felt the relief washing over him like summer rain and I let myself smile at him, just a tiny bit.

15

DRAKE

I had craved holding Saraya close to me for so long that now I finally was, it felt like a dream. It almost made the fact that I had just murdered someone in cold blood right in front of her disappear.

Almost.

But I pushed that to the back of my mind as I enjoyed her heat against me, her sweet cinnamon scent filling my nose. A scent that promised me everything would be well. That one day, sometime in the future, we would be fine. Her curves promised me something else too, but I couldn't think about that with her pressed against my groin just now. A tiny part of me was still a gentleman. So I told her about my life and started at the beginning.

WYXIAN NEVER WANTED ANYTHING TO DO WITH ME AS A CHILD. I was ten when my mother presented me to Black Court, and I met him and my half-siblings.

I put on what I thought were my best clothes and even brushed my hair with a tool I'd made out of thin wooden sticks. But my mother is not a domesticated deity. She's not made for a fae palace, even in a dark one like Black Court. She wore nothing, from memory, except a necklace my father had given her as an offering when he first came to the throne. Which was, I imagine, the day I was conceived.

We walked in on presentation day, which is the one day of the year all young fae who've come of age to marry are presented by their parents. So the entire nobility of the Black Court was there.

We walked in and the entire throne room quietened. A servant rushed over to my mother, offering her a shawl to cover herself, but she waved them away, took my hand, and walked me down the long carpet. Even at that age, and having never been around many other people, I knew their faces were filled with contempt for me. I can't possibly imagine what we looked like to them: feral creatures, dirty and uncouth.

But my mother walked in like she owned the place. That is the way of Goddesses, I suppose.

I remember seeing my father for the first time, the young, powerful king, as I stood in front of his black throne. He looked so strong, so powerful, with a beautiful wife by his side. There was Sage, standing primly even at six, Ivy and Dattan fidgeting in the corner, and Daxian standing stiff-backed in beautifully embroidered clothes. I wanted my half-siblings to like me, to want me, to accept me.

But my father looked me straight in the eye and said, "You

are not my son."

The room went dark and my mother gripped my hand so tightly I swore it would bruise. I did feel sad, but the thing was, I *was* a little feral creature, and I couldn't take my eyes off Daxian. Not him, exactly, but what he was wearing. And so I pointed at him and said, "You can't climb a tree in those clothes."

Daxian's face screwed up in a child-like rage, and he said, "Yes, I can!"

I just frowned at him and thought, *That poor kid.*

The queen placed a hand on Daxian's shoulder and said, "This is the Crown Prince of Black Court, heir to the throne. This is Prince Dattan and Prince Ivy. *These* are Wyxian's only true born sons."

Looking at her face, I thought it looked a bit odd, but I hadn't been around enough people to know it was arrogance. I didn't even have the wherewithal to know that I was being mocked and rejected to my face. But I didn't have to. My mother got angry for me.

I looked up at her and saw a vicious smirk on her face—as if she knew something no one else did. Wyxian was just staring at her. I know now that it was probably a mixture of lust and anger, but he couldn't do anything about it. My mother gave a mocking curtsey, had me clumsily bow, and we left without another word.

As we made our way home, we basically pretended the whole thing never happened. For the next three years, I lived my life as I always did, playing about the grove with the animals and plants, thinking about you, making adjustments to my treehouse, and making clothes and gifts for my mother.

And then, as I mentioned before, the grove was no longer enough. I wanted to find my mate and travel the world with her. And I knew I had to go over the mountains to get to you. I set out one night without a thought for my mother because she'd raised me to be independent. But when she realised I had gone and gave chase, I felt such a thrill that I think it made me more excited to escape, and I headed right into the mountains.

Her roaming territory ends at the base of the Silent Mountains, so she couldn't pursue me into the human realm. She visited Wyxian and told him I was heading into Lobrathia to terrorise the humans there like the feral monster I was expected to be.

My father tracked me down and caught me as I was sleeping high in a tree in the Temari Forest. They dragged me back, kicking and screaming to my mother, who then came with us to Dacre Liversblood in his tower at Obsidian palace.

Even then, Wyxian did not suspect the prophescy about his firstborn son was about me. I don't think he expected a deity to lie about my timing of birth.

While Dacre didn't require my parents for the binding tattoos, he did require them both to bind my mind, to remove the urge to find my mate and the memories of me wanting you in the past. That's why the magic fell apart after Wyxian died and my memories were released.

So that brings me to after the binding. I didn't remember why I didn't trust my mother anymore, and I could see that my new tattoos were keeping a powerful side of me at bay.

So now I was angry.

There was a permanent storm cloud above my home, and at first, I ran away to try and rid myself of it and the strange heaviness that was sitting at the back of my mind—like a thorn in my side that I couldn't get out. Something was pricking at me, and I couldn't do anything about it. But once I left, the storm cloud followed me. I figured it was a way that Dacre found to channel the massive amount of magic that was being held off me. I was generating a large amount of power, and it needed somewhere to go.

I roamed the fae realms, simply looking. Looking for something that I didn't realise I would never find there. But that urge to seek, to hunt, led me all around, to each realm, even into the demon kingdoms. I learned to play cards and collected money that way. Eventually, I found Slade and then Lysander, helped them get out of their terrible situations, and together, we roamed the countryside, causing trouble.

Eventually, my father wrangled us into attending the Academy, where I met the other fae males, and quickly they realised I wasn't like the rest. Chalamey Springfoot, the Dean, saw that I had potential for something. We'd sit and play cards together, it was the only way he could get me to converse with him. I think he recognised that I needed a father figure. But after a few months, it was clear there was no point in forcing me to stay at the school and the Dean had me taken out. My father had no choice but to enlist me in his army.

I remember that first day he saw me in the training field. Fighting four on one, my opponents were all lying in the dust, and I turned around to see him standing there with his generals. They had been called to observe me. And just like that, the ageing commander of the elite forces took me under his wing and I learned what I needed about leading from him. I was never comfortable leading because I'd much rather work alone or with a small team, but they respected me, and I had a knack for tactics. I guess all that time spent in the wild had helped me develop those skills even though it was just play for me at the time.

Wyxian gave me a Darkcleaver ring and made me Commander of his Elites.

"Thank you...father," I said to him, but the words felt foreign in my mouth. I had wanted to test the word out, garner its measure.

But Wyxian's smile was tight and I knew in that moment, his intention.

The ring was not to claim me as his son, but to claim me as his weapon. He loved me for what I could do, not for being his blood. It was a bittersweet day because though I knew the truth, if I squinted just so, I could pretend that he loved me as he did Daxian.

I never addressed him as *father* again. Not until the day he died.

Then last November, we got the news that Daxian's marriage was set with a human princess, and I had no idea why it enraged me so. But it had been set thirty years before, so that was that. We set out for Lobrathia and I met you for the first time.

SARAYA LISTENED TO MY STORY QUIETLY AS WE RODE BACK TO THE demon palace, nodding here and there, but I had no idea what she thought about it. Finally, she knew the whole truth, and here we were, husband and wife. The thought settled in my stomach like a spiked ball, because here we *also* were, stuck in a court of monsters. But those monsters didn't know they'd enslaved the worst monster of all.

And Goddess help them if they took the rest of my runes off.

16
SARAYA

C hildbirth is to women what war is to men.

Some do not return from the ordeal, and those who do are changed for life. All bear the scars, and though they might heal from them, they will bear the memory of it for the rest of their lives.

So when Drake told me his life's story, I suppose I understood what he may have felt. Drake was a war commander who had a natural inclination for the job due to his upbringing. His story tore at my heart, the thought of a miniature version of him being shirked at Black Court by his own father. Then that very male had gone on to instate him as a trusted Commander.

It felt unfair to me. It felt dirty. But maybe that's how the dark fae people thought. Maybe that was their way. Surely Drake felt a betrayal on some level? His father had welcomed him into his court, but it was not as a son. That exchange during the acceptance of his ring had proved that.

As we headed back to our suite, Drake was silent and brooding after the mission we'd been sent on. He headed immediately to bathe. But when he returned, he frowned at the door and told me Tarangi was running towards our rooms, smelling of blood. I ran to open the door.

When she skidded to a stop, the girl was a sobbing mess. "Princess Saraya, you have to help me please!"

I immediately scanned her body for injury. "What's wrong, Tarangi?"

"It's Fessima, one of the Ellythian slaves...she's given birth, but the afterbirth won't come out. She's bleeding. There's so much blood everywhere, oh Goddess, please help her."

I immediately strode out the door. "Take me to her."

My chain pulled taut, and angrily, I turned around to see Drake staring at us.

"Drake." My voice was low in warning.

"Are you sure, Saraya?" he asked, black eyes assessing.

I strode up to him and looked him directly in the eye. "I am a *midwife*. Of course I am fucking sure."

He twitched in surprise.

"When will you learn, Drakus Silverhand? My first priority is to a childbearing woman in need. Each and every. Single. Time. And you *will* allow me back my magic so I may use it."

He nodded. "Of course."

Without another word, I turned and gestured for Tarangi to lead us. Wide-eyed and frightened out of her wits, she hurried forward, Drake close behind me.

She led us deep into another wing of the palace that I knew was Havrok's side. Anger and nervousness built up in me like a rising tide. Havrok bred his human slaves with less respect for their lives than even a farmer with his livestock. He only cared for the warriors they produced, and as for the female children, well, I couldn't even imagine what became of them.

I knew we'd reached the room when a group of young women were clustered around a door, some of them crying and hugging each other. When they saw us approach, one of them shrieked, and she was grabbed by another two girls. But they weren't looking at me. They were staring in terror at Drake.

"They're here to help!" Tarangi cried to them. "Make way! Make way."

The girls parted to let us through and I heard a groan through the wooden door. I whirled around, barking orders like I was the commander and Drake was one of my own men. "Stay outside. Let my magic back for as long as you can."

He only nodded sincerely, leaning against the wall, simultaneously lengthening my chain. Tarangi yanked open the door.

I took one look and immediately knew I only had minutes. A young Ellythian woman lay on the birthing bed, no older than twenty with a worryingly ashen face. Beneath her, there was not a spot of white on the sheets, for all was covered in crimson.

The slave midwife was massaging the mother's uterus and looked up with dread in her eyes. I ran over to her, noting the mangled mess that was the placenta in a bowl.

"Fessima is unconscious now," she said softly. "I had to manually remove the afterbirth. I don't know what else to do…"

I felt my magic rush back into me and nodded at her. "Give me a moment." Glancing at the mother, Fessima, I closed my eyes and looked into her body.

Inside her uterus, I clamped the muscles and vessels with my magic. The trickling bleeding stopped.

The midwife gave a soft 'oh.'

"That's me. You can let go now."

She did so and I inspected the muscular lining of the uterus. There were many reasons why a woman might bleed after labour. Most of the time, it was because the uterus was tired. Other times it was because there was a piece of placenta still left inside. And given the piecemeal placenta currently sitting inside that bowl on the bed, I was guessing that was it. The midwife had to retrieve the placenta herself, meaning that it had not detached on its own after birth.

I saw why immediately.

In a rare condition called a *placenta accreta,* the placenta had attached itself deep into the muscular lining of the uterus during pregnancy. Normally placentas attach just to the surface lining of the uterus so it can transfer nutrients from the mother to the baby but still separate itself from the womb after the baby is born.

But in this case, the placenta had buried its fingers so deeply into the uterine muscle that it would not come out of its own accord. I'd only ever seen it once in Lobrathia. But then again, this child had a demon father, and I suspected such a union might result in abnormalities like this.

I would have to carefully prise the portions of the placenta out. It would take meticulous care and a lot of magic, so I worked fast. Scanning section by section, I checked the lining of the uterus for placental tissue and prised it away one cell at at time, making sure the blood vessels I left behind were closed off and unable to bleed further.

The entire time, I was wary that Fessima had an incredibly fast and weak pulse, as her body was trying to use the blood it had left to keep itself alive. I was only halfway through the job when I felt my magic snuff out like a lid placed on a candle.

"No!" I opened my eyes, ran to the door and yanked it open.

Drake stood in the same position against the wall, his tanned face drawn, a fine sheen of sweat across his forehead. The girls stood a distance away, clutching each other.

"I need more time, Drake."

His voice was a little strained. "I can do it. Keep going."

I frowned at him in worry for only a moment before I rushed back into the room, my magic stuttering back to life.

The midwife was busy cleaning up the room while Tarangi was sitting by the bedside, holding Fessima's hand. I resumed my position by the bed and kept going, all the while feeling an odd resistance against my magic. By the time I was done clearing the uterus, I was sweating profusely. I wiped my forehead on my sleeve before passing my attention to Fessima's heart.

"Where is the baby?" I asked as I checked her blood pressure and encouraged her cells to support her while she recovered. "We need to get fluid into Fessima. I need to wake her up."

"The baby has been taken to a wet nurse," the midwife said with a sigh. "It was a boy."

"Return him," I said shortly. "He's surely fed by now. His mother needs his skin against hers. It will help her recover."

"But—"

"It will help her recover, midwife," I said sternly.

The midwife, only a little older than me, curtseyed politely. "Yes, Your Highness." She rushed out of the room, and I returned to Fessima, pushing blood with oxygen into her brain and encouraging her to wake up.

"You need to drink water," I said as her eyes fluttered open. "Right now, as much as you can."

Tarangi hurried to the pitcher and poured a cup.

"My baby?" Fessima gasped, eyes darting around the room.

"He's fine. He's on his way back to you."

"I thought I was dead." She let Tarangi help her drink from the cup.

"I stopped the bleeding. You should live, but only if we can get the fluid into you."

"Call the fae mage," urged Tarangi. "I saw him heal a warrior with a severed arm. It was the same thing. It was like he put his blood back into him.

Before I could reply, Tarangi's eyes looked over my shoulder and widened. Immediately she fell to her knees, bowing her head down. I knew who it was before the cold voice shot across the room.

"Just *what* do you think you're doing?"

I turned, slowly, mostly to use the time to calm myself.

Glacine stood in the doorway. Today she wore a long black dress, with her dark hair braided. She also wore a deep frown, her mouth twisted in distaste. With her was a familiar face, one of her two maids from Quartz, Tenna, a young woman who used to hold me down while Glacine whipped me. Her blonde hair was tied into a bun and she had a ledger and quill in hand. The sight of them turned my blood into lava.

"I am saving Fessima's life," I said carefully. "She's lost too much blood, she needs a healer."

Glacine waved a hand. "No need. Strike her off the list,

Tenna. Empty the room, we need it for the next woman in labour."

Her business like manner enraged me and I gaped at her. Tarangi quietly sobbed into her hand.

"She will die!" I exclaimed. "If the obsidian mage could just be allowed to come and—"

"No." Glacine's voice was incredulous. "You are not in charge here, *concubine*. And if you speak out of turn again, I will have you punished—"

Drake appeared at the door, looming behind Glacine. "*What* did you say to my mate?"

Tenna shot away from Drake. But Glacine crossed her arms and stood her ground. "You cannot hurt me, Lord Drakus. The king will have your head."

Rage tore through me at the delay. "Enough!" I cried. "A woman is dying while you bicker with us."

Glacine whirled around, her nostrils flaring, and in that moment I decided that I would take *great* pleasure in slicing her throat open, right through that scorpion tattoo. But for the sake of Fessima's life, I could bite my tongue. Glacine was saying no just to spite me.

"Think about it, Glacine," I urged. "Why would you lose one of your breeding women when you could save her? She proved she can bear strong children! It would be a useless waste to let her die."

Glacine's eyes searched the room, flicking to Tarangi on the floor, then to Fessima's pale face. I could see the wheels of her mind turning, assessing.

"Fetch the mage," she shot to Tenna, who jumped. "Hurry, this has delayed my rounds as it is. He is in the lower dungeon."

With that, she turned around, pushed past Drake and left.

I blew out a relieved breath. Thank the goddess Glacine wasn't stupid. She was many things, my old stepmother, but an idiot was not one of them.

Tarangi bounded onto her feet and swung her arms around me. "Thank you thank you thank you, Princess."

I patted her back. "It's alright, love. Hopefully he can help."

Drake was watching us. He gave me a tight smile and ran a hand through his dark hair.

"Are you alright?" I asked tentatively as Tarangi took a seat by Fessima's side once again.

"Never better."

"Apparently, Dacre can magically give her blood somehow. I'm not sure how she'll do without it."

"Dacre is a questionable fae," Drake muttered. "But an excellent mage."

Clearly, if he could bind Drake in the way he had done. But I couldn't think about that now. I patted him on the shoulder and rushed back into the room to clean Fessima up.

Thankfully, Glacine was long gone when the midwife returned with the baby, and we placed the sleeping child skin to skin on Fessima's bare chest. Both of them settled in a satisfying way that was palpable.

"Never separate a mother and baby at birth if you can help it," I advised the midwife. "Especially if either is unwell. They always do much better when in contact with one another."

She nodded in earnest. "The first-concubine gave us orders to take the babes long ago. She did not want the mothers forming an attachment to them."

"That is awful," I muttered. But I expected no less from her.

"Not as awful as the way they train the boys," she said pointedly.

"What do they do to the female children?" I couldn't bear not knowing.

She leaned in towards me and said with an embarrassed grimace, "They go to a different sort of school, Your Highness."

Concubines. My stomach churned. To have that sole duty as your only prospect was a type of nightmare I could never endure. Something had to be done about it. It couldn't go on. But how could I do anything in my chained position? Drake was right. We needed to gain the king's trust. That was the only way Havrok's entire system would change.

After a few tense minutes, chains jangled in the corridor. We straightened to Dacre Liversblood in glowing black handcuffs, being chaperoned into the room by two demon warriors.

"Lord Mage," I said as if we were nobility meeting in a palace and not slaves in the demon realm. Dacre seemed to appreciate this because he cast me a smile, the fae runes inked on his face stretching.

"Your Highness." He swept a bow. "Thank you for sending for me. I have heard much. All rumour, of course. I would be pleased to converse with you...in better circumstances."

"Indeed, as would I. There are many questions you might be able to answer for both Drake and me. But we have a matter of great urgency I need your assistance with." I gestured to Fessima, who was too weary to keep her eyes open. "I was told you have some skill with blood loss."

"Of course." He swept forward, and to my chagrin, the

warriors followed close behind. "I'll need my magic." He turned to look at the guard with bumpy lime green skin.

"I'll lower it a quarter turn only," the warrior replied, fishing a key out of a loop on his belt. I watched closely as the demon fit the key into a lock on the shackle and indeed, only turned it a quarter of the way around. The glow around his shackles dimmed only a fraction.

Dacre's face was gentlemanly disappointment. He flexed his tattooed fingers. "It will do."

Tarangi got out of the way and we all watched with great interest as Dacre placed his hands to hover over Fessima's abdomen.

Even without my own magic, the hairs on my arms raised as I felt a shift in the air. I wished I could have seen its effect magically myself, but I could only look on as, with great intensity, Dacre unleashed healing magic over Fessima, her face gaining back its colour by the minute. Quite quickly, she was pink, and I went over to feel her pulse. I found it strong and bounding. We all sighed in relief as Fessima opened her eyes.

"I feel better." She smiled up at me and then saw Dacre and clutched her babe, still on her chest, in fear.

Dacre gallantly bowed. "All in a day's work, Madam." The demon with the key swung the mage back around and relocked his shackles.

"Your magic is a wonder, My Lord," I said softly. "Thank you."

"We must talk again, Your Highness."

"Oh, I will make sure of it."

I would not forget the fact that he was the one who had taken Drake's memories away. If it had been me in Drake's place, I would have been livid.

Dacre seemed to see the wariness in my gaze because he said, "I must warn you, Your Highness. If Drake's runes are ever completely undone—"

"Enough." The two demons yanked Dacre's chains and hauled him out of the room. He turned his head to cast me a grimace one last time.

"It was lucky we had him," muttered the midwife, standing in a daze next to me. "This happens all the time."

I turned to her, a heat flaring up in me. "All the time?"

"We grieve weekly, Your Highness. The placentas always get stuck." Tears welled in her eyes. "I've always thought it was the babe's demon blood. They are clingy, hungry creatures. It only makes sense the placenta would infiltrate the mother's body like a parasite and cling on for all it was worth."

"What doesn't make sense is killing women for your own ends," I muttered.

All she could do was nod. This poor midwife could only stand by and watch these women bleed to death at birth. I couldn't imagine anything worse. I was still shaken by the exchange with Glacine. She held a great and terrible power in this place. A power no one should have had. She chose death for these women and I could hardly believe the evil of it. I gripped the midwife's forearm. "Call me for each birth, you understand? Day or night, call me, and I will come."

The look in her eyes seared my soul. Whatever became of me in this place, I was going to help these women get out.

17
SARAYA

We had a chance to rest until the mahogany clock Drake had procured told us it was nine p.m. A pounding at the door woke me from where I'd been sleeping on the couch with Opal, Drake snoozing on the couch opposite.

To my surprise, it was Tarangi and Flora.

"There's a small party tonight," Flora beamed at me. "To celebrate the Lord of the Kill's latest victory. We are here to get you ready."

I turned and raised my eyebrows at Drake, who sighed and laid back down on the couch as if he were going back to sleep, but my chains began lengthening.

"Alright then," I said, leading them to the bedroom. "I suppose I won't be allowed to wear pants?"

"Oh, that would be an insult, Your Highness," said Flora earnestly. "The king has very strict requirements for female dress."

"Is transparency one of those requirements?" I said

glumly as Flora skipped to my wardrobe and began oohing and aahing at the contents.

"It's preferred," said Tarangi, crossing her arms over her own transparent dress. "But we don't have to. I'm sure there's *something* not completely awful in there."

"This one!" Flora swung out a scrap of silk with a flourish.

"That's a bare-breasted dress, Your Highness," Tarangi said in a deadpan voice. "Maybe not, Flora."

"But Her Highness has lovely breasts!"

"*Flora*," Tarangi chastised.

I couldn't help but laugh. "Thank you, Flora. But if we can cover the breasts, that would be preferable."

"Fair," said Flora lightly. "I don't think the Lord of the Kill would like them on display anyway. He seems the possessive type of lord."

Irritation spun through me. "Lord Drakus *does not* and *will not* ever determine what I wear. *That* is my choice."

Tarangi grinned in appreciation at me while Flora's eyes went wide and glanced towards the living room where Drake was most likely listening to every word. Not that I cared. I charged forward to see what heinous outfit I could find. Drake had told me that we needed to play the part here in order to get our way and eventually get out. So play the part I would.

"Are there no demon ladies around here?" I asked. "I've only ever seen lords."

"They prefer human consorts," Tarangi said in a low voice. "It's like a status symbol. And they're not called ladies. The demon lords have their wives, but they are really the 'first concubine' in charge of the rest. Like King Havrok's wife."

"So she's not a queen?" I asked, turning this information over in my mind.

Tarangi made a face and shook her head. "Not in this court. I've heard it's possible in others, but His Highness prefers it this way. It is his law."

So Glacine bore no title. I had some small satisfaction at that, given how she'd made a point to taunt me about my lack of royal title on the first day.

"So I am Lord Drake's first concubine? That is my title?"

Tarangi shifted uncomfortably while Flora hummed to herself and draped her favourites of my clothes over her arm.

I nodded in determination. "Then show me how the best first concubines dress."

Flora tittered excitedly and showed me her selection. They were all ridiculous and revealing. One was even crotchless. So naturally, I chose the worst of them. Or the best, according to Flora.

I sat on a chair in front of the mirror and Tarangi helped me to arrange my waves so they fell down my back prettily.

My black dress was half string, half fabric. My back was covered, but a panel in the front was absent so that red and purple jewels were strung over my breasts and stomach, holding the sides of the dress together. Black silk fell to my feet, with deep slits up to the thigh on both sides. The girls then placed silk slippers on my feet that laced up all the way to my thigh. I had to admit, demon dressmakers had a sense of imagination. It would have been scandalous had I not already worn the string of jewels that had been my wedding attire.

So it didn't feel like too much when I traipsed out into the living room where Drake was now sitting, ready to go in a black shirt and pants. When he saw me, he jumped to his feet.

"No."

Tarangi and Flora hurried out the door, casting me terrified glances as they did.

"I beg your pardon?" I asked, striding forward. "We should get going."

But Drake didn't move, and the need to tease him got the better of me. I sauntered up to him, practising playing the part of 'first concubine.' I got close enough that I could smell the sandalwood soap he'd used that evening and poked him playfully in the chest.

In my most seductive voice, I said, "Do I not make an excellent first concubine, My Lord?"

To my satisfaction, his body went unnaturally still and his throat bobbed as he swallowed. "You don't have to do this."

"I will do anything to save my father, Drakus. Even if it means dressing like a harlot. My stepmother called me a whore when she took us from the human realm, did she not? Perhaps I'll prove her right. Although..." I cocked my head. "I can't really be a whore if I'm sleeping with my husband."

I heard the sharp intake of breath before a long exhale.

"Do you think you can control your lusty mate bond for tonight, Drake?" I dramatically batted my eyelashes. "Because I'm going to great lengths to have them believe the magic of the mating bond has taken me over."

He flashed me a cocky smile and unexpectedly took my chin in firm, warm fingers. Heat pooled in my core as his breath tickled my lips as he spoke. "Be careful playing with me, Saraya. People have a tendency to lose games played against me."

I could have kissed him then. His lips were close enough. The bond was pushing me to, but I forced the lust back down and made a delicate sound at the back of my throat.

"Lysander mentioned something like that when he told me about how you won him in a card game." I leaned into him. "Well, that means we have a good chance at tricking them, don't we?"

"We have to make them believe the mate bond is in full play." He let go of me.

"Oh, I fully intend to do that."

But the heat was already twirling in my core at the proximity, at the implication of his touch on me. I couldn't deny that I wanted to be close to him, couldn't deny that my imagination was taking me into the realm of what it was that husbands and wives were supposed to be doing in bed. But I also knew it was the magic of the mate bond that was doing it. It was just magic, not my own free will. It couldn't be true desire.

Drake's nostrils flared and I suddenly realised that we'd been staring at each other. I shook myself out of my stupor, hastily looking anywhere except his face.

Just in time, there was a pounding at the door. Drake took my hand, and heat enveloped my entire being. This was the problem. I wouldn't even have to act tonight. All I would be doing was giving into the mate bond. The realisation settled in me like silk fluttering down around my form. I'd just give in to it, and I knew it would be enjoyable. It was a small cost to pay, after all, to get Havrok to trust us.

In that moment, the slave collar somehow didn't chafe so much.

Drake yanked open the door and found two demon warriors sweeping a bow. Both were of the grey-skinned variety with white irises and bulging muscles. I glanced at Drake's own arms and knew with a pleasant flutter in my stomach that his muscles were sizeable in comparison.

Perhaps the monster element in him made his physique so intimidating. The demons took great pains not to look at me, I noticed, as they turned and led us out of our room, and I had to stifle the urge to smirk.

A heavy presence came up against my mind, and even without my magic, I knew Drake was waiting just outside my mental defences. I thought for a moment and decided he probably needed to tell me something without the demons hearing. Letting him in might be beneficial. I had never done it before, and maybe him being my mate made it easier, but he surged in like water when I opened a tiny door into my mind.

"*Are you enjoying this?*" he asked, mind to mind, not showing me any emotion.

"*I thought you had something important to say,*" I chastised. "*But yes, some parts of it are funny, I guess. Mostly, you, though.*"

"*You think I'm funny?*" he asked, affronted.

I smirked without looking at him. "*You're hilarious, actually.*"

Silence.

I squeezed his hand and simultaneously sensed his surprise.

"*Oh, the things I'm going to do to you tonight, Saraya.*"

I gaped at him, offended, simultaneously feeling a tingle between my legs.

"*You're right.*" It was his turn to smirk. "*I'm very funny.*"

Returning him a sour look, I decided it was best not to entertain him in my mind and shoved him back out. He obliged and said nothing more. I didn't know who I was angrier at. Him for baiting me, or at myself for the flutter in my stomach that was now incessant *and* the drawing towards him I now felt. There was a vicious desire between us.

I would have to be careful.

The demons led us to a drawing-room: all black tiles and walls with silver finishings. When we entered, the seats were arranged in the same way the podiums were arranged in the throne room. The other five demon lords and their first concubines were present in their own chairs, being served food and alcohol by human slaves.

The seventh chair, a regal wing-back, obviously meant for the king, sat empty at the head of the group.

As we turned in, the other lords began a round of applause. And then I saw it. Lord Gangrene's severed head had been mounted to the far wall behind the king's chair, alongside a row of other, older heads, shrivelled with age.

I suppressed a gag, but Drake did not miss a step as he strode in and shook the first lord's hand. The others stood in anticipation.

"Lord of Pleasure," Drake said by way of greeting to the first. He was a navy-skinned waifish demon. His first concubine, a milk pale, lovely young lady, cast her gaze down in a way that seemed to be considered good manners for women here. Appalled at this realisation, I offered her my hand.

"Lovely to meet you."

She stared at my hand for a moment before jumping to her feet. "The pleasure is mine." Her voice was as sweet as syrup.

The Lord of Pleasure ignored that particular interaction, so I made it a point to introduce myself to each first concubine, ignoring the lords completely. A turning of the tables seemed warranted. We turned to the Lord of the Feast, the silver furry demon, who was not married apparently, because he was sitting with his giant clawed hand on Lysander's leg.

I struggled to hide my surprise as Feast introduced himself. But I offered my hand to Lysander, and he took it, lightly kissing it, and turned his blue eyes up to me. There were bags under his eyes, but they glimmered with good humour. I squeezed his large hand in return, somehow comforted by the fact he was here with us and still in one piece. His presence here would mean that he was favoured and I hoped that meant he was being treated well. There were certainly no wounds or signs of mistreatment on his shirtless body at the moment.

We swiftly moved on to the Lord of Punishment, the Lord of Sacrifice, and lastly, the Lord of Gold, Braxus. Who *did*, in fact, take the opportunity to seductively kiss my hand. Drake growled softly and the demon lord bowed his apologies, his yellow eyes snaking down my body.

We took our seat at the head of the group as slaves hurried over to us, offering Drake a glass with a green-coloured liquid.

"Oh, do be careful with the demon spirits," cooed Lord Braxus. "They can be quite caustic—"

But Drake took the glass and downed it in one go. He placed the glass back on the tray with a nod at the girl. The other lords stared at him. "It's pleasant enough. Bring me another."

The Lord of Gold raised his dark brows but said nothing.

Havrok arrived through the side door, Glacine trailing behind him in a red gown, and we all hastily stood. With a pang, I noticed two eerily familiar faces, Havlem and Yarnat, the queen's guards from Lobrathia. But now, their faces were a pale green colour, their armour bearing a scorpion insignia. I would *never*, for the rest of my life, forget how they'd barred me from leaving my palace to go and help Bluebell, in labour with twins. Firey rage tore through me anew at the memory. Bluebell and her babies ended up being fine, but it could have

161

easily ended poorly. Regardless, they were both deserving of death, in my eyes.

For their part, they both avoided my eye and stared straight ahead as they stood guard by the door. The last time I had spoken to them, I had told them I would kill Glacine. And I still held that promise close to my heart, a sacred talisman for both my parents.

I'd already seen Teen, no doubt, Marissa, Glacine's other maid, was around here somewhere too.

"Reaper bless the king!" the lords shouted.

I glanced around the room in alarm, not knowing this ritual. But Havrok gave Drake a smirk and gestured to the servants.

"Eat and drink, My Lords, then we shall talk business." He settled into his chair and pulled Glacine into his lap, then, with his other hand, accepted a glass from an offered tray.

I couldn't help but stare at the way Glacine twisted seductively in the demon king's lap to give him a passionate kiss. My stomach churned violently at the image of her flaunting her union with this creature in front of me. I ground my teeth in anger and tore my eyes away.

This seemed to be an average sort of meeting because the lords and their concubines were quite adept and comfortable in making fun for themselves, gossiping, drinking, and eating. Drake and I ate what was offered to us, and he drank the liquors of strange colours, seemingly unaffected by them.

It was all fun and games until Lord Braxus tugged down his pants and his first concubine fell to her knees before him.

A few other first concubines were made to do the same in some weird show of power. I was extremely thankful that Lysander's seat was on the other side of the room and I pointedly avoided looking over there. But it was clear, Lysander knew this game and he played it with a smile.

I felt Drake tapping on the door to my mind. I let him in.

"Should I do the same?" I asked dourly, not knowing where to look.

A pause and then, *"Only if you want to."*

Scoffing, I glanced again at Glacine, who was now straddling Havrok with her back to me. I decided then and there that two could play at this game. Besides, Drake needed punishment, as he was getting too cocky for his own good. It wouldn't mean anything, of course. This was all an act. We had to look the part.

Without warning, I climbed into Drake's lap, straddling him. With relish, I sensed him tense. So I smirked, and before he could stop me, I leaned in and pressed my lips to his. The rising, glittering sense of pleasure was instant, and it reeled me in. He tasted like spirits and salt.

While I'd only really kissed a man once before, that one blacksmith, the brother of one of my patients, I *had* seen plenty of the activity in Madame Yolande's brothel. I'd also like to think that I'm a quick study. So, when Drake's lips parted in surprise, I took the opportunity to sweep my tongue softly across his. He grabbed my hips to pull me closer and it took all the discipline I had to pull back. Hiding my desire, I smirked at him as he stared back at me, lips parted, and slid back into my place next to him, looking about the walls of the room as if nothing had happened.

I swallowed down the lump that had formed in my throat, a delicious curl of desire making me want to crawl into Drake's lap again and stay there. The sensation of his lips against mine was now seared into my brain. I could still taste him, and to my great chagrin, I began wondering what it

163

would feel like to be naked beneath him, our bed sheets tangled around us.

It looked like Drake must have also been taken by similar thoughts because he sat frozen for a few moments before sliding an arm around me, his fingers curling around my hip.

I bade my heart to settle down.

To distract myself, I stole a glance at Havrok and Glacine. Havrok was smirking as if this was exactly what he wanted to see from us. Glacine was smug as if that act from me confirmed all she's ever thought about what I am. In her tiny mind, she probably thought that back in Quartz I snuck out at night to be with some city boy. Little did she know that I had never actually done anything like that. Since I had been trained to be a midwife of the city, all the men around me I considered husbands or brothers of my patients and therefore were out of bounds. I had always been focused on my work, despite whatever male attention. I think that fact was hard for her to understand.

But I also knew how to play politics. Even if it was this demonic, heinous sort. Drake leaned down and pressed his lips against the soft skin of my neck. Shivers erupted, spreading out from where his lips had been, and I trembled against my will. I was irate at his audacity, but the revenge was a good one, I'll give him that.

But Havrok clapped his enormous hands and I almost snapped my neck to looking at him.

"Three points on the agenda," he called. "The first is that I must congratulate our Lord of the Kill for his latest exploit." Havrok gestured at the wall behind him and the five other lords raised their glasses to Drake. "My thanks, with this gift to your mate." A servant hurried forward with a black velvet jewellery box. She opened it in front of me, revealing a magnificent ruby studded bracelet.

"Wow," I said, genuinely surprised, trying to guess the meaning of it. But I had to be submissive here. "Thank you, Your Highness." The slave clipped the bracelet around my wrist and Havrok moved on.

"Next, my annual ball is in two weeks. All the outer nobility will also attend. I want this year's to be the biggest and grandest the demon lands have ever seen." He grinned savagely. My eyes met Glacine's, and she gave me a long, slow, cruel smile. My stomach turned upon itself.

Drake pressed a large hand against my thigh as if he felt my apprehension. She was planning something. She knew something. The last time she smiled at me like that was when she had known I was fated to marry a fae prince against my will. I clenched my teeth, refusing to let her see me falter. The wounds on my back stung anew. I forced myself to meet her gaze steadily and then looked back at Havrok.

The king was smiling at Drake.

"My next move is to take over the human kingdom of Kaalon. I want to see if their women's peaches are as sweet as the humans boast."

The blood drained from my face as the demon lords laughed at the lewd joke. *Kaalon.* He wanted to take over the human realm one by one. That meant Lobrathia was successfully taken.

What *had* happened to the nobility after they'd run for their lives from the palace? Had they all made it to Kaalon, or did they flee to Waelan in the north? Either way, Kaalon was now in danger.

But Havrok wouldn't take his eyes off Drake.

"Lord Drakus, you took over Lobrathia with such proficiency and with only a small number of fae. I want you to do the same with Kaalon. Bring me the head of this pathetic King Osring and his wife."

Terror shot up my spine. I wanted to hurl. I wanted to cry. Osring was like an uncle to me. He and his wife were now frail, the queen bedridden. They did not deserve this. Havrok wanted to take the entire human realm or as much of it as he could. And now he wanted Drake to take it for him.

"Do you accept this task, Lord of the Kill?"

Drake had no choice. *We* had no choice. Havrok had to trust Drake.

My mate inclined his head. "Of course."

I was stupid to think this was a game. This was life and death.

18

SARAYA

Being a midwife required me to maintain my composure at all costs. In the face of life and death, a midwife is always the voice of reason in the room. But tonight, everything fell down upon me like an avalanche of despair. Not only had my own life crumbled around me, but now this devastation was to extend to the entire human realm.

It was this thought that had me livid as I confronted Drake back in our rooms.

"He can't make us do this, Drake." Furious tears trickled from my eyes. Angrily, I wiped them away. Opal looked between us in fright. "King Osring is like family to me. I cannot. How do we—" I pulled at my hair, exasperated. "Drake, you cannot kill him."

Drake—my *husband*—simply leaned against the wall. A statue of resolve.

"Say something," I hissed at him.

He surged towards me. I would have recoiled due to the ferocity with which he came at me, but I couldn't because grabbed my face in both hands.

"I will do what I must, Saraya."

"No," I whispered. "I will not let you."

"You will have to come with me. I will not be separated from you."

"No," I repeated breathlessly. "Let go of me."

He obliged, stepping backwards.

"We leave in the morning. Get some rest." And with that, he turned, picked up Opal and left for the bedroom.

I seethed at his retreating back, but all at once, I felt him knocking at my mind again. Reluctantly I let him in.

"They are watching," he said into my mind, *"and listening. There is magic in that bracelet he gave you."*

Startled, I stared down at the circlet of rubies around my wrist. My own reflection shone back at me. I hadn't even detected it.

"Are you sure?" I silently asked.

"Yes. Don't look at it too much. Even if you take it off, it will listen. We must keep up the show."

I sighed and wiped my eyes, thinking of my father, who was still trapped down here with us. More pretending it was, then. *"We'll use it to our advantage."*

I felt him smile and heard him gesturing to Opal in the bedroom. I gave them a moment so she could hide and headed into the bathroom to wash off the night's grime. I had seen far more than I had ever wanted to, and that was saying something because I had been frequenting brothels in Lobrathia since I was a teenager.

Back in the bedroom, I climbed into bed while Drake took his turn in the bathroom. I carefully took off the bracelet and laid it on the bedside table, wondering how we could use the thing to our advantage. Havrok needed to be sure we were compliant and dutiful. I would have to continue being unsure about the Kaalon invasion, while Drake would have to continue his bloodthirsty monster act.

But Glacine's smile during the party haunted me. It was a smile that said she was up to something. And knowing her, it was going to affect me badly. As Drake returned, shirtless, I eyed his twisting, binding runes, especially the still coloured-in parts around his biceps and shoulders. There was yet more to his monster nature than I could see right now.

As he climbed into bed, discreetly checking Opal in the open drawer where her illusory magic would have to hide her all the time now, I made a show of turning my back on him and wiping my eyes with an exaggerated sniff.

He seemed to understand the ruse because the mattress depressed on my side, and for the first time, he sidled up next to me and pulled me possessively close to him. The round of my bottom was pressed against his groin, and I hid a grumble because I knew this act was definitely to his advantage. Though his warmth around me *was* comforting. Maybe because it reminded me that I wasn't alone in this hell hole. His hand curled around my stomach and I felt his breath on my ear as he moved to kiss me.

"Don't, you devil," I said half-heartedly.

He ignored me, gently tucked my hair behind my ear, and kissed me on the neck.

"Goodnight, beautiful."

My stomach flopped on itself. Desire rippled through me, from abdomen to toes, and I found myself leaning back into him. He growled, but it was more like a cat purring with pleasure.

I convinced myself it was just the mate bond spurring us on, but I also knew that I fell asleep faster than I ever had.

WE WOKE UP IN THE EXACT SAME POSITION. WITH THE MOST reluctance I'd ever seen from him, he removed his arm from around me and rolled out of bed, the chain chiming like an obscene morning bell.

I stifled a yawn and we both quietly readied ourselves.

Drake would have to be Opal's vehicle now since I was forever being watched by the blasted ruby bracelet. The smartest thing to do was wear it and show Havrok what we were up to.

The fact that Drake wanted to bring Opal along meant that he had some semblance of a plan. Monster or not, he had explicitly told me that as his mate, he would do what *I* wanted no matter what. I had to believe that was true because the thought of taking over Peach Tree City and murdering the man who I'd seen as an uncle was the worst possible thing to come to mind.

My mother had been killed by Glacine. My father was just as good as dead. And now Osring? Everyone close to me, everyone I loved, had been taken away. I couldn't take one more. I just couldn't. There had to be some way I could get a message to him. To warn him, so he could get his armies ready or to flee northwards.

Usually, we sent carrier pigeons or messengers on horseback with our mail and I had since learned that the fae used ravens. I turned to the drawer where Opal was probably waking up, still under her illusion, away from the prying eyes of Havrok's bracelet. Her fractures had since healed with my assistance and her own natural healing, so we had already taken the splint off. The beginnings of a plan came together. I knocked on the door to Drake's mind.

THE DEMON CAPTAIN, ARGOTH, WAS ONCE AGAIN ASSIGNED TO Drake and escorted us to the military compound adjacent to the palace.

Drake reassumed the role of army commander with such a fierceness that I finally understood why he was revered in the Black Court. I took a step back and watched from afar. My chain lengthened just so that I could still hear but be out of the way.

He had the demon warriors line up in a single file, and he and Argoth walked along a line of thirty warriors, assessing them. The demon captain gave their various strengths and attributes. From them, Drake expertly chose ten and asked for their names, which he seemed to memorise instantly.

I was seriously impressed, to say the least. Drake had taken over Quartz City with a reasonably small company of warriors and I wondered how he'd done it. Now was my chance to see it first hand. But he didn't know these creatures personally. Surely that would put the plan a step behind.

As I observed, Drake put together a plan with the demon captain over a parchment map of the human realm. Our demon contingent would escort us to the quarry portal. Once in the human realm, we would cross the Kaalothian river into Kaalon and head straight into Peach Tree City

This was good news because we would now get to see the exact route to the quarry portal. This would be our route once we were ready to escape this place. At least one part of the escape plan would be finalised.

As we got onto our reptilian haxim creature once again, I relayed this to Drake in his mind. He patted his pocket absently, and I knew Opal was likely to be nervously rolling around in there. Drake had instructed her to look at the map and listen as he made plans with the demons. She would need to know exactly how to get to the capital of Kaalon by herself.

"There is more than one portal out of the demon realm," Drake replied as we set off in the opposite direction, what I guessed was north. Though, without a sun or stars, I had no idea how these demons navigated. *"I've used another portal before…when I used to frequent the demon realm."*

"You used to come down here often?" I asked.

I felt a smirk coming from him. *"Before Havrok took the throne, yes. This is where I found my friends, after all. Their black markets are impressive. Their gambling even more so."*

"Dear Goddess."

"There are no Gods or Goddesses down here. Only demon kings and their chosen."

I grimaced at that.

"What are we going to do, Drake?" I asked nervously. We were heading straight to Kaalon, and I had barely a plan in place to save Osring and his family. The entire thing relied on Opal.

"I don't know yet," he replied honestly. *"But with Opal's help, I think we can scrounge something up. I was able to make a backpack for her. But…you're sure she could understand that map?"*

"Yes. She was always with me when I took the fae academy classes. Once I fell asleep and she drew a picture on my page for me.

It was a little wonky, but I knew then that she could understand a lot."

"Lumzen are quite clever. If she does understand, Osring might very well stand a chance."

We reached the portal a little over two hours later.

Having been unconscious on my way through the quarry portal the first time, I had not seen what the thing looked like. And on the demon's side, the portal could be seen from kilometres away.

In the middle of a barren landscape, a mass of swirling blue energy as wide as double story manse stood strong. I felt the magic coming out of it in powerful waves. I had never seen that much magic in one spot, and I felt all the sicker knowing who they had been stealing it from for over a hundred years.

Demons pulled carts and wagons of luminous quartz through the portal, heading straight for Havrok's palace. I wondered where they were storing it all, along with the magic they'd been stealing.

We slid off our haxim and handed his reins over to an eleventh warrior who would return all the reptilian steeds back to the palace.

The land underfoot was like desert sand found in the far north of the human realm, except it was black and ashy. The demon warriors trudged right up to the portal and straight through it, disappearing immediately. With an uneasy glance at him, Drake and I stepped up to the blue and white magic.

"Scared, Princess?" Drake teased, reaching for my hand as if to comfort me.

"I fear nothing," I shot back and slapped away his hand, striding forward. I was determined not to let the pulsing magic get to me. These warriors already thought females were weak, and if I was to spend days with them travelling to Kaalon, I couldn't very well have them jeering at me too.

The magic of the portal enveloped me in an intense heat that had me sweating right away. My heart beat irregularly and I felt my blood pressure rise as a vice-like grip clamped around my form. But within seconds, it dissipated, and that light died down. Once my eyes adjusted, I realised I was in the heart of the quarry. Within the dry darkness, speckled luminous quartz lights of all different colours peeked out from the rock.

I looked up to find the midnight sky was a sea of stars bordered by thick clouds that I knew were waiting for Drake. The demons led us to a rope and pulley system my ancestors had installed hundreds of years ago. Two demons bear-climbed all the way to the top of the quarry so that they could pull the enclosed platform up. I knew that there were a number of ways to get in and out of the quarry from inspecting the place with my father, but no doubt the demons had decided this was the quickest and least strenuous for us.

When we reached the top, I sighed in relief as cool, fresh air lapped at my face, and I took what must have been the first full and proper breath in days.

Turning my face towards the heavens was like some sort of gift from the Goddess. I had no idea how much I had missed it, and to my great and happy surprise, before Drake's magical clouds came and blocked it from view, a fat, full moon sat proudly.

I was so close to my home. Quartz was less than ten kilometres from the quarry. The humans of my city, the staff of the palace, Agatha, Bluebell and the twins. They had to be around there somewhere if they weren't dead already. I wondered what had become of Lobrathia's military. Who was alive and who was dead?

We were given horses, and quite quickly, we were trotting for the eastern border, leaving my home behind us.

WE REACHED THE RIVER A FEW HOURS BEFORE DAWN AND DRAKE directed the warriors to make camp for the day because demons needed shade from the sun. That was their one weakness, which I kept at the back of my mind to use at some stage. But, decades of scoping out the land astrally had them knowledgeable of the landscape because Argoth expertly led us to a broad cave.

It was an excellent hiding place, and deep within the cave, Drake pulled me and two pallets a little away from the warriors. Before we went to bed, Drake whispered to Opal, tucked the letter I had quickly penned—a message to Osring—into a backpack Drake had fashioned, and sent her to Peach Tree City.

Anxiety rippled through me at the thought of her running through Kaalon all alone, but it was really the only thing we could do to warn them. She was clever. I had to tell myself that she would be fine.

Side by side, we went to bed and fell into an uneasy sleep. At least I did because I don't think Drake slept at all.

An hour before dawn, a glowing presence shone at the corner of my mind. I sat up bolt upright.

19
SARAYA

Arishnie, my warrior midwife mentor, stood in her ghostly blue-green form before me. Drake, too, immediately sat up. Arishnie's eyes widened as she took in the chain leading from my neck to Drake's wrist.

"Oh, Saraya, what happened?" she whispered.

I glanced at Drake, who stared at Arishnie as a cat stares at a mouse. But the demon warriors slept metres from us. I would have to be careful. Knocking on the door to his mind, he let me in.

"I need to go into astral form to speak to Arishnie."

"This is the ghost from the Order of Temari?" he asked, eyes taking in her armour, her sword, her muscled arms.

"It's her. I'll need my magic."

"Of course, it's yours."

The fire of my magic sputtered to life within me. But I knew the time would be limited, so I acted quickly. Lying back down on my pallet, I ascended into my astral form. A thump sounded next to my physical body. Startled, I looked back down to see both mine and Drake's bodies lying as if asleep and Drake sitting up in his own transparent astral form, our chains, now ghostly, still binding us.

"How—"

"I think," said Drake, looking back at his body. "It might be—"

"The mate bond?"

He smiled as if he enjoyed hearing those words coming from my mouth. "I think so."

I turned back to Arishnie. "We must make haste. This chain keeps my magic at bay. Drake has to—"

"Then let's go." Arishnie nodded and flew up into the cavern ceiling. I quickly made to follow, dragging Drake with me. To his credit, he was a quick learner, and we managed to ascend into the night sky above the cavern.

"Tell me everything," Arishnie demanded.

I told her an abridged version of our story and the ruse we were now keeping up to get Havrok to trust us.

"But there are human women being kept as breeding slaves, Arishnie," I hissed, an angry heat flaring in me. "I stopped one from bleeding to death the other night, but more will follow. It's awful."

Arishnie gripping her sword tightly was the only thing that told me she was overcome with furious emotion. "This is worse than I—" Arishnie looked upwards abruptly and twitched as if something had stung her. "She summons us, Saraya."

My heart leapt into my chest. "She *she*?"

"The Goddess Umali, yes. Come. Quickly."

I exchanged a look with Drake, who, for the first time since I'd known him, looked apprehensive. Leading the way, I flew up after Arishnie into the night sky and south-west-wards towards the Temari forest.

I glanced at Drake, happy to be able to share this with him, this experience of flying over the world as birds do, the countryside but a tapestry beneath us. When he smiled at me back, truly enjoying himself, it felt like I was flying higher than I had before.

When the sea came into view, it was a truly breathtaking sight with the light of the full moon glittering over the waves.

But as we slowed down, we glided over the forest rather than descending into it as I had expected.

"Are we not going to the temple?" I called.

"No, this is a matter for the wilds," Arishnie called back over her shoulder.

My stomach jolted at that, and we touched down upon the sand.

Arishnie turned to petition me. "I had hoped to ease you into this Saraya, perhaps in a year's time at least, but am I overruled."

That truly boggled my mind. "What on earth do you mean, Arishnie? The Goddess knows about what I said?"

"She is a Goddess, Saraya. She hears all, especially anything to do with her own subjects."

"But I thought Gods could not interfere in human goings-on?"

"They cannot do so directly, but there are minor ways they can influence people."

Drake remained silent as he followed and I could sense his curiosity through our mate bond.

Arishnie turned and led us across the sand and down to the water. The sound of the waves crashing was like music to my ears after the humid silence that had become a constant companion in the demon realm. Arishnie turned and faced the ocean, turning her face to the moon and closing her eyes. I mirrored her.

A sudden calm fell upon the beach. The tide seemed to hold its breath.

Then she appeared.

Emerging out of the water, she stalked towards us like something out of a dream.

Her bare midnight blue skin was covered only by a garland of skulls. Wild, onyx hair reached down to her thighs, swaying as she walked. In one hand, she held a bright sword. In the other, she carried a severed demon's head.

Even in astral form, the sheer force of her presence fell upon me like the weight of a crashing wave. I could not help but fall to my knees. Behind me, Drake did the same.

Darkness falls upon the human realm, Saraya.

Arishnie bent the knee. "Goddess, she is too young—"

Her voice crashed upon my ears louder than any wave. *There is no other. Everywhere we turn, there are women who suffer at the hands of monsters.* I could tell that she had turned to me. I looked up at her. *Will you let them, Saraya?*

"No," I whispered as tears filled my eyes. "I cannot. I will not. I will do anything."

The goddess Umali came to stand before me and held her palm out in blessing, dark eyes fixed on me. The command rang through me like an earth-shattering bell.

May your feet be as thunder,
May your strike be as lightning,
May your heart be as Umali.

You will lead,
You will hunt,

You will anoint,
You will destroy in my name.

Do you accept the High Priestess pledge?

I struggled to find my breath, but when I did, my voice came out calmer than I expected. "I do, with all my heart and soul, I do."

Then give me your hand.

I did as she bade, and she pricked my thumb with the sharp point of her black nail. To my surprise, blood welled from my finger as if it were my actual skin and not just my astral form.

Then I anoint you, High Priestess of the Order of Te'mari.

With her hand, she pressed my own bleeding thumb to my forehead. Magic bled through me like honey, sticky and potent. I was humbled before the density of that power, and I was struck with a reverence that took my breath away once again.

Rise.

It felt like it took all my strength, but I climbed to my feet and faced my Goddess. Her voice resounded in my brain.

If you fail, Saraya, the human realm will not recover. All will be lost.

"I will not fail these women. I will not."

Then go and do your duty.

She turned and slowly walked back into the ocean. I watched her every step, enamoured.

"I'm sorry, Saraya," Arishnie said after the goddess was enveloped by the ocean and the air around us turned light again.

I whirled to face the spectre of the old warrior. "Sorry for what?"

"For everything that happened. Our path has always been a tough one, and yours tougher still."

I nodded. "Perhaps. But this path was decided for me—" I turned to glance at Drake, who had gone pale, "—for us. This path was drawn for us before we were born. What could we have done?"

"Heavy are the shoulders of those who bear destiny."

I shook my head. "I'm not so sure about that. Because I have no idea how I'm going to help those women escape, and we still have the matter of the task Havrok sent us here for. We can't get out of it."

"There has to be some way," Arishnie said, clutching her sword like she wished she could use it on something.

But a memory struck me. What Drake had said to me after I told him about the Order of Temari. "What does this word, *Temari* mean?"

Arishnie smiled at an old memory. "In old Ellythian, it is pronounced Te'mari. It is the essence of Umali. It means feminine rage."

My blood surged as if my body recognised those words on a core level, what they meant to me, and how that power could be wielded. I felt Drake's realisation through the bond.

He stepped forward. "There was a legendary blade named Te'mari, wasn't there?"

Arishnie regarded him up and down and seemed to come to some sort of conclusion in her head. "The lost blade, yes. It could only be wielded by a woman. It was said to be a powerful weapon. We never did find it in my time. But there is another matter I wanted to speak to you of. Dawn approaches. I must be quick."

"What is it?" I stepped forward. I needed to know everything I could to help us get out of this situation with Havrok.

"You inherited both your father's magical heritage as well as your mother's."

I shook my head. "My father had no magic that I know of."

"No, but his ancestors did, and their blood sings in you. Heightened perhaps, by the Ellythian magic."

Lightning does not yield. Volantius House had once wielded lightning. My father's ancestors weilded weapons made of electricity.

To the east, the sky began to lighten with the predawn.

"I cannot stay," Arishnie said quickly. "But please, find yourself above ground at the next full moon— because I cannot get to you down there. You must—"

But Arishnie didn't get to finish her sentence because she dissolved into nothing.

20

DRAKE

Of all the dark and terrifying creatures that walked upon the earth, the goddess Umali was the most frightening thing I'd ever seen.

But the most frightening thing on the earth stood in front of the most beautiful thing. My Saraya, now High Priestess of the Order of Te'mari, at only nineteen. Who was now staring blankly at the spot the spectre of her warrior mentor had just stood moments ago, the sound of the ocean crashing around us.

I couldn't talk though. I had been made Commander of Black Court's elite guard at twenty. I couldn't have been prouder of my mate. Though she and I knew the responsibility was a big one. My own mother was a minor deity and I knew full well the wrath a Goddess could wield.

"We should head back, Saraya," I said gently.

She turned towards me, wiping her eyes, and nodded. Together, we ascended into the dawn sky above Lobrathia to fly back to the Kaalon border. Never having astral travelled before, this was such a thrill. Naturally, if I'd learned this as a child, all I would have ever done was visit Saraya in the human realm every day. But the fae were not capable of astral travel. Our blood was tied to the land and our spirits could not leave our bodies in this way. The fact that I was only half-fae was probably how I was allowed to do this tag-a-long with Saraya at all.

We flew as high as we could and as fast as we could, the land tangled out under us like the patchwork blanket Queen Xenita had made for my littlest half brother, Wren, before his birth. Something sour twisted in me. Did Xenita know that my father, her husband, was dead? If we were to fight the demons off, I would need the entire dark fae army at my back.

For the thousandth time, I wondered where Daxian was. After I'd seen my father's corpse being dragged through the human palace, I imagined that Daxian had somehow gotten away. If he was smart, he would have run back across the Silent Mountains and alerted the Academy, which would then have sent word to Black Court.

"Saraya," I began as an idea grew in me. "We should make for Black—"

My magic was dissipating. The tourmaline cuff around my wrist dampened my own magic, which in turn made me unable to give Saraya's magic back to her. And it was her magic that was allowing us to astral travel. "Oh no."

"What is it?" she asked, concerned. But we weren't even near the Kaalon border. What would happen if my magic failed—

It didn't take me long to find that out because all at once, we were both sucked into a dark vortex. Saraya gave out a muffled scream.

When I woke, I felt like I was floating on air, but I could

tell the hard floor of the cave was beneath my back. I sought out Saraya with my mind and felt her presence next to me.

"Oh my Goddess," she whispered. "This has never happened to me before, Drake. I feel like my head is going to explode."

I suddenly remembered Havrok's spying bracelet, still on Saraya's wrist. So I entered her mind again so we wouldn't be overheard.

"You have to ground yourself." I pushed myself up to sit. My head swam as a wave of dizziness washed over me. *"I've seen this happen before to fae who've tried to astral travel. It goes away after a while."* Her face was pale, her eyes unfocused.

"Maybe I didn't come back into my body properly?" she asked.

"Sleep is the only thing that will fix it, as well as feeling everything around you. Here." I pulled on a strand of her dark hair.

"Ow! What in hell's name, Drake!" she hissed out loud

"Sorry, pain always works to get you back into your body."

"You just wanted to pull my hair, didn't you?"

"Maybe." I had to suppress a chuckle. *"Go back to sleep. It'll help."* I pulled her back against me, and she gave a half-hearted protest before giving in to the mate bond and letting me hold her. The feeling of her chest rising and falling with each breath calmed me and settled the monster that was trying to rear up and protect her from the demons sleeping in the cave with us.

It was like the world narrowed into focus where it was just her, existing perfectly, right where she belonged. My eyes began to flutter shut, to my surprise, and I was lulled to sleep by her scent and her sound.

Even so, I was still acutely aware of the breathing of every single one of the ten demon warriors sleeping in the cave with us, and the fact that given a chance, the monster in me would execute them all.

I WOKE US UP WHEN I FELT ARGOTH ROLL TO STANDING FROM HIS pallet. Saraya was groggy, wiping her eyes and yawning, so I decided to shock her again. I pressed my lips to the soft corner of her mouth and she jumped out of the pallet, simultaneously landing a punch to my gut.

"You sly monster!" she exclaimed, staring down at me with her hands on her hips. On her wrist, the ruby bracelet twinkled in the dusk light. Behind her, the demon warriors were pretending not to watch us.

"Well, it woke you up, didn't it?" I said as I got to my feet and pulled my boots on. And then I made my voice a little louder. "And don't say you didn't like it."

She scowled at me. "I need to go to the bathroom."

We rolled up our sleeping things and trudged out after the warriors to our horses. They were passing around some type of demon flatbread while Saraya stalked away from them. She seemed to suddenly realise that we were out in the wild because she uncrossed her arms and looked helplessly out at the bushland.

"Oh, my sweet princess," I sang. "Never had to use a hole in the ground?"

"That sounds awful in your monster-y rasp, you know," she shot back. The timbre of my voice *had* changed a little since my binding runes had come off, but I knew it wasn't the worst it could get. If, God forbid, the rest of my bindings came off, I doubted I'd be understandable at all.

"The goddess didn't grant me a penis," Saraya said primly. "So I'm not as lucky as you."

"Oh, I don't know, having lady parts would be some fun, I imagine."

"You've got no idea. Now, lengthen this chain, at *least* ten metres. I don't need you to hear me attend to my business."

"Ten metres?" I said, pretending to be horrified. "I could never be *that* far from my mate! I won't allow it. I'm coming with you." I headed into the scrub.

"Drakus Silverhand, do you want me to break your nose?" she cried after me.

"I might rather like a love slap."

"It'll be my knuckles, sir, not a slap. Better still, give me one of those demon blades and let me have at you. We never *have* fought one another, have we?"

I abruptly stopped when I found a good spot, and she walked right into my back. She gruffed as I checked the surrounding land for any concerns. Finding none, brought out my magic to make a neat hole in the soil.

"Will you need any assistance?" I asked.

Saraya sighed when she saw my work. "Only if you can let me borrow your dick for this."

I grinned at her use of the word. She was a midwife, I reminded myself, body parts were her bread and butter. "I mean, you can borrow it anytime—"

She shoved me out of the clearing. "*Ten metres!*" she shouted after me.

Chuckling, I strode away, lengthening the chain as she'd requested.

After Saraya was ready, we rode double saddle on one of the horses the demons had no doubt commandeered from Saraya's palace. I spoke to her mind to mind.

187

"*Before my magic failed, I was going to suggest we fly to Black Court to see what happened to Daxian and the rest of my fae warriors. I'm sure they would've headed south immediately.*"

"*Daxian isn't as clever as you think he is,*" she replied sourly.

I had wanted to kill my half-brother ever since he'd been engaged to Saraya. Daxian was an arrogant princely prick, to say the least, but so was every other prince of the fae realms.

THE KAALOTHIAN RIVER WAS BROAD ENOUGH THAT WE WOULD need a barge to cross. The demons had arrested the human barge workers on both sides and commandeered the vessels. If this was the case, no doubt Osring already suspected that the demons would have a plan to take over more than just Lobrathia.

If he was smart, he would have fled as far north as he could, to Kusha even, the northernmost aspect of the continent. That entire territory was hidden behind an ancient wall and there was no way the demons could breach it unless they sailed around. And demons hated open water. They would never bother with the ocean for anything other than obtaining slaves from Ellythia.

I relayed my thoughts to Saraya, but she shook her head. "*Osring would never leave his country.*" She sounded so sure. "*He has too much honour for that. He would rather die than run.*"

"*We need to convince him to flee, Saraya. Otherwise, our plan will never work. What's their military like?*"

"*Three thousand strong, the last I heard. He'll have moved them all to the city, no doubt. And I don't think they have secret tunnels like we did in Quartz.*"

"*You might not be right about that part,*" I said thoughtfully. "*Because they were built around the same time. Your magical human ancestors might have been of the same mind.*"

"*Even so, those entrances will be well hidden. I doubt I'd be able to find any in time to be of use. How* did *you take over Quartz anyway?*"

"*Magic and steel mostly,*" I said ruefully. "*It's not hard when the people you're taking over don't have much of either.*"

Under cover of night, we travelled undisturbed, past the river towns. But one thing troubled me.

The Kingdom of Kaalon was incredibly quiet. With my heightened hearing and smell, I should have been sensing more than I was. My insides prickled unccmfortably, but I said nothing to anyone, just making sure that when we saw a town or village, we skirted wide enough around them that the demons would not see or hear much of what went on within. Demons were terribly silent when they travelled and their senses better than humans. If somethirg was going on here, I wanted them kept in the dark about it.

Meanwhile, I had already learned something valuable in Havrok's decision to use a small force for this job. He didn't want to make a brute force attack because he didn't have the warriors to do it. He had dispensed his entire force to Lobrathia and didn't have many more to hold another kingdom.

It was no wonder he was desperate to keep breeding more.

But I wondered what his plan was for the rest of the realm if this was the case. Perhaps he just planned to hold the two? But surely, he knew the humans in the neighbouring kingdoms would retaliate. I'd have to find out more information when we got back to the demon palace.

Approaching the capital, I smelled the famous peach trees kilometres before I saw them. The sweet fragrance wrapped itself around us and I couldn't wait to eat one. The demon meat, fungus, and root crops diet was only serving to make me hungrier than before. On one of our rest breaks, we hopped down and collected a bag of peaches, and even the demon warriors ate as much as they could, juices dripping down their snouts and fang-filled mouths. They were sweet and filled with nutrition. Funnily enough, I had not tasted anything like them even in Blossom Court, where fruits of all types were abundant. It was just as well. We would need every ounce of energy we could muster if we were going to get King Osring and his wife out of this predicament. Both Saraya and I would need to think fast.

Travelling at a swift pace, we reached Peach Tree City proper a few hours before dawn.

21

SARAYA

I knew something was wrong right away.

Being Lobrathia's neighbouring kingdom, the capital of Kaalon, Peach Tree City, was a place I was very familiar with. Approaching the city from the south in the dark of night, we should have seen a multitude of quartz lights in orange and yellow, shining brightly from the battlements and up on the hill within the palace windows.

But the city was a blanket of darkness.

Worse still, on our way here, although we had skirted past villages at a distance, we had not seen any other sign of human movement.

A shadow formed a fist over my heart as Drake pulled our horse to a stop before we exited the line of trees we were in. He held a fist up to halt the demon contingent.

"Something's very wrong," I muttered.

"You're sure no one got here before us?" Drake directed to Argoth.

The captain made a rumbling sound in his chest with a

drop in pitch at the end that I'd learned was their way of saying 'no.'

"We'll head in cautiously on foot," said Drake to the others. "Stick to the shadows, could be a trap."

They grumbled in assent and we tied the group of horses to low branches in the surrounding forest. Creeping forward, we kept low and headed right for the city gates.

To my surprise, the grand wooden gates stood wide open, a maw of black emptiness welcoming us in. There was not a soul, not a sound or smell that I could make out. An eerie feeling encompassed the entire city, and it stood as if in mourning. As we stuck to the walls, the demons around us jittered nervously. These particular warriors had been otherwise stoic in nature, but now they stepped from foot to foot and grunted with uncertainty. I couldn't help but feel the same. This felt awfully wrong. I hoped Opal had found a place to hide safely.

"Where is everyone?" I whispered to Drake as we came up with echoing footsteps to the city square, a hexagonal tiled area they often gathered in on peach harvest days.

But something was more than wrong about this, because even if the people had fled the city, the quartz lights should have been here. But everything was absent, even dirt and debris. Everything was too clean. I relayed my suspicions to Drake mind to mind.

He abruptly turned to Argoth. "We need to scout the place. We'll split into four groups and head to cardinal points. Meet back here in half an hour to report.

Since there were only ten demons, the captain decided he would come with Drake and me. My stomach churned and I wondered if there was a way to separate from him and run off. If we both had weapons, we might have stood a chance against ten demons, but I knew the reality cf it. Ten was still too many to run from. And we had no supplies or anything.

So after Drake sniffed the air, he decided we would go eastwards with the captain. Off we trudged, eyes darting, noses sniffing, and on high alert for some type of ambush. I was honestly waiting for something to jump out at me from the shadows because a sense of being watched had me prickling with anticipation.

We paused at an intersection, and behind me, there was a thump and sick crunching sound. I whirled around to see the demon captain falling to the ground. Drake looked innocently at me.

"Was that necessary?" I asked mind to mind putting a hand over Havrok's bracelet, staring at the captain's crumpled form. *"Is he dead?"*

"No," said Drake replied, glancing casually down. *"It needed to be —"* He suddenly looked at his feet.

"What is it?" I squinted at his leg, looking for some sign of danger.

"Fluffy just crawled up my leg and onto my shoulder. Unless it's some other kitten-sized creature."

Relief swept through me, cool and distant. *"Thank the Goddess."* I moved my arm and stepped away from them so the bracelet wouldn't pick up their interaction.

Drake whispered and Opal began chattering non-stop, gesturing with her paw, moving her eyes this way and that.

I tried to make sense of what she was trying to say. Drake unhooked her backpack, the letter still tucked in there, untouched. Then it struck me.

"It's an illusion," I told him. *"That's what she's saying."*

"A very good one," Drake said, frowning. *"But too good. Everything's too clean. That's what gives it away."*

E.P. BALI

"How the hell has it come about? By what magic?"

"It has the smell of old magic," said Drake. *"It's so out of place here that I didn't realise what it was. Smells like the sea mixed with blood."*

I crinkled my nose at that. Drake had a strange way of describing abstract things. "So that means they're still here? Under illusion, maybe?"

"I'll see if I can sniff it out. Give me a moment. I know Osring's scent."

I was impressed. Drake had only met Osring once before.

Head bent low, he scouted through the area, leading me up to the palace. I knew he had the scent when his whole body tensed and then he began moving quickly. He led us into the housing district, where townhouses were set in rows.

"The illusion is concentrated here," Drake said absently, inspecting the window of a house.

"That's strange," I said, peering around the door. *"It's a random place to be —"*

"Saraya!" a familiar female voice hissed.

We whirled around to find a young red-headed woman I recognised immediately.

"Tembry!" I made to run to her, but the chain linking me to Drake stopped me short. Alarmed, I looked back. Drake grimaced before whispering to Opal and gesturing to my wrist. A cloud of black surrounded the bracelet before it fell off my arm. Drake waved a hand and it flew far into the distance.

Only then did he let me run towards Tembry, who was waiting under the eave of a blacksmith's shop.

"Tembry, oh Goddess!"

Sobbing, Tembry and I grabbed each other, half choking one another to death.

"I thought you were dead!" she cried.

"We must be quiet," Drake urged.

Tembry pulled away from me and wiped her eyes on her sleeve. "I'm sorry. Yes. I know. I'm just so relieved you're here! Wait, isn't Blythe with you?"

A cold chill swept through me. "No. But she's—" I was going to say 'safe', but she wasn't. None of us were. "What happened back in Quartz? I haven't had the chance to speak to her."

The blood drained from Tembry's face. "After Jerali led us and the nobles out of the secret tunnel, Blythe and Jerali went back into the palace. Jerali wanted to take the palace back, but..." She covered her mouth, silent sobs wracking her body. I felt like I was going to vomit. Jerali going back in made sense. The armsmaster was a full-blooded warrior, through and through. But Blythe as well? She was a good fighter...but now they'd landed themselves as prisoners. Shame crept through me. I should have been able to save them both by now.

But Drake interrupted, his voice grim. "We can't stay, Tembry. We can't delay here."

My heart plummeted into my stomach because I knew it was true. It would be impossible to leave their demons in the dust. They would just follow us.

"Tembry, where is King Osring?" I said, barely keeping it together, as once again, the people I loved were dying around me. "You must take us to him right away."

She nodded. "Follow me."

Only the thought of Tembry and baby Delilah being safe made my feet move. My friend led us to an old cottage connected to the blacksmith's forge. With brows raised, I followed her in, Drake right on my tail. When we entered the cottage, we headed straight to the back door. But instead of leading to a back garden like I'd imagined, we were back out on one of the streets of Peach Tree City. Except this time, luminous quartz lights speckled from windows and outside houses, people and carts bustled about, a bard sang in a tavern nearby.

This was the city that I had known and loved as my childhood summertime retreat.

"I don't understand, Tem," I said as she rushed us down the cobblestoned street to a large manse.

"His majesty will explain, Sara," she called over her shoulder. "But the visitor's alarm went off, and they sent me to bring you in because they knew you would trust me. Wait til you see Delilah. She didn't take well to the breast at first but now growing so fast!"

I wiped a tear from my own eye, just so happy to see her alive and well.

She ushered us inside the manse and up a set of carpeted stairs into an upper room.

Brightly lit luminous quartz lanterns were strung all over the walls and sitting by a double bed was King Osring, more wiry and hunched than I remembered, his scattering of hair now white, looking over his son, Adlain. The prince was a skinny young man of thirty, he'd always been kind to me, although always consumed by his academic studies. He had a soup spoon in hand and was feeding his sickly elderly mother, Queen Irma, tucked up bed.

"Uncle!" I cried. "Aunty!"

"Saraya?" Osring's eyes widened when he saw us and he heaved himself onto his feet with his walking stick. "Oh Saraya, thank the Father you are alive!"

I rushed forward to embrace him.

"I've kept her safe," Drake said behind me, reaching out to shake Osring's hand. My adopted uncle took it with raised brows.

But I knew we couldn't waste any time. "Uncle, Adlain, the demons are here to take over. The demon king is forcing Drake to assassinate you and take over Kaalon!"

But Osring seemed unsurprised by this information and I helped him sit back down. He nodded. "I know, Saraya. We headed straight here after Jerali Jones helped us escape through the hidden tunnel in your palace. It only made sense they would attempt to take us over next."

"So all of you got out?"

"All of the royalty. Along with your maid with her parents and her baby—who have been taken in by some kind people in the city—Helena, Junni, and the others stayed here awhile before they escaped back to their kingdoms. Helena is preparing for war."

A sense of relief flooded through me at the thought of Queen Helena rallying her troops for us. "But how have you hidden the city?"

"A genius construction of our ancestors," Adlain said, rising to his feet. I reached for his hand and he kissed it with a bow.

"I had always known it was there," Osring continued, "but never really thought I'd need it in this day and age. A bit of my own blood on an old stone, and here we are, a hidden dimension."

"I imagine it helped them quite a bit in the old days when fae and demon attacks were prevalent."

"But there is a problem, Saraya," Adlain said, brushing a hand through his chestnut hair.

Osring held my eye seriously and I hung on to his every

word. "A week after our escape, a fae raven delivered this letter to me." He took out a piece of parchment that had clearly been folded and refolded many times. I recognised the black dragon wax seal as the royal seal of the Black Court. I took it gingerly and held it so Drake could see too. In a rushed cursive was written:

> *The Green Reaper has awakened. Prepare.*
> —*King Daxian Darkcleaver of Black Court*

Drake froze next to me.

So Daxian was alive. He'd clearly made it safely back to Black Court if he'd been made king. But this message... a spider-like shadow scuttled up my spine. I looked from Drake to Osring.

"Surely not?" I said in disbelief. "The Reaper is just a bedtime story. The story of the fae who went bad? Who divided the fae realm into light and dark?"

"It is not just a story, Saraya." Drake's voice held a current of such darkness, I stared at him. "The Green Reaper is very much real. I have seen him."

Even Osring frowned at that.

"My mother's tree sits above his crypt," he explained. "She was forced to be the sworn guardian of his remains. I was born on the grounds there."

Surprise bled from me, raw and foreboding. "Are you serious, Drake?"

He nodded. "For fifty years he's been recovering from the injuries he suffered in an old war. I went down there as a child. I saw his desiccated body, even touched the thing. You should have seen the way I ran for my life when I saw one of his eyes twitch."

Osring and I stared at each other in disbelief.

"But what does he have to do with us?" I asked. "What does he have to do with Havrok?"

"He was emperor of the demon kingdom, was he not, fae?" asked Osring to Drake. "His intention was to spread his darkness over this earth, to increase his lands and take over the human realm."

"That is correct, Your Highness. Saraya..." Drake turned to look at me and spoke with urgency. "Havrok is a liege lord to the Green Reaper. It must have been him who began collecting magic from the humans and ordering the demon king to do the same. As soon as Havrok captured us, I knew there had to be a bigger story behind it. It's him, the Green Reaper."

I gripped Drake's arm. "Tarangi told me that the Reaper opened the quarry portal— I thought she meant Havrok."

And, *Reaper save the king*, the demon lords had called out. I'd thought nothing of it at the time. But now, this information shot through me like an arrow. Finally we knew who the real culprit was and his motive.

"So he's been asleep for fifty odd years," I said, my mind rapidly calculating this new equation. "But now he's awake. What do you think he'll do?"

"It's difficult to say, but we have to get out of Havrok's court as soon as we can."

"Then you must run," said Osring slapping his hand on his leg. "Go south, petition the fae courts."

"I cannot," Drake said. "I am bound by magic to Havrok. He can call me back at any time, and I would have to obey. He calls me even now. I can feel the command. We must leave Saraya."

"But you came here to kill me," said Osring wryly. "What will you do about that?"

Drake reached up to his shoulder and grabbed the invisible form of Opal sitting there. She appeared with a sigh, thankful to be seen again.

"Havrok wants your heads," Drake said. "So it's heads we'll give him."

2 2
SARAYA

"**A**mbush!" Drake shouted at the top of his lungs.

With Havrok's bracelet lying where it could see us, Opal sat on my shoulder, invisible but wielding a complex illusion involving five dead soldiers and two real ones in a ruse of fighting Drake. I had to admit, the illusion was good, and especially in the dark, it looked very real. Behind me, Captain Argoth groaned and groggily scrambled to his feet.

It had been a quick and teary goodbye with Uncle Osring, Adlain, and Tembry— I didn't even have time to see Delilah and Aunt Irma was too poorly to understand what was going on. But our plan had come together rapidly, once Drake told us his idea.

So in the dark of the fake Peach Tree City, I made a show of screaming and collapsing to the ground as Opal sent a soldier swinging at me.

Drake plucked me off the cobblestones, swung me over his shoulder so my backside was in the air, and Opal managed to climb up to my back and hang on for dear life.

The sound of pounding feet and male shouts resounded in the distance.

"There's too many of them!" Drake called. "Retreat!"

Captain Argoth grunted as Drake swung a mesh bag at him. He caught it just in time, following us at a run to the city square.

My head bounced along in the most jarring way, but it wasn't long before we reached the square—Opal making it sound like shouts and boots were coming from behind us. Ahead, the demons were calling out.

"Retreat!" Argoth shouted to the demons waiting in the square. "Go!"

Demon boots pounded as they followed their captain's orders, and if I weren't bouncing so vigorously, I would have sighed in relief. They had believed it. And with Opal's illusion, they would believe the two rocks Drake had picked out to be the heads of my aunt and uncle.

We sprinted through the empty city behind the demons and eventually ended up in the forest where we'd tied our horses. As we all scrambled onto our steeds, Drake slung me in front of him and I pretended to cry out in pain as if I'd been injured.

The sky had begun lightening in the east and the demons made haste, setting a swift pace through the forest surrounding the city. We rode, my body slumped against Drake— who I knew was very satisfied with the act of holding me incredibly close— and Opal clutched onto the pommel of the saddle in front of me. I knew the demons had no idea what they were doing. The plan had been to find shelter in the city once we'd taken it over. But it had taken longer to get here than we'd thought and they needed a place to hide from the dawn sun.

If Drake didn't have his blasted controlling rune, we could have trapped these demons in the sun and made a run for it. But as it stood, Drake had to keep up the ruse of helping them.

They might not have known this land, but I did, and it was the perfect way to gain their trust. South of Peach Tree City was a training facility for their military. In it were log cabins the senior military staff used for accommodation. Naturally, it would be abandoned right now.

I relayed this mentally to Drake, who called a halt.

The demons gathered around, and I clutched my stomach, giving a false grimace, and explained about the training grounds. There was a palpable lessening in the tension of the group. Drake took the lead and I directed him southwest.

WHEN WE REACHED THE LOG CABINS, THE DEMONS BARGED THEIR way in as fast as they could, pillaging any food and weapons they could find, making a general mess before shutting out any light and settling down to sleep for the day. We found ourselves in a cabin with Captain Argoth, who immediately opened the mesh sack. Inside were the rocks, nicely disguised as the severed heads of the king and queen of Kaalon.

"We found them hiding out in a cottage," Drake explained in a falsely bored voice. "They were refusing to leave the city with their people who had long fled. Both are old and sickly, unable to travel. Their soldiers were easy to kill."

I pretended to sit distraught and silent next to him. Drake then produced a solid gold signet ring with the orange tree of

Osring's House on it. The captain took it, nodding. In the face of severed heads and a ring, it was terribly convincing.

We drew the curtains and went to bed. In our case, pushing two single beds together, so Drake and I weren't uncomfortable with chains hanging on the floor between us.

"He believed it," Drake said through our mental bond. *"I can't believe it worked."*

"I can," I said tiredly. *"I tricked everyone at the Mountain Academy with Opal's magic. It was so convincing that Briar saw me naked by accident one time and thought I was a eunuch."*

Drake sat bolt upright in bed. "What did you just say?"

I chuckled, and Opal gave a tiny warble of fright next to me. "Sh!" I said to her. Captain Argoth was sleeping only two doors down. Then I spoke to Drake mind to mind again. *"It's alright, Drake, don't get all matey with me. It was an accident. You saw me once in the bathroom too, remember?"*

Drake lay back down, but I knew his heart was pounding in the chest. *"Did you just say 'don't get matey with me?'"*

"I did. And Briar is a funny boy—fae, I mean."

"I know him," Drake said with murder in his eyes. *"The Nightclaw family lived close to my childhood home."*

I flapped a hand. *"Well, I walk around half-naked in the demon court anyway. I don't see your problem."*

"It's a big fucking problem, Saraya. You're mine.*"*

His voice took such a possessive cadence, that I turned and gave him a push away from me. But his voice had also sent a confusing flutter of desire soaring through me. I said, *"I'm no one's. I'm my own person, Drakus Silverhand."* But the words came out more harshly than I intended.

The corners of Drake's mouth turned downwards just a bit as he rolled onto his back away from me. I lay back down, suddenly feeling cold. To my horror, I realised that I'd gotten used to his warmth at my back. What *did* I actually feel for Drake? His gaze, his body, gave me a fluttery sort of feeling, and I *wanted* his physical touch. Craved it, even. Like I did now. I liked it when he touched me.

But how could I, in the face of everything that had happened, give in to those feelings? Everyone I loved had either left or died. Giving myself to someone else was something I couldn't let myself do. The way it tore at my heart to lose my mother, my father, send my sister away, and lose everyone else. I didn't *want* to give myself to him in that way. Husband, mate or not, I just couldn't completely give in like that. It would be dangerous for me.

I let out a long exhale as emotions roiled in my stomach. I couldn't deny that Drake's presence made me feel better, his touch even more so. Maybe it was selfish of me, but I knew he liked my touch too.

So I hefted myself up and turned to look at him over my shoulder, considering if my next move was going to be heinous or not. He looked back at me, those black eyes boring into mine, his face a little glum. Trying to make light of it, I grabbed his arm and rolled him onto his side, so he was against my back again. He rolled easily, but I could tell he was a little confused and more than a little satisfied. Sighing as the cold seeped away and his heat melted through me, I closed my eyes, clutching his muscled arm with one hand. With his arm around me like that, I couldn't help but wonder what he would feel like against my naked skin— with his hands caressing all of my body. I shifted at the thought.

"Saraya," Drake's whispered in warning.

I froze, realising my backside was rubbing against his groin. The sudden urge to roll over and kiss him swept me up and I half turned.

His scent, his eyes, his mere presence drew me in. It would be all too easy to pull my clothes off right here and curl my legs around him. He would plunge himself inside me and we could make love. Drake would be a good lover, I had no doubt about that.

He sensed my desire, because he made a soft growl and put a hand around my head and leaned in, pressing his lips against mine. Softly at first, then hungrily. I reached up and fisted my hands in his hair, meeting his tongue with mine. I suddenly found my hands pulling his shirt up, the hard planes of his muscled stomach rippling under my fingers. Drake made a sound of approval and pulled my own shirt up, pulled away from me and lowered his head to my side, licking and kissing the curve of my abdomen. I gasped—

And then Opal let out a loud snore.

I yanked myself away, swearing. Drake threw himself away from me, running a frustrated hand through his hair.

"Dear Gods, Saraya." His voice was no more than a rasp.

I groaned and rolled away from him, tugging my clothes back in place, breathing deeply to try and steady myself. Both of us had almost lost complete control. I needed to calm down and will the desire away. "We'd better sleep," I muttered angrily. Angry at myself more than anything. "Goodnight, Drake."

A heavy sigh, and then Drake clearly couldn't help himself because he rolled back over, putting his arm around me. But, noticeably, kept his groin well away.

It took a long while for me to fall asleep.

THAT NIGHT WE MADE OUR RETURN JOURNEY BACK OVER THE Kaalothian River and into the quartz quarry. This time, my stomach twisted as I saw human figures toiling away in there.

The sound of leather striking skin assaulted my ears. I twitched so violently at the sound that Drake reflexively reached for my hand. I let him take it without complaint. I couldn't breathe. I couldn't move, nor think as we both witnessed the worst thing imaginable. Demons were whipping human miners as they chipped the quartz out of the rock.

My stomach churned as the old scars on my back twinged in memory. Still I could not move. The demons ahead of us turned around impatiently.

"Sara?" Drake was in front of me, my face in his hands. "Breathe, my Princess," he whispered. "You are with me. You are safe."

The whip. That Goddess forsaken sound had more hold upon me than anything else in my life. It rendered me immobile. Reminded me of the feeling of leather on my skin. It was more than pain. It was helplessness. Powerlessness.

"*Princess.*" Drake's voice was a plea and it made me focus on his face. His eyes were hazel, the whites of them returned. "Come back to me."

Unbidden, I took a sharp intake of breath and swallowed the lump in my throat. Nodding, I said, "I'm sorry. I just—" I looked back at the human men, mining under duress. I broached Drake's mind and he let me in, as always. *"I will get them out of this. I swear it."*

He let go of my face and stepped back, his eyes clouding over with the all-black once again. His lips curved into a vicious smile and he replied into my mind, *"And I will be there with you."*

My stomach flopped on itself as Drake looked around the quarry, a bloodthirsty look taking over his face. He would enjoy it too. Perhaps a little too much.

But the hand that reached for mine was gentle and we followed after the demons, grumbling under their breath about the delay.

As we took the wooden platform down to the portal, I glanced back in the direction of Lobrathia one last time, wondering what had become of my home. Of Agatha and the other midwives. Of the mothers and families I had looked after. Of Bluebell with her twins. What was going on in the city? If any of them *were* slain, I would avenge them. Each and every single one. But for now, we had to go back to the demon palace.

The lotus is patient. Before it rises up through the mud, it *must* be patient.

Back through the gleaming portal we went and onto a new set of waiting haxim reptiles. We reached Havrok's palace an hour later.

Captain Argoth took us directly to see Havrok and presented the heads and signet ring.

Havrok nodded as if this was what he had expected.

"Well done, Lord of the Kill," he said, leaning back in his chair and assessing us. I made a show of looking teary and miserable, staring at my feet. "And you seem to have broken in your first concubine while you were at it."

I bristled at that but kept my eyes on the black marble floor.

"As your reward, you may take your pick of the royal concubines."

Something sour crept its way into my heart. The image of Drake sleeping with another woman came unbidden into my mind. Anger unfurled in me and, conflicted about my own reaction, I frowned deeply at my feet.

But Drake's rasping voice was a hair's breadth away from open anger, "*No.*"

Havrok raised his brows. "Lord Braxus has also requested your first concubine in a swap."

I felt the sheer anger emanating from Drake like a fiery tornado of power. Without thinking, I reached out and grabbed his hand.

"Stand down, Lord Drakus," Havrok warned.

Drake's fingers curled tightly around mine as I felt, for the first time, Havrok's control surrounding him and pushing him into magical submission.

"*I* said to Braxus," Havrok said, not taking this white eyes off Drake, "That I would allow it, but only *after* my big event."

As my own anger unfurled in me, Drake bristled, only able to hold himself back because of the controlling rune. I didn't know how I felt about his possessiveness. It was a pleasant feeling to be wanted, but this level of desire was all at once overwhelming.

"There is one thing we must discuss, Lord Drakus." Havrok motioned for Drake to sit in the chair that was designated as ours. After we were seated, with Drake's protective arm around me tightly, Havrok took a long sip from his chalice.

"In three days is my annual ball. It is a show of the kingdom's wealth and success, and with the securing of Kaalon, we no doubt have much to celebrate." He lifted his drink. "This year, we celebrate the new Lord of the Kill."

Drake stilled beside me, and I knew he forced himself to incline his head and say, "Thank you, Your Majesty."

E.P. BALI

"Thank me when your binding runes are undone."

A vile chill swept through my spine. Drake's hand suddenly clutched my hip.

"This will be my grandest event," Havrok said greedily. "The Obsidian Court mage will, in front of the entire court and wider nobility, make a spectacle of taking the rest of your binding runes off." He motioned to Drake's tattoos, and I stared in horror. "And we will see the true monster emerge."

Drake's breathing became slow and exaggerated as if control was taking a great toll on him.

"He will become more bestial," Havrok said suggestively to me. "You will have to be careful. These things do not happen often, you understand. The Green Reaper will also be in attendance. Your mate will be masked and hidden among other women, a grand experiment! The first of its kind to see what really happens when a Niyati truly meets a Tyaag. To see a real monster at play, that is something we all want to see. Hmm?"

He was asking the question as if he weren't toying with our lives. I didn't know the words he had just used. They sounded like fae words, but I had never heard them before.

"What does he mean?" I asked Drake in his mind. *"What is he saying?"*

But Drake didn't, or wasn't in a state to, reply.

"And I hear that your First has saved the life of one of my breeders. To show my gratitude, I will allow her a visit with her father."

It was my turn to tense, as every cell in my body stood to attention. Havrok gestured to one of the slaves who hurried outside. Moments later, a smirking Glacine brought in my father in his wheeled chair.

Eldon Voltanius looked paler than I'd ever seen him— as

if all the life had been sapped out of his skin. His eyes were closed but sunken into their sockets, his hair now all grey. He had been obviously cleaned and dressed by someone, but it did not take away from how awful he looked. I thought my heart was going to split into two.

I couldn't bear the thought that he was still being used and manipulated by Glacine, even in his catatonic state. I wanted to run up to him, to hold his hand, to tell him I had not forgotten him or our family. That I knew he was still in there somewhere. But Glacine standing over him made my feet stick to the floor. There was no way I was going near her and that God-awful smirk.

Havrok waved a casual hand. "The poison keeps him compliant, but it's a shame it's affected him physically. He is unable to breed at present, but we will persist before we put him down."

Fire swept up my spine as my stomach churned. He spoke about my father's life like he was an animal. Drake snatched up my hand. "Calm yourself," he said out loud. His tone was sharp and his grip firm. I knew it was a part of the act. I knew he wanted to help me, but it still hurt.

It hurt that I was once again powerless to do anything but let others do what they pleased to those I loved. To determine the course of my life. I gripped Drake's hand right back.

I had sworn a vow when Slade had told me that my father had been taking poison instead of medicine. And I would stand by that vow. Glacine would be dead by my hand before the end of this.

It wasn't until Havrok dismissed us and we were back in our rooms that Drake answered my question. He swung around and grabbed me by both arms. His intensity frightened me for only a second before I realised he was actually frightened.

"We need to leave," he said, his voice hoarse. "Saraya, they *must not* remove my runes. They can't."

"Why? We can't leave Drake, you know that. Slade, Blythe and Jerali—"

"I will be a danger to you, Saraya, don't you understand? I will not be in control. I will only want to claim you as my mate, claim you as mine. Consummate our union. I'll hurt you."

"I trust you, Drake," I urged, surprised by my own truth. "I know you won't hurt me."

He let go of me and began pacing the room, an angry lion, pent-up energy being released in his stride. "You cannot trust me in my monster form."

"It's been so long, though, Drake. Your runes have bound you since you were thirteen. It might be alright—"

"But I *remember*, Saraya." He shook his head and looked at me helplessly. "You have to understand, once puberty hit, I was a mess. I was a monster devoid of rational thinking. It was like being pure instinct. My actions were not determined by logic, only by feeling. And whatever I wanted, I got. That's why they bound me in the first place. I was *unable* to be controlled, *even* by my mother, a Goddess!"

My heart raced in my chest. The vision of Havrok's mad spectacle. Me as Havrok had described, in a mask, disguised amongst other human slaves, Drake, a snarling creature, hunting for me as he had hunted Gangrene. Seeking me out. And finding me.

"We can't run, you know that," I said quietly. "The controlling rune. We have to go through with it."

"There has to be another way."

Opal crooned and fled to Drake, who, with great control, roughly patted the creature. "You too, Fluffy. Small creatures aren't safe around monsters. I'd probably…"

But he didn't need to say it. I knew what a monster would do if they saw Opal. My stomach churned violently. My father was still here, along with Lysander. I had been anointed as High Priestess by Umali. I was not only a warrior anymore. I had to be a leader of women. Running away was not an option for me. Whatever we were going to do, we had to end it.

"It's not just you and me, Drake," I said. "It's not just us that's captive here."

"We can't save everyone, Saraya."

But I looked at Drake in the eye, the image of not only Blythe and Jerali but also Sarone, Tarangi, and the other girls fighting for their lives as they were bred against their will, in the forefront of my mind.

"I am High Priestess Warrior of the Order of Temari, Drake," I said firmly. "If there is a way out of this, I am going to find it. You'll become the monster you were born to be and I'll be here to deal with it. But I'm not leaving you or *any* of these girls to deal with this alone."

Before my eyes, his shoulders lowered a little, relief sweeping through his form, tentative and quiet. He was worried he would attack me and fearful that I would shirk him. But I had signed an oath to him in blood. Whatever my mess of feelings was, I was still wed to him. As far as I was concerned, I was his wife and my mother had taught me to honour my vows.

Wild and violent things like Drake are the fodder of my patron Goddess. I hadn't forgotten what Arishnie had told me about what *Te'mari* meant in old Ellythian. And I had

213

been raised up by Umali for a reason— that wasn't coincidence.

In three days, the monster that was Drake's true form was going to come straight for me. But Drake's true form hadn't met *me* yet.

23
SARAYA

I n the three days leading up to the ball, Tarangi had run to my room twice to help a woman post-birth. And each time, the problem had been the same: Placenta Accreta. I had pulled Drake along with me each time, and quietly he came and sweated to give me back my magic, forcing the tourmaline shackles to give way to him. Glacine, on her supervision of the women, had ignored me, each and every time.

In those three days, the cogs in my brain turned, working through the issue that we now had.

The afternoon before Havrok's spectacle, Captain Argoth came to our door. In his hands, he held a black tourmaline key, and with it, he undid Drake's wrist shackles and my slave collar. Before I could even think to stop him, he bound my hands with a set of black tourmaline shackles laced with gold and silver.

"To block the mate bond," he said gruffly. "You will sleep separately tonight."

As he clasped the shackles closed, I felt as if a cloud had fallen over me, heavy and damp. My throat went tight as I felt

Drake's emotions cut off from my mind. He had always allowed me free and open access to his feelings, and I felt the absence of them now like a wet blanket covering me.

Drake cast me a final look that I couldn't read before heading out the door with Argoth. Opal nervously dug her invisible claws into my shoulder.

"Wait!" I do not know what possessed me. Perhaps it was the fact that Drake was leaving me for the first time since we arrived here. Perhaps it was the fear of what would come, but I flew towards Drake. He turned, and I flung my arms around his neck, pressing my lips against his.

Automatically, his arms encircled me, holding me satisfyingly close. I sighed as my insides melted. He parted his lips and kissed me back, his touch like the caress of sweet honey. The space between my thighs tingled madly.

"My Lord…" Argoth's voice was impatient.

Demon scumbag.

Remembering we were being watched, I pulled away from Drake. But he came with me, following my lips with his.

I turned my head away and his kisses continued down my neck.

"Drake," I said.

"Saraya," he huffed between kisses.

I shoved him into the wall away from me, and the look of utter shock and irritation on his face made me grin like an idiot, despite the situation. I pointedly glanced at Argoth, whose mouth had dropped open.

"I will see you soon, Drakus," I said formally.

Drake cleared his throat and nodded stiffly. "Bye, Princess."

As he turned away, his voice echoed in my ears.

I WAS CUDDLING WITH OPAL ON THE LOUNGE WHEN AN aggressive knock came at the door. To my great displeasure when I opened it, standing there was a familiar, scowling face.

Marissa stood with her arms crossed, her lips twisted above her black slave collar. She wore the same sheer gossamer gown the other slaves did, her chestnut hair twisted into a bun. "The king's first concubine requests a meeting with all the other first concubines," she snapped at me. "You need to be dressed in the uniform."

Having not seen her for many months, I took a moment to look at her. But some things—some people— never changed. "Good to see you too, Marissa," I said smoothly. "And I'm not changing my clothes." I stepped out of the door and closed it. I was wearing one of Drake's modified outfits. A white cotton shirt and black pants.

"You can't go like that," she snapped back.

It was with some satisfaction I could see that she wanted to strike me. If she did, it wouldn't end well for her, even with my shackles on. "Who's going to stop me? Lead the way, please."

She remained in front of me for the moment, looking me up and down like I was the most disgusting thing she'd ever seen.

I won't pretend that her or Glacine's treatment of me didn't have an effect. All I could do was simply push it to the back of the crevices of my mind as often as I could. But in reality that only meant it festered there, a heavy mould at the edges of me. I felt every scar on my back when these dark thoughts came out. I think it was a part of the whole reason I could never heal those wounds.

But one thing also came to mind.

That is the noblest thing a person can do in this life. Drake had said those words about protecting those you love. At the time, I hadn't thought too much of it, dismissing it even, as pretty words. But the more I'd gotten to know Drake, the more I realised he never spoke pleasantly for the sake of it. He was always honest with me, and the mate bond confirmed that every time.

If he thought Glacine ripping my back open shouldn't be a reminder of my life's failures but of my noble intentions, perhaps I could think that way too.

So I stuck my chin in the air and stepped up to Marissa, so we were nose to nose. My voice took on a rare tone of deep venom. "Don't *ever* think for one second that I've forgotten what you are. What you did. What you do in her name. Woman or not, evil never wins, Marissa. The demons will never win while I'm alive. Got it?"

Fear flickered in her eyes for the briefest moment before she sneered down her nose at me. "We'll see what happens to you after the ball, *Saraya.* And when he tears you open, I'll be happy to watch."

I recoiled from her as if she'd slapped me, my mouth twisting in disgust at her awful words.

Satisfied, she pushed passed me and stalked down the corridor. Aghast, I stared at her for a moment before I felt Opal's soft warble in my ear.

Drake won't hurt you, that warble was saying. *He didn't hurt me, remember.*

Squaring my shoulders, I slipped Opal back into my room, shut the door, and hurried after Marissa.

IT TURNED OUT THAT THE FIRST CONCUBINES MET IN GLACINE'S personal chambers once a month. They were all sitting in their velvet chairs, with Glacine at the head. I could see my seat waiting for me opposite Braxus's first concubine, which unfortunately meant it was adjacent to Glacine's chair.

A servant offered me a drink and I took the pink liquid with no intention of drinking—it smelled like over ripe fruit. Glacine's face was a courtier's cold, wide smile as she looked me pointedly up and down. She wore a striking, sheer black dress and magnificent red quartz necklace and earrings— it had always been her preferred jewellery.

I wondered again at her parentage. *Eyesmith*, Tarangi had said, was her surname. I wondered how I could use this information to my advantage— perhaps to see if I could get Blythe and Jerali Jones out of their captivity.

As I took my seat, I saw that each first concubine wore a sheer black gossamer dress that left nothing to the imagination, coupled with rich jewels representing how wealthy their demon lord was.

"It is a requirement you wear the uniform." Glacine's voice was velvet smooth and sickly sweet. "Do you know the punishment for disobedience in this court?"

I gritted my teeth as Glacine's smile grew wider. "We call it the demon of nine tails. And I'm afraid it is well past time you were taught a lesson. I have been far too lenient with you." She gestured to Marissa, who, grinning, brought out a long wooden box from a side table. Glacine lifted the lid and my stomach dropped to my feet. It was a leather whip. But instead of a single strap of leather at the end, it was split into nine whips, joined by a single handle.

My breath was ragged as I exhaled, but I composed myself enough to say, "You are not the king. It seems I outrank you here. I can wear what I want."

She smirked, stroking the whip. "I will remind you that you are not a princess any longer. *We* own Lobrathia now. The seat of the king is owned by Havrok. *You* are nothing. "

The words were bruising because I knew, on some level, she was right. If Voltanius House did not hold Quartz City, then we were not in power, and I was not a princess. But I swallowed that bitter taste down.

Because even then, I was *not* nothing. I was still my mother's daughter. Still a princess of Ellythia on her side. *And,* I was High Priestess of the Order of Temari.

But in this single moment in time, it didn't matter.

"Get on your knees," Glacine hissed.

No.

I wanted to scream. I wanted to swear at her, to slug her across the jaw, throw her across the room. But all I could do was sit on my hands and grit my teeth like a child. That's how she had always made me feel. Small. Pathetic. The vision of the whip in her hand disabled me completely.

When I did not move, Glacine aggressively motioned to the other concubines, her alabaster cheeks reddening. "Get her down. Now." Her voice was knife sharp and cut me to the core.

They moved reluctantly, but I could tell they had done this before because they each took my stiff body, turned me around, and forced me onto my knees with the ease of practice. One of them shoved my elbows onto my chair.

I wanted to punch someone, but my disbelief would not let me.

I wanted to kick them, but my honour would not let me.

I wanted to run, but something sickly and dark held me in place.

Glacine was everything I was not. And because of it, here she was getting her way and winning, once again.

My shirt was rolled upwards with expert hands that I sensed were Marissa's.

I squeezed my eyes shut and thought of my mother.

Raw, blinding pain cracked across my skin and I bit the fabric of my shirt. *Lightning does not yield.* I said in my mind. *Lightning does not yield. Lightning does not yield.* Try as I might, I could not stop the tears. I didn't want to make a sound as Glacine struck me again, but a whimper fell out of my mouth and I could feel Glacine and Marissa's satisfaction.

Another strike and a fire raged across my back. I couldn't move. My limbs were water. My head was mush.

You're in shock, something at the back of my mind screamed. *Get up, get moving, fight!*

But there was nothing left in me to fight. And I couldn't numb my back with my magic like I used to. The pain rendered me completely immobile.

"That will do." Glacine's voice was far away. "Take her back to her rooms, wipe the blood. There will be time for more lessons in the coming weeks."

Someone got me to my feet and the pain of my shirt falling back down over my back brought everything to a sharp focus. Glacine's red quartz earrings, necklace, and bracelets were all glowing with a brilliance that couldn't have been possible even if they were charged under the sun. I had never seen her after a whipping, I had always put my head down and left.

It all fell together.

The sun was not the only way to charge the luminous quartz.

So was pain. And Glacine had been using my pain as fuel for the last five years.

24

SARAYA

That night I lay in bed with Opal curled against my side. The entire suite felt far too big, the air too cold and frigid. Needless to say, as my back stung like a million blades were stuck into it, I struggled to sleep. One of the first concubines had dressed it with a wet moss the demons used for wounds. So I lay there, watching Opal breathe, peaceful in her own lumzen dreams.

We awoke on the day of the ball and I felt as if a thousand weights were bearing down on me, my thoughts muddled with exhaustion. After I forced down my breakfast of mushrooms, Flora and Tarangi presented themselves at my door once again.

As usual, Flora tittered excitedly about the party and Tarangi gazed upon me with a mixture of admiration and sadness.

When I undressed in front of them, both girls went silent. Then Flora began crying. I calmly asked Tarangi to help me to re-dress my wounds with whatever she could find. Fighting her own tears, she obliged.

They dressed me in a gown and mask of Havrok's choosing. A part of the game was that I would be dressed exactly the same as the other women so that the audience couldn't tell who was who. They wanted a mystery, a drama, a spectacle.

The crimson silk draped around me like water. There was a plunging neckline, showing an ample amount of my breasts, the silk draped there, fitted tight around my hips, and then fell to the floor in a cascade, one long silt up mid-thigh. There was a perfumed silk ribbon around my throat to try and conceal my scent and a lacy red mask fit around my eyes.

Tarangi arranged my hair into a long, loose plait and tinted my lips and cheeks red. Lastly, there were soft red slippers.

Looking at myself in the mirror reminded me of the dress I wore the first time I returned to the Quartz Palace to taunt Drake. Even then, I had wanted to seduce him and didn't know why. He had seen the scars on my back and my little seduction act had failed. I wished my sister were here. Her humour had gotten us through the darkest of times after our mother had died.

"How does one keep going when, at every turn, they fail?" I murmured.

Tarangi looked up at me from where she was adjusting my shoe. "Because we have hope that one day it will all be better. That someone will answer our prayers and have the courage to fight."

I smiled at her, my vision going blurry. The courage to fight.

Lightning does not yield.

"He's not going to kill you, is he, Your Highness?" asked

Flora, clasping her hands under her chin. "He wouldn't really do that, would he?"

I swallowed my tears away. "I don't really know," I said honestly.

"But he cares for you," said Flora, sniffing. "I've seen it. He would do anything for you, even if he scares the rest of us. I think it's true love, by the way he looks at you. I think he will love you even if he is a monster."

"How can you tell how he looks at her if his eyes are black all the way around?" asked Tarangi. "I can't see anything in them."

"Well, I can," the younger girl insisted. She nodded earnestly at me. "He will know which one is you right away. And he will whisk you away into his arms and make sweet love to you in your bed."

I snorted and hastily turned it into a cough.

"He wants to do that, doesn't he?" Flora wiggled her eyebrows. "Oh please, I hope it's true!"

"You're a sweet thing, Flora," I said, bopping her on the nose. I didn't have the heart to tell her I highly doubted this was what would happen.

Making love was the last thing a monster did. It would be a ravenous, vigorous, heated type of sex. I could feel that under his skin, Drake was capable of it—wanted it. I might have never had sex myself before, but I had frequented brothels enough to know what sex of all different types looked like. I had looked at it all clinically at the time, never really having known anyone I wanted to try it with.

But I wanted to try it with Drake. I had for awhile now.

The moment Drakus Silverhand had come into my life, the moment I had seen him, everything had changed for me, and I hadn't even known it at the time.

Heat unfurled in me as desire flooded my veins. I shoved it back down right away. Drake would sense my lust immediately and it would make everything worse. I had to keep a cool head.

Flora and Tarangi escorted me to the back of the palace. With my stomach flopping on itself, over and over again, and Opal invisible on my shoulder, I followed them, expecting to be taken to the stadium directly. They instead led me to a little section at the side of the stadium, into a wide garden.

The battering noise of the crowd inside the stadium made my heart gallop in my chest like a raging stallion. I clenched my fists, as another wave of pain from the wounds on my back stabbed at me.

Two guards stood on either side of a wall-off section.

"In there, Your Highness," Tarangi whispered, nervously glancing around us.

I turned to my two companions.

"Thank you, girls," I said, suddenly wanting to hug them.

Tarangi took my hand and kissed it and Flora, to my surprise, began crying anew. "It's alright," I whispered.

Tarangi's eyes became shiny as she pulled me away from the guards' listening ears and whispered, "Your Highness, if you figure out a way to get out of here, you'll take us with you, won't you?"

Her voice was so earnest and desperate I almost broke down into a sob right there and then. But I swallowed it all down and forced myself into a midwife-cool voice. "When I find a way, I'll be taking you two and *everyone* back to their homes."

"I want to stay with *you*," Tarangi said.

"Me too!" cried Flora before clamping a hand over her mouth.

I nodded firmly. "Whatever you like. But I'm sure your parents are looking for you too."

Tarangi nodded in an absent way, her eyes searching mine. One of the guards barked at us and we all jumped.

"I'd better go, but I will see you afterwards, all right?"

They nodded eagerly.

"And...just be watchful for...anything and everything." What I didn't say was, if we *all* were getting out of here, it was going to be an all-out bloody massacre. There were too many demons and too many humans. I smiled at them with a confidence I wasn't sure I felt. "Off you go, see you soon."

They trotted off in a hurry, casting worried looks back at me. Once I'd lost sight of them, the roar of the crowd filled my consciousness again and I strode into the walled garden.

I was met with an oasis of colour. The grass was lush, and hundreds of flowers of all colours dotted the bushes.

Milling around were a group of young women, roughly my height and build. To my horror, I saw that they all wore wigs to match my wavy plait and had all been *painted*. The girls nervously touched each other's bronzed skin, painted the exact shade as mine.

I reached out and touched the petal of a pink rose and felt its fibrous texture. It wasn't a real rose at all. Rather, it was made out of some type of cotton material. Looking around, I realised the entire garden was fake. Opal cooed quietly from my shoulder and I knew she was surprised to see an illusion of a different form.

"Rather impressive, isn't it?" drawled a throaty voice from behind me. I slowly turned around to see the Lord of Gold, Braxus, leering at me in his party wear. A bare chest, loose flowing pants, and a sash that he wore over one shoulder, around his back, and draped over the opposite forearm. His eyes, which were fixed greedily on me, quickly flicked left, then right before lunging at me.

But I had been trained from toddlerhood by first my mother, then Jerali Jones, the best armsmaster in the human realm. I darted out of his grip, leaving him to stumble, almost falling face-first onto the dirt.

"You little—"

I ran, bolting into the group of girls, sending them shrieking. There was no battle for me to win here. Braxus would have his way if he could get to me, but it was just my luck that thirty-odd girls had been made to look exactly like me.

Making my way deep into the group, Braxus was forced to retreat, cursing about Ellythians and their wiles.

The girls moved glumly about. I tried to ignore their nervous murmurs as the sounds of a cheering and stomping crowd were all we could hear.

I was suddenly very aware of Opal on my shoulder. Drake would sniff her out immediately and know which one I was. But did I *want* him to find me? That assessment would have to be made when he appeared in his true form. I needed to see how he was first—if he was a real threat to me or not. But it didn't matter. Drake himself had said that he would need to stay away from Opal lest he didn't think kindly of her.

Turning away from the girls so they wouldn't see me apparently talking to myself, I said, "I think you should hide in the garden, Ope."

She made a sound that told me she didn't want to.

"It's safer. Go on. Come find me when this is over."

She warbled miserably but slipped off my shoulder all the same.

A few minutes later, the warriors strode through the garden and we parted like a wave to let them through. They opened the partition in the stadium wall and herded us into a dark, low ceilinged corridor. The guards shoved us all through, and with flaming torches, one of them led the way, deep into the corridor.

"All on the square! Stay within the lines or yer fallin' off!"

We hurried to comply, squeezing into a tight group on the wooden slab on the ground. For some reason, it felt like we were going to our deaths. Sacrificed in some weird ritual. I suppose in reality, that's what it was.

Two guards hefted a lever and, all at once, a panel in the ceiling above us opened and we all gasped as blinding light streamed through.

The wooden slab jerked and shakily began to rise. One of the girls shrieked but we held ourselves tightly together as we were risen on the platform right through the floor of the stadium. I blinked as millions of quartz lights blinded my eyes and cool air brushed my face. The platform continued to rise above the stadium floor and into the air, before shuddering to a stop.

Once my eyes adjusted to the light and the crowd's beating and screaming, I saw Havrok's penchant for theatrics on full display.

Stationed near the front of the group, on the platform above the grounds, I could see quite clearly into the area below. The landscape was more like a savage version of an obstacle course. Back at home, Jerali Jones made the soldiers work through a series of obstacles made out of wood that was designed to make them stronger and prepare their bodies for battle.

But this wasn't intended to push the person using it. Rather, it looked like its purpose was to kill them. The entire course spanned about one hundred paces. From my position, I saw Drake right away.

He was bound to a high-backed chair, his wrists chained to the armrest. He wore only loose, black pants, leaving his muscled chest bare for all to see the curling tree branch tattoos around his biceps and chest. His eyes were closed as if he were in meditation, which was probably a good idea— trying to concentrate on anything but what was about to happen. Six demon warriors stood behind him and at their centre stood a shackled Dacre Liversblood, tattooed face looking grim with his instrument pouch in hand.

Between us stood one hundred paces of murderous intent divided into five sections.

In the first, closest to Drake, prowled two snarling beasts. I had only seen lions in pictures before, but these were gross mutations of them. I knew that because, although they bore the head of a lion, complete with a mane and snarling face, these creatures were also twice the size of a regular lion, grey skin stretched over rippling muscles. They paced back and forth, irritable and aggressive.

The second compartment contained five demonic warriors, standing surefooted and silent, each with two swords in hand, one with two axes. There were large boulders scattered here as if to provide some barrier to ease out the fight.

The third and middle compartment contained four naked human women swaying as if drugged. One was a full Ellythian with deep mahogany skin, one looked mixed race, like me, with bronzed skin, and the other two were pale-skinned. The obstacle here was clearly one of seduction and it made my throat close up to think of it.

Would I have to watch Drake having sex with other

women? Would his monster form take over to such an extent that he just couldn't help himself? I really hoped not because even the thought of it had me wanting to vomit. I didn't think that was a memory I could ever get out of my mind.

The final compartment before mine made me frown because the three rectangular shapes, which I took to likely be cages, had been covered with heavy canvas that had been chained down. I was guessing that something awfully dark was going to be revealed when Drake got to this section.

Tearing my eyes off Drake, still sitting with his eyes closed on his platform, I looked into the stands where the spectators all sat. The lower levels were comprised of minor demons, both male and female, their strange features and animalistic shapes revelling and bucking in the entertainment that was to come.

In the upper levels sat demons that had more human shapes. The demonic nobility from around Havrok's kingdom all wore elaborate masks and clothing made of a multitude of materials. Dresses of silk, chiffon, and furs, masks with glittering jewels, feathers, and sequins.

Human slaves were delivering the nobility alcohol while to the side, demon musicians began to play anharmonic melodies that strained my ears, on string and wind instruments I had never seen before.

Sitting high above them all was Havrok on his throne, drinking deeply from a goblet. Glacine sat next to him in a white dove mask and white jewelled gown— as if she were an innocent debutante.

Havrok's five other lords sat slightly beneath him, all with their first concubines sitting on their knees, wearing elaborate, shining costumes and beautiful masks.

Oddly, Havrok's throne had been pushed to the side,

allowing for a centrepiece throne to sit as emperor above everyone. It was made of twisted black wood with odd little red veins curling all around it.

Within minutes of our group of fake Sarayas arriving, Havrok abruptly rose from his throne and made a signal. The musicians stopped playing, but one of them picked up a large demonic horn and played six flat notes.

Quiet descended over the entire arena. Even the minor demons immediately froze in their spots.

Every single one of the nobility rose in a cascade of colour and silk. They cast their eyes downwards and a palpable tension rose, making the very air go taut. Two girls next to me shuffled nervously and grasped each other's hands.

Just as I began to wonder what was going on, a dark power swept over the arena, suffocating us all.

25
SARAYA

It was as if the very air had been sucked out of the arena, the oxygen had been replaced by a malodorous blanket.

It was the odour of rotting flesh mixed with the smell of something burning.

A malefic being appeared on the black throne and I had no doubt in my mind that this was the Green Reaper. *This* was the being who had ordered the demons to steal and collect human magic for the last century.

He appeared as a narrow-shouldered male in a black robe that covered him from neck to toe. But above his collar was no visible head. Instead, a blazing emerald green fire burned, verdant flames licking viciously up into the air. Rotten hands rested on the ends of the armrests. He very clearly nodded, slowly, just once.

Havrok sat back down and everyone else followed suit. He raised his hand to signal to the musicians and a large demon began beating on drums with a fast beat. Just when I thought the beat couldn't get any faster, the drummer abruptly cut it off. Havrok stood and bowed to the Green

Reaper, who remained still in his seat, although the flames of his head crackled and spat.

"Drakus Silverhand, Lord of the Kill, will finally, today, put aside his fae heritage and assume his rightful form. The monster is ready to be unleashed and we will all bear witness to the spectacle event!"

The crowd cheered and clapped, although it seemed a little strained, affected no doubt by the presence of the Green Reaper, sitting like murderous death on his throne above them all.

"Fae mage, commence the unbinding ritual!"

The crowd cheered once again as Dacre was prodded forward by his guard. He said something to Drake, who, with his eyes now open, replied.

Dacre nodded and knelt on the floor, taking out a quill, the end of which finished at a knife-sharp point. I held my breath as he began where he finished last time, at the point where Drake's tattoos were thickest and darkest.

Blood welled and spilled in a long line down Drake's bicep, and I found I could not take my eyes away, even from such a distance. But after a moment, the musicians began their music, a slow and melancholy beat, and I found myself searching Drake's face. I couldn't tell where exactly his all-black gaze was looking—but I knew he was looking for me. His vision was good, but with me standing in the second row behind a line of girls, I didn't know if he'd be able to find me that easily.

"This is it!" one of the girls murmured to my left. "I wonder if the change will be obvious."

"Do you think he'll attack us?" someone asked nervously.

"No," jeered another as if that were the stupidest thing

she'd ever heard. "He'll be horny for his mate. He'll probably try and lift your dress!"

Giggles. Stupid, imbecilic giggles.

"Which one is the real Saraya anyway?" someone piped up. "Speak up! Where are you?"

"It's me," came a high-pitched voice down the back.

"No, it's me!" cried another.

Dear Goddess, some of these girls had been living down here for so long that they had no idea what the real world was like. That this *wasn't* normal. That they deserved full and happy lives of their own choosing. But I knew many of them had been born down here, they had no way of knowing any different.

As Dacre worked and more blood dripped, my eyes searched the stands. I avoided the green flames that always seemed to be at the side of my eye, but I quickly found Sarone and the other two Ellythian girls who were Havrok's favourites. They were in their regular positions, kneeling, but a little behind Glacine. As I watched, Glacine leaned down and backhanded Sarone.

Anger twisted in me, thick and sharp. But from the little I could see, Sarone had no reaction to give to Glacine, and I'm sure that infuriated her even more. My heart lifted. If anyone could lead these human slaves in a coup, it was Sarone. They trusted her, loved and admired her. If the time came to take action, I would need her by my side quickly.

Looking back at Drake, his fists were now clenched, a fine sheen of sweat over the hard planes of his naked abdomen. Dacre had unbound the tattoos of the right side of his chest and was now cutting away at the left. The thick solid black lines were now fine lines of swirling tree branches, but

235

somehow now they looked jagged and vicious. I couldn't imagine the pain he was in.

Dacre cut the final lines before my very eyes. Drake's head immediately dropped onto his chest as if he'd fainted or fallen asleep. The mage quickly stepped away, wildly gesturing to the warriors to get back.

Havrok stood from his throne, and the music cut off. "Lord of the Kill!" he called. "Come forth, take up your true form!"

The warriors were quite clearly hurrying down the steps away from the platform as fast as they could.

Drake twitched a little and then slowly lifted his head. The fine capillaries around his eyes turned inflamed and dark.

When he opened his eyes, they were no longer a fixed black all the way around. They swirled with specks of silver light.

An animalistic rumble sounded from deep within his chest, his teeth bared in a feral snarl.

My heart hammered, threatening to tear free from my chest. I was pulled towards him like a fish on a line such that I leaned forward into the girl in front of me. She was so fixated on Drake that she didn't even shove me away.

We watched on as Drake roared into the arena, straining every muscle on his body. I held my breath as his arms pulled at the solid metal chains binding him to the stone chair. He turned crimson with rage and the stone began to crack under his strength.

As if they had anticipated this, more warriors hauled on pulleys from below, similar to the ones we had in the quartz quarry. They dropped Drake into the first section of the obstacle course that came before the lion-monsters. Just as they did, Drake tore free of his chains with a snarl. The stone armrests of the chair crumbled and the chains snapped, falling useless to the floor.

Someone opened a sliding door between the two compartments, and seeing the exit, Drake rushed through, right into the waiting monsters' den.

I gripped the shoulder of the girl in front of me. We were all watching, fixated now, as Drake stood in front of the lions and cocked his head. But the lions didn't attack. Both merely fell to their bellies in submission.

The lump that had appeared in my throat eased a little as a talkative girl in our group gasped loudly. "Oh my God, they're letting him go!"

"What is going on?" someone else said. "Why are they not attacking him?"

I swore internally as Havrok gestured to someone next to the second compartment, and this door slid open from the top.

Drake headed into where the five demon warriors stood in fighting stances. They rushed at him all at once. But Drake was fast, so incredibly fast that I couldn't see what exactly he was doing. All I saw was one warrior fall to his knees, his head bent at an odd angle, the second was disemboweled, the third's chest was opened and his heart flew across the compartment, the fourth attempted to run, but a sword skewered him through the neck. The fifth held his hands up in submission, but Drake crushed his skull against the earth.

I tensed at the raw display of violence. It wasn't something I wanted to see of Drake, even though I knew he was capable of doing it. But with blood all over his hands and five demon warriors scattered over the sand, the crowd roared as if this were the type of spectacle they wanted to see. For a moment, Drake looked up at the crowd in a turn of the head that, in complete antithesis of what he'd just done, was strangely curious.

The third door slid silently open and his head snapped towards it. He prowled through, his stride promising more violence. However, the four naked women were in this compartment, and they waited nervously at the centre.

Drake halted as he entered and we watched him take each woman in, his breathing deep as if he were scenting them. One of them tentatively stepped forward, the full-blooded Ellythian girl, and Drake's head swivelled to pay full attention to her. He stalked forward, hips swaggering in the most masculine way, and I found the backs of my eyes burning. If he took her in this section I—

But Drake pushed angrily past her and waited for the next door to open. Only it did not. Above us, Havrok raised his hand in pause. Hoping, perhaps, Drake would get frustrated and mate with them for a bit of a show. Except when the door didn't open, Drake simply leapt up and scrambled over the wall.

Magic twinkled above the compartment wall as if there was some sort of barrier there. Drake snarled angrily, his blue magic enveloping him in a shield, and he pushed through it, throwing himself across the wall and landing on his feet in a crouch on the other side. *On our side.*

Drake looked up and saw our gaggle of red-silked girls standing on the platform and cocked his head again.

Our platform began to lower, and two girls in front of me screamed. We were being lowered to the ground floor, right in front of him. Drake remained in a crouch and sniffed. He turned to look at the covered cages to my left and sniffed again.

Even before our platform reached the ground, girls began

jumping off and tried to flee into the furthest corner of our compartment, huddling amongst themselves. I wondered if I should follow a group and do the same, but then someone yanked off the covers of the cages, and I stopped dead when I saw what was in them.

The first held Lysander, gagged and shackled, wearing only a loincloth.

The second held Slade also gagged, with a slave collar and head-to-toe chains, his chest bare. Next to him was pale-faced, shackled Blythe.

In the third cage, held down by four heavy chains, one for each limb, stood Jerali Jones, snarling like a beast.

A sob escaped me because in the fourth cage sat my father, grey-faced and sitting still in his wheelchair.

"Behold!" cried Havrok. "Friends of Lord Drakus and the human Lobrathian ex-Princess Saraya Voltanius. Watch the Lord of the Kill destroy them!"

Their cage doors magically swung open.

I could barely breathe through the raw pain that now held my body. I wanted to run to my father, to Blythe, to Jerali Jones and tell them I was sorry. To try and protect them. But between them and me stood Drake—who was now walking towards my father's cage.

I wanted to run towards my father, to protect him, but I suddenly realised the air around me was absent of human bodies. The girls had all fled to the sides of the compartment, and I stood alone in the middle. But Drake wasn't paying attention to me at all, as I thought he would.

Instead, he stood in front of my father's cage and outstretched a broad hand. Before my very eyes, sickly blue streaks streamed from my father, through the air and straight into Drake. A vile blue colour appeared under Drake's skin, from his throat down his chest. Sweat gleamed across Drake's torso and his breathing was heavy but steady.

The realisation of what he was doing was like a vice around my heart.

Drake was taking my father's poison into himself.

I looked back at my father with a gleaming hope rising in me. A hope I dare not let myself fall into. But as I watched, my father blinked, and his brows knitted together.

An expression he had not made for months.

Without warning, from above me, a powerful force grabbed my body in a tight magical grip. I gasped in shock, looking into the stands. But my vision went black and I was sucked into an abyss, and the only thing I saw was the glint of a verdant flame.

When I opened my eyes, I was enclosed in four walls of darkness with an oily smoke coiling around the edges of things.

I knew this was the astral realm, but not in the way that I'd ever been in it. This was a dimension unto itself, a creation of someone powerful. A space above and beyond the earthly plane.

The Green Reaper appeared before me, and this close, I could see that his robe was not black. Instead, it was a green so dark it only appeared black. But here, his green flaming head was no longer present and I immediately saw why he would choose that form instead of *this*.

The only thing set into the smooth skin of his face were eyes. Three pairs of blinking eyes set beneath each other. Each one was blood red all the way through. And of his pale ears, the fae tips had been brutally slashed off, and the raw angle was such that it made me suspect he had done it himself.

I wanted to vomit.

When he spoke to me, it was mind to mind in a voice that grated upon the folds of my brain.

"I see you, Saraya Voltanius. I see what you are. I see what you fear."

Images were forced into my mind. The faces of my friends, dead, Drake dead in my arms, my father dead, Glacine laughing.

"Your mate is healing your father. But what use will it be if I do this?"

The astral plane disappeared around me like evaporating smoke, and jarringly, I was back in the real world. Invisible hands held my head and forcefully turned it to look at my father sitting in his wheelchair.

A blood-red line appeared around my father's throat, and slowly, so slowly, his head tipped off his neck and rolled to the ground.

I couldn't hear the scream that erupted from my throat. My world came collapsing around me. That knot I had folded myself into to keep my mind together suddenly unravelled.

"I want to see what you're capable of, Warrior Midwife. What would happen if I took these off? I will be watching.*"*

My shackles clanked as they fell off. The world felt lighter, and I knew the Green Reaper had left.

My magic rushed back to me in a tsunami of sheer, trembling power. All I wanted, was to destroy.

26

SARAYA

The first thing I saw was Drake. Power crackled in my arteries, desperate to be unleashed, but everything else inside me froze for a moment. I took off my mask and threw it to the dirt.

Drake was standing in front of me, staring with radical concentration at my face with those silver twinkling black eyes. The power emanating from him was like nothing I'd felt before, like the heat that burned in the fires of hell. Ripples of raw, violent magic made the particles in the very air around us tremble. It hit me in the chest so hard I could barely breathe. The sensation completely disabled me.

But my magic responded in kind, spiralling upwards and outwards, meeting him, drawing him in. To my surprise, static electricity rippled in my fingers.

Drake did something that I did not expect. He raised a large hand and brushed my cheek with his fingers as if marvelling that I was standing there before him. I realised with a pang that he was holding his breath, and so was I.

"Drake," I whispered.

Something blue caught my eye and I saw the evidence of the poison he'd taken from my father swirling eerily under the skin of his chest. Tears brimmed in my eyes as heat rose in me. My father was dead. Both my parents had now been murdered.

Drake abruptly raised his other hand and cupped both my cheeks, leaning down to press his forehead against mine.

When he whispered, his voice was a guttural rasp so deep it made the hairs on my arms raise on their ends. "I would destroy the entire world for you."

Before I could react, he was gone. In one swift movement, he leapt onto my father's cage and then, with impossible agility, into the crowd.

The demon nobility screamed, scattering to get away from Drake. But Drake was preternaturally fast and leapt up to Havrok's throne within seconds.

Then they were all running for their lives.

Because Drake had leapt onto the armrests of Havrok's throne and ripped the demon king's head clean off.

Then it was chaos as everyone tried to escape the arena. Warriors swarmed towards Drake, but they did not realise that the Green Reaper had taken off *my* shackles.

My forehead grew hot and I imagined my Priestess mark was becoming visible. With a dark smile that I had never before felt on my face, I raised my hand to the demonic sky. Electricity jolted through me, a shrieking and violent sort of energy that seemed at once familiar and foreign.

My blood sang because my ancestors had once done this, and now the world would see this type of power wielded by a human again. The first thing I did was turn off the pain from the wounds on my back and rapidly knit together the slowly healing gash on my thigh.

Then, I raised my hand and manifested my blade. It appeared with a crack of static, humming with a new electric intensity.

As quickly as I could, I ran to a stunned Jerali Jones and cut down my armsmaster's chains. They fell away with sparks of light as my sword struck them. I could see numerous wounds marking Jerali's skin, but once my old armsmaster was free, Jerali leapt forward with a snarl, looking for someone to fight.

There would be time to catch up later.

I went to Lysander and cut down his chains too, followed by Slade and Blythe, who lunged to hug me. But we had no time to speak as demons bolted towards us. Their captains were shouting orders, but the screams of the nobility drowned them out because Drake, like a completely rabid animal, was up in the stands killing whoever came at him with his bare hands.

A contingent of demon warriors came for us, led by a captain. Whether it was the sheer anger sparking in me or the fact that my priestess magic had just been returned, when I reached out with my mind and felt the consciousness of all ten demon warriors, I was able to wipe them out with one mental, electrical blow. They all collapsed to the ground, their weapons clattering out of their hands. My four friends behind me wasted no time. They surged forward and grabbed two swords each, and whirled around to find Drake.

I turned and saw the body of my father, still sitting in his wheelchair.

All I could do was scream with rage.

Lightning crackled out of my palms, and I suddenly understood the power of my father's ancestors.

Lightning does not yield. And the lotus had been patient for a while now. *This* was my time.

I ran for Drake, who was now being swamped by a horde of warriors who clearly didn't know what else they could do but try to attack the monster who had killed their king.

Although Glacine had done what she did best and was no where in sight, Sarone and the other two Ellythian slaves had remained frozen on their knees by the throne, the severed head of Havrok lying in front of them. But their focus was on me. Jerali, Lysander, and Slade ran behind me, striking and stabbing anyone who came up to them. But there was still a huge contingent flowing towards Drake, still fighting on the stands, his blue magic flashing as he fought.

That mad, crackling power lit up both my hands and my sword. Without even thinking, I directed my left palm towards the demon warriors in front of me.

White-hot lightning flashed so brightly it burned my own eyes. It sizzled across the stands, and when it faded, thirty warriors fell to the floor, dead.

"That's a handy power," I heard Slade mutter from behind me.

The demons behind them cried out and surged towards me. My sword, now imbued with lightning, crackled as I slashed at the first, but the power in it was such that when his sword met mine, he flew backwards with the flash. Demons recoiled from the blast before surging towards me. But with each strike, my sword blasted demons through the air over and over again. Before long, I had cut a path through the mass and reached Drake, fighting warriors on the other side of Havrok's throne.

I flew for Sarone and the other two girls. "Grab a sword. Fight. We're breaking Havrok's kingdom apart today."

Sarone leapt up and grabbed my arm.

"Something isn't right," she said. "Why would the Green Reaper let us do this?"

"We don't have time to think about it," I said, then turned to Jerali, who just turned around having stabbed a demon. "Help Sarone free the slaves and gladiators," I instructed. "Take them through the quarry portal to Kaalon. The city is under an illusion. Osring will take you in."

The armsmaster grabbed my wrist, grey eyes intent on me. "I tried to take the palace back. There were just too many demons. But aren't you coming with us?"

I shook my head, looking at Drake unflinchingly strike and cut countless warriors. "I need to get him help," I said. "He won't be any good in the human realm like this. You guys need to get out of here and see what forces can be brought together."

"You need to take him to his mother," Lysander said with a grunt as he felled his own demon. "Go straight to the border of Black Court and Obsidian. He'll know the way."

"Will he?" Slade asked darkly.

We all turned to look at Drake and we saw the rabid monster he had become, a creature made for violence. How would he be after the fight?

"I'll be fine," I said, not entirely sure if I meant it.

Something clawed up my leg. To my relief, it was Opal, wide-eyed and stuttering with fear. I took her in my palm.

"Opal, I need you to go with them."

She shook her head and made a sound that told me a sad *no.*

I gestured to the fighting that was going on around me. "You know it's the right thing to do, Ope. They'll need your help to get out of the portal. There's too many humans to save. We'll meet again, I promise."

She cast me a wistful look before turning and leaping onto Jerali's shoulder.

"We're acquainted." Jerali patted Opal on the head. "Are you sure about this, Sara?"

"Go," I urged. "We'll deal with these ones. There'll be more inside."

Jerali Jones saw that my decision had been made. And Goddess bless my armsmaster because Lysander, Sarone, and the other two Ellythians all followed Jerali, wielding their swords like they'd been born for it, heading back into the palace. Slade had a protective arm around Blythe as they ran, but I barely had time to ponder that.

I turned to fight beside Drake, whose eyes seemed to take me in for a fleeting moment before he continued chopping down the rest of the horde. I flew at the remaining guards, my lightning blade flashing again and again.

Eventually, the rest of the demons scattered, running away from us instead. But Drake's bloodlust wasn't sated because he ran after them, pouncing upon the shoulders of one, knocking him to the ground and ripping his head off. I groaned in irritation as I sprinted after him as he bounded into the palace, clearly looking for more demons to slay.

Watching him carve a bloody path through the black marble halls, I realised that he had some type of reason or logic to his actions. He wasn't just blindly killing everyone. Female slaves cowered against the walls when we came upon them, but he ignored them completely.

"Gather in front of the palace," I called to them. "You are leaving. Sarone will come get you!"

And then we came upon the Lord of Feast, Lysander's demon lord, shouting through his pig-like snout in the red light of the entrance hall. A circle of demon guards had gathered around him and his first concubine. Drake prowled into the hall, with me close behind.

The demon lord's brown eyes flashed when he saw us. "Get him, you fools!" Feast shouted at the demons. "Your king commands it!"

I could have rolled my eyes. Naturally, he had decided to take up Havrok's crown for himself. Drake merely snarled and in a blur of movement, began throwing demons across the room. I took the left flank, blasting lightning and striking with my sword.

Within a minute, the Lord of the Feast was staring blankly at Drake and me, advancing on him. His concubine fled outside. I was about to tell Feast to leave when Drake let out a mad growl and flew at the demon, taking him by the collar.

"No one touches Lysander," he snarled. He twisted Feast's head and it broke with a sickening crack. He thudded to the floor, eyes glazed over.

Drake prowled the entrance hall, but it was empty. I cast an eye around, but a majority of the warriors seemed to have either fled or had been killed at the arena. Havrok's palace forces had been decimated.

In that case, I trusted Lysander, Slade, and Jerali to take care of the hundred-odd slaves that were in this palace and lead them to safety. They would do their job as best as they could. Then, there was only one thing left for me to do.

I approached Drake tentatively.

"Let's go, Drake," I said softly. "Lysander said we should go to see your mother."

He froze, his back facing me, and then turned around so slowly that I held my breath. I evaporated my lightning sword as his swirling eyes appraised me. Swallowing the lump in my throat and holding out my hand, I said, "Will you take me to your home?"

27
DRAKE

My mind was a thunderous storm. There was a roaring in my ears that felt like an untethered hurricane and a raucous sheet of rain pounding upon me that urged me to move.

It had come on slowly. As pain sliced through the layers of my skin, something uncoiled around my mind, like a python unravelling after a long sleep.

What came out had taken over.

All I wanted to do was kill, maim and destroy. And, of course, find my mate and claim her as mine. It was a burning sort of yearning that pulled me forward, guided by pure instinct. As long as I found her, everything would be alright. The darkness would go away.

But several things had stood between her and me, so I knocked them away and found her. When I laid my eyes on her, not her physical form, but her energy, the shape of her magic, something seemed wrong.

There were two things that needed fixing.

The first thing had been, that someone tied to her by blood

had been bound with poison. So I took the poison, because I knew I could.

The second issue had been a black smoking something sitting on the throne high above us. I knew I needed to get rid of it at all costs, and that had been that. Anything that affected my mate would be destroyed. There had been some magic on that shadow's arm that had tried to influence me, but it hadn't realised that nothing could control me now.

And now it was all done, all I could smell was *her*. My mate was a sweet torture that filled me up with *need*. A need to consume her.

But a kernel of thought struck me as I looked into those emerald eyes. It suddenly reminded me of home, a single leaf I had seen growing from a stray rose bush. But it was my mate's words that were pushing me to think something.

"Go to your home...Black Court...Obsidian Court."

I honed in on the sounds her mouth was making.

"Drake?" Her lips were like honey around my name, and I could not help but lean towards her. I wanted to hear her say my name again.

"Saraya?"

"Yes, it's me." Her voice held a note of sharpness. She was impatient with me, I realised through the storm that was my mind. Why was my mate impatient with me? That was bad. I should be paying more attention.

"Drake!" Her voice cut through the storm like a lightning strike. Within her magical presence, I saw that my mate had the power of lightning now. Her eyes were narrowed upon me, her face, stern. My strong, strong mate. I shook my head in confusion, trying to clear the water out of my ears.

What did she want me to do?

"Go to your home." Her voice came from far away, but the

hand she placed around my wrist was very much real and close. Her soft warmth pulsed through me, and I could feel her heart hammering in her chest. Feel the breath that went in and out of her. She pulled my arm, and I let her move me wherever she wanted me to go.

Then we were outside again and the scent of reptiles came towards me over the cacophony of smell that was the blood and flesh of demons. The huge lizard-like creatures scented me and pranced nervously, but one of them fell to his knees with a knowing huff. I recognised him and understood his mind.

On. Travel. Go. The reptile was thinking. *Over sand.*

I made a sound to reassure it and my mate swung herself onto the creature. I swung up after her, possessively tugging her closer to me.

She squirmed in protest, but I wasn't letting anyone take her from me again. She was mine now, forever. The flesh of her thigh was now exposed because of the clothing she wore. Gooseflesh puckered all over her skin, and I placed a hand on it to try and warm her. She expelled her breath forcefully, but at that moment, the reptile groaned and got to its feet, and I had to place my arms around her curved body to stop her from falling off. The beast began to walk onwards and I sensed it was heading for the last place it had taken us.

"Wait!" my mate cried.

The beast ceased its movement and my mate tried to look back at me. I tried to look at her face to sense what she was trying to communicate, but underneath the clouds dampening my mind, there was a need to take her…home. So, though her words were not clear, I settled on the Black Grove, my childhood home.

I instructed the beast to turn southeast and follow its nose to where there was water that tasted like light. The beast obliged and ambled off.

WE RODE FOR ONE HOUR, AND THAT ENTIRE TIME, I SAT CONTENT, my nose in my mate's hair, my body flush against her softness. Her magic caressed me in a pleasurable way. It was seeking me out as well and I took great pleasure in that fact. But her physical body, on the other hand, sat still and hunched as if burdened by something.

And then I remembered that back at the arena, I had recognised her sire and taken the poison from him, as was my duty to my mate's family. But he had been killed anyway.

My sire had been lost to death as well. I wanted to comfort her, so I nuzzled into her neck, and her muscles loosened, leaning into me, and she made a pleasurable sound. But all at once, she sat upright and pushed me away with her back.

I frowned the rest of the way to the portal.

When we reached the Dead Forest, Saraya stiffened in front of me.

"Do not be afraid," I said.

She flinched. "I am *not* afraid, *Drakus*. And if I was, I wouldn't let you know."

Drakus. That's right, that was what they called me. The name my mother had given me. How could I have forgotten that?

So I smiled at my mate's back as the beast let us down. Patting him on the snout, I instructed him to return to his home because that's where his food was. He agreed and began the travel north.

I walked back to my mate, who was staring at the tall scraggly trees that plunged like blades into the black sky. I scented a few dark creatures in the air, so I reached for her hand. She took it with a sigh, and I could tell immediately that she wasn't happy about the hand. I wondered if it was because of the dried demon blood still on it.

Hesitantly, I let go of her but made sure she was by my side as we headed into the forest. The blood would be washed off within moments anyway.

The creatures that were lurking nearby fled at the sight, or at the scent of me. I sensed them moving away from the vicinity with amusing haste.

When we reached the spangled tree which contained the portal, I leaned forward and whispered a word of command into its bark. The ancient tree groaned in reply before a trickle of water began running down its trunk. Within seconds, the trickle became a flood of water that sparkled with its own white light.

"Where is it coming from?" My mate was squinting up into the branches. But I had no idea where the water came from, so I merely grabbed her around the waist, and jumped straight into the water.

She had no time to react as the water pounded down on us for a single second before we landed on the grass on the other side, completely dry. I had managed to land, pulling her on top of me. She now quickly scrambled off my body, giving me a dark look.

We were at the foot of the Silent Mountains on the Black Court side. From there, it was an hour's walk to the Black Grove, and we walked the entire way in comfortable silence.

When we reached our home, I marvelled at how little of it

had changed. The smell of dark lilies and silver ferns filled my nose, fae mice scurried in the undergrowth.

Old memories flapped at the back of my mind like ravens trying to get my attention. But I would not let them. Nothing had changed since I had last been here, some five years ago, when I had left to find my fortune out in the real world. There had been an itch I could not scratch and I had searched the entire fae realm for peace and never found it. I now knew why. I had been looking for my mate.

But Saraya was in front of me now. She reached up, put her small hands on either side of my face, and I closed my eyes to relish the feeling of her.

But her voice was urgent. "*Drake.* I know you're in there somewhere. Come out and play with me."

My eyes flew open to see a beautiful smirk on her lips. And it was like the clouds parting for the sunlight as a clarity whipped through me like a cold wind. The roar of the storm faded.

Just a little.

"Saraya." I smiled at her, and she scowled back at me.

"Look up," she said, pointing to the sky.

I obliged and saw, for the first time in seven years, a black sky filled with stars. Thousands upon thousands of them.

A finger reached up and closed my jaw that was hanging open. I grabbed her hand and held it to my chest so she could feel how fast my heart was beating. "I haven't seen this since I was a child...since..."

"Dacre bound you and the clouds came," she said.

I looked at her. "You're finally here," I breathed. "Finally with me in my home."

"Your eyes sort of look like that, did you know?" she said, touching the skin at the edge of my eyes.

I leaned into her, her beauty making my breath hitch. "Like what?"

"Like little stars. I wonder why."

"Maybe it's because I'm looking at you."

"Haha. You could never be a poet, Drake, did you know?" She turned around as if to inspect the Grove. "When Dacre first started with the procedure, your eyes were closed. What were you thinking about?"

I frowned, trying to push my mind to think about something from *before*. It was almost like I was a different person then. A different creature entirely. What *had* I been thinking about before my true mind emerged unbound? When the answer came, I grinned at her smugly.

"I was thinking about you, of course."

But I didn't tell her that I'd been thinking of plunging myself deep inside of her, thrusting into an oblivion of pleasure while she groaned sweetly under me.

She turned and crossed her arms. "They told me you'd want nothing more than to mate with me. That you would force me to—am I in danger from you?"

I recoiled from the question as if she'd stabbed me with her own blade. But I remembered that *before*, the fae side of me had been worried that I *would* actually harm her. I slashed my hand through the air to help her understand how serious I was. "Never. I could never *harm* my mate. It is my sole duty to stop anyone from doing that."

It was my sole duty to pleasure her for the rest our days.

She gave a long sigh that moved her shoulders, and I felt such a strong urge to move towards her that I let myself take a single step. She was still unsure of me, even though her magic and her body gave her true feelings away. She wanted me as much as I wanted her. I wondered what type of noises she would make as she came. But she was speaking again and I had to pay attention.

"The Green Reaper came to me in the astral realm," she said earnestly. "He gave my magic back, provoked me. He *wanted* us to kill Havrok, but why?"

Politics was not something my mind wanted to fathom right now. It wanted to go to bed, to lie with Saraya on my chest. To eat suppleberries and see her tongue go bright pink with the juice. But my mate was asking me about something important and I had to wrangle my mind into submission. So instead of thinking about Saraya's tongue, I thought about where we had come from. And the old man who had lain in a tomb under my mother's tree for fifty-odd years.

"It's likely that he wanted a new ruler over that kingdom. Perhaps he was not happy with Havrok."

She nodded as if she thought I was going to say that. So my mind moved to more important matters. "Are you hungry?"

28
SARAYA

The Black Grove was like some twisted version of a forest in a fairy-tale.

Towering, ancient trees seemed to groan under their own weight. The air smelled of fertile, wet earth and something fuzzy that stroked the inside of my nose. I felt the same on my skin, a delicate buzz of power.

Magic, I realised.

Because this, of course, was the domain of a deity. Drake's mother.

After the dry wasteland that was the demon kingdom, this lush fertility was a pleasant oasis to my eyes. There was a multitude of flowers and fruit trees that liked to dance under their own magic, and Drake seemed to have names for all of them.

He went around to each one, brushing his fingers on rough bark and murmuring to them as if they were old friends. A pang of sadness surprised me, as this person who I'd just seen savagely murder a whole demon military had a childhood so solitary that he'd come to intimately know every blade of grass in this grove. His posture was relaxed, his face soft and his touch gentle.

I followed him through the old trees, the gigantic ferns and fresh blooming flowers that glowed in the dark like a collection of multicoloured quartz crystals. At the same time, I couldn't help but feel like the plants were watching me, not with any malicious intent, but with a sort of curiosity. Stopping to look at a pink rose, I admired the way its edges were limned with light. It was mesmerising and eerie all at the same time. Suddenly, it turned towards me of its own accord and startled, I jumped back.

Drake was by my side within seconds, flicking the rose with his fingers. "They know of you," his voice was a guttural rasp in my ear that made my stomach jolt. I remembered how we'd kissed when he'd been taken away before the Havrok's big event. "They play tricks sometimes."

"Did you...speak to them about me?"

He nodded, then reached for my hand. I let him guide me through his forest home.

"Are you taking me to your mother?" I asked tentatively, glaring at a vine that was wandering too close to me.

He shook his head, grunting. "She is off on travels. I can't feel her here."

I supposed, when she came back, meeting my mother-in-law would be an interesting event. The goddess Umali was one thing—an ethereal creature I could never hope to understand. She only spoke when she needed to and presented herself at the right time. Perhaps this demigoddess was similar in that way. I wondered what she knew of me already.

Drake took us a little way into the forest, and tiredly, I followed. We stopped under a magnificent tree with sprawling branches stretching out so high above us, I couldn't even see the top properly.

Drake pressed my hand against the rough bark and said to me, "Home."

The tree groaned with a rich, earth-deep sound that told me, *welcome*. It gave a shudder, the leaves swooshing above us, and with a little *pop*, dozens of ridges stuck out of the bark, cascading upwards. I remembered Drake had told me he lived in a tree house as a boy.

"It's a ladder!" I exclaimed.

Drake smiled at me, and even with those monstrous, sparkling all-black eyes, he looked ten years younger. I couldn't help but smile back.

A sudden wave of desire flew through me as Drake's eyes zoned in on my lips. I couldn't tell if I was feeling his desire or my own, so I cleared my throat and said, "Should I go up first?"

He shook his head as if coming out of a reverie and nodded.

The rungs were thankfully easy to climb up, and with the pre-dawn light beginning to purple the sky, I hoisted myself up one by one and dared not look down.

"I will catch you, Princess, if you fall," a guttural rasp reassured me from right under my backside. I was about to berate him for his closeness but realised that perhaps he wouldn't understand. In his monster form, he seemed to not appreciate personal boundaries. It was no matter. There would be plenty of time to put him in his place if he got too handsy.

But a nagging feeling at the back of my mind jeered at me. I wasn't really sure if I *wanted* to berate him for being handsy. I'd spent the entire previous night longing for his body to be next to mine. My own hands had skimmed the surfaces where he would often carefully hold me at night. And worse still, I had wondered what it would be like to feel his skin flush against mine, his lips pressed along the parts of me where his eyes often wandered.

Lately, images of what it would be like to have sex with Drake flashed through my mind's eye. He had never pressured me nor pushed for it, although it was supposedly his right as my husband. I'm sure he was thinking about it, and all last night, his distance had made me crave the ultimate version of intimacy with him.

As a result, I had barely slept—and the thought of him being by my side once again made me feel *better*.

These thoughts were as surprising to me as everything that had happened tonight. The tourmaline shackles had been supposed to mask the magic of the mate bond. And what had happened? Even without the mate-magic for that period of time, I couldn't deny that I had *still* cared for him and wanted him close to me. I felt okay that I had been married to him without any say in the matter.

Sometimes, when we were together, it seemed like the rest of the world fell away. I wondered if that was how it had happened between my own parents, a slow-growing of feelings that blossomed into love.

My father. My throat closed over and my hand missed the next rung. I careened sideways with a gasp.

But suddenly, heat enveloped me, strong hands holding me steady and secure. I realised Drake's hard body was somehow *behind* me, holding me in place, both of our feet on the same rung.

I looked down and saw the tree must have intuitively

pushed out its rung, so it had become wider—a sort of landing.

"Goddess," I breathed.

"No, it's me," said Drake honestly.

A choked laugh worked its way out of my throat and managed to turn itself into a sob. I covered my mouth, reminding myself to breathe. But there was nothing I could do about my father. I had stood there while—

Then Drake's arm was around my waist, his lips soft against my neck, giving me tiny kisses. He was comforting me in the best way he could, and I let him, leaning into his warmth, a solidity that promised strength. We just stood there for a moment before I realised how precariously we were balanced so high in the air. I looked upwards and saw the solid floor of the treehouse, with a circular entrance carved into the bottom, so you climbed right up into the centre of it. It was ten steps away.

I cleared my throat. "I'm sorry, this is not the right place to do this. Let's get up there."

Drake kissed the line of my jaw and I wiped my nose on my sleeve, placing a hand on the next rung. Silently, I finished the climb, my thighs burning only a little before I found myself inside a cosy room filled with yellow quartz lights beaming down on me.

I crawled into the room and stood. Drake leapt in behind me. He reached for me, turned me around and pulled me towards him. He took my face in his hands, and to my surprise, his eyes were not black anymore. They were his fae eyes—hazel irises in white sclera.

"Never apologise to me," he whispered, "for showing your true emotions."

A slight warmth spread through me before the face of my

father swam into my mind's eye and raw sorrow chased any warmth away, biting and sour. I don't know how I found my voice, but I had to say what I felt. "You tried to save my father, Drake. Taking on the poison into you." I touched his bare chest where the blue poison still showed, roiling under his skin in slow swirls.

"I knew it would not harm me," he said. "I...knew it would rid him of the illness. For all the good it did, though."

Because my father had been murdered by the Reaper anyway. I swallowed away the lump in my throat, wanting to take this chance to talk to Drake now that his eyes and his mind, too, were clear. "The Green Reaper wanted to force my hand. He wanted to anger me and used my father as a pawn to do it. In the end, my father was so powerless. I can't bear that. What he must think of me—"

"You do him proud every day." Drake brushed his knuckles against my cheek. "You do both your parents proud. You saved those women. I remember hearing you tell that arms master from your home to take them to Kaalon."

"Along with Lysander and Slade, I knew they could do it."

"The armsmaster was hard to capture back in Lobrathia," he admitted. "But do not worry, I will send a raven to find them." He then gestured to the room. "This was the treehouse I made into a home."

I gaped at him for a moment because, looking around the room, it was clear there were rooms branching off the main one. It looked more like a townhouse. "You made this?"

Drake nodded, taking my hand and leading me around. "Mother built the foundation, but I built all the inside components...I had a lot of time on my hands."

I imagined a little boy scuttling down the ladder each day,

playing, and running back home into a refuge that was infinitely safe, building new pieces of it a little at a time. But ultimately, he was always alone.

"There's a kitchen," he said proudly, pointing out a smooth wooden bench, neatly stacked with wooden bowls, spoons, and cutting utensils, covered in dust. "I carved them myself, and here is where I watched the sunrise."

He led me into another room where wood and ferns had been fashioned into a lounge. There was no fourth wall in this room, only a balcony rail and a view of the forest. We were high enough in this large tree that the canopy of the rest of the forest was entirely visible, stretching out as far as the eye could see. As we watched, the dawn sky lazily presented itself in hues of orange and pink.

"It's beautiful," I said.

He squeezed my hand. "I'm going to get some food." He led me out of this room and towards a small hatch in the wall. "This is my slide."

I raised my eyebrows as he opened the hatch, revealing a winding slope made of curved wood.

"You *slide* down this?" I asked, shocked.

He nodded, hazel eyes dancing. "Want to see?"

I stifled a yawn. "If that means I have to climb back up, I'm going to say no."

He frowned in thought. "The elevator broke before I left, but I will fix it."

I marvelled at the fae male standing in front of me, his eyes searching his elaborate treehouse as he thought.

"Can I stay here?" I asked.

His grin was so wide that it showed all of his white teeth. He swept forward and grabbed me, hoisting in into his arms and swinging me around in a wide circle. When he set me back down, my head spun. "I've been waiting for you to say that for my whole life, Princess."

I couldn't help but chuckle.

"I'll be back."

He literally threw himself down the chute.

I sat on the couch, which had been worn smooth with years of use. My eyes prickled with tiredness, and my back began to ache as I eased the numbing off it to give myself a magical rest, and the pain returned, vicious and biting. That chasm between me and those wounds seemed wider and darker than before. I wondered if there would ever be a time where I would be able to breach that gap and heal them. But it was too raw right now, and the pain to bright.

I rested my head on the armrest which I imagined Drake had done in the same way as a boy. He had left this place at fourteen, I remembered, which meant that everything here had been built before then.

In the quiet stillness of the dawn, the only sound was the leaves rustling and the tree creaking. I was truly alone, and I realised that a gaping void lay at the centre of me—the place in my heart where my parents had been. They were both gone now. My only family in the world was Altara, who was safe and far away in Ellythia, perhaps not to be seen again for quite some time.

That thought choked me—to feel truly alone in the world, a vast landscape so big around me. Havrok was dead too. The Green Reaper was probably lurking about, all of this a part of some bigger plan that he had. He said that he knew who I was. That he'd been watching me.

I suddenly sat upright as I realised Drake had said the Green Reaper's crypt was below his mother's tree. This was his home, meaning the tree and therefore the crypt had to be

E.P. BALI

close by. My skin crawled at that realisation and I drew my knees up, hugging my legs close. My magic was back, so that was a positive, along with a strange new power to wield electricity. I would have to test that out and see what more I was capable of. The moon currently sat half full, meaning I still had awhile before I could see Arishnie again and ask her more questions.

A rustling woke me from a doze and I realised I must have fallen asleep, curled up in that same position, as the thought of the Green Reaper crept like shadows across my mind.

But Drake jumped up the ladder of the treehouse, a bundle in his hand and a grin on his face. Any tension in my body melted away. He had that effect on me, I realised. The sight of him had a palpable effect on my muscles.

I was not alone.

He laid out his yield before me, and together we ate his favourite things. Ripe mangoes, which he fed me pieces of, oddities of pink fruits which he called suppleberries along with nuts and seeds, all washed down with cool water from a nearby spring.

Drake tapped his own forehead. "Your Priestess mark is permanent now, did you know? I thought it would go away after awhile, but it hasn't."

Surprise filled me as I touched my own forehead. The centre of it was slightly warmer than the rest. "I had no idea. I guess it needed my magic shackles off to take effect?"

"Seems likely. Everyone will know what you are now."

I nodded absently, a sudden fatigue washing over me.

"I'll go hunting for dinner," he said, licking his fingers. My eyes caught on his mouth, and he paused, a coy smile on his lips.

I shook myself out of the desire lancing through me. "I

266

think I need sleep. You don't happen to have clothes lying around, do you?" I was still wearing the red silk dress from Havrok's spectacle, which was now stained with demon blood and dirt.

He nodded. "It's quick for me to make."

Drake *was* quick to fashion me a long nightdress out of his collection of cotton. He'd been hoarding it for winter months, he told me, but he'd left before he could use it all up.

He showed me his bed, which was a stack of furs and handmade blankets in the corner. With a wave of his hand, his blue magic swirled and the dust was gone, the space refreshed and cosy. He arranged it so we would both fit, which I appreciated, but didn't mention.

We laid down, me on my side. He curled around me, kissing my ear. My stomach turned on itself pleasantly, and somehow, despite everything that had happened, his kisses promised me that maybe sometime in the far future, everything would be better.

29

SARAYA

I woke up, frowning into the darkness. A single orange quartz lamp glowed on a nightstand casting a comfortable glow. I had slept the entire day away.

Stretching, I got out of bed, and with no Drake in sight, I decided to try his ridiculous slide. Barefoot, I made my way to the chute, sat down on the slide, and pushed myself down into the dark. It was impossibly slippery, made slick with some type of lacquer. I sped down, the wind beating at my face and my stomach leaping into my throat. I couldn't suppress the grin as I made out the end of the slide in the dark and, suddenly realising the great speed with which I was approaching the end, let out a little yelp before tumbling out into a bed of soft leaves.

Giggling like a child, I righted myself and turned my face to the night sky. I closed my eyes, feeling the jagged pounding of my heart.

The night was warm, the smell of citrus in the air and the feel of soft moss underfoot. A cool breeze stirred across my skin and, encased in Drake's clothes, the desire to find him came over me, and I wondered what he was doing.

Tentatively, I headed out into the woods, squinting into the dark by the light of glowing flowers. An owl hooted in the distance, but I sensed no threat within the forest—anything malicious had probably run at the first scent of Drake.

It wasn't long before a faint blue light shone through the trees, and curiously, I headed towards it, wondering what sort of strange fae thing I was about to see. Emerging between two ferns, ripples of magnificent turquoise water came into view —a lake glowing with its own light in a clearing. But I halted in my step because Drake was inside the pool, sitting there with a frog in his hand, petting it with a finger.

"Hello, Saraya," he said without looking up.

The cadence of his voice sent a cascade of warm feathers over my body, and I found myself clearing my throat. "Hello."

Drake turned, his rippling muscles shiny with water, and sent the frog into the grass. As it hopped away, I wondered if I should leave him to it, but a single thought stopped me.

I wanted to get in the pool. The space between my thighs tingled.

Drake was not looking at me. Instead, his all dark eyes were turned up to the waxing moon. Before I could stop myself, I pulled off my nightdress. With not a stitch of clothing on, I stepped carefully into the pool. The last thing I needed was to slip right here.

A memory came wandering into my mind. I had done this before. The first time Drake had seen me naked, in fact, was when I was wading into another pool to complete a ritual. But that all felt like a lifetime ago. So much had happened since then.

Drake surged smoothly forward to meet me. He couldn't help himself, and I guess neither could I.

"What are you smiling about?" he breathed.

I realised that I was, in fact, smiling and licked my lips as the surprisingly warm water caressed first my knees, then my thighs, then my waist. When the water lapped at my nipples, I was standing right in front of him. I couldn't help it— a delicious curl of desire rose up my abdomen, and I reached out to touch his chest, where the now hollow lines of black ink met his tanned skin.

"Saraya," he breathed.

"Hm?" With horror, I realised I was unabashedly stroking his chest, and I jerked my hand back. "Sorry, I—"

"No." He grabbed my hand and pressed it against his chest, but on the other side, where I could now feel his heart pounding against my fingers. "I want you to touch me…if…you want to." He swallowed, and I looked up into his starry eyes.

I found myself smiling again. "Your eyes match the sky."

We both looked up at the stars twinkling above us, and I imagined how odd it would be for him to see the night sky now, after seven years of seeing just clouds. I couldn't help but look at his face, the line of his jaw, cleanly shaven, the slope of his nose, the glow of his skin. Since his runes had come off, he looked…more alive. Perhaps more like himself.

"Does it feel better?" I asked. "To be yourself now?"

He looked back down at me and moved a little closer. "What feels better is having you here."

The heat moving in me was almost unbearable. I had to feel his warmth against me. I stepped forward and pressed myself against him, my nipples flush against his smooth skin. He hissed, and both of his muscled arms immediately came around me, holding me close. I tilted my head up to look at him, my breath heavy.

"You take my breath away, Saraya," he whispered before sweeping his lips down and pressing them against mine. I opened for him, sighing in the back of my throat as the feeling of his tongue in my mouth consumed me.

But that only made him hungrier.

He pushed the both of us back to the left side of the pool, where my back came against a soft mossy earthen wall. His kiss turned deeper and I yearned for him to be even closer to me. I spread my legs and curled them around him, running my fingers down the hard planes of his biceps. He growled and kissed his way down my neck. Sweet, burning desire filled my core, and I knew nothing but the sensation of him against me, of his manhood pressing hard against my stomach. "Drake…"

He abruptly lifted his head off my neck and looked at me. "Yes? Is it too much? I'm—"

"No," I said firmly. I pulled his mouth against mine and brushed my lips across his. I pulled back. "I love the feeling of you against me."

"All I can think about is you." His voice was so deep that I felt it in my bones. "But if we continue, I will *have* you, you understand that?"

I nodded and pressed a kiss against his neck. "I know. I want you to have me." He kissed me harder and with an urgency I'd never seen in him before, devouring my lips, my neck, my breasts. When I felt the tip of his manhood pressing at my core, I let out a hiss.

"Saraya," he whispered, his forehead against mine. "I was made to worship you."

Some deep-rooted emptiness in me dissolved and I sucked in a breath as he eased himself into me.

I tilted my head back and moaned as I melted into him, his thick length stretching me out slowly. I had anticipated some measure of pain in having sex for the first time, but this…this was a beautiful sort of burn that melted into a heavenly fullness.

He filled me up so completely the sensation was my whole world. He sucked on my neck and began thrusting himself into my core, slowly at first. Pleasure soaked through every cell of my body, and I wanted nothing but to be filled up by him over and over again.

It was a fulfilling, satisfying sensation that came from this fae monster desiring me as much as I desired him. Of me being the source of his ultimate pleasure. The type of pleasure that made his eyes sparkle with little bursts of light and made his muscles go taut.

The sensation of him finally inside me was everything I hadn't realised I needed. I had needed Drake the first time I had seen him in the entrance hall of my palace. But I had not known that ache in me was for him. His place was with me and mine with him.

I cried out as rivulets of heaven swamped my being, enveloping me so completely I wanted to burst into a million pieces. Drake groaned into my mouth and we moved together, faster and faster, making waves in the water around us.

"I'm going to look into your eyes as I cum inside you, my princess," he whispered.

My sweet release came so abruptly that I gasped his name out loud, clinging onto him for dear life. But he didn't stop, he was ferocious in his desire for me and I could tell he was holding back for fear of causing me hurt. His strokes lengthened as he found his own release, and I tilted my hips to urge him deeper. He pumped into me until he groaned deep in his chest and thrust himself a final time.

I sighed with happiness as our chests heaved, our hearts pounded, and the cool water settled around us like silk. He tilted my chin up and kissed me deeply.

When he pulled back, he whispered against my lips, "You are so perfect, Saraya."

I smiled shyly up at him. "When I'm with you, I feel different."

"Different, how?"

"Like I can do anything."

He looked up at the sky and, smiling, said. "You could do anything without me, Saraya. I think I just remind you of that fact."

A sudden burning on my right hand made me gasp. I inspected my arm, and to my utter and complete shock, light erupted from my fingers up to my wrist. Drake was also startled by a sudden light erupting from his own hand.

Suddenly, he laughed.

I gaped at him and then at my hand. As the light died down something had been marked on to the back of my hand. A twisted black tree, its branches curling up each finger.

It was a magical ink, a delicate mirror of Drake's own tree tattoo.

"It's a mate marking!" Drake chuckled, tracing the fine, curling lines. "Look at mine!" he said excitedly. Sure enough, on the back of his left hand, written over his old tattoo, was a lotus haloed by a crescent moon. I traced my finger along the

273

delicate leaves with a smile. The implication of the marking was clear: I was his, and he was mine.

Drake brought my hand to his lips and kissed my new tattoo. "Our bond needed to be consummated before it was official."

I couldn't help but grin at him.

WE WERE WALKING BACK TO THE TREEHOUSE, HAND IN HAND AND completely naked, when Drake paused and abruptly pulled me to crouch behind a bush.

"Fae larks," he whispered, pushing a fern down so I could see two silver birds flying in an odd pattern around a glittering rosebush. They chirped softly to one another. "They only turn up when…" he cleared his throat. "I used to watch them from these very bushes when I was a boy. The way they flew in concentric circles, it was like I was watching life itself in its rawest form. And I…wondered why I was built to want to take that life away. And then I would think of you, and I knew that I would never harm you, and I knew that there must be good things in the world that were worth living for." He abruptly turned away from them. "I'm sorry, I'm talking too much. Let's go."

"No." His face fell just a little, so I quickly said, "I mean, I like hearing your thoughts. You have a unique way of looking at things."

A slow, playful smile spread across his lips, and he placed his hand over his heart in mock surprise. "Are you…giving me a compliment, Princess? Colour me shocked."

I swatted him on the arm. "Don't get used to it."

30
SARAYA

The next day, Drake and I were digging up wild potatoes from one of his old crop patches when he looked up abruptly, a small frown on his face. "My mother is here."

"Does she often go away?" I asked, brushing off a potato and putting it into a carved wooden bowl.

He nodded, wiping his hands on his pants before offering a hand to me. "Sometimes, she moves about her territory. We should go and pay our respects."

I took his hand and we moved through the forest, my heart pounding at the thought of finally meeting his mother.

As the undergrowth thinned, so did the light, and we came to a small grove shrouded in darkness. The air was frigid with cold, dry enough to crack the skin, and so unnaturally silent that the hairs on my arms stood on end.

Within its eerie heart stood a tree the likes of which I had never seen before. Black as the void, her trunk spanned ten paces across, thick branches curving wickedly upwards, ending in sharp tips that reminded me of Drake's own silver finger blades. She bore no leaf, no sprouting buds. She was all hard edges and thorny sides.

I could not help but think that on this hard ground, beneath which the crypt of the Green Reaper lay, Drake had *played* here as a child. He had been weaned on this very darkness. It was no wonder he was as brutal a monster as he appeared.

But how long had Drake's mother stood sentinel over the Green Reaper's body? Why was the crypt here, and whose side was she on exactly?

Like mist creeping across the twilight, the deity of the Black Widow Tree appeared out of nothing.

Lithe and strong, her skin was a blue-tinged silver, like moonlight on a tombstone. She wore a gown of shadow that shifted and roiled around a willowy figure. She wore her white hair in a long, tangled braid over her shoulder and her eyes were the endless black I saw in Drake when his monstrous side emerged.

"I heard foul whispers on the wind." Her voice was like the creaking of old branches in winter as she walked towards us. "Lobrathia has fallen to the demon king, and in turn, the demon king has fallen to Drakus Silverhand, unbound once again."

Drake took a knee. "I have returned with my mate, Goddess Mother."

The Goddess stood before us now and my magic prickled within me, sharp and goading. I was compelled to sink onto the hard black ground beside Drake.

"And what a mate she is," the deity whispered. Icy cold fingers reached under my chin and tilted my head upward.

"Let me look at you, Saraya Yasani Voltanius, High Priestess of the Order of Te'mari."

Her eyes bore into mine and I saw in those onyx orbs an ancient and terrible wisdom swathed in cold ruthlessness. "Ellythian emerald eyes always spoke of great power. It is no wonder you are Umali's chosen."

Her magic was overwhelming me, gathering in my ribs, my lungs, seeking, looking, and finding.

"You have come to find out about my son."

Abruptly, she whirled away. Drake and I got to our feet. He reached for my hand and warmth spread up my arm and into my chest. We listened as his mother spoke with a breezy and distant cadence.

"Do you know why I became known as The Black Widow? Because the men I lie with die early deaths. But I chose to bed Wyxian Darkcleaver because I knew that together with my blood, we would make a creature powerful enough to defy the Green Reaper. And all greatness requires sacrifice."

"The Green Reaper was there in the demon court," I said tightly. "He spoke to me. Wanted to see what power I had."

The Black Widow regarded us with a slight, animalistic tilt of the head. "Of course he did. And he will replace the demon king with another. Worse than Havrok. That was always his way."

"You saw him awaken?" Drake asked, stepping forward. I let go of his hand. "You knew this would happen?"

The Black Widow nodded once, and anger curled through me. She could have warned us. Could have told Drake about this. But she had chosen not to.

"The Green Reaper is a creature known as a *Niyati*," she said, and a memory chimed in my mind. Havrok had used

277

the same word. "A being who is a destructive turning point in the world, who has the potential to wield incredible carnage.

"When such creatures are created, a balance must be made. They must be bound to a mate, or the land faces a terrible destruction. Raw power can never be left untethered. There is a push and pull, a give and a take. A dark to the light.

"When a Niyati is made, a tethering energy must be bound to it. Otherwise, it is likely to destroy everything around it. So each *Niyati* must have a *Tyaag*."

Drake stiffened next to me as I heard the second word Havrok had used to describe us.

"When Drakus was born, he was such a creature— a Niyati. The Jacaranda tree told your father about it, but...I had him believe the prophecy was about Daxian. He never would have gone to great lengths to find a Tyaag if he believed it was Drake. To condemn one of their females to be sacrificed goes against fae kind, so he went to war with humans in order to give them no choice but to give us one of their women instead. Once the blood contract was made, it was done, and the Tyaag was created. Unborn Saraya was set as the sacrifice."

A dark and sour wind shifted through my very core. I had been used as a sacrificial lamb, a pawn for the whims of a fae king. *Wyxian* had planned to use me. Had known all along and was now also dead because of me. A pang of terrible sadness erupted through me, and I didn't know who to feel worse for.

"What will the Reaper do, Mother? You can tell me that at least." Drake's voice was tight with leashed anger. I guessed he knew that speaking out of turn to this Goddess Mother wouldn't help.

"He will make a move for the largest collection of Quartz

in the fae realms," the Black Widow said lightly. "Black Court. Already the new king is petitioning the dark fae realm for their forces. "

I exhaled slowly, processing this information. I did not think Daxian would make a particularly wise leader. Then again, in an unexpected move, he had warned Osring about the Reaper having awoken. Perhaps I underestimated him.

The Goddess waved a silver hand at Drake. "Let me talk to my daughter-in-law alone, Drakus."

Drake hesitated, but I knew that whatever she needed to tell me would be important, so I smiled at him. "It's alright."

She waited until Drake was far out of sight before she said, "You must reject Drakus as your mate."

It felt as if she had struck me a blow with brass knuckles. "I beg your *pardon*?"

"If you don't, you will destroy him."

I refrained from letting my anger get the better of me. I needed to be calm with this goddess. "And how would I do that?"

Her eyes were like ice sticks boring into me. "Drake's power will never come into full force while you are with him. Even now I see his power is dampened with you by his side."

My mind raced to understand what she was saying. "I mean, he gains his senses back when he is with me. He's not—"

"As much of a monster?" A wry smile curled around her silver lips. "*That* is who he is. A monster is who he was born to be. If he is to defeat the Green Reaper, he will need his full power behind him."

I stared at her. "He is the one who needs to defeat the Green Reaper? It *has* to be him?"

"The Green Reaper severed his bond with his own Tyaag.

That is why he is so powerful. So, he can only be killed by another of his own kind. Drake will only be a match for the Green Reaper in his monstrous form. And he can only take that on if you sever your bond. He must be free."

"But, I am his mate…that means we are *made* to be together. I thought that was what 'mate' meant. And you just said a—a Niyati needs a Tyaag to keep him…"

But she shook her head as if she pitied me, and it made red anger knot in my gut. "Exactly. He will never reach his full destructive power while you are by his side, tethering him. If he is to succeed against the Green Reaper, you must leave him. He must be allowed to become the monster he was born to be. Niyati are as good as Gods when they are free. You saw the power of Green Reaper. He is indefeatable at present."

I sat on a fallen log, off to the side. My heart felt like it was cleaving in two as I thought of what Drake would say to this. He would never agree. After what we'd said to each other last night? After what we'd both been through together? After what *he'd* been through?

But she must have known what I was thinking. "It is best if you do not tell him, Saraya. It will cloud his judgement."

I looked at her helplessly, my heart aching. "You ask too much of me. I don't think—"

"Put it out of your mind for the moment." She waved her hand in a dismissive way that irked me to no end. "You needn't do it today. In the meantime, I need you to help him retrieve something for me." She turned her head to the left and her voice carried on the wind. "Come back, my son."

Drake was beside me in an instant, his hazel eyes searching my face for any clue as to what his Mother Goddess might have said to me.

"There is a task you two must complete. If we are to rid this land of the Green Reaper, you must know two things. The first is that he cannot be killed, only contained."

"Everything can be killed," Drake's rasp was gravel against stone.

The Black Widow smiled at him. "He recovered from his last war under my roots, I am well aware of what he is." She held up a finger. "Which is a malevolent being like no other, Drakus. But as I say, there is a way to incapacitate him for all eternity."

"And what is that?" he asked.

"The Darkmaul Dagger."

Drake cocked his head in a way that told me he got that particular quirk from his mother. "That is myth."

"It is very real and, at present, missing. Dacre Liversblood will know about it. I sense he has returned to Obsidian Court after your business at Havrok's palace."

"Then that is where we will go," I said firmly. "We should speak to Dacre."

The Black Widow smiled at me with bone-white teeth. "You humans are such strange creatures. It is such a shame I am limited to my territory."

Drake squeezed my hand. "But Mother, I only just got Saraya to myself. Perhaps we could stay a little—"

His mother turned and cast him a dry look over her shoulder. "I watched fae rise and fall over the centuries, Drakus. What you do is of no consequence to me. As long as you rid this land of the Green Reaper, I will have no qualms with you." She began to fade.

"So this is why you made Drake?" I asked quickly. "As an opponent to the Green Reaper? That was his sole purpose?"

The Black Widow turned and was face to face with me

within half a breath. I jerked backwards. "You are High Priestess of Warrior Midwives, Saraya Voltanius. You, of all people, should know when nature creates one thing, it must create its opposite. When nature creates a predator, it must create its prey." She resumed her fade into the mist and her deep voice echoed all around us. "When life was created, death was created by default."

And when Drake was created, so was I.

WHEN WE RETURNED TO THE TREEHOUSE, VIA THE ELEVATOR pulley device Drake had repaired, he strode straight to the balcony with urgency. Startled, I followed him and promptly stopped dead on the threshold because something—or someone—was waiting for us. A tawny owl, half my height and eyes fiery with intelligence, was perched on the railing.

When he spoke through his beak, his voice was surprisingly deep and masculine. "Greetings, Princess Saraya of Lobrathia. I bring news from your sister."

Startled, I simply stared at him. But Drake seemed unperturbed and strode forward, sweeping a bow. "Greetings, sir. I have not met with one of your kind in some time."

"No, indeed," the owl replied, inclining his body in a reciprocal bow. "We keep to our territory. But the Princess Altara is of the blood. I was urged to follow her orders."

I couldn't help the tears that sprung into my eyes as I heard Altara's name. "Oh Goddess, I have to sit down."

Drake whirled towards me as I took a seat on the couch, a look of concern on his face. "What's wrong?"

"I just—" I swallowed the lump in my throat. "We never

had time to talk about it, but I sent my sister to Ellythia. She left the same day I did. Is she well…sir?"

The tawny owl bowed once again where he sat on the balcony railing, his talons flexing around the rail. "Quite well. But we heard tell of the demons in Lobrathia. I have been trying to track your movements for weeks." He cleared his throat. "Her message reads thus:

"Dear Sara, it's Tara here.

I'm well and happy at the Ellythian school. I've learned so much and met so many people, and I can't wait to share it with you. So much has happened, I wish we could speak in person, but wing-brother here will have to speak in my stead. We heard the demons have taken over Lobrathia. Please tell me the truth of it. I hope you are okay. Tell wing-brother everything that has happened, and he will relay it to me. Goddess, I hope you are alive and well, but the reports we are receiving here are telling me anything but.

Praying and hoping,

Altara."

I stared open-mouthed at the owl as the room disappeared from around me and Altara's beautiful face swam into my vision. I was thankful that she was well and it was lucky that she was not here. Thank the goddess she went away when she did.

"And she really is well?" I asked the owl.

"A few difficulties were to be expected, but she is as right as rain, Your Highness, I assure you."

"Do you have a reply message, Sara?" Drake asked.

"I will relay it exactly," the owl said regally. "As lengthy as you require."

I nodded and cleared my throat. After a moment of gathering my thoughts, I spoke what I would have written in a letter.

It was long, but it had to relay everything that had happened, and I left nothing out.

At the end, I paused, then nodded to myself. "And tell her that I intend to take back Lobrathia as Queen."

Drake glanced at me in a way that suggested he was not in the least surprised. I had never shared this intention before, but the feeling had been growing in me since we'd visited Kaalon and had seen Uncle Osring cowering under that protective illusion.

But the owl also seemed unperturbed, and only nodded when I was done. He gave his thanks when Drake offered to find him a rat to eat. I had to turn away for that part, of course.

When he was finished eating, Drake snaked an arm around my waist and we watched the tawny owl, or wing-brother as Altara had referred to him, leap into the sky and fly westwards until he was nothing but a speck in the blue sky.

"You know I will stand by you, Saraya," Drake murmured. "Whatever it is that you intend, I will always be where I belong, next to you."

I smiled at him as emotion swelled in my throat. "I know we didn't talk about it earlier...but I feel in my heart that it is the right thing to do...although I don't even know where to start."

"I always intended to help you get Lobrathia back, and it only makes sense you would do it as Queen. And...well, it's a good thing your mate is commander of Black Court's elite forces then, isn't it?" He scratched his chin. "But if you are Queen, what will that make me?"

I grinned. "That will make you Queen-Consort. You'll be a prince."

Drake grumbled in his throat in mock annoyance. "That will ruin my reputation completely. But, if you insist."

31

DRAKE

S araya and I set out for the east, with bags over our shoulders filled with food and clothes. My raging mind was clear around Saraya and I was able to focus on the task at hand.

Obsidian Court was three days travel, but I wanted to track my zekar stallion, Razor, whom I had scented on the wind before we even left the grove. I knew he'd come back to the fae realm to wait for me, the loyal beast.

When it came to my mate, honesty was important. We were one now, and as such, so were our minds and everything in them. So, as I bent to brush my fingers over an old hoof mark in the earth, I said to Saraya, "She told you to leave me, didn't she?" I tried to ease the frown off my face, but I couldn't hide my dismay.

I could tell my mate was surprised by the upturn in her voice. "How did you know?"

"I know her," I said darkly, leading her through the forest. I suppressed the urge to take her hand. "She is a goddess. She cares nothing for mortal lives." My tone was bitter as I remembered the type of childhood I had. Worshipping a mother who could never really be a true mother to me. "Since I was a child my mother has been hinting at my Niyati nature. And after that...well, I've been around, Saraya. The Green Reaper tried to keep his story secret, but all fae know the legend— how he rejected his Tyaag and in doing so, became God-like in power. It wasn't a stretch to imagine she would want the same for me." I paused in my step and couldn't help it. I surged towards my mate and took her beautiful face in my hands. I *had* to make her understand how much she meant to me. How much I did not care about any fucked up power. "But you must *never* for a moment think to do such a thing. There has to be a way around it."

My body stirred at the closeness of my mate, her smell reminding me of the zap of lightning and the sweet cinnamon that grew in wild tropical forests. It drew me in, and I leaned down and pressed my lips to hers. She couldn't help but return the kiss.

I reached around and held her close as her tongue encouraged me to pursue deeper. Her hands tangled in my hair, and I guided her towards an oak, pressing my body against her luscious softness before turning her around and pushing her front against the oak.

She sighed as my hands slipped below her cotton shirt, the one I'd made for her. Fingers skimming the skin of her breasts, I enjoyed the taste of her neck on my tongue. Desire coursed through me like a raging fire totally taking over my body.

I hooked my fingers into her pants and she laughed breathlessly. "Drake, we should really—"

"More." My voice was ragged as I kissed my way from her supple cheek to the nape of her neck, my thumbs making circles on the sensitive skin below her wide hip bones. "I've wanted you for so long, Saraya. Let me have you."

She moaned and the sound was like the sweet music of the Gods.

"Drake," she whispered, her voice like Ellythian silk around my name.

All I wanted was to be close to her. I raised my head and placed my cheek against hers. "Yes?"

"You're terrible," she panted, reaching around to dig her fingernails into my back and pull me close.

And that spurred me on, stoking my raging fire. I made a satisfied rumble deep in my chest, and I pulled off her shirt and slid her pants down her legs. Before we knew it, we were both naked, my hands cupping her heavy breasts, my manhood pressed against her round behind.

She was already slick with desire and I just knew I had to taste her.

I roughly turned her around and took a second to enjoy the confused look on her face before I sunk to my knees and pressed a kiss against her sex.

She gasped, and I tugged one of her legs and placed it around my shoulder. Eager with anticipation, I swept my tongue down her sweet lips.

"Oh Goddess," she breathed.

"Your Goddess isn't here," I said darkly against her beautiful core. "Only me. And I can feel how much you want me too."

She sucked in a delicious breath as I worshipped the centre of her, the evidence of her desire dripping freely. I growled in pleasure at the sweet taste of her, the scent of her filling my mouth.

I lapped it up like nectar.

She panted and I sucked. She moaned softly, and I quickly learned where she liked it best. I flicked my tongue over and over on her sweet nub while she gripped my hair and ground her centre against my face.

I growled, encouraging her to find her pleasure against my mouth. I flicked my tongue and she quivered, crying out, finding release. I relished the sight of my mate, my everything, finding pleasure through me, and only me.

She pulled her leg off my shoulder. "Take me, Drake," she panted. "All of me."

Thoroughly ready to be inside her, I swung her around, so her precious, marked back was safe against my chest and pushed myself into her, the quiet squeak from her throat making me even harder. With a fiery realisation, I saw that there were fresh wounds on her skin. I growled and paused in my thrust.

"Who did this?"

"Not now, Drake," she panted. "Please."

I wanted to protect her from everything. I wanted to see only desire and pleasure on her face, not the raw fear and panic I sensed from her when Glacine was around. It had been her, I knew it. She'd done it when we'd been separated The fae-human mutant still affected my mate, but I would do everything I could to help her find revenge.

The wounds and scars against my chest reminded me of my mate's sheer strength, her power. I wanted her even more. I wanted to be consumed by her.

So obliging her request and, avoiding her new wounds, I

slammed my rock-hard self inside her heavenly wet heat until pleasure made me feel as if I were floating high in the cloudless sky above the Grove. I held her breasts in my palms, her softness urging me on. I reached a pinnacle, roaring her name. She groaned in release, and I spilled myself into her, filling her up with my—I pulled out with a cry, stepping away from her.

My mate spun around in shock, still recovering from the release. "What! What is it?"

But the shock and horror were still tolling in me like a bell from the depths of hell. How could I be so selfish?

I looked at my manhood and then at her in horror. "Saraya, I filled you with my seed. I didn't even think! Yesterday and then again today, I didn't—"

"Oh." To my surprise, she let out a laugh. She grabbed her shirt from the ground and looked around the forest floor. "I'm a midwife, Drake. I don't make mistakes like that."

Relief flooded me like summer rain. I lurched forward and pulled my mate into my arms, holding her more tightly than I ever had. "I just couldn't imagine you being pregnant at a time like this. I should have thought of it before. I'm sorry."

The thought of it made my stomach roil violently. I could never make such a mistake again.

She kissed me on the chest, and my heart swelled. "I can stop my body from releasing an egg. A perk of my magic."

Surprise filled me and I let out a slow exhale of deep relief. "Thank the Gods for that. I don't ever want to put you in danger."

Pulling back, she gave me a delicious grin that made my heart skip a beat. "I'm sure I could fight just as well, being pregnant."

I couldn't help but grin and bent to pick up her pants and took her hand, leading her down the path where there was a stream. "I'm sure you could. We've never fought, have we? We should train together."

Her grin turned into a smirk as we emerged through bushes to the sparkling brook. "Not worried that I'll beat you on your ass like I did Daxian?"

We began washing in the surprisingly warm water shaded by leafy trees.

"I am a little worried, actually." I let out a laugh. "Perhaps I shouldn't have mentioned it."

She smirked in satisfaction. "I'll catch you unawares, be on your guard."

Knowing she meant it, I splashed her with water. "*You* be on *your* guard, Princess."

We quickly dried ourselves off, collected our packs, and made our way down the path again, where I quickly picked up Razor's scent.

COMING OUT OF THE WILD FOREST THAT I CALLED HOME AS A child, we tracked the zekar for an hour across the wild and unforgiving land that was the Black Court countryside. The soil was deep red so dark it was black to non-fae eyes, which I explained to Saraya was coloured that way because of the incredible amount of iron in the soil.

Our tolerance to iron was what separated the Dark fae from the Solar fae. In those realms, sending a gift of iron was a declaration of war. The dark fae were more brutish people and usually sent the severed head of one of the bordering liege lords if they wanted to wage war. Twilight Court was the only peaceful court in this realm, and the remaining four kept an uneasy truce for the moment. The current truce had been dependent on the huge supply of luminous quartz Black Court was supposed to be bringing in because of Saraya's supposed engagement to Daxian. Saraya wondered out loud what my blasted half-brother was up to now and whether the rest of the fae realms knew what had happened in Lobrathia.

"We will have to be careful in our travels," I murmured as we strode down the empty road. "There are fae who support the Reaper."

"Could we not send a fae raven?" she asked. "That's how you've previously communicated with Dacre, right?

"All incoming and outgoing ravens will be monitored from now on. They'll be read by the Obsidian spymasters even before they reach the recipient."

"Who's side is Dacre on, then? He'll have to do whatever his king says, right? If he sides with the Reaper, he won't give us any information about the dagger."

"Dacre has questionable ethics, but he owes me," I replied. "He won't have a choice but to tell me the truth."

We continued on in silence until I found Razor grazing in a green field on the side of the road.

As we approached, my oldest friend raised his head and eyed us with a blue gaze and an acute intelligence that I knew Saraya had never seen in any 'horse' before.

I broke into a run.

Knowing my mate was following close, albeit in alarm, I leapt over the fence separating us and embraced Razor around his neck.

Took your time, Razor said, absently chewing grass.

I was occupied. I laughed. *Near-death situation and all.*

Razor snorted like he didn't believe me and then told me what had happened after the demons had attacked us in Lobrathia.

Behind me, Saraya climbed to sit on the fence, watching us warily.

Razor was the biggest stallion of any zekar I'd personally ever seen. Corded muscle winded its way up his legs and chest, and he had a magnificent black silky mane. But the most noticeable thing about him was a pale, jagged scar that cut his face in two. Razor and I had been in many a melee in our youth, and that particular scar was caused by a beast in Eclipse Court four times his size. Naturally we killed that beast after a bloody battle.

But it was time to introduce my oldest friend to the now most important soul in my life. "Look who I found. This is my mate, Saraya. Princess, meet Razor, my oldest friend."

Saraya appraised my friend.

She smells nice. Does this mean she is mine too?

Fuck off. She's only mine.

I turned to Saraya and laughed through my nose. "He thinks you smell nice, but I put him in his place."

My mate smiled as Razor followed me towards where she was perched on the log fence. "A pleasure to meet you, Razor."

I beamed at Saraya. "He said he was waiting for me. He came here after the battle finished. Killed a few demons too."

She looked at me with surprise. "He's very clever."

"I've known him since foalhood. He was born in the Grove, same as me. We're land brothers in that way."

She made an impressed noise as Razor snorted.

But then a cleaving sadness came through the mate bond and a burning that told me Saraya wanted to cry.

I think I moved too quickly because when I shot to her side, my poor mate almost fell off the fence. Quickly I braced her, keeping her in place as she wiped her eyes.

"I'm just thinking about Opal and my own horse, Silent-foot," she sniffed. "We've been through a lot together too. And I don't know where they are."

I was also worried about Fluffy, who I'd come to care about during my time with her. But Razor trotted up to Saraya and nuzzled her face with his massive head. She let out a sad laugh.

"The beings we love have a way of finding their way back to us," I said nostalgically, taking her hand and kissing it. "Razor thinks so too."

She nodded sadly.

"Can you ride bareback?" I asked.

"I've done it once or twice." She eyed Razor nervously, but the beast politely turned around and waited for us to get on.

RAZOR WAS SO ATTUNED TO ME THAT I DIDN'T HAVE TO GUIDE him at all. Because of all our exploits together, he knew the trails I preferred, and so it felt as if we were passengers being taken to Obsidian Court.

We rode for a full day and made camp in a thicket well off the road. We made vigorous love again that night and fell into an easy sleep. Razor was sharp-eared in his sleep and always alerted me if anything unusual strayed close to us.

We set off again the next day and quickly reached the Black-Obsidian border.

Just as a river separated Lobrathia and Kaalon, Black and Obsidian Courts were separated by a wide fjord, the bridge which, not to my surprise, was heavily guarded by Black Court's border lord, Viscount Nightclaw, and a contingent of his guards.

Hidden behind a line of black and silver-leafed trees, Saraya and I slid off Razor, and I showed her the guards.

Politely, I knocked on the back door of Saraya's defensive mind-shield. She let me in right away.

"*Border patrols,*" I said, mind-to-mind. "*The Viscount Nightclaw would have been ordered to be prepared for an attack from the Reaper.*"

Saraya shifted on the spot as she eyed the group of armed fae around the bridge. "*But why are they patrolling the Obsidian Court border? Shouldn't they be keeping an eye on the mountain passes and portals instead? That's how the demons will get in, right?*"

I passed her a grim look. "*Obsidian Court was in support of the Reaper the last time, meaning that they will fight for him alongside the demons.*"

Her mouth dropped open. Naturally, she was new to the less than civilised political aspect of the dark fae realm. "*I just assumed all the fae were against him.*"

I shook my head sadly. Roaming the two fae realms as a teenager, I had to learn the politics between them rather quickly. I'd gotten into many a tight spot not paying attention to power dynamics. "*The Reaper started his life as a fae, so he has his share of allies of like mind. Midnight and Obsidian might take up the Reaper's colours once again. It depends where each king feels his allegiance lies. Perhaps we'll find out when we get there.*"

As we strode out of the lines towards the bridge, Saraya took in a sharp breath, staring at the Viscount and his round son, mounted on horses next to each other, no doubt on the daily inspection of their patrols.

Concerned, I asked her what was wrong.

"I know him," she whispered, "from the Academy."

3 2

SARAYA

A s I looked at the fae guarding the river crossing, I now
knew why the name Viscount Nightclaw had sounded
so familiar when Drake had first mentioned it.

He was the father of my dormmate back at the Mountain
Academy—the rotund, romance-novel-reading Briar—who
was now sitting on a chestnut pony next to his father.

I found that I had no trouble trusting Drake completely.
Perhaps this feeling might have surprised me, but we'd been
through so much together down in the demon court. The
entire time, he'd seemed too sure of himself, so confident in
the unknown. The only time he'd ever shown a lack of confidence was with me in regards to my feelings about being his
mate.

I had not forgotten about what we had been talking about
before Drake had taken me against the tree in the Grove. Just
as I had begun to feel comfortable being his mate, his mother
had gone and sprung her advice on me.

The Green Reaper was hundreds of years old. If, in all that
time, he hadn't found a way to get around the sacrifice of his

Tyaag to gain his power, then there was likely no way we were going to find one.

It made my stomach twist to think about it.

But I trusted Drake in matters of fae politics, so when he bade me to get back on Razor and led us, with him on foot, right towards the Nightclaws, I wasn't afraid.

They spotted us right away, of course. Surrounded by ten guards, they waited in front of the bridge.

I didn't think Briar would recognise me. He wasn't the brightest fae. Even when he'd seen me stark naked at the Academy, he'd not suspected that I was a female.

To my surprise, the guards drew their weapons as we approached, and startled, I appraised the Viscount sitting on an onyx stallion. Briar's father was the spitting image of him —a rotund fae with a shock of black hair tied back in a ponytail. His cheeks were pink against the cold, and they both wore fur-lined cloaks and black hilted blades.

When we reached ten paces from them, the Viscount raised a fist. "Halt there, Commander!"

Razor halted as asked and I nervously looked at Drake.

"Who is your charge?" called the Viscount.

The warriors were on their guard and never took their eyes off Drake. And in truth, both the Viscount and Briar eyed us uncertainly.

"My mate," Drake said evenly, though his voice was magically carried over the dirt.

The Viscount's brows shot up into his hairline. "Indeed? That is news. Approach, please."

Drake nodded, and Razor stepped forward until we were right in front of them.

"Gooday, Viscount." Drake's voice was deeper than before. I cast a glance at him and realised his eyes had once again returned to their monstrous black form. The fae shifted nervously, perturbed by his new appearance.

"Apologies," the Viscount said, and he sounded sincere. "But you will understand my hesitancy. News of your capture and subsequent upheaval of Havrok's court has reached us, naturally. Congratulations on finding your mate."

I looked up to see Briar staring at me. His father turned his attention to me. "And who do I have the pleasure of meeting?"

"This is Princess Saraya Voltanius," Drake rasped. "My wife and mate."

A tiny pulse of pleasure shot through me as Drake gave my name and title. The Viscount and the fae guards were surprised because whispers broke out immediately.

"Princess Saraya of Lobrathia?" the Viscount asked me. "King Daxian's betrothed?"

Drake growled low in his throat, but I had never forgotten my etiquette. I bowed where I sat on Razor's back. "The one and same, my Lord. A turn of events occurred when the demon king stormed the Lobrathian palace. It was revealed that Drakus was bonded to me. He is…was, Wyxian's firstborn son, not Daxian. We were married at Havrok's court."

Briar and his father exchanged a look before the Viscount said, "This is very unexpected news, Your Highness. But forgive me, should you not be on your way to Black Court to explain this to the king? I'm sure he is very confused. He is raising an army against the Green Reaper, hence our border patrols."

"We have private business with the Obsidian mage, Dacre Liversblood," Drake said, his voice like gravel. I could tell he was getting impatient.

"He is the one who bound Drake's powers, you see," I

E.P. BALI

said quickly. "The bindings kept his monstrous side at bay, but they have been undone. We wish to ask Dacre some questions."

The air grew heavy around us, and the Viscount seemed to understand the implications rather quickly. "Of course, of course." His eyes shifted nervously between me and what I was sure was Drake's murderous expression.

"You had better let us through, My Lord." I used my eyes to indicate Drake's preternaturally still, viscous form. "We will return to Black Court palace as soon as we have our information."

"Have we met before, Princess?" Briar piped up. "Or do you have a brother?"

"No, my Lord, I do not have a brother." That part wasn't a lie.

He nodded, giving me a tiny smile.

I had always liked Briar, he had been my first friend at the Mountain Academy, and I felt bad not telling him the truth, but this was neither the time nor the place for it.

The Viscount moved his soldiers aside and I inclined my head as Drake leapt back up behind me in a way that had the fae guards staring at him. We continued across the wide bridge.

Drake kissed me on the neck and murmured in my ear. "Look at you, warning people not to make me angry."

"Oh, you noticed that did you?" I asked. "I saw your eyes were black again. I couldn't have you very well killing our allies, could I?"

He made a rumble of assent in his throat. "When I'm with you, close to you, I'm okay. But away from you, it all comes out."

How could I ever forget the moment Drake's bonds came

off in Havrok's arena? The way he'd moved and fought and killed? And it was this very thing that his mother wanted him to become. Without me, he'd be monstrous all the time and be a match for the Green Reaper. I shivered on Razor's back as we reached the other side of the bridge.

The Obsidian lands started off much like Black Court countryside. Black rolling hills, strange bent trees with charred trunks, and that coal-coloured soil. But eventually, Drake pointed out the huge chunks of rock the land was named after. Obsidian stone was sporadic at first, then it was everywhere, tall natural columns, wide caves, and shining boulders. There was a volcano off the eastern coast, Drake said, and for decades the Obsidian fae had been bringing the rock over to the mainland.

The area was mostly barren as Drake said that most Obsidian folk lived by the sea, where the land was more fertile and kinder for living on. Out here, there were foul creatures who prowled, including dark goblins who would kill anything on sight for eating. They worked in packs, like scavengers, and the only time I saw a group of them, they were running in the opposite direction from Drake.

Drake, for his part, thought out loud about lassoing one of them to ask for news, but I quickly dissuaded him from it, his black eyes clearing with every word I spoke. It was a reminder to me of what Drake really was. That we still would have to be careful about his monstrous nature.

We stopped for breaks twice, but I got the feeling that both Drake and Razor did that only for my benefit. Neither seemed to tire and they looked to enjoy each other's company as I saw one time, when Drake was laughing at something Razor had said as I came out of the bushes after relieving myself.

We reached Obsidian Palace late after sundown. It was

eerie, walking up the long road to the palace. Our path was bordered by eerie black pines, and a chill wind didn't stir the branches. Seven square gates of obsidian arched over the wide paved road.

"It's supposed to ward away evildoers." Drake chuckled softly. "But most of the evildoers are already *in* the palace."

The entire sprawling palace was a ten-storied monument hewn out of Obsidian. I imagined that it would shine brilliantly in the light of the sun. Prince Fern hailed from here, I remembered from the Mountain Academy. It was an odd thing, to have lived and studied with the five princes. Now, Fern and his family was supposedly siding with the Reaper. Fern was physically the largest of the princes. When I had been put with the princes group of training, he'd been the one who taught me wrestling techniques. It would be a strange thing now, to think of him as an enemy in actual war.

Drake pointed to the highest tower, where the flickering glow of fire was faintly visible.

"Dacre is up all night," Drake murmured. "He sleeps during the day."

But the smell of smoke wasn't coming from Dacre's tower. The entire palace was surrounded by a moat, in which a fire burned night and day. The light danced all around the bottom of the palace, making the entire thing look like an ethereal thing from another time and place.

Well, I had to remind myself that I *was* in the fae realm. To me, this *was* another time and place.

We rode up to the arched front gate as Drake waved a hand around us. A cloud of curling shadow surrounded Razor's form, not unlike the way Opal used her magic to hide us on our travels. But while Opal's magic was light and shimmering, Drake's magic was dense and cloudy.

Drake tapped on the door to my mind, and I let him in. *"Don't make a sound, my love. We'll need to get in unseen."*

I nodded, trying to see through the shadow that now surrounded us, but with no luck. Also, trying not to be surprised at the new term of endearment.

Somehow, both Drake and Razor were navigating as if the shadows weren't even there because Razor suddenly took a sharp turn right.

"Do you trust me, my princess?"

I grinned wryly. "By now, I would say yes."

He hummed with satisfaction. "If this were not important, I would take you here and now."

Heat crept onto my cheeks as arousal drifted up from my core. But Drake only chuckled and said, "Don't scream." He slapped one hand over my mouth and grabbed me around the waist with the other, and shot us up into the sky.

I *did* almost scream.

It was like when we astral travelled and shot through the air, only this time it was shockingly real. Perhaps that experience had prepared me for this. But I could never have been prepared for the way my stomach dropped into my nether regions as we zipped upwards with a blast of the chilly night air. With my eyes tightly shut, I got the odd feeling of huge wings stretching out around us. Wings made of black storm clouds.

We slowed to a stop, and as I opened my eyes, I felt Drake landing on something solid. I made to turn to punch him for not warning me, but he held me so incredibly tight that I could not twist far enough to angle my fist at him.

Abruptly, the shadow around us dissolved, and my boots touched stone. Warmth enveloped me as I found myself in a large circular stone room. In the corner was a roaring hearth, over which a squat cauldron sat bubbling. Branches and collections of herbs hung from the rafters, and before me was a square wooden table laden with papers, books, and instruments. In the corner, sitting hunched on a stool with knitting needles and black wool in hand, was Dacre Liversblood, free of his demonic shackles.

There was an objectionable *sqwark* and I saw something black sitting on Dacre's shoulder.

"You two shouldn't be here. They'll capture you on sight."

"Nice to see you're alive, you old goat," Drake shot at him. "And we weren't seen." Drake let go of me and strolled towards the fae mage who was deftly knitting the sleeve of a small black cardigan, tattooed fingers flying.

Dacre grumbled and tied the wool off, snipping it with shears. The creature on his shoulder jumped onto the square table, and I reluctantly approached. The place gave off a dangerous feeling, as if some dark thing would leap out at me from the shadows at any moment. As Dacre shook out the tiny cardigan, frowning at it, I saw that the creature was a tiny black monkey. As we watched, Dacre held the cardigan out to the monkey and helped him slip it on. It fit perfectly. Only then did the Obsidian mage look up at us.

"You're here for the Darkmaul Dagger." His voice was a low drone as he picked up a pipe from the table and began filling it with a mixture from a tin.

"Yes," Drake replied.

I glanced between them in surprise. How on earth did he know?

"I'm afraid it is not here," the mage said. "That dagger was split in two and both pieces are lost."

My shoulders sagged. This was the last thing I was expecting.

"Who's side are you on, Dacre?" I asked suddenly. "Drake says you follow the Green—"

"Do not speak his name, your Highness," Dacre interrupted, turning to me. "His eyes are his specialty, did you know? He sees a lot more than people suspect."

Goosebumps scattered all over my arms as I remembered the way the Green Reaper had somehow known things about me.

"And word is, there was a kraasputin going around with your name on his lips."

I cringed inwardly before I felt Drake's warmth come up from behind me. "I believe my mate asked you a question."

The mage nodded, waving his pipe. "I do not yet know, Drakus. Time will tell."

"So, will you tell us about the dagger or not?" I asked.

"Well…" Dacre strode to the tower window we'd come from, peering out of it. "You could hunt anything, Drakus, could you not?"

Drake stepped beside me and cocked his head. "I've only ever hunted organic material. Flesh-like."

The mage shook his head. "Only because you've never had to hunt an object. Theoretically, you only need its scent."

I saw the realisation blossom like a spring bloom across Drake's face. "You're right."

Dacre smiled, his face tattoos stretching, and he crooked a finger. "Come here." He brought out an old wooden box, elaborately carved.

Before he opened it, I saw that on it was carved a symbol bearing an eye and the initials *EH*. Inside was a red velvet interior, the perfect shape for a dagger.

Drake stared at the box and sniffed at it. His brows raised

and he looked at the mage with an expression I could not read.

"I know," Dacre sighed. "Oh, I know."

Suddenly, there was a rapid knock at the door and I jumped. Both Drake and the mage stilled, staring at the door before Dacre waved a hand, and it swung open.

Across the room, standing there in a crisp white cape, was a middle-aged human man. Handsome, brown salt and pepper hair with a full beard. His black vest bore an upside-down white crescent moon.

He swept a bow. "My name is Roland White. I am Head-master of Morktalis Academy. I am here about the position I offered you at my school."

"Of course, come in, Headmaster." Dacre gave us a pointed look.

Quicker than I thought was possible, Drake pulled me into his arms, and his dark shadow enveloped us again. I could tell we were out of the window when Drake stepped up through the window before we plummeted to the ground. My stomach flopped on itself multiple times before we landed with a thud on the grass. When the shadows dissolved, we were on the other side of the fence with Razor, who was waiting patiently.

"That," murmured Drake, "was a dangerous man. I didn't want him seeing you."

I nodded carefully. It was then that I noticed Drake was holding the black box from the mage's tower. He tucked it into a saddle bag he'd made out of leaves and vines on the way here.

"How old do fae typically live?" I asked. "You called Dacre old, but he looks young."

"Fae usually live up until a hundred years of age. But

mages like Dacre and fae with great amounts of magic can live for hundreds of years. Depends how powerful they are."

"And what's this school that dangerous man mentioned?"

"It's a dark school in its own dimension. They always have a dark fae tenure on offer. Their previous one is no doubt dead. Dacre is naturally a good candidate."

"In another dimension..." I repeated lamely.

Drake glanced at me and grinned. "The portals don't just lead us to different parts of *this* world, but to other worlds as well. Chrysalis and Sacrilis are the other magic schools."

"And they teach you magic? Huh. Perhaps I should take a visit. I'd like to learn more magic."

Drake put his arm around my shoulder. "I'll take you to Chrysalis if you like. It's on a tropical island and the school is a gigantic monolith of diamond. Perhaps after all this is done."

I grinned up at him, imagining how a gigantic diamond would sparkle under a tropical sun. "I'd like that."

But he'd said: *After all this is done.*

What would that take, exactly?

W e were finding a place to camp for the night when a
fell wind stirred the air. Drake lunged to come to
my side while I reflexively summoned my lightning blade.

But the voice that came to us on the wind was familiar as
it echoed and shifted. The creaking of ancient trees under a
cold wind—it was Drake's mother.

> *Return to Black Court palace immediately.*
> *Attack is imminent.*

We arrived in Black Court capital city after four days of
travel.

I had never, in my entire life, imagined royal architecture
like that of Black Palace. If I had thought Havrok's abode or
Obsidian Palace was something to behold, I was sincerely
mistaken.

A colossal black stone dragon reared on its hind legs,
wings spread out wide, monstrous jaws roaring up into the

sky. Nestled in front of it was the black stone affair that was the ten-story palace—conical turrets, sloping rooves, and tall columns standing sentinel along the front aspect. There was no gate and no moat. Instead, the palace sat on a hill, overlooking the land like a king, casting a shadow over the city through which we now rode.

The fae of Black City recognised both Drake and Razor on sight. Crowds parted for us and the fae stopped in the street, their beautiful faces gaping and whispering in each other's ears. Males tipped their hats or nodded to Drake, who nodded back. I wondered what rumours they'd heard about our capture and escape from the demon court. Viscount Nightclaw had hinted that they already knew about the goings-on in the demon realm. But what did they think about it?

Drake seemed unperturbed by both the attention and the knowledge we were about to present to Court, so all I could do was try and keep an even expression and not show my own nerves.

We were going to meet my ex-fiancé and mother-in-law and I couldn't help but think they would take it as an insult that I was now returning as Drake's mate.

"It's Monday," Drake murmured as we exited the city and made our way up the winding road to the palace entrance. "That means the entire court will be in attendance. They use today to make announcements and such."

"I can't believe Daxian was coronated so quickly," I murmured.

"With war on the horizon, it would be the smartest thing for the council to do."

Black Court was certainly prepared for war. We had

passed three watchtowers, each teeming with fae warriors who had come to greet Drake, their Elite Forces Commander, immediately. He had ordered them to send word ahead of us, to let Daxian know that we were on our way.

Warriors dressed in black with the gold-wreathed dragon of the Darkcleavers on their chests respectfully saluted Drake all the way up the main drive to the palace. One of the captains of the guard met us at the palace entrance as we climbed off Razor.

Drake and the captain shook hands, and I could tell he was startled by Drake's new, darker appearance. He certainly felt different to me, now that he was unbound, and the black, sparkling eyes and gravelling voice made an impression. These people had known him for years. The difference for them was surely more profound.

"We've been eagerly waiting for you, Lord Commander," the captain said.

Drake shook hands with the fae and gripped him on the shoulder. "I'm glad to see you well, Callan. What were our losses at Quartz?"

Callan swallowed before answering, "Five of our elites, my Lord."

"I will visit their families and thank them personally," Drake promised. "There's much to discuss so I'll hold a meeting. Let me get the lay of the land first."

The captain gave a firm nod and graciously indicated that we should proceed inside. My heart pounding in my chest, I glanced down at my clothes. It seemed that I was destined to never make a grand entrance at any court because, yet again, I was attending a foreign court in the worst sort of clothes and in desperate need of a proper bath.

Sighing, Drake hovered protectively by my side as we headed into the cool shadow that was Black Court's entrance hall.

"I'm hardly dressed for this," I murmured to Drake as royal fae servants in court finery stared, fae eyes looking me up and down.

"We're at war," Drake said as he observed the hall, "no one will care what you're wearing."

When the throne room came into view, I knew at once that I'd made a mistake in not wearing a gown of some sort because everyone gathered at the end, by the two spectacular black and gold thrones, was wearing their court best. I had never seen fae courtiers before, and these fine bodies were dressed in shades of silver, grey, and black that seemed to sparkle with their own light. So much for being at war. I wondered how they dressed for events.

Inwardly cringing, we made our way in, stopping briefly so Drake could speak to the herald.

As we walked down a silver carpet that glittered under a magnificent yellow quartz chandelier, I knocked on the door to Drake's mind.

"I'll declare my intentions to take back my throne. How do you think Daxian will receive us?"

"It's hard to say. I don't know what's happened here since the Quartz City invasion."

When we reached the throne, it was clear by the palpable tension and the whispers that they had been waiting for us. But it was not the judgemental courtiers' eyes that had a burning horror curling around my heart.

It was Daxian's appearance. The last time I had seen him, he was a student at the Warrior Academy, arrogant, cocky, and terribly handsome in that supernatural way of the fae people. Today, he sat on his father's throne, shoulders hunched in a gold-embroidered black shirt and vest, a crown of gold and black sitting on his brown hair.

But the most startling thing was the black patch that he wore over his left eye, with a long scar extending down from it, cleaving down his cheek. It looked like someone had tried to take his eye out and succeeded. His other eye, a brilliant turquoise, had a slight darkness beneath. Next to me, I sensed Drake's surprise.

Flanking Daxian, was his mother, the epitome of feminine beauty, golden skinned with long, curling brown hair down to her waist,, now the Dowager Queen Mother of Black Court, Xenita Darkcleaver. She had always reminded me of Glacine in her icy, imperious manner. On Daxian's other side were his younger brothers Ivy and Dattan. Both were armed and wore solemn, observant faces, with their arms clasped formally behind their backs.

As the court herald stamped his wooden staff, goosebumps spread over me. This would be the first time my new title would be announced.

I curtseyed in my pants, though I'm sure it looked ridiculous. Drake swept a bow.

"Her Royal Highness, Crown Princess Saraya Yasani Voltanius, Queen Apparent of Lobrathia. And His Royal Highness Prince Drakus Voltanius of Lobrathia and Lord Commander of Black Court Elite Forces."

The crowd around us erupted into whispers and I glanced at Drake in surprise. He had told the herald that he had taken my name. My throat burned and my eyes prickled.

Drake said into my mind, *I love you, Saraya Voltanius.*

Damn him, I would have cried right there and then. But

with a few deep breaths, I held it together as Daxian assessed us with a sharp eye. I looked to Xenita, and I saw her mouth was pressed into a firm line. She was not happy about this, naturally being another woman's son, I was sure she never had any affection for Drake.

Daxian suddenly let out a prolonged sigh and stood, but did not come to kiss my hand as would have been proper. "Welcome to Black Court, Your Highness," he said to me. He took a firm swallow as he continued. "You seem intent on taking our Commander from us."

"Your mother came," Xenita explained coldly. "Told us of her ruse about Drakus actually being born before Daxian. I cursed her name, and she laughed at me. She said we would need you both if we were to win this war. But alas, a demon wedding is not a valid wedding here."

I bristled. She was trying to discredit us.

"We signed the blood contract set by our fathers." Drake's voice was impossibly deep and I could see an anger burning within him. He gestured to my right hand, and I showed them my new magical markings. "Princess Saraya is my mate as proven by her mark. That is the law for our people, whether anyone likes it or not."

Both Daxian and Xenita seemed taken aback by Drake's voice and his appearance. A palpable heaviness shifted in the air. It would be a bad move for them to insult him. I tried to warn Daxian with my eyes, and got ready to intercept Drake if he got out of hand, but Daxian seemed to understand on his own because he changed the subject and addressed me.

"You intend to take back Lobrathia as Queen?"

I nodded. "It is the only way forward from here."

"But by the law of *your own people*, a woman may not take

313

the crown." His tone was only curious, and it felt strange not to hear any arrogance in his voice.

"There is no Lobrathian law anymore, as far as I am aware. Any law that once was is now dead. I am respected by the people of Quartz. I worked as a midwife among them for years. They will support me in my claim, as will Kaalon and Waelan Kingdoms at the very least."

Daxian nodded again. He was the opposite of how I remembered him. He looked so young, a scarred young fae now standing there, unprepared on the throne of his father. No doubt he never thought he would come to it this early. Whatever anger he might have had about me first tricking him about being Sam Sourbottom at the Academy and then about finding out he was actually not his father's firstborn was long gone, given way to grief and the more pressing matter of war.

"I am sorry for the loss of King Wyxian," I said gently. "It was an awful shock. We saw just before they captured and took us into the quarry portal."

Xenita's nostrils flared in anger and grief, and it was then that I noticed under her black gown the pronounced curve of a pregnant abdomen. Very much full term. I swallowed my surprise and inclined my head to her. "Congratulations, Your Grace, on your pregnancy."

She met me eye to eye. "Wyxian's last seed is in me, yes." She tilted her chin up in pride.

I gave her a small smile, which she did not return. My stomach churned. Perhaps some part of her blamed me for her husband's death. If he had not been there to have me married, he would be safe in the fae kingdom and alive. The thought hovered over me like a shadow.

Daxian cleared his throat and nodded as if he'd made a

decision. "I wish to talk in private with Their Highnesses. Court is dismissed for the day."

I was acutely aware that every fae noble in the room had been paying undivided attention to our exchange. Xenita opened her mouth to object, but the Herald stamped his staff and she, with the courtiers, had no choice but to head out.

"Gods save the king!" the Herald shouted.

The courtiers repeated the sentiment and dispersed in a whisper of silver and black glitter, murmuring amongst themselves.

Daxian beckoned to us. "Come this way. Mother, go rest."

Xenita, clearly livid at being dismissed, but holding it in with all the strength of her pursed lips, swept away on the arm of Ivy.

I glanced at Drake before following the new king into a chamber branching off the side of the hall.

It was as opulent as the rest, with black and gold gilded furniture, an elaborate painting of an epic battle, and a magnificently carved black dragon hanging on the back wall.

Daxian deftly picked up a tray from the side, set it on the long mahogany meeting table, and quickly poured three glasses of wine. He picked up a glass and began pacing the room. With raised brows, I watched him, the image of an anxious regent. This Daxian was unsure of himself, his shoulders hunched, his handsome face drawn with anxiety and grief. He ceased his pacing and stopped before us, set his glass down, and gripped the back of the chair in front of him, looking at each of us in turn.

My eye was suddenly drawn to his index finger, where sat a golden ring with his family's black dragon sigil wreathed in black flames with a crown atop the dragon's head. I cocked my head. For my bridal ritual, I had asked Drake to give me something of Daxian's and he returned with a golden ring, similar to this one. Except *that* ring had a plain black dragon, not one with flames or a crown. Something stirred in my memory but Daxian began speaking hurriedly and I concentrated on what he was saying.

"It was a massacre," he said hoarsely. "I scrambled together the last of our warriors and made a run for it to the Mountain Academy. One of them lodged an axe in my head. It missed my brain, but I lost my eye in the process. They patched us up best they could at the Academy, but...they couldn't save my eye."

My heart stuttered in my chest. Daxian had come close to death. The fact he was still living was a miracle.

"I know you have pledged to Lobrathia, but I need you here, Drake." I felt my mate's surprise through our bond as Daxian swallowed and continued, "Obsidian and Eclipse Courts have pledged to the Green Reaper. Midnight Court is still uncertain. I am alone here, Drake." His voice broke. "*Alone.*"

A hand clenched at my heart as I saw the position he was in. Eclipse and Obsidian were on either side of Black Court. Their direct neighbours were enemies.

"You are not alone, Dax," Drake replied smoothly, pulling out a seat for me and then sitting in the second himself. "I will still lead your forces. I have seen what the Reaper is capable of."

I sat down and took a glass from the tray. "We will fight with you, Daxian. It's clear we have to do this together."

"With what army, Saraya?" Daxian asked. "You have none. The demons completely took your palace by surprise. Have you even counted your losses? While you were stuck down in Havrok's court, I've been up here, the laughing stock of Black Court, once our apparently false engagement was broken. I had to return here with whatever warriors I could muster and tell my mother that Father was dead. Do you have any idea what that was like?" He was gripping his wine glass so hard I thought it might shatter. "And now, *now*, the Reaper is intent on taking us over and *then* the entire human realm. What the fuck are we supposed to do? Twilight Court has not even returned my raven. I might have to actually call for help from fucking Blossom Court next. And now my mother will have to go through the birth ritual by herself..." he shook his head and roughly rubbed his face.

I looked at Drake quizzically. "Birth ritual?"

Drake nodded. "For fae parents, birth is a little different than for humans. They must go into the void themselves and retrieve their children from the ether. Their ancestors watch over them."

I felt sick to my stomach. Now that her husband was dead, Xenita would have to go into this void herself. Sighing, I looked at what options we had. The human realm had soldiers aplenty. "I'll write to the kingdoms in the human realms," I said in what I hoped was a reassuring voice. "Kaalon and Waelan should come to our aid. Even Traenara, if King Omni is still alive after the fight. They all will have men they can spare."

Daxian's turquoise gaze fixed on mine. "Omni is alive. We parted ways at the river." He swallowed another gulp of wine. "I know we've had...our problems, Saraya. I'm sorry about the Kraasputin incident."

I shrugged. After all that had happened between then and now, I couldn't help but forgive him. "From my part, I deceived you as well. I'm sorry for the golem."

"The golem dissolved after we found it out, it was good

317

magic." He tapped his forehead. "What is this sign you bear now? And what went on at the demon court? All I have is rumours."

Glancing at Drake, I thought it was best to tell Daxian the full story. He had been my fiancé at the time, and I felt I owed him answers. "You'll need to sit down for this."

34
SARAYA

fter we spoke at length, Daxian put us in one of his guest rooms to freshen up while he met with the king's council. He even provided two maids for me and a squire for Drake. All at once, I was reminded of Tembry and Blythe, who were hopefully all safe back at Kaalon with Opal, along with Jerali Jones and the other humans, now refugees.

Tembry was probably busy raising baby Delilah, and I hoped that Sarone and the other slaves were doing what they could to make a life for themselves. Blythe had seemed quite friendly with Slade during their time together in the demon realm and I was sad I couldn't be with her to talk about it.

And Lobrathia. Now a demon city, I wondered what had become of the humans there. Were they being used as slaves and kicked out of their homes? Was it a complete mess over there? I had no idea what was going on and all I wanted to do was charge over there with a massive army and beat them out of the palace. Destroy them all. Surely there would be unrest with Havrok dead?

I said as such to Drake, mind-to-mind, as we lay in bath-

.P. BALI

tubs in separate rooms. *"Do you think one of the other lords will have taken the demon throne?"*

"That's the demon way," Drake said. *"Probably Braxus. They are used to changing kings as a person would change clothes. But what of Kaalon—do you really think Osring will send us men?"*

"He will. Once he realises the Green Reaper will head straight for Kaalon after Black Court, he will have no choice. But what are the chances here, Drake? Is it really as dire as Daxian says it is? How will the Reaper take Black Court?"

"He'll be rallying an army as we speak," Drake said darkly. *"No doubt, he's gone off to petition Midnight Court. All three Courts coming at us would have us in a chokehold. We have a lot of warriors, but not enough. Even with me here, without anyone else coming to our aid, it will be a massacre. We need Twilight on our side at the very least."*

My stomach twisted as I was trying to decide what to put into my letter to Kaalon, Serus, and Waelan Kingdoms. Even if they agreed to help us, would they be able to get here on time?

"Not to mention the amount of luminous quartz," I said, suddenly remembering. *"It stores magic, so they can use that to attack as well?"*

"That's right. And the Reaper will have a colossal amount of it to share from his haul at the quartz quarry. Which reminds me, send your letters, and we'll be off to inspect what we're working with."

We finished our baths and got dressed. I penned four identical letters and a fifth for Altara, and then Drake took me up to the raven master's office in one of the high towers. The raven master, an elderly fae with coarse white hair and pale blue eyes, eagerly helped us find ravens to travel north and west. He proudly showed us his flock, and once all five birds were up in the sky, we headed straight back for Daxian's council chambers.

The room was full of fae males, only a few of whom I'd seen before. I was pleased to see Briar and his kindly father, the Viscount Nightclaw, and my other Academy dormmate, Emery, and his father, the Duke Nightsong. Emery was a lanky, dark-haired fae who had been a cheery companion but terrified of Drake while we were at school. All the males stood and bowed upon my entry.

All except one, who bowed in his seat.

Next to Emery was a large black bloodhound, upon the back of which a tiny creature sat cross-legged in a cloth nest.

About the size of a human three-year-old, he was undoubtedly fae, with pointed ears, but his skin was dark as night. He wore a black mage's robe and a wrapping of purple cloth around his head. Warm, purple eyes appraised Drake and me and his dark lips twitched into a smile.

It was to this being that Drakus immediately shot, bending down on one knee with his head bowed.

"Drakus, my boy," the tiny fae growled. "Good to see you, though unbound. Wonder what you can do on the field now, eh? We heard you laid Havrok's court to waste." His eyes shone with pride.

"Some of that my mate is responsible for," Drake said with a smile.

I inclined my head to the creature whose eyes flicked to my forehead. He openly smiled, showing a mouth full of white teeth.

"Saraya," Drake said, "this is Chalamey Springfoot, Dean of Mountain Academy."

"If you had arrived at the Academy on time, we would

have met, your Highness," Chalamey said sternly, waving a tiny finger at me.

My smile faltered. *He knew.*

Briar and Emery both frowned deeply, snapping to attention at the Dean's words. The other lords were also looking between us sharply now.

"I thought it best if you told them," said Daxian, taking a seat. "It'll go smoother that way."

I took a deep breath and nodded.

"Briar," I said, looking at my friend, who had now turned white. "When we met at the border, I failed to mention that yes, you have seen me before. I look familiar because I was attending the Academy under disguise as a fae male. I was inducted to the Order of Temari, the Warrior Midwives, by the goddess Umali and I was required to train with the best. I was disguised as Sam Sourbottom and I am sorry for my deception."

Briar and Emery gaped at me, unable to find their words.

Then after a moment, "It was a good disguise." Emery looked me up and down, his gaze only briefly stopping at my breasts.

I gave a short laugh. "It's lucky I had the magic to do so. And Opal, of course, was a great help."

"I don't know what to say--" began Briar

"Hold on," said Duke Nightsong, frowning at Daxian. "Not the same, Sam Sourbottom, who beat the king in—"

"Yes, yes, we know," grumbled Daxian. "She is very good with a sword."

I suppressed my smile and inclined my head to the Duke. "I was trained from toddlerhood, my Lord."

"So was Daxian!" Viscount Nightclaw exclaimed.

"Perhaps we should move on to more important matters,"

Daxian said ruefully, "we may compare cocks later." He waved a hand at me. "Metaphorically speaking, Your Highness."

I pressed my lips together to try and control my grin. "Of course, Your Highness."

It was then that everyone shifted their attention to Daxian, and the room suddenly went quiet. Drake and I took the last two seats next to the king.

The meeting ended up being a brief on where we currently sat. Daxian said that Twilight Court had said they would come to our aid and were on their way with reinforcements, which was a great relief. Eclipse, Obsidian, and to our great concern, Midnight Courts were still ignoring our letters.

I spoke my part about my own missives to the human realm, at which the fae raised their brows but nodded their thanks. In all the years we had existed on each side of the mountain range, we had never needed to call upon one another for aid. But now, it seemed all rules, even the unspoken ones, were thrown to the wind.

Through our mate bond, I asked Drake whether we should tell them all about the Darkmaul dagger. Drake was wary, and we decided to keep it quiet. There were still hidden Reaper sympathisers in Black Court.

Suddenly, what had happened at the Mountain Academy when it was discovered that I had betrayed the fae made sense. At the time, all the nobles' sons had immediately left the Academy and run home that night. I hadn't really understood why they had chosen to do that. But the knowledge that the dark fae courts weren't all on the same side changed my perspective. The princes had all seemed friendly at court.

In hindsight, they *had* stuck together in groups. Daxian was friends with Skelton, the prince of Twilight Court, and

Ashwood, the prince of Midnight. But the Obsidian and Eclipse princes, Fern and Naxon, kept a little apart. Their loyalties had been clear even then. As Reaper loyalists, they would be in danger if something happened. Given reason, one of the other courts could very well hold them for ransom.

After the meeting was done, Daxian led Drake on an inspection of the palace, and I dutifully followed, keeping my eyes peeled for every and any detail.

Eventually, he led us deep under the castle, where their stock of luminous quartz was usually kept under lock and key. Under this level was a gargantuan chamber built into the earth—and old, I could tell from the colour of the rock. It was filled with stacks of luminous quartz in all colours.

Now, fae blacksmiths had been given full access and worked night and day to make fortified quartz weapons. Mages filled the swords, spears, and arrows with magic so that warriors who used the weapons would be able to fight with greater strength, arrows would fly further, and specialist warriors would be able to use magical attacks. We needed to be able to compete with the other courts, who were no doubt fortifying their own weapons in the same way.

"Here," said Daxian, indicating a line of finished swords. "Take your pick. With the way you fight, if you could ramp up the power behind your own magic, you'll be unstoppable on the field. We have carriers for them and everything."

I picked up one and hefted it. Too light. I wanted to use my astral sword. "Can I take some quartz instead? I might be able to manifest my own modifications."

Daxian shrugged and then picked two purple quartz bracelets from a box on a table. "Take these as well. It'll give a kick to your punches."

I smiled in thanks and he placed them both into my palm.

It felt a little odd accepting a gift from my ex-fiancé, especially jewellery. I felt Daxian's eyes on me for a moment before he turned away. I wondered what he was thinking and glanced at Drake, but my mate only had sympathy in his eyes for his half-brother.

3 5
SARAYA

That night was a full moon.

While Drake attended a meeting with Daxian, I excused myself as dusk fell and found my way outside to the back of the palace.

I shivered in the crisp air, the smell of winter approaching on the wind. The grounds were neatly kept and lined with the Darkcleaver's signature flower— black tulips that swayed to some song only they could hear. Beyond were greenhouses where Xenita supposedly kept the Corpse Flowers she was known for. They had to be kept separate and isolated because once a month, they emitted a heinous rotting smell.

The fae used quartz in a way humans never had. We really just used them for light and decoration, but here in the fae realm, the fae took things to the next level. Sculptures of quartz crystals formed dioramas depicting scenes from old fae tales. I stopped beside one just off the path—two lovers in a passionate embrace though the female had a dagger behind her back.

I was reminded that Glacine also used the magic of quartz.

In all the time she had been whipping me, I had never suspected that the red quartz jewellery she favoured was a storage space for the magic she was collecting from my pain. The red lights she favoured in her room completely disguised the glow of her red jewellery. I had always been tired and drained after a whipping, but that was to be expected when one had suffered great pain. I had no reason to think she was stealing my magic.

And I knew she was using it proficiently because she'd somehow disappeared without a trace, twice now. First from the Quartz Invasion and second from the melee at Havrok's ball. One second she'd been there, and the next, she was not.

But where had she gone?

I looked down at my own quartz bracelets, a rare purple I hadn't commonly seen around because it was too dark for producing light. But they sparkled prettily in the night, and I wondered how Glacine had channelled the pain into her own jewellery and how I could do the same with my own magic. If there was a way I could be even more powerful, I needed to learn it.

It was at that moment that Arishnie found me.

"Saraya!" For the first time, my warrior mentor's broad face was burdened with worry.

"I'm alright, Arishnie." I smiled grimly. "We escaped the demon lands and fled here. The human slaves were able to get out too. I'm hoping they're all safe in Kaalon by now."

Arishnie's round face relaxed and she released the tight grip on her sword hilt. "And what's the damage?"

I ticked the list off my fingers. "A new king for the demons, though we don't know who. Still no way for me to take back Lobrathia, and the dark fae are on the verge of war against the Green Reaper."

Arishnie's face paled under her transparent sheen. "Where did you hear this name?"

"Not, just hear," I said glumly. "I saw him. He spoke to me. He's awake, apparently, after a fifty-year slumber." I told Arishnie about the events at Havrok's court. Her face got grimmer and grimmer as I went on.

"This is worse than anything I could have expected." She began pacing back and forth before me.

"I can fight, Arishnie," I urged. "We already know this. But there's more to war than that. I don't know what to do."

"We have a lot to get through tonight, Saraya. There is much you need to know before the Reaper comes."

"Last time we spoke, you got cut off saying something important."

She nodded earnestly. "I wanted to remind you that Voltanius House has its own magic and that it was likely you had inherited that aspect too. Especially after being made High Priestess of Umali's Order, lightning is one of her manifestations."

I raised my hand, summoning a charge of tiny lightning. Fibres of white light crackled around my hand. "It happened for the first time when the Reaper wanted to take my shackles off." I let the electricity go and rubbed the tickle out of my skin, disturbed at the memory. "He said, 'I want to see what you can do.'"

Arishnie expelled a heavy breath. "He's been watching you, Saraya. It's impossible to know how much he knows. Even here…" She looked around the palace gardens where, in the distance, fae servants walked, going about their business.

"We need to be careful," I said, keeping my voice low. "But what choice do we have? I have no hope of outmatching him if I don't try."

"Saraya," Arishnie warned, "no one will be able to do this on their own. You'll need to work together. Back in my time, the Reaper stuck to the fae realm, but every so often, he would terrorise the humans. Obsidian Court would attack Kaalon or Lobrathia."

"He was waiting to collect more magic from us," I said darkly.

Arishnie nodded. "It was clear then what his intention was. He wanted more land and was testing the waters. He was a dark general who wanted to influence the fae, but Black and Twilight Courts would not follow his plan. He couldn't take over the entirety of the human realm without them all by his side. He clearly found a different path and decided to use the demon kingdoms instead. Clever, I'll give him that."

The Black Widow's voice breezed into my mind. Drake was the only one who could match him. I pushed away the sour feeling in my stomach. There had to be another way. "What can I do with my lightning other than zapping people to death?"

"I saw your ancestors use electricity in many different ways," Arishnie said, smiling faintly. "I'm going to advise you on a few. You can shock a person to death, yes, but with your knowledge of human anatomy, what else does electricity do?"

Revelation spun through me, bright and glimmering. "Neurons," I breathed. "Nerves in the body and brain."

"Those are now yours to manipulate."

I beamed. "But most of the soldiers will be males, not females."

Arishnie cocked her head. "Have you not figured it out by now, Saraya? You are now the High Priestess of our Order.

That mark you bear comes with great benefit. Gender is no issue for your power anymore."

I felt my magic rising within me, buzzing like a hive of bees under my skin. I looked at my hands. To be able to manipulate a male body as well as a female's...I practically had no limits. "I had wondered why I knocked out so many demon guards so easily," I admitted. "This is a great advantage."

"And it's not so much the physical body that this is advantageous for," Arishnie said, tapping her temple with a finger. "The benefit here is the manipulation of the mind. *This* is what the Green Reaper is known for. He plays within the astral realm, your fears, your desires."

I spun with that knowledge. "Is that why the other fae follow him so readily? He's manipulating them?"

"With promises, yes. If you know a man inside and out, you can manipulate them to do what you please."

And he knew all about us. About *me*. With his astral eyes, he was no doubt astral projecting, unseen, maybe, finding out all manner of things. And *we* knew nothing about him. That would have to change. I would have to find out everything about him, too.

"One more thing." Something had been turning over in my mind since Drake told me about the fae birth ritual. "If Xenita will allow me, I will go into the ether with her in place of her husband. I feel it is my duty."

Arishnie smiled proudly at me. "That is noble of you."

"Though I do not know the first thing about how it works."

"The mother will pull you in as she would her husband. You will then act as if you are in your physical form.

Anything that happens to you, including damage, will happen to your real body. It's unique in that way."

"A new experience will do me good, I suppose."

Arishnie walked with me about the garden. "There are three High Priestess skills I will teach you tonight. We'd better get started."

"I need to take back Lobrathia, Arishnie. But the entire kingdom is overrun with demons, and I have no army. We simply do not have the numbers."

"In the days of old with the warrior midwives, it would only have taken seven of us to do it," Arishnie said nostalgically. "Because it is not with strength that we won our war, but with our minds."

"Being Priestess, that means I can initiate new warrior midwives, doesn't it?"

Arishnie smiled. "It does, but the ritual is a difficult one. You'll have to memorise it."

"I'll do anything to get back Lobrathia, you know that."

"Well, you'll need that attitude to get this done. Let's start."

Once Arishnie advised me on the ritual to initiate warrior midwives, we began talking about my power of lightning.

"In old days of Lobrathia," she said, "the lightning kings would use their power to shield the city. This was the way the Reaper never was able to take control of the human realm. Both Kaalon and Quartz had magical defences that couldn't be breached. *This* is why the Reaper planned on taking human magic away. It's a genius plan and it worked well."

It clicked for me then. "Kaalon had a grand illusion over the entire city," I said. "That's how they're keeping safe now. But Quartz didn't have that."

"No," Arishnie said. "The old Kings used a shield of

331

Lightning around the city. It was impenetrable. They could even set off targeted attacks from a distance."

I froze on the spot. "A shield that big?" I couldn't contain my excitement. "Do you think I could do the same?"

My mentor gestured to the purple bracelets. "Have you tried drawing and filling the quartz?"

I frowned down at the bracelets, trying to focus on the magic I felt tingling against the skin under the jewellery. I honed in on the crystal, mentally pulling on it as I would pull on a rope, imagining its power coming into me. Suddenly, purple sparks flashed out of my fingertips, brighter than I'd ever seen. I jumped backwards.

"Holy Goddess!"

The bolts were seared into my vision and it took me moments to blink the image of them away. I could already use lightning to attack. I had done so at Havrok's Court on instinct. It would only be a minor manipulation of its path to place it around something like a shield.

When I looked up at Arishnie, she gave me a savage grin. "How much quartz can you get your hands on?"

36
DRAKE

Daxian, Chamaley Springfoot, and I headed out for the final inspection of the city's fortifications on horseback, my mentor on his fae hound.

The monstrous storm that had raged in my mind since my binding runes came off calmed when I was by Saraya's side. But with her back in the palace and me out here, I struggled to maintain clarity of mind.

Move, the storm said, *fight*.

Constantly keeping a tight rein on a raging stallion, it took great effort to listen to the words of those around me. My focus was best for fighting. So it was a great effort that I asked Chalamey, sitting cross-legged on his faehound, Bubble, to repeat what he'd just said to me.

"Your mind is a fire, Drakus Silverhand," my mentor said.

Daxian glanced at us in that twitchy way he seemed to always have now. He smelled sharp, like he was ready for a fight. His heartbeat was almost erratic, his breath shallow. He was always sweating. It was obvious that his black crown sat heavily on his head. I think he was still jumpy from the attack that had him lose his eye.

Once again, my mind was chasing birds of thought. I had to focus.

"I know, Dean," I grumbled. "It is worse when my mate is not near me."

"Hm." His tone was curious. "How many soldiers do we have?"

I rattled off the figures. "But ten out on injury."

"How many manning the watchtowers?"

I gave the numbers without thinking.

"Hm." Chalamey stared at me with those unnerving purple eyes. "So your penchant for war and strategy has only been sharpened by your unbinding."

It seemed so.

When I had first arrived at the Academy, a wild and untamed creature not made for sitting in a classroom, Chalamey had brought me into his office and produced a deck of cards. He said, if I won against him, he would let me off certain classes.

And so it had begun. I learned the games quickly and strategy even more quickly.

Soon, I was winning exorbitant amounts of money from the princes who thought they could best the erratic fae from the wild. But for me, cards had been a way to focus my mind when it wanted to run off and do something adventurous. Somehow, Chalamey had known exactly how to keep me in a chair. Through cards, he taught me discipline. Clever bastard. But that's how the Dean was, and that's why he was here to help us instead of at his home in Sky Court.

We were out of the city and on our way to the first watchtower when I broached a topic I did not want prying fae ears to listen in on.

"What do either of you know of the Darkmaul dagger?"

Daxian glanced at me with a frown. "The weapon used to slay Oberry the Gruesome in that myth?"

Oberry the Gruesome was a monster of fae legend. He had terrorised the ancient fae before Fern the First had put him to bed with the dagger.

But Chalamey tutted. "No myth. Truth."

The wind around us was crisp, the smell of tension palpable, to me, at least. We had no idea when the Reaper would come, but our ravens for Obsidian and Eclipse were disappearing into thin air now, and Viscount Nightclaw said his men had heard war horns across the river.

They were coming. And I estimated that we had days at best.

"Do we know where the dagger is?" I pressed. "My mother insists it is the only way to entrap the Reaper. I cannot find its scent, though I've looked into its box."

Chalamey eyed me significantly. "You will not *find* the dagger, Drakus. It finds, it chooses."

I swore under my breath. "Dacre Liversblood said it had been split in two."

"That is because it requires two beings to wield it."

"But Fern the First slew Oberry by himself," Daxian said, adjusting his eyepatch.

"He did not," Chalamey said. "His wife, Lily Silverfoot, seduced Oberry, lured him into Blossom Court, and as they lay together in the ancient grove, Fern came from behind and the two of them thrust both pieces of the dagger in at the same time. Lily Quickfoot knew what her husband did not—that men will follow their lust over any fear."

335

Rage tore through me so fiercely that below me, Razor tossed his head. "*What is wrong with you?*" he grumbled at me.

I growled. Unbidden to me came the image of Saraya beneath another male. There was no way in heaven or high hell that I would ever engage in a plan like that.

Both Chalamey and Daxian were staring at me.

I shook my head to try and get the image out.

"Focus, Drake," Daxian said. "I need you here, with us. Not wherever it is you go in that monster brain of yours now. I'm starting to believe the rumours about you ripping Havrok's head off."

I said nothing as we came upon the watchtower and Daxian rode on forward to speak to the captain. Chalamey eyed me. He knew very well that ripping Havrok's head off was exactly what I had done. He knew my nature.

"Do you fear for me, Dean?" I said, laughing darkly. "Fear for my shrivelled black soul?"

Chalamey tipped his head back and laughed. "You are a son of a deity, the mate of a High Priestess. Fear for you? No, but I do fear for your mate. Her path may very well be more difficult than yours."

I bade Razor to stop. Chalamey continued on Bubble for a few paces before stopping and looking back at me.

"What do you mean?"

He smiled. "She is Umali's chosen, Drakus. The path of tempests, of storms and rage. Her path will be the same. Wild. Unpredictable. Terrifying."

Brooding, we trekked along the circumference of the city. I checked the soldiers with Daxian and then, with Chalamey, checked the magical defences and pre-emptive attack mechanisms.

The magical fortifications around the city were absolute.

They would hold against a radical assault, giving us time to inspect our enemy and see how they wanted to attack.

While Obsidian and Eclipse Courts will physically attack the city, the Reaper would no doubt head for an internal assault, infiltrating the minds of the warriors, fighting a completely different battle.

My Black Court warriors were renowned for their physical fighting ability. We were the Court who established the Mountain Academy, after all. But our friends from Twilight Court would fight on the astral front. They would all sit down in the town hall and show their mental prowess. They would guard the city with their mental shields.

While fae could not astral travel, the Reaper would all but pull them out of their bodies. And then, only the Gods themselves knew what would become of us.

We were deep in the forest, on our way back to the palace, when Daxian paused on the trail and got off his zekar stallion.

I followed suit.

He looked seriously and Chalamey and I. "I needed to speak to you both where there was no chance of us being heard."

My ears perked up at the odd note in his voice. Nervousness. Anger.

Chalamey stepped Bubble forward, his tiny ears twitching.

Daxian's nostrils flared and he swung around, looking to the north at the mountains. "The Queen Mother wishes for me to take up the Green. She has been harassing me at every turn."

I went so still that the poison I'd drained from King Eldon's body bubbled uncomfortably in my chest. I glanced at Chalamey, but my pygmy fae mentor was nodding. "I expected her to feel that way. The Flamekeepers always favoured the Reaper."

I remembered that Xenita's natal home was in the Court of Flames and her family, the Flamekeepers had ruled it for centuries. Word was that Wyxian's father thought the union would make Obsidian and Eclipse Courts more friendly towards us.

"By pledging to the Reaper," Chalamey said softly, "you will avoid much carnage. There would be no war against Black Court."

I glanced at my mentor sharply, but he and Daxian were squaring off.

"But I cannot," Daxian hissed, slashing his hand through the air violently. "It was the one thing Father instilled in me. His one desire was to follow in the path of his ancestors. 'We are Black Court,' he used to say. 'We have always been our own fae. No one but us will rule our hearts.'"

My father had been a good ruler. Relief flooded through me at Daxian's response, and Chalamey nodded sagely. "Good boy."

Daxian didn't even look annoyed.

Only the Dean of Mountain Academy could get away with speaking to a king that way. Even a nervous king like Daxian. But the crux of it was that Xenita was siding with the Reaper, and that meant anyone who sided with her politically would also. We would just have to hope that the rest of our liege lords would be loyal to Darkcleaver house.

"But." Daxian was looking at me. "It seems we are alone in this battle. Are we all dying for our honour, Drake?"

Chalamey grumbled into a flask he'd taken out.

"Twilight Court will come. And the humans will come,

Dax," I said. "Lysander and Slade will bring them from Kaalon."

Daxian nodded slowly. "Us and the humans against three dark fae courts. These odds are not good."

"We have Drakus," Chalamey said, and I glanced at him in surprise, "born for war. And his mate, Goddess chosen. The enemy does not have those things."

"No, they just have the Reaper," Daxian sighed. "I'm having a feast tonight. If we are to die, then at least let us eat well before it."

As we continued back to the palace, my heart sat heavily in my chest as I thought about Daxian's words. *Were* we all going to our death over the Reaper's war?

The younger Darkcleaver children, Sage and Wren, had been sent to Sky Court ages ago. Xenita had refused to go and now I saw why. She wanted to be here to see the Reaper return. At least if we all died, the Darkcleaver line would not die with us. Wren would likely be the Reaper's chosen king.

My stomach churned at these dark thoughts. It wasn't going to happen. I wouldn't let it. Chalamey was right. Both sides had a Niyati, but only one side had a Tyaag. Traditionally, *Tyaag* meant sacrifice, but they were also people of great power. Lily Silverfoot had orchestrated Obery's death—with my Saraya doing her own preparations with her lightning shields and me already bouncing in my boots for a battle, we stood a chance. Twilight would side with us, I knew. Three courts against two. Those were odds I could work with.

37
SARAYA

A s night fell, the tension in the palace was palpable. Scouts had reported that both Obsidian and Eclipse Courts had crossed the border into Black Territory and had made camp for the night. Everyone was armed to the teeth with quartz-enforced weapons and ready for battle. With quartz spurring their travel, Drake expected the enemy to at dawn.

It felt awfully like the moments before Quartz City had been attacked by enemy demons. The very air waited with a heavy presence, my skin constantly marked with goose-bumps. Smiles were nervous when anyone could bear to smile in the first place.

We were in our rooms, changing into fresh shirts for Daxian's feast, when a knock came at the door.

"Raven master," Drake muttered to me before he strode to the door and opened it.

The old fae bowed, his wispy white hair flopping back as he straightened. His expression was strained. I supposed he was under a lot of stress with losing all those ravens to the enemy courts. "Your Highnesses, a return letter from the Human Realm."

I ran forward to take the parchment from him, breaking the orange peach tree seal and opening it. There was only one picture, and I showed it to Drake in horror. It was a drawing of two penises, with squiggly lines coming out of the top of them and, next to those, a triangle.

Drake took one look and chuckled as the raven master left. "It's in pictorial code," he explained. "Lysander made it up when we were teenagers. It means, 'We are coming.' And they must be at the mountain pass."

I scoffed in mild disgust. But I had to admit it was marginally clever. "Gets the point across, I suppose."

"Indeed." But Drake could not wipe the smile off his face, and I knew that hearing his sergeants would be returning was the best possible news he could get. "Do you think they'll be bringing Kaalon's army?"

"Harder to say, and harder still to ask without the risk of interception."

Drake nodded. "Either way, they'll be here at the same time as the enemy."

THE FEAST HALL WAS CLAMOURING WITH ARMED FAE MALES. There were some females in the military, but those who had powerful magic were favoured. The liege lords had sent their wives and children home or as far away as possible, but the rest of the female nobility would wait with Xenita in a safe hold under the palace when the battle began. Even Chalamey Springfoot had left, back to his native home in Sky Court.

"We will meet again, Princess," he had said, eyeing me with a smile.

Fae musicians played a bawdy tune, and the bard sang a song about a salacious fae maiden and a tree sprite that had me shaking my head. The food was piled high on silver plates, and drink flowed freely. Drake returned to me after a round of playing cards with some of his warriors. I noticed that whenever they played with him, he declined to play with money and they agreed it was for the best. Somehow, Drake won every hand. The times he did lose, no one said anything. It seemed to be the general consensus that he lost on purpose.

"Fae are not affected by alcohol as humans are," Drake sat down next to me as I observed the king's table. "It clears the system within hours. We have to keep drinking to feel the effects."

"Convenient," I replied as we began to eat.

"Your Highness," came a soft voice.

I jerked around to see Briar, standing uncertainly with a plate of food.

"You should call me by my name," I chided him, patting the seat next to me.

As he hastily sat, I could feel Drake watching the round fae with hawk like eyes. No doubt he was remembering that Briar had seen me naked that one time at the Academy.

"I'm...I'm glad you're here, S-Saraya," Briar said, tugging on his bun of black hair— the way he always wore it. "We need all the help we can get."

"You forgive me?" I asked sheepishly. "About pretending to be a male?"

Briar shrugged his wide shoulders. "You did what you had to do. And look, it's gotten you here, with all these powers everyone is talking about." He turned to me excitedly, "Is it true you can summon lightning?"

I grinned at him and raised my fingers, allowing a thread of electricity to circle around my finger. My control was getting better and having practised for hours with Arishnie yesterday, I was almost fully confident with it now.

"Whoa!" Briar choked and without thinking, slapped me on the back. "That's amazing!"

I laughed and for a moment, it felt like we were back at the Academy, having dinner together and joking around. But Briar seemed to realise we weren't at the Academy and who it was that he'd just thumped on the back.

He covered his mouth, "Oh Gods, I'm so sorry—"

I thumped him on the back in turn, choking on my own laugh. "You were my first fae friend, Briar, you can hit me all you like."

A low growl came from the seat next to me, and Drake, although he seemed to be concentrating on his food, I knew his full attention was on me. Briar blanched.

"Ignore him, " I said, giving Drake a pointed look of disapproval. "I'm glad you're here as well, Bry. I miss the Academy sometimes."

Briar calmed down enough to grace me with a smile. "You do?"

I grinned at him and we ate together and reminisced about our time at the warrior school..

An hour later, the party was in full swing. Xenita had left to rest, rubbing her pregnant stomach. Daxian and his younger brothers Dattan and Ivy were sitting with their liege lords, eating and still drinking.

Daxian swayed to the music, one arm around Ivy, the other holding a goblet of strong whiskey. I frowned as I thought about how much he would have had to drink to be *this* drunk. Ivy's face was drawn tight and he clutched his own chalice with white knuckles. Daxian was the picture of a male who—

And then it hit me with all the force of a battering ram to the gut.

Daxian didn't think we were going to win. He was the picture of a man who thought this was his last night on earth. He intended to die here.

Bile rose up my throat and I clutched at my stomach.

Drake was at my side with a flash. "What's wrong?"

I looked up at him, his black eyes dissolving into hazel right in front of me. It was a constant reminder that when he was around me, he changed.

There was a shout in the entrance hall, and a warrior ran in. "It's a rider! A rider from Twilight Court!"

Drake was out the door before anyone else, leaving the rest of us to hurry behind him.

The rider was sopping wet, his grey cloak sticking to his lithe body.

I recognised the brown face of Prince Skelton immediately, cradling an injured shoulder covered in blood and rainwater.

"Dead," he choked. "My entire court was massacred. They made me leave. Father *forced* me to leave. I had no choice. Kill me. Kill me right now for abandoning my family—"

He babbled as Daxian pushed past everyone and put strong arms around him, his face tight with suppressed emotion. I stood transfixed, listening to the horror unfolding.

Then Drake was there, pulling Skelton's wet cloak off and pushing him towards the hearth at the side of the hall. "When?" Drake rasped.

Skelton looked up at Drake as if in shock. His face

blanched with cold and trauma. "I rode with my father's magic on my heels. Two days."

Drake stood, whirled around, and spoke to every fae in the room. "I think that's enough for the night. Everyone who's not on duty, get to bed."

As everyone hurried to comply and servants rushed Skelton from the hall, my mate then strode towards me, pulling me out of the room by the elbow. He spoke to me mind-to-mind. *"Saraya, I need you to leave. We will not win this battle."*

My heart sank deeper in my chest. I let him steer me out of the hall and then shook him off. *"No,"* I said firmly.

Silently, we made for our rooms. We couldn't be seen having an argument on the eve of battle.

When we arrived, I whirled around and said, "You would have me leave you? Leave my friends?"

He looked truly scary in the yellow quartz light, his body rippling with power, his body practically quivering with concentrated energy.

I vaguely found myself wondering who would come out best if we ever got into a physical fight and really tried to hurt one another.

Despite his appearance, I did feel safer with him. All the time he'd been captor in my own palace in Quartz City, I'd known that he'd never truly harm me. Perhaps that was why I had pushed him so much.

"I…" Drake sighed heavily. "Saraya, as your mate, my first instinct is to protect you. Understand this, please?"

I closed my eyes. He *was* my mate, and it was clouding his judgement, his power. "Drake, my place is beside Xenita. I am the reason her children are fatherless. If I had not left to go on

345

my own, Wyxian would never have been there, he would never have—"

Drake grabbed me by my face. "You cannot blame yourself for Wyxian's death—"

I shook off his hands and stepped away from him. "Drake, it's not only that. I am the High Priestess of the Order of Te'mari. My place is beside a pregnant woman who needs me. Xenita is long past due for her baby and the stress of the war would no doubt make her go into labour. I see her having early pains already. I need to be here for when active labour starts. It's her sixth. It will go quickly."

Drake's eyes were a stark and bright hazel. "Saraya, we don't have the dagger. We don't have the men. We are walking into a graveyard tomorrow. The warriors know it. A few have fled already. Those who remain are ready to die for the honour of House Darkcleaver. What would you have me do?" His voice cracked and he looked at me desperately.

I fought the burning in my eyes like a seasoned warrior, then made an effort to smile at him. "Just hold me tonight."

Drake's shoulders sagged, his face melting into a mixture of sadness and desire. He rubbed his face and nodded. He took off his shirt and got into bed. "Come here," he said softly.

I licked my lips and came forward, kicked my boots off, and lay on my side against his chest. His arms came around me in that easy, comforting way. The way our magic twined together when we were close was like the sea meeting the shore. It spiralled and tickled, beamed upwards in my chest, making me feel giddy. I pulled back to look at Drake's face and brushed my lips across his lips. An unexpected tear slid from my eye.

"Oh, my princess," Drake whispered, kissing my tears away.

My throat was thick with sorrow I didn't—couldn't express. Drake kissed my cheeks. He always knew how to make me feel better. The thought of him leaving, the thought of him dying in this war…I had to feel his skin against mine. I had to have him. I pulled my shirt off, then my pants, and like the desperate woman I suddenly was, I pulled Drake's pants off to find that he was already hard, his manhood springing upwards. I straddled him.

Not taking his eyes off mine, he reached down and eased his hard length into me. I threw my head back and moaned to the ceiling as my body relaxed around his girth. Drake pulled my face down to his.

He kissed me deeply, thrusting into me slowly. "You can't fathom how much I need you, Saraya," he whispered against my lips. He pulled back and thrust in me again. "All of you. I could never leave you." He increased his speed, groaning out each word with another thrust. "All. I. Want. In. This. Life. Is. You."

Suddenly, he rolled us over, and all at once, he was on top of me.

But I wanted more of him. I pulled my thighs towards my chest, and with a growl, Drake adjusted his arms, pinning my legs with his shoulders.

The result allowed him to slide inside me so deeply that I groaned deep in my own chest.

He filled me over and over again, pleasure building up, first starting in my core and then spreading upwards, encompassing the whole of me. He whispered my name, and I whispered his. In a blind fervour, we came together. He buried his face in my neck, and I screwed my eyes shut tight, begging them not to betray me.

Afterwards, he held onto me like his life depended on it. I sighed at the feeling of his skin on mine. I never wanted to forget this.

"The fae lark back at your home," I said softly, "You never told me why they came to the Grove."

He hesitated, delaying his answer by tracing the thin lines of the mating bond on my arm.

"Fae larks appear wherever there are strong feelings of love. I...felt that for you."

Emotion filled my throat, hot and aching.

But I knew what had to be done. I had known for a while. It tore my heart to pieces, but I could not see these people die just because I wanted Drake to be with me. In my heart, I knew the only way we would win this war against the Reaper was if Drake was allowed to take on his full power without me as his mate.

38
SARAYA

They came before dawn.

Deep war horns blared in the distance as Drake and I parted ways at the entrance hall. The horns meant the army had breached the magical protections. We had to hurry. Drake had refused armour, instead wearing a number of weapons, including a sword. I frowned when I saw its hilt because on it was a plain black dragon on a field of gold. When I pointed it out, he hurriedly said, "That's my Commander's symbol."

Recognition hit me with a blow to the gut. *"Looks like I beat Daxian to giving you a ring."*

I thought he had been making a joke. Instead of giving me Daxian's ring, Drake had given me *his* ring, back in Quartz before my supposed wedding to Daxian. Even then, his subconscious had known and wanted me. I didn't even know where that ring was now. Probably stolen by some thieving demon. But I put it out of my mind. I had to. I had to. I had to.

Drake reached for me and kissed me fiercely before his eyes clouded over with that starry all-black. If I was going to do it, the time was now, right now. Drake needed to be out there in full force if we were going to win this. If we were going to survive. I needed to reject him. I opened my mouth, but my throat closed over. I gritted my teeth.

Just do it.

My weakness might get us all killed. I clenched my fists, bracing myself against the vile words I needed to say.

I reject you as my mate.

My mouth opened, but my tongue was heavy in my mouth, and my vocal cords were frozen in time.

But Drake was pulled away by one of his captains, and they strode out of the hall into chaos.

I took a moment to watch him stride away. The warriors were grim-faced, their movements tense. I should have done it. Drake was weaker because of me. They might all die because I couldn't say six simple words.

"Saraya."

I whirled around to see Daxian, in full black fae plate armour, striding towards me. It was beautiful, with a dragon scale design all the way around. Although his face was pale, his jaw was set, and his shoulders were straight.

Today, he looked like a king, and despite it all, that made me smile. "My mother has gone into labour."

That wiped the smile off my face. "I'll go to her immediately."

He nodded and, without hesitation, offered me his hand. Surprised, I took it, and we shook.

"We may never see each other again, Saraya," Daxian said in a voice that did not waver. "I want you to know that I harbour no ill will towards you."

My eyes burned. "Nor I for you." I swallowed. "I'm going to activate my lightning protection around the palace. Make sure you tell your soldiers they cannot touch it." I had another trick up my sleeve, but I didn't want to reveal it just yet.

He nodded. "Thank you. Look after my mother, please. And…when my new sister arrives, tell her…that her brother fought for her."

I could not control the tears that slipped from me, but I didn't try to hide them either. "We will meet again, Daxian."

He smiled ruefully. "If not in this life, then the next, perhaps." Stepping back, he bowed, and strode to his warriors.

I wiped my eyes on my sleeve, my breath shaky as I watched them all leave into the dark. Once the entrance hall emptied, I strode out onto the front steps and raised my hands. In the way I had practiced with Arishnie, drawing out the lightning from inside of me, I triggered the points of power I had set around the palace last night, drawing them upwards into a wide arc. Beams of brilliant blue-white light travelled upwards in a static hum, and between the beams, a sheet of electricity vibrated boldly. I had staked head-sized quartz stones into the ground around the entire perimeter of the palace so that the shield would run off their power and not mine.

Satisfied, I hurried down the marble steps that would lead me to the Queen Mother's safehold. I wondered if Xenita would actually let me help her. All I knew of her was that she reminded me of Glacine, in that icy, I-have-my-own-agenda courtier way of hers. Drake had told me that she was willing to side with the Reaper as that is what her family had historically done. She might very well shun me.

The metal door was open, two female warriors herding the noblewomen and children in. When I arrived in the wide room, I was regarded coldly by the courtiers, who held their children closely to their breasts. An infant cried, and I glanced curiously at the bundle of blankets in the mother's arms. Fae infants rarely went out in public, so I had never seen one before.

On the far wall was a wide set magical window that made it look like we were in a room high in the wings of the palace, with an excellent view of the city. Warriors were streaming through the streets, guiding the city folk to board their houses, gathering into their units, and heading out to the plain where the battle would be fought.

My heart gave a sick pang as I knew both Briar and Emery would be with their fathers. No males could be spared to sit and watch, so both boys were somewhere in there, wondering if they would live to see another day.

"I do not wish to be touched!" a familiar voice snapped. "Just bring the water."

Xenita was in an adjoining chamber, and her maids, their eyes wide in nervousness, nodded and let me in.

Xenita was dressed as she always was, hunched over a bed, her head bowed. Her ladies-in-waiting scrambled about the room. Two girls were heaving a shallow bowl of water onto a table.

In the distance, a bell rang. My heart sank, but I suppressed the urge to look into the magical window because I knew what I would see.

"The city bell! The protections are breached!" a maid cried. "They are—"

"Calm yourself, Tulip," snapped Xenita. She turned and

saw me standing by the door. Her cheeks were pink and her face held a vibrant magical glow. She cast me a look, her eyes flicking to my priestess mark. "Why are you here?"

I stepped forward. "I am High Priestess of the Order of Temari. It would be my duty, my honour, to accompany you in your journey."

Xenita inhaled deeply as she registered what I was saying. Finally, she said, "The ether is not for the faint-hearted." She looked me up and down, from my priestess mark down to my new leather boots. "It may very well kill you."

I hid my uncertainty. "We shall see. But I *will* protect you with my life."

There was a moment of tense silence as Xenita simply looked at me, her hand on her stomach, her entire face and body glowing with what must have been fae birthing magic.

"You may join me," she said imperiously. "If Daxian can forgive you, perhaps I may look past your previous transgressions as well. For the moment, at least."

As I exhaled in relief, Xenita Darkcleaver strode to the centre of the room and held out her hands in front of her, palms up. She cast a look over her shoulder at me.

Taking my queue, I took my place in front of the Queen Mother, placing my palms on top of hers. Her breath smelled of raspberries as she expelled a slow and measured breath. This was her sixth baby. She knew exactly what she was doing and raspberry leaf tea was something we always told our women to drink as well.

"Goddess, protect us," she whispered. "Pan, protect us. Ancestors, watch over us." Her breath caught, but she swallowed the rise of emotion down. "Wyxian, watch over your unborn child and your widow."

My own throat went tight as I said my own prayer.

"Great Umali, grant us all the power of the raging storm. The strength of the queentide. May all quiver from the thunder of our roar."

I felt Xenita shift in mild surprise before me. But it was short-lived because her magic quickly reached out for me, taking root deep in my being. It was an ancient, glittering marvel of dark and light magic woven into the fabric of reality. And all at once, I was pulled out of my body.

Abruptly, my vision cleared and darkness yielded to dim light. I found that I was seated, gently rocking from side to side. A two person boat. Sailing on black water. We gaped at the infinite shadowy maw that had become our world. Well, *I* was gaping. The Queen Mother was eyeing this place like a long-forgotten enemy.

But there were rocky walls on either side. It was a cave, I realised, just so incredibly huge that I felt like an insect on a miniature boat travelling through the ocean. Surrounded by darkness, Xenita grabbed the glowing wooden stick that sat between us—able to guide this boat using it. We sailed along, and just ahead, two shadows came into view high above us, on either side of the black river.

I realised with a pang that it was a set of two gigantic doors suspended in mid-air, easily big enough to accept our boat with space on the side. Xenita was not surprised, simply looking at each door as we went.

We sailed along, passing another set of doors, then one on its own at our left. Finally, the river picked up its pace, and ahead, facing us this time, was a large wooden door. It lowered as we approached, blocking our way down the river.

"You should not have come with me," Xenita whispered. "There is no going back now."

"I am High Priestess of the Order of Temari," I said softly. "I do not fear the dark."

After a pause, she said, "And I am a Darkcleaver of Black Court, I do not fear the void."

I nodded at her. "Then lead the way, Your Grace."

The door opened inwards and we sailed right through. On this side, the sky was a deep blood red, and the air was warm and humid. Immediately, I got the undeniable feeling that we were being watched. I whirled around, the hairs on the back of my neck prickling terribly. But in the vast ocean of dark water, I saw nothing on any horizon. The water stretched out as far as I could see. But that didn't change the fact that we were in a tiny boat in the middle of nowhere.

"Are you ready, Princess?" Xenita asked darkly.

I gripped my side of the boat and turned to look at her. "What do you mean?"

She simply held her hand out, and with a flash of light, a ruby-hilted sword appeared in her hand. I gaped at her.

"On this plane, you can summon anything you like. It's only fair considering what is to come. Look." She angled her sword towards the middle distance.

I summoned my own sword, my heart racing in my chest, and then I turned to look before us.

Through the red light, a shadow appeared on the water.

Xenita grabbed the guiding stick between us and jammed it right, causing the boat to veer sharply in that direction. I grabbed the side of the boat, my stomach lurching as we sped away from the shadow that was slowly solidifying into something huge. The wind struck me in the face as Xenita increased our speed.

I turned to look over my shoulder.

"Do *not* look at them, girl!" Xenita cried over the wind battering at our faces. "Not yet. We must get to the exit first."

"But what are they?" I shouted back.

"Wyxian called them the ship of fears. They are beings who represent every fear you have. You must execute them all once we get to the exit, and only you and your aides can kill them."

My brows furrowed as I thought on this.

On the horizon, a shadow appeared, and within ten minutes of zooming over the water, it came into view. The yawning mouth of a gigantic cave.

"That is where my child is," Xenita said, staring into the darkness with her chin set stubbornly.

I nodded.

"When we land inside, do not look at the ship behind us. Let them follow, but do not engage with them."

I rubbed my arms, bidding the goosebumps away. I didn't like the fact that there were things following us and I could do nothing about it.

We approached the cave's mouth, jagged, rocky teeth forming a border all around us. I felt as if I were sailing into the belly of an awful monster. Xenita did not hesitate. Its darkness swallowed us. But once my eyes adjusted, I saw that just inside was a sandy beach.

Xenita steered us with a sure hand, and we sailed right up onto the sand.

Wobbling, I got out, splashing into the water and climbing onto the wet sand. I pulled the boat higher up the shore and went to help Xenita. She, albeit reluctantly, took my hand and allowed me to help her hop ashore.

We stumbled onto the beach, looking around the seemingly empty landscape. Which way now?

"Xenita," came a male whisper on the breeze.

"Saraya!"

I would recognise that voice anywhere.

It was my mother's.

Whirling around, a group of people waited for us.

39

DRAKE

azor pranced excitedly as I mounted him.

We were both bred for war, and now, war was here. Saraya's face just before I left her in the entrance hall haunted my mind's eye. Her expression was nervous, conflicted, thinking. Was she thinking about what my mother had told her? I had no doubt about it. It pained me that it had made her upset, but on some level, I was satisfied that she had not done as my mother had asked and rejected me as her mate. Even though the magical ink on her hand sat firm and bold, she could technically abandon me, and the tattoo would fade away.

But even as I left the stables and trotted out into the city, my thoughts about Saraya became muddled, and I allowed myself to succumb to the war rage that had been hovering at the edge of my mind.

It engulfed me as a snake engulfs its prey, and I was ashamed to say that I loved every moment of it. The exciting terror at Havrok's palace seemed too long ago.

I met our warriors outside the city, where a scout was

galloping up and down the city's line, blowing his horn continuously. I watched the units assemble, making sure everything was aligned as we had planned.

Warriors on horseback made our front lines, armed with spears. Behind them were warriors with swords and axes. And behind those, the soldiers working on horseback.

And far behind us, our archers stood ready with their quartz-infused long-range bows. Inside the city hall, our mental defences sat ready in meditation.

After circling around, I cantered to the front of our army, where Daxian, our liege lords, and generals sat on their war horses.

Daxian gave me a grim nod, his twin swords strapped to his back, like mine. I also wore a baldric with daggers. I was ready for a long fight. Eager for it.

Daxian signalled the captain with the horn to retreat and now silence swept the plain. I was acutely aware of every movement. Darkcleaver House flags rustled, horses snorted and stepped, steel scraped, fae warriors held their breath. The enemy had been working on our magical shields for an hour now. I imagined they had exhausted their mages to get through. That's how we'd set it up. Briefly, I wondered if Dacre was out there somewhere. It was more likely that he had fled.

The scent of foreign fae warriors wafted in the breeze. Obsidian weapons, Eclipse steel, Midnight Court zekar.

Something shifted on the horizon, and the flag bearers came into view, three of them, galloping on their horses, standards raised. Then the ground began to tremble with what I estimated were four thousand stampeding steeds. Daxian gripped the sword at his hip, our generals and sergeants exhaled, and next to me Duke Nightsong growled in his chest.

The line of warriors came into view, black armour on a dark plain. Pre-dawn light began to purple the sky to the east. I knew that by the time the sun cleared the horizon, many would be dead.

My eyes found each flag along the horizon. Obsidian's silver serpent on a field of black, Eclipse's red crescent-moon on a field of black, and Midnight's gold phoenix on a field of black.

We were outnumbered three to one.

The three kings had come themselves, as was proper. Their silver, red, and gold armour glinting from the light of the flame torches. They rode to the centre of the entire force and slowed to a stop, leaving a good one hundred paces between our front lines and theirs.

It was King Fern Gulfblade from Obsidian Court who spoke with a magically enhanced voice that flew to us across the grassy field. "Black Court is called to submit to our emperor and saviour, The Green Reaper!"

Under the storm of my mind, four words came to mind. My mate's house.

Lightning does not yield.

I snarled in anticipation.

Daxian set his shoulders like the warrior I knew he was and he magically enhanced his voice, roared across the field. "We will not. The Darkcleavers have always been our own fae. We have always owned our own land. And we always will."

A cheer erupted from our warriors. The Darkcleavers always had loyal subjects. They had always been worthy rulers.

But where was my mark? Where was the Green Reaper? I could not see him on the field as of yet.

"Then we have no choice," King Gulfblade called. "We will take your land and your people in the name of the Green General."

Daxian's voice did not falter. "Then you have chosen evil. And we will not stand down." Daxian put his helmet on.

I growled in approval. Razor pawed the grass.

Let this be done, he said to me. *Let us have blood.*

If the Reaper was not here, I would set my sights on another mark for now.

Midnight's King, Shadowwing, was a turn cloak and a coward. He could have fought with us. Could have fought for our autonomy. But had chosen cowardice. I unsheathed one of my swords and pointed it at him. He was a sharp, stocky man, and across the battlefield, I saw his eyes flash angrily at me.

I gave him a taunting, promising smile in return.

The three kings across the field gave the command to charge.

Daxian raised his blade and roared.

Razor galloped out with enthusiasm and focus, with eyes only for Shadowwing's horse, a vicious chestnut zekar.

Our forces met as the sky turned red with the sunrise.

I came on them first, pushing spears away to stab and slash with both my swords. Razor kicked and bit, and we worked our way towards the traitor King Shadowwing.

Daxian was behind me, and on some level, I knew that I should be protecting him. But my half-brother was fighting in a way that I had not ever seen before. There was blood on his face and his sword, and he roared with the insane fury of a person who thought this was their last battle. I allowed myself a fleeting moment of pride before I unleashed myself on the warriors around me—mere annoyances at this stage.

Magic flew through the air, severing someone's neck next to me. One of my warriors. I located the perpetrator, plucked a spear from a fallen soldier on horseback, and threw it, piercing the fae in the gut.

Magic was not as satisfying a way to kill as my bare hands were, but this battle called for it. So I brought my power out, and a thundering filled my being as a dark blue shock of power expanded outwards in a bright dome, killing any enemy within fifty paces.

A shocked pause overtook everyone outside the dome before they ran. Pleased, I pursued.

The battle raged. Magic flew, flames sprung, fae warriors screamed. The smell of blood filled the air, and then—

A high-pitched bugle sounded behind us, to the north. I knew at once it was a human-made horn.

Activity on the battlefield paused as the human military contingent from Kaalon came rampaging down the western path, and in the lead were Slade with Lysander trumpeting a merry tune on a golden bugle.

I growled in approval before ramming my fist into an enemy's nose. Shadowwing was close now, and I saw at his side was a fae male I knew well from the Academy, Prince Ashwood, looking terrified. I briefly wondered if I should spare him. As heirs, the princes were not meant to be on the battlefield. I made my way up to him, blasted his guards away, and took him by the neck.

Shaking him roughly, I said, "Run."

The look of terror on his face was enough to make up for me not getting my kill. He turned on his heel and ran back into his lines. In order to avoid the raging desire to chase him,

I turned to the Midnight King, currently slashing at two of my warriors.

I ran for him with a cry, watching Lysander and Slade from the side of my eye. The humans were no match for full-blooded fae warriors, but somehow they still fought valiantly, slashing their swords aggressively.

The battlefield surged, and through my blood lust, I realised with dismay that our left flank had broken where no reinforcement had come. Our right held firm where the humans had engaged in battle.

We needed to cut the snake off at its head. If we could kill the three kings, perhaps their forces would dissipate with the lack of leadership, and Midnight Court was the one that might just do it.

But just as I reached Shadowwing's ring of guards, the quality of the air changed and gave me pause. I elbowed a warrior that tried to come up behind me, cocking my head to consider.

The air smelled of burning flesh, and a voice like dark and rotten things vibrated through the air. "Halt!"

Everyone knew who it was right away.

The entire battlefield magically froze mid-fight, swords hanging in the air, faces contorted in rage or pain. All around the field, all I heard was the sound of thousands of thumping hearts.

High above us, against a cloudy morning sky, a silver chariot emerged, drawn by a glittering, semi-transparent winged zekar.

My eyes were drawn to the two beings standing in the chariot, one with a green flaming head, the second, with a very normal human head.

The Green Reaper's voice echoed all around us. "I will

give you one last chance to side with me, Darkcleaver King. Or we will lay your city to waste."

A flame of fury tore up within me as I recognised Glacine by the Reaper's side. She was dressed in green armour, her pale face calculating.

I wanted to locate Daxian, but I couldn't turn my head to look around the battlefield. This type of power would have taken a serious amount of quartz to work. Grunting, I pushed against the magic holding me, shoving my magic against it with all my might. It yielded to me and I turned my head, inch by inch, to my right, to where Daxian was surrounded by our warriors and Duke Nightsong. Whatever was holding the rest of us was not holding him.

My half-brother waved his sword in the air angrily. "Never!" he cried.

"Very well," boomed the Green Reaper.

Suddenly, lightning fell from the sky, narrowly missing the chariot. The zekar scrambled, terrified by the sudden electricity.

I frowned because there was no storm in the air.

Saraya.

The chariot did a sharp U-turn in the sky, the zekar reeling from the attack, before whisking the chariot away and dissolving into nothing. My mate, my powerful, clever mate, had set up an attack without her being here.

Whatever magic the Reaper had used to hold the entire battlefield broke and both sides re-launched into their attacks.

But it was useless because our front lines were breaking and Midnight's army was now past us, swarming towards the city, closely followed by Eclipse's warriors in the wings. We couldn't hold them. We had to hope Saraya's lightning shield around the palace would hold, because the Black Court army was not.

And then an ear-shattering roar split the air in two.

Everyone remaining on the field stopped dead. With the Green Reaper gone, his undeniable dark presence had dissolved, leaving clean air behind. But the air filled with a heavy presence once again. Far in the distance, came a second fiery roar. The ground trembled. Something was hurtling towards us on the horizon. My senses picked up what the others could not. Smoke, fire, molten earth made sentient.

"What the fuck is that?" Lysander called loudly from my right.

Everyone, including our enemy, ran.

40

SARAYA

A group of spectres was gathered on the beach behind us. Most of them were fae, by their pointed ears and ethereally beautiful faces, but two of them were human.

I recognised King Wyxian immediately, standing in front of the group, but a little way from him was the clear and obvious figure of my mother, and next to her, my father.

An involuntary sob tore through my throat. I ran.

Xenita called out a sharp warning to me. "Do not touch them!"

I barely heard her as I stumbled across the sand, eyes only on the ghostly forms of my parents. But just as I reached them—

"Do not come any closer, my love!" My father's deep boom swept across me and made me halt mid-step in the sand.

"Mother," I choked. "Father, I am sorry."

I hugged myself, taking in my parents. My mother's kind, round, beautiful face, the curves of her figure. She was wearing the long white Ellythian silk dress we put her in on the day she died. My father stood proud and tall, his beard full, his eyes clear and intent on me— focused like I'd not seen them in years.

I was vaguely aware of Xenita striding up to Wyxian, her voice thick and hushed with grief and a little relief, I think.

Because relief was exactly what I felt.

My parents looked well. There was only happiness in their faces, no pain, no harrowed suffering. They looked perfect, and a jagged edge in my heart healed. Next to me, Xenita was furiously whispering to Wyxian

"Saraya, you must listen to me." My mother spoke so quickly that I had to concentrate to understand her words. "You must find Umali's blade. The Te'mari Blade. It's the same one I defended you with after your birth. The Sky Court queen will know where it is. It is guarded—"

"We must go." Wyxian's voice reverberated towards us, hitting me in the gut.

I didn't want to go, I tried to control my face, but it crinkled with emotion. "What do you mean?" I said, taking a step forward. "Umali's blade? But what—"

Then Xenita was tugging on my elbow, nervously glancing behind us.

"Saraya, my beautiful girl," my mother said, her voice heavy and urgent. "I am so proud of you. Go, fight for what is right. I will be watching."

My father nodded and smiled at me. My heart felt heavy in my chest. I needed to ask them more questions, needed to know if they were happy and to tell them that I wished that they were here. But all the words in the world could not capture the laceration of being torn away from them once again.

Xenita was pulling me away now. "Y-Yes, Mother," I stammered, holding back the sob for all I was worth.

As I turned away, I saw that Wyxian's ghost was standing with us and Xenita was eyeing the remaining ghosts like a general surveying her soldiers.

She pointed at my father. "I choose you, King Eldon."

I frowned at Xenita, looking between her and my father. But my father looked equally surprised. "Are you sure?"

"I must choose two ancestors to watch our backs in the tunnel. Naturally, I will be choosing my husband. But as for the second…" she waved her hand at the mixture of fae ghosts listening to our conversation. "But I have had five babies previously. They've all had a turn. And…" she turned to my father. "It seems only fair the two fathers get to come along. Besides, the princess will need help to get through this."

The tears that rushed to my eyes were unexpected, but Xenita was already turning away as if her choice was a trivial thing. I blew out a breath and looked at my father's ghost.

He beamed at me, and for the first time in half a decade, he looked like the capable and bright warrior king he had once been. He flexed his hands. "Lead the way, Fae Queen." A two-handed broad sword flashed into his hands and he nodded at me.

"Goodbye, Mother," I said, blinking the blurriness in my eyes away. "I wish Altara could have seen you."

She smiled at me and my heart beat irregularly in my chest at the sheer love that I felt from her. "One day, my love."

I grinned back and, summoning all the discipline I had in my bones, turned away from her and followed Xenita, now picking up her dress and stomping across the beach.

As Wyxian and my father fell behind us, I muttered an

apology to Wyxian. "I'm sorry things happened the way they did, King Darkcleaver."

He gave me a nod. "The blame lies with only one person, Princess Saraya. The Green Reaper. I am glad the humans and the fae are working together."

I nodded absently. There *was* only one enemy now, and I wondered how the battle outside was going. Chances were, by the time Xenita and I came out of this, the fighting would be over. It was lucky I had put the reinforcements around the palace when I did. It may very well be our last stand. While human bones and muscle might yield, my lightning never would— while the quartz was there to power it, that is.

Xenita led us up the beach towards the rocky wall and I followed with the two kings behind me. Before us was a narrow tunnel entrance.

Xenita audibly gulped and summoned that ruby-hilted blade of hers.

"Thank you," I said in a low voice.

"Don't thank me yet," she said curtly. "Because now, we fight for our lives."

She walked straight in.

Before I could stop myself, I summoned my blade and followed. Impossibly quickly, everything went incredibly dark and terribly silent.

"Xenita?" I hissed.

"I'm here, Saraya." My father's voice was hushed. "I'm right behind you, keep walking, and do not halt."

Gulping. I put one step in front of the other, hearing only my breathing in my ears.

Left.

Right.

Left.

Right.

And then my feet found no ground and with a lurch, I was falling.

A scream escaped from my mouth as I fell through the air. Somewhere very far away, Xenita was also screaming. Through the darkness, we fell, falling from nothing into nothing— and then a force struck me, sending me careening sideways.

I noticed too late what it was, and before I knew it, leather struck my skin again, binding me, holding me, choking me. Leather wrapped itself around my torso completely, pinning my arms down to my sides, digging painfully into my flesh. The wounds on my back stung anew and I was immobilised. Falling, in the pitch black, the feeling of death consumed me. I couldn't think. Couldn't move. Couldn't see.

Then I slammed into a body of water with a painful slap.

Ice cold water was on all sides of me, and still unable to see anything, my body sunk down, down, down. I gasped and found that I could breathe normally. The sensation was disarming and confusing until I *did* see something in that sea of darkness.

My father's glowing figure floated above me.

"Father!" I gasped.

"You are doing well, Sara," he said seriously, eyes darting around. Then he stilled, looking somewhere over my shoulder. He whispered, "They are coming."

I squinted to try and see better, the sharp sting of fear making me twist within my leather bonds.

Something grabbed my foot.

I thrashed like a mad woman. My father lunged with a cry through the strange water, his sword slicing. The grip around my ankle released and I continued to try and muscle my way out of the bonds. But they were like steel and would not budge.

I whirled around on the water's floor. Figures were approaching us in the distance, glowing with a sickly brown, and appearing stretched out in the water. I needed to get up and fight. I needed to get out of these Goddess forsaken bonds. My father stood protectively in front of me, his sword held at the ready.

My mind needed to focus. I needed to use my brain. Wriggling wasn't working. I needed to cut through the leather but I didn't have the use of my arms. My hands were stuck uselessly by my thigh but they were not covered. I quickly manifested an axe into my right hand and dropped it onto the ground. I angled it towards my bonds and began madly sawing the leather against it. But I was still in the strange watery environment and my movements were buffered and painfully slow.

The stretched out glowing beings prowled closer. It was then that I turned and realised they were behind us, too.

"Be vigilant, Saraya," my father hissed. "Whatever hurts you here, will actually hurt your physical body."

Something cracked through the air and pain burned through my arm. I whirled around to see one of the shadows had struck me with a whip, a very real wound on my shoulder, bleeding.

On some deep-rooted instinct, I froze, my breath caught in my throat. I felt thirteen years old again.

"I'm sorry for not protecting you when I should have," my father cried, bringing me back to reality. "I failed as a father. But allow me to rectify that mistake now." He leapt towards the shadows.

A pain like no other shot through me, but it was not from

371

any physical assault, it felt like my heart was tearing in two. I threw myself anew into the task of sawing through the bonds and quickly, I was able to release my forearms enough to summon a sword and cut through the rest.

I turned, stabbing through a mud coloured spectre coming up behind me. It dissolved. My father was battling with the horde on his side so I ran towards him, my steps bounding in slow motion through the water. But they were gathering, more of them pouring in from the dark.

"Go, Sara!" my father cried, deftly cutting, swiping, and stabbing his way through them.

"No!" I cried, swinging at another two.

But the horde was endless.

"They will not stop, my love."

My heart clenched and I pressed my lips together. I couldn't leave him for dead again, I just—

"I'm already dead, Sara," my father grunted as if he knew what I was thinking. "But you are not! Run, my precious girl."

And so I let him. I let him protect me the way he might have if he were alive. I bit my tongue and turned away. As I bounded through the water, an old wound inside of me ached anew.

"Saraya?" Xenita's voice cut through the water, and in the dark, something glinted.

Xenita's pale face loomed in the distance, her eyes wide. "Come! Quickly and climb!"

Wyxian was nowhere to be seen.

It was then that I made out a golden ladder standing before her. Leading up into the dark. Xenita began climbing up and I hastened to follow.

"Forgive me, Sara!" my father called behind me.

"That's all the dead are ever after," Xenita panted, shaking her head in dismay as she climbed as fast as she could. "Forgiveness."

I said nothing as we climbed for our lives, never looking back down. My father, my poor father. My heart clenched impossibly tight, the feeling over just leaving him behind tearing me open. I knew he was already dead. I knew he was just a ghost, but I would never get to look upon him again, never get to talk about what it was that had happened. I hadn't even asked him if he knew about the poison. But all that was lost to me. All that was left was for me to let him go. To let those unresolved questions go.

We emerged onto an impossibly bright plane. An infinite blue sky spread out above and a field of grass spread out before of us. At its centre, something glowed with the light of the sun.

Xenita led me up to it and it slowly came into focus as my eyes adjusted. I realised it was a tree made of golden light. Colossal, the size of my palace back in Lobrathia. Hundreds of tiny glowing orbs the size of apples dangled from the branches.

"There she is," Xenita breathed. She raised her hand in a summoning motion and a small object flashed into being. Now, her hand swung a tiny white lantern made of what looked like carved bone.

I followed her line of sight to a particular branch. She held up the bone lantern and an orb jiggled on its stem. As we watched, it wrested itself free and floated right down to us. It headed straight into the cage and Xenita clicked the door shut.

"We did it!" The Queen Mother grinned at the orb. "Let's

go home, High Priestess. The water will take us back to our physical bodies."

With success racing in our veins, we waded straight into the pool. The water was pleasantly warm and light on my skin, and when Xenita bent and ducked her head under, I followed suit. Through the light-filled water, we swam directly towards the base of the pond, where fractals of light were splintering around something shiny.

A strong current sucked us in and we were pulled towards the crystalline floor.

Before I could figure out what was going on, we landed on our knees on dry land, not a drop of water on our bodies. I glanced at Xenita. She was now holding a bundle of blankets in her arms. A throaty newborn cry filled the air, but Xenita's face was a mask of horror as she looked around us.

I too looked around and realised we had not emerged back into our physical bodies. We were once again surrounded by darkness.

Xenita whirled around. "No!" she breathed. "No. No. No. It can't be!"

"What is it?" I asked, trying to see what had gone wrong.

And then I realised.

This was the same dark gaseous void that the Reaper had brought me into that night he came to Havrok's court.

My heart plummeted into my bowels. I summoned my sword as, in the distance, someone began laughing.

The voice we heard I couldn't mistake for anyone but the Green Reaper.

"You are strong, Princess. But while the lightning around the palace is stopping me and my warriors from physically entering, you are no match for my mental attack."

Every cell in my body lit up with fiery heat. I summoned my sword. But next to me, the newborn gurgled unhappily.

"It's alright," Xenita cooed, laying the baby on the ground. She expertly began tying a long piece of cloth around her body, placed the newborn against her chest, and strapped her in, tying the pieces together at her waist.

Just as she'd secured the babe, five warriors emerged from the darkness, tall creatures with blood-red eyes and pale athletic muscle. With a jolt, I realised their ears were pointed.

They were fae.

Mutated by the Reaper, perhaps, but their heritage was obvious. They were armed with vicious curved swords. They formed a loose circle around us. Xenita summoned her sword, and I glanced her way and saw that her mobility would be greatly reduced. I would have to cover her and the baby.

"We are going to destroy you, Priestess," the first demon-fae rasped. "We will desecrate your body. Then we will kill the fae queen and her infant and toss them into the void."

Anything that happened to us here happened to our actual bodies too.

The thought of these creatures killing this newborn baby and her mother was all I needed. I inhaled as the fuel for my rage filled me, my veins filling with that fell electricity I knew I could use to kill them. I let it flood my being, and it crackled, travelling down my arms, into my hands, and down into the sword. I had killed a legion of demon warriors in Havrok's court. I had no doubt I could do it again. My priestess mark heated up.

Goddess Umali, grant me the power of a hurricane, the speed of a tornado, the vengeance of a storm.

"You only have two swords," another demon rasped. "You are no match for us."

375

"Wrong," I said lightly, as my magic swirled in rings around me. "We have three."

In my left hand, I conjured another astral sword, this one pure white. "Get behind me, Xenita," I ordered. She did so without question.

"Tell me one more time what you're going to do to me?" My voice was a cold wind across a barrow-down.

"We're going to kill all three of you." They rushed at us from all sides.

The volcano that was my rage erupted.

Lightning struck in seven points, shattering bodies, making the astral plane around us tremble. Xenita screamed, but the demons didn't even have time to cry out as the smell of singed flesh filled the air.

Satisfied, I angled both my swords into the air and shot out another bolt of electricity into the astral void. The plane cracked open with a roar, and light flooded my eyes. I flung myself over Xenita, shielding her and the babe from the shattering, and the sound of breaking glass filled our ears. Pain burst across my back.

The air around us suddenly lifted, and when I opened my eyes, I instantly saw that we were back in the safehold under the palace. Relief poured through me, calming the residual electricity still running through my body. I stepped away from the Queen Mother and my body thrummed. I rubbed my arms down as the maids swept towards Xenita to check on her and the baby.

"They're fine," I mumbled. "We're fine."

Wide-eyed and panting, Xenita, with her arms still protectively around her baby, stared at me blankly at first, and slowly, colour filled her cheeks.

"I thought we were dead," she whispered to me. "I really

thought we were going to die, but you saved us. You really are—"

It was then that outside, the fae courtiers began screaming. I turned to run outside, but Xenita pushed her maids away and grabbed my arm in a vicious grip. When I looked at her in surprise, her face was twisted in fear.

"I have done something terrible, Saraya," she whispered, tears filling her blue eyes. "I am sorry."

"What do you mean?" My voice came out hoarse.

A tear slid down her cheeks and she sunk to the floor, clutching the bundle at her chest. She began rambling through her sobbing. "I wanted to pledge for the Green but Daxian wouldn't listen! Last night I called the fire wraiths. *I called upon the family fire wraiths!* I have docmed us all!" she screamed. "Gods, please forgive me, please forgive me!"

I realised with a pang what she was saying. Before her marriage, Xenita had been princess of the Court of Flames.

I fled for the window.

Xenita screamed after me. "Priestess, I am sorry!"

41
SARAYA

Fire wraith.

Those words were the only thing I could think of as I observed the carnage of the city through the magical window.

Two huge beasts, easily as tall as the Black Court palace itself, made of pure fire, fangs, and fists that pummelled through the air, raged through the battle lines. Warriors from both sides were scattering, fleeing for their lives as Xenita's family guardians swatted warriors away like flies.

One tiny figure flew through the air straight for one wraith. I gasped as they made contact. On impact, both were blown away from one another. The wraith flew through the air and fell to the ground with a cloud of dust fifty feet tall.

A moment later, the shockwave hit us, and the very foundations of the palace shook. Two courtiers screamed. The children wailed.

I knew only one person who was crazy enough to take that monster on.

I ran for the door, yanked it open, and flew up the steps, ignoring the cries of the female guards. I could feel my protections around the palace remaining strong, and even now, my lightning begged to be unleashed. Now that I had the hang of it, it wanted to be used. *Yearned* for it.

But as I ran out of the entrance hall, I shoved that all away because I only had a mind for Drake.

Obsidian Court warriors swarmed outside the palace, electricity zapping them as they attempted to get through. Sparks flew as I approached the shield, and I didn't give it a second thought as I surrounded myself with a ball of lightning, and enveloped by the hum, I charged through my own shield. The warriors in my way flew through the air as soon as my electric bubble touched them. The rest scrambled away.

I ran through the streets of the city, the tiny spec that was Drake and the two fire wraiths still visible fighting on the battle plain.

Just as I reached them, Drake jumped into the air and, with a closed fist enveloped in a colossal ball of blue magic that sizzled, punched the beast on its jaw.

They were launched backwards from the blow. Someone was calling out to me from the side, but I couldn't take my eyes off the fight.

Because this time, when the beast hurtled onto the earth, it was with an enormous, earth shattering crash. The ground itself shook, and a sound like nothing else I'd ever heard penetrated the air. It was a cracking, a cleaving, a breaking.

It was the sound of the earth breaking.

I threw myself to the ground, covering my head, curled in the fetal position, my lightning shield still around me. Rock and stone hit my shield but it held strong.

When the dust settled, I looked up.

A sudden silence had come over the battlefield.

Both the fire wraiths and Drake had disappeared.

Voices shouted out. Before me, the earth dropped away. It had been broken into two.

Then I saw it. Silver-tipped fingers gripped the ledge of earth from inside the crack.

When I cried my mate's name, the sound that came from my throat was a blood-curdling scream. I ran for my mate and slid over rock and dirt to the edge. The beast's fall had cleaved a fissure in the earth. A fissure with no visible end. And hanging by his fingers from the edge was Drake.

The cries from the others on the field faded from my mind.

"Drake!" I screamed, grabbing his forearm. My heart stopped in my chest. The fire wraith was hanging by a gnarled claw from Drake's legs. I pulled on his forearm, but try as I might, there was no way I could pull him up.

"Saraya," Drake whispered, his eyes turning hazel, his face contorting with sadness.

I choked on a sob. "I can't pull you up."

His hazel eyes were clear but pained. His fingers began to slip from the ledge. A million thoughts ran through my mind at once. There was no way he was surviving whatever was down there. He needed to be stronger, faster. He needed to survive this. I needed him to survive this.

I knew what I had to do.

I forced the words out from gritted teeth, my vision blurring. "I reject you as my mate."

A pause in the turn of the earth. A pause in all things. The air fled from my lungs, my heart sliced into two. I had said it.

The look of sheer devastation on his face lasted one full second before his eyes clouded over with that all-black darkness, but this time it was speckled with vicious red twinkling lights.

Drake let go of the edge. He plunged into the dark, his fingers still outstretched for me, his expression hewn out of stone.

42
JERALI JONES

The scream that came from Saraya as I hurtled towards her was like nothing I'd ever heard before. But it didn't matter. I had to get her away from the edge of that newborn crevice. She was still dangling over the side, her arm outstretched.

I skidded to a stop on my knees, grabbed her, and hauled her into my arms, away from the drop.

"You can do nothing, Saraya," I cried.

"No!" she screamed, clawing at me. It was the sound of a heart breaking into two. I pulled her against my chest and she fought against me, sobbing, screaming, a feral mess of rage and pain.

But something sharp zapped at me, and a burnt smell came from Saraya. Having seen what she was capable of at Havrok's Court, I pushed her away, scrambling back. I shouted out a warning to Blythe and Slade, who were running towards me.

But Saraya was standing now, lightning crackling around her form in silver and blue bolts. She screamed, her eyes squeezed shut, and lightning shot from her arms and into the sky, her eyes opening up and revealing stunning light within them.

"Holy Goddess," I whispered.

"She's angry," Blythe sobbed. "Someone do something!"

But anyone could tell that Saraya was above reason.

"Stop, Saraya!" Blythe shouted. "You'll hurt someone!"

But she *wanted* to hurt someone. The enemy fae were either at the edges of the field, staring in shock, or trying to get into the palace.

The ground trembled beneath my feet; Saraya's body seemed to split in two. Lightning roared, and she turned and directed it towards the soldiers rallying around the palace.

Her magic seemed to seek them out, because she found each one of them, and struck. Screams filled the air, and then fae were running. Saraya had become something completely out of this world. She hardly looked human.

"Saraya!" Blythe screamed in terror.

Lightning crackled and fizzed and struck. Fae screamed and died before our eyes.

"You're killing everyone Saraya, stop!" Blythe's voice was scared, frightened, and small, almost child-like. The lightning rumbled to a close and Saraya turned to face us. Lysander came up behind us with Daxian and his generals. Saraya's eyes became clear and she took one look at us before crumpling to the ground.

We ran for her. Our princess.

"Who is that?" she asked, her voice barely a rasp.

"Me!" Blythe grabbed her, sobbing in her neck. "It's me, Blythe. Please stop!"

"Peaches," she whispered. "You smell like peaches."

Then her eyes shut and she went limp.

Blythe was blubbering, "Saraya, I'm sorry—"

"We have to go." Slade's deep bass.

"They've taken the city," I said, picking up our princess.

I turned to see the fae standing behind me— a blood-soaked Lysander, a panting Slade, and a grimacing Daxian and his men.

"We lost," Blythe panted next to me. "Where will we go?"

Lysander surged towards me, a frown on his face, "Is she alive?"

"Just fainted," I said, and to my chagrin the blond fae pulled her into his arms, cradling her like a baby.

It was then that Saraya gave a violent twitch and though her eyes remained closed, she clutched at Lysander's armour and managed to choke out, "We must go to Sky Court!"

Surprise coursed through us all.

"What?" Lysander choked.

"Sky Court, my mother… my mother said…" she went limp again.

She'd spoken to Yasani. Saraya had spoken to her mother. Who would forever be, in my eyes, the greatest woman I'd ever met. "Then that's where we're headed," I said aggressively, daring anyone to contradict me.

"Fae King!" I called to the tall young brute with one eye. "Which way to Sky Court?"

He frowned, as his one-eye assessed me. Then he shook his head. "The portal is there, but—"

"I know where it is," Slade said uncertainly, looking at the unconscious Saraya.

"Then let's go," I barked.

"Then go," the Black Court King nodded. "But look after Saraya, she is your queen now. She told us she intended to take back Lobrathia."

My heart leapt into my throat. I knew it! I would follow her to the end to get Quartz back.

"I am heading back," said Daxian firmly. "I won't leave my city."

"Your Highness!" Lysander said, aghast. "You can't—"

"My mother is in there," he said angrily. "And if Saraya is here that means my newborn sister has been born. I must go to them. Saraya gave me instruction on maintaining the shield. I will wait them out." His generals nodded. Lysander and Slade glanced at one another. I had come to know both of them well during our escape from Havrok's Court and then some weeks in Kaalon. They were good fae, and even better warriors. By now, I trusted them enough to lead me through their realm.

"Let's go." I urged.

By now, both fae knew *me* well enough to listen when I spoke a command. So they should.

We parted ways east of the field. Daxian and his generals squared their shoulders and headed back towards the city. While we, Lysander, Blythe, Saraya, and I, followed Slade into the dark forest outside of the battlefield. Whatever was coming, at least we could face it together.

THE END

OF

—BOOK 2 of THE WARRIOR MIDWIFE TRILOGY—

Thank you for continuing on Saraya and Drake's journey with me! I really hope you enjoyed this instalment.

Join me for the final piece of their story in: The Warrior Queen, get your copy now.

For updates on Altara's story, sign up to the email newsletter at:

www.ektaabali.com/warriormidwife

Signing up to my mailing list means that you get first peek at everything I produce, including book covers, new releases, exclusive excerpts and bonus material that I don't post anywhere else.

ACKNOWLEDGMENTS

My first thank you always goes to my parents, who are infinitely patient and kind with me.

Thank you to my brother, Anmol, for his listening ear and constant support.

To the wonderful artists who have worked on the illustrations in this novel: Carly and Jess as well as Najlakay for his wonderful maps.

To my copyeditor, Maryssa, your insight, enthusiasm, feedback and professionalism is always appreciated.

A massive thank you to my fae-eyed proofreaders: Sheree, Breanna, Amy, Sammy and Molly. You guys are all gems and I wouldn't have been able to produce a high quality novel without you!

ABOUT THE AUTHOR

Ektaa P. Bali was born in Fiji and spent most of her life in Melbourne, Australia.

After graduating Killester College in 2008, she studied nursing and midwifery at Deakin University, going on to spend eight years as a midwife in various hospitals.

She published her first novel in 2020, the beginning of a middle grade fantasy series, before going on to pursue her true passion: Young & New Adult Fantasy.

The Warrior Priestess is her fourth novel in the Chrysalis-verse.

She currently lives in Brisbane, Australia.

facebook.com/ektaabaliauthor
instagram.com/ektaabaliauthor

ALSO BY E.P. BALI

NA Fantasy

The Ellythian Princesses:

#1 The Warrior Midwife

#2 The Warrior Priestess

#3 The Warrior Queen

#1 The Archer Princess

#2 The Archer Witch

#3 The Archer Queen

YA Fantasy

The Travellers:

#1 The Chrysalis Key

#2 The Allure of Power

#3 The Wings of Darkness

Middle Grade Fantasy

The Pacific Princesses fantasy adventure series:

#1 The Unicorn Princess

#2 The Fae Princess

#3 The Mermaid Princess

#4 The Tale of the Three Princesses